Gerard Gilbert is a journalist. From 1992 to 2016 he was a critic and feature writer for *The Independent* and is currently working for its online version and for the 'I' newspaper. This is his first novel.

The Concierge

Gerard Gilbert

The Concierge

Pegasus

PEGASUS PAPERBACK

© Copyright 2017
Gerard Gilbert

The right of Gerard Gilbert to be identified as author of
this work has been asserted by him in accordance with the
Copyright, Designs and Patents Act 1988

A CIP catalogue record for this title is
available from the British Library

ISBN-978 1 91090 306 3

*Pegasus is an imprint of
Pegasus Elliot MacKenzie Publishers Ltd.*
www.pegasuspublishers.com

First Published in 2017

**Pegasus
Sheraton House Castle Park
Cambridge CB3 0AX England**

Printed & Bound in Great Britain

To Michael and Roberta, my parents, with love and gratitude

Based on an original idea by Q.

PROLOGUE

The Italian coastguard vessel is top-heavy and clumsy-looking but slices through the choppy waters like a knife, unlike the unseaworthy rust bucket that they had all just been rescued from. Four hours out of Tripoli the engines had failed, and they'd spent most of the morning drifting around in slow circles, rolling and pitching, feeling sicker and sicker. The children had finally stopped crying, too busy vomiting on the rusty decks.

Omar had counted about 150 of them, mostly Africans, pitifully under-dressed for the late winter weather, their teeth chattering beneath woolly hats pulled low over their faces, but also a few Arabs like himself. At least he hadn't paid 500 dinar for the 'privilege' – the people smugglers had a good idea of who he was, and even upgraded the boat in his honour – God knows what they had intended them to sail in. A half-deflated rubber dinghy perhaps. This old fishing boat was on its last legs anyway.

Despite the cramped conditions Omar had been given a lot of space by the others; there was something about this self-possessed young man that said *leave well alone*. The impenetrable dark eyes betrayed not one milligram of weakness, in fact they betrayed nothing at all, and the scar down the left side of his face spoke of the battlefields some of them were escaping. Except it had been done to him with a knife by a Yazidi woman whose daughter he had taken for his own. He had killed them both on the spot.

Eventually the Guardia Costiera's ship appeared on the horizon. They had known it was coming because a helicopter had circled above them earlier, those Africans still able to, standing and waving their arms, but it seemed to take ages to actually arrive. Finally alongside, men in white overalls, surgical masks and blue disposable gloves had gestured for them to stay where they were, and thrown gold-coloured foil blankets and life jackets into a sea of outstretched arms. Omar didn't move. He was warmly dressed and in no hurry. Everything was unfolding exactly as he had been told.

The fishing boat's course was set for Calabria on the Italian mainland, but if picked up they would most likely be taken to Sicily, the contacts in Tripoli said. This is confirmed when Omar overhears one of the Africans ask in English where they are headed. One of the coastguards, impassive behind mirrored dark glasses, replies brusquely, "Sicilia." If he has any pity for this human flotsam, he doesn't show it.

At the port of Trapani they are greeted by a phalanx of officials in every hue – nurses in maroon, doctors in white, police in blue and civil immigration services in grey. Omar watches the nurses tie surgical masks over the mouths of the Africans as they march onto the tarmac. Another nurse rolls up the sleeve of each migrant and attaches a wristband. A man shines a torch into their eyes and ears and waves them forward. The processing has begun.

Omar's name isn't really Omar, but it is now. He is not really Syrian, but he now will be. He's a Syrian fleeing the fighting in his homeland, but beyond that he won't say a word. He has no ID and when they ask for his fingerprints he will clench his fists, and the immigration people will recognise the signal; he doesn't want to stay in Italy but head northwards to more generous and better ordered countries like Germany and Sweden, and the officials will look the other way. One less migrant for their overburdened economy to cope with.

Except that Omar does indeed want very much to stay in Italy. He is headed for a rendezvous in Rome, and this is very much not the last time that the Italian state will hear of him.

CHAPTER ONE

At about five o'clock in the afternoon, as the street lamps take over from the fast-fading March sunshine, Nicola gets unsteadily to her feet, shakes the cramp out of her legs and leads Topaz to one of the quieter Mayfair back streets off Piccadilly. Topaz trots by her side at the other end of a length of twine that Nicola has fashioned into a lead, not that the dog really needs a lead because she would never leave her mistress's side. Till death us do part, thinks Nicola. Did she think that or did she say it out loud? She can no longer tell these days.

On the rare occasions she thought about it, Nicola had always assumed she would outlive Topaz, but now she's not so sure. She's hungry and she's cold. The evening rush hour is gathering pace and if they don't move they are in danger of being trampled underfoot at her usual pitch between Green Park underground station and the Ritz. And anyway people are too preoccupied in getting home, thinking of missed trains or what to cook for dinner, to drop coins into Nicola's upturned flat-cap.

This side street opposite Fortnum & Mason still has some well-to-do shoppers and window-gazers who might spare her their loose change. She'll head back on to Piccadilly at seven, maybe stopping to exchange a few words with H, whose pitch is under the arcade of the Ritz itself, and whose ostentatious positioning means he wages a continuous war with the police and the hotel doormen. He is hilarious, but he's always getting himself arrested or beaten up, occasionally at the same time.

Topaz is a sheepdog crossed with something else, her long-suffering demeanour earning regular pats on the head, which she graciously acknowledges with her almost comically mournful eyes. The animal lovers then feel obliged to say something to Nicola and perhaps drop a few coins into the hat. It's the do-gooders, the

Christians and the women aghast to find one of their sex living on the street, who are the time-wasters, wanting to know her life story, how she became reduced to begging, and with suggestions as to how she might get herself back on her feet. There is often a church involved, or a feminist sanctuary where, they say crouching beside her, she would be looked after – and which sounded as boring as a month of Sundays back home with her parents. No spare change from this lot, of course.

Nicola is ruminating like this when she spots two men she knows by sight and likes to call 'Gervaise' and 'Cecil' on account of the way they dress in expensive suits with open shirt collars. Sauntering with their hands in their pockets, they remind her of a black and white photograph that their history teacher had shown the class at school in Bolton. It was taken in the 1930s; two haughty Eton schoolboys in top hats standing by their trunks, hands in their pockets, surrounded by mocking street urchins. "Who do you think had the last laugh?" asked the teacher, who seriously hated Tories, toffs and southerners.

Except Nicola's toffs aren't sauntering today, but striding away from Piccadilly, into the bowels of Mayfair, heads down and talking intently. 'Cecil' is sleek and tanned with full thick hair swept back; he has never looked at her. She knows the type; she might as well be invisible.

'Gervaise' is the slightly taller, gaunter man, with receding temples and nervous darting eyes, which did seem to take in Nicola, although both men would be surprised to learn that this bedraggled woman in her late thirties – actually the same age as them – notices anything at all, such was her bent-over posture and the practised forlorn stare aimed about a foot in front of her begging cap. Experience had taught Nicola that this passive approach to begging was ultimately more effective than the challenging variety. H, who was always making sarcastic remarks to non-payers, never made much money, despite his high-profile pitch.

One day, out of the blue, this man, the one she called 'Gervaise' had given her a folded fifty-pound note. "Here you go," he'd said, his voice unexpectedly gentle.

"God bless," Nicola had said, although she didn't think God had anything to do with it. Perhaps he was the devil. That had been a while ago now, and when he was alone, without 'Cecil'.

"God bless." She also used that on the guilty looking ones who maybe went to church on Sunday and were obviously struggling as to whether they should give to this woman. She'll only spend it on cider and cigarettes, they thought, but then again Jesus commanded us not to pass on the other side.

"God bless." It sent them scuttling on their way, like a sharp slap on the backs of their legs.

CHAPTER TWO

'Cecil' is in fact Maximilian Draycott – Max for short – and 'Gervaise' is Harry Kimber. And it isn't true that Max never notices Nicola. The men have talked about her, speculated on how she had ended up on the streets. Care home, followed by heroin and a spot of light prostitution, was Max's hypothesis. Harry had argued for a few stints in psychiatric wards. Once she cropped up in one of their games of 'would you shag her?' The answer was 'no', not even after a good bath.

Actually Nicola comes from a stable home – a tidy 1930s council house with a large well-tended garden that backed on to fields, and both parents had decent jobs; she was even considered to speak quite 'posh' in Bolton, mainly because she never used swear words. But her mother and father had been older parents and she was an only child. They were 'respectable' but they only ever did things together – 'a world unto their own', as her mother had once declared so proudly. They didn't have friends. There were cousins supposedly but distant, and nobody ever came over. Nicola couldn't wait to leave home.

Squats and bar work had been her lot for twenty years, before the bar work dried up because the drink was playing havoc with her time keeping and her looks. She hasn't touched a drop in three years now, not since being given Topaz, a rescue dog from one of the squats near the Elephant and Castle that she noticed recently was being redeveloped into luxury flats 'for exciting inner-city living'. Nicola knows all about exciting inner-city living.

She notices Max and Harry turn into the lobby of a big hotel where she had tried begging once. A burly East European with thick arms and a bull neck had moved her on in no uncertain terms and she had given it a wide berth ever since. "Russians," H had said with a knowing look. "Heavy duty; stick to nice old cockneys – they have a bit of humanity."

Actually H was wrong; the security guard is Lithuanian, one of two identical twins who discreetly works the lobby and keeps an eye out for trouble. Adomas, the one who told Nicola to move on 'because her dog seems such a nice dog and it would be a pity for anything to happen to it', now clocks Max and Harry as they enter the hotel for the third consecutive night, and walk over to the same sofa as on previous occasions.

The first evening they had waited an hour and a half – one leg crossed elegantly over the opposite knee, identical posture, and not a trace of impatience for whomever they were waiting. Occasionally one would flick his suit cuff and glance at his watch, but that was all. Adomas was impressed. The hotel's rich customers were not patient; they didn't need to be, of course. If Adomas were rich – when he gets rich, he remembers to tell himself – he too will be impatient. There would be so much time – so many evening like this one – to make up for.

Last night the men had returned and Adomas had made enquiries at the reception desk. They were waiting for the Arab party that had booked out the entire second floor for one week. They are in luck today, then, he thinks, watching one of them turn to look at the other.

Max is inspecting Harry's blue, off-the-peg suit that he personally helped him select. He has had to teach Harry how to dress, escorting him round Crombie on Conduit Street, down Savile Row, through Burlington Arcade and along Jermyn Street to Turnbull & Asser – Henry Higgins to Harry's Eliza Doolittle.

Both men wear their shirts open at the neck – the uniform of the hedge fund managers. The Arabs and the hedgies are the same in this respect: smart casual, as they say on the sort of invitation that Harry throws in the bin without a second glance.

The younger Saudis like the preppie look: chinos and Gucci loafers and cashmere sweaters draped over their shoulders, as if they were about to re-join their yachts after a meal ashore, instead of preparing to step out into the chilly London night.

Max's eyes run down Harry's suit trousers to the cashmere socks and the shoes, which aren't as polished as he'd like them to be. Harry himself has been staring across the lobby and into the bar, where a good-looking couple are sitting on stools as the barman mixes them a cocktail. They're both smiling at the man as he performs with the shaker and the scene looks like a corny advert.

"I could do with one of those," he says, pointing with his head towards the bar. Max follows his gaze.

"The woman or the drink? How's it going on that score, by the way? Still picking up girls on dating apps?"

"Not so much", says Harry, suppressing a yawn. "And actually I was referring to the cocktail."

Max himself is trying to cut down on alcohol – a thought that has him flicking his cuff to read his activity tracker. He has just over 2,000 units of activity left to meet his daily target of ten thousand. He slept well last night, according to the device, which he syncs daily to its iPhone app, with just one vertiginous spike on the graph highlighting the time he padded off to the loo at about three in the morning. Is he too young to get his prostate checked?

On his other wrist Max wears a rose-gold Rolex Cellini, whose face he now twists towards his incipient jowls – he's putting on weight, Rachel tells him on an almost nightly basis. Harry in turn flicks his cuff to reveal his own, much cheaper, Rolex – a silver Submariner that Max had helped him purchase, more than £5,000 worth of stainless steel to duplicate the watch on his iPhone. Harry, who hadn't owned a watch since his schooldays, who had once asked strangers the time with the same ease that he bummed cigarettes off them, is still faintly in awe of the timepiece.

"Another no-show," he says under his breath. Max doesn't reply, looking over instead to where two pumped-up hotel security men are staring into the middle distance – not looking but all seeing. He has spoken to them, pumping them to find out if the Arabs are actually inhabiting the entire floor booked in their names two weeks ago. They merely stared at him through unreadable blue eyes, paler than death, implacably silent, except to say that no, they weren't Russian but Lithuanian.

As usual, the receptionists would neither confirm nor deny the arrival of the Saudis. This is the third evening on the trot that Max and Harry have made their way to this lobby, the previous two times to no avail. No excuses offered or sought; the Arabs had simply changed their collective mind. Gone to Cairo or New York or – God help them, thinks Max – Paris.

Down at heel, shabby, stuck in-the-1980s Paris – Max's favourite lament every time he takes the Eurostar from the Gare du Nord. Like most people in their industry, Max has a poor opinion of the French. Their time-serving, unimaginative bureaucrats don't understand hedge funds, he says, and blame what they see as Anglo-Saxon opportunists for the mess that the French politicians have themselves made of their economy. They'd like to destroy the industry completely and for this reason Max hates them – a hatred fuelled by fear, the fear that they might one day get their self-serving way. Would Brexit be the trigger for this worst-case scenario? Max was quietly confident that it wouldn't make any difference to the hedge fund industry in general. Their investors had taken a big hit from the referendum vote – Max and Harry had taken a punt on remain.

But Max loves London – it looks so smart; so rich, so clean, not like the old days. Okay, so you never heard English being spoken any more, not in Mayfair at least, but that only confirmed him in his view that he was now where he needed to be – among the global super-rich, the one-per-centers. A real world city.

Harry's not so sure he likes London anymore; it feels more crowded and at the same time the centre feels like a playground for tourists and a racetrack for playboys in Ferraris. Brexit had helped to slam the brakes on Central London property, but all the same it had been nearly a decade of ever increasing house prices – until recently he'd been making a hundred grand a year doing nothing, by simply being the owner of a terraced house in Hammersmith.

"Holy fuck they're here."

Max shoots to his feet as an Arab in tight white jeans and cowboy boots, a bit gay and a bit Nashville, with thick greasy hair tumbling down over the collar of a cream jacket, is heading straight towards them with a clenched scowl on his face. He nods to Max. "His excellency will be down shortly," is all he says, whipping out his phone and speaking in Arabic.

Cream Jacket pirouettes on his Cuban heels and turns his back on them. Then with an almost courtly sweep of his arm, he pirouettes back again, and Max and Harry realise they are being introduced to a short, rotund, moustachioed man in Arab dress. His flesh looks unnaturally soft, like a children's toy, or another species of human. The super-wealthy.

"Your excellency," says Max, bowing his head to this other-worldly being. Harry follows his lead, but without saying anything, and is offered a small, soft, limp hand. For one crazy second he wonders whether he should curtsy.

"Max, how are you?" says the Saudi, putting an arm around the middle of Max's back, and guiding him towards the hotel entrance.

It's all happening very quickly now. Having given up all expectation that this rendezvous would ever take place, Harry is now confused. The Saudi and Max sweep off, followed by two minders and, behind them, two women both in Western dress – jeans and cashmere. Harry feels a pair of eyes on him now. It is the younger of the two women, who is looking over her shoulder at him in amusement. She looks away when Harry returns her dark, chestnut gaze.

He's not sure what to do so he hangs back, following the two women, who are ushered out of the doors by one of the minders. The man inspects Harry for a moment from behind dark glasses, and then ushers him out too. A brand new black-on-black Rolls Royce Phantom is waiting immediately outside the hotel entrance, gawped at by a young tourist, who raises his phone as if to take a picture and then thinks better of it when he notices the minders.

The Saudi and Max step in, and Harry spots a second car directly behind – an intimidating black Mercedes 4x4 with privacy-glass windows. The two women head for this, but the minder nods at the back door of the Rolls, where the Saudi and Max are already in deep conversation and Harry slips in beside Max. Softness, fibre optic lights woven into the ceiling and the deep, rich odour of fine leather. The unmistakeable smell of wealth.

They only drive for a couple of minutes, lapping Berkeley Square for no good reason that Harry can see, pulling up beside a house on Charles Street. "This is the one, your excellency," says Max, pointing through the privacy glass. The driver lowers the window and the Saudi gazes, expressionless, for a while at the redbrick town house. Harry notices the full lips and slightly bulging eyes. Max wonders if he's blown it.

"How much?" the Saudi asks.

"Eight thousand square feet... seven bathrooms... marble throughout... fully furnished to the highest standard by a very gifted young Italian interior designer... swimming pool and cinema in the sub-terrain floor... It's beautiful. Do you want to go inside?"

"How much?" repeats the Saudi softly. Harry can't help staring at the large pink diamond ring on one of his fingers.

"Twenty-five million pounds sterling. In dollars that's..."

"Very good. Now let's eat." He softly lifts the fingers of his already raised hand and the driver, who has been watching for such a signal, puts the Rolls into gear, and they glide off. Deal done.

Max knows where they're going – to Novikov as usual. After much bowing and scraping, and a spot of flirtatious banter between the Saudi and the blonde Russian maître d', two suitably well-sited tables are found – one for the men and one for the ladies. Harry takes another look at the Arab girl, but she is studiously ignoring him now and staring into her menu, the ghost of that same ironic smile on her lips. She has lustrous long black hair that Harry would like to run his hands through, push his face into and smell. She looks so naturally beautiful among the bottle blondes on the surrounding tables, their faces paralysed with the botulinum toxin so regularly injected into the muscles of their faces. Max kicks him under the table.

There's a mix-up as menus printed in Russian are swiftly exchanged for ones in English, before they order vast quantities of tempura and maki. The Saudi, it seems, is drinking tonight and two bottles of 2007 Chassagne Montrachet are brought to the table. Harry takes one more glance at the girl's table, and now she is looking at him. She holds his stare with dark eyes. She nods very slightly and looks away. The girls are drinking bottled water, Harry notices.

Max is admiring the Saudi's diamond ring. He himself had brokered the stone in Geneva last year, and now the man has had it set in platinum. Before the first tuna maki has been nibbled, Max has received an order for a new diamond – preferably another pink but anything really unusual will do.

"Sixty grand for me and twenty for you," says Max as they eventually hit the pavement, a respectful ten minutes after the Arab party has made their departure, leaving them at the table with the unpaid bill. Just under one grand seems a small price for such a bounteous windfall and anyway it will be a business expense claimed as investor entertainment. Harry uses the company credit card and folds the receipt into his jacket pocket.

"Beats working for a living," he says as they step out into the Mayfair night. He thinks it will take some poor bastard a year to earn what he's just hoovered up in one night; it would probably take his mother two years. Follow the money – it was one of Max's favourite appropriated sayings.

"They never even looked inside the house," continues Harry. Then he notices Max appraising him as if seeing him for the first time – not a sensation Harry ever relishes; Harry likes Max to take him for granted.

"This is just to start," Max says at last, in deadly earnest. "This is fucking peanuts." He's a bit drunk, as is Harry.

"We need to get in with the Russians," blathers Harry, who has downed most of a bottle of the Chassagne Montrachet.

"The Russians have their own people," Max says sternly. "They have got all their own concierges now. They love their art.

But the Saudis have simpler tastes. Right... I've got to rush. Ring the agent in the morning and offer twenty-two mill. Don't let him talk you up... I know he'll take that. And can you give Rachel a quick ring... tell her I've gone to Geneva to see a man about a diamond."

Harry doesn't understand why Max can't call Rachel himself, but somehow it seems to have fallen to Harry to liaise with Max's wife about Max's comings and goings. Part of Harry's amorphous role seemed to be that of a glorified secretary. "I'll see you on Friday," says Max.

"A good evening's work," says Harry.

Max navigates his iPhone apps and books an Uber Lux. In the back of the pristine black S-Class Mercedes, as new as a toy taken out of its plastic wrapper but a cheap feeling compared to the Saudi's Roller, he texts his friend Simon, asking what time his plane is leaving for Geneva.

"On board by 11:30. S," a text pings back less than a minute later. Max smiles and wonders once again how Simon, a trader like himself, manages to run a private jet. He leases it, he knows that, but not much more than that: aeroplanes don't interest Max – especially when he can bum a lift in one, like tonight. Cars don't interest him either, not to own anyway. Stuff in general doesn't engage him – it merely exists in order to be traded.

The guy at the passport desk, who has a little goatee beard and an ill-fitting suit, bristles involuntarily against whatever it is that Max represents, but waves him through. No luggage. And at twenty past eleven he slides into a deep leather seat opposite Simon, who has brought a girl along for the ride.

"Max, this is Genevieve... Genevieve, Max," says Simon absently, pouring Max a flute of champagne. "Genevieve is going to Geneva." Simon then pours one for the girl, who is all long legs and short sequined dress. She looks she might have been plucked straight out of a nightclub. Genevieve giggles. She looks stoned.

"We have a slot – ten minutes to take off," comes a relaxed, mature male voice – the timbre of airline pilots the world over.

Simon scoops up his laptop and starts to stare into it, light reflecting on his face, which registers neither boredom nor interest – just a flaccid compulsion. He is a currency trader – "stat-arb trader" is how he puts it himself. What he really means is that it never stops – this automated pair trading of the yen, dollar, euro, rouble and pound sterling, these never stable G8 rates of exchange whose smallest movements can be bet for or against. Unlike Max, Simon had made a fortune on Brexit. He'd made the right call. "You should mix more with the common people," he'd said to Max a few days after the vote. He meant girls like Genevieve. "It was obvious to me we'd vote leave." But Max doesn't envy him his sickness, however well remunerated.

"Put it down," the girl says woozily, standing up and folding herself in Simon's lap. The tiniest flicker of irritation passes over Simon's face before being supplanted by a big fat, indulgent smile. They kiss noisily, tongues slurping and the laptop down by his side seemingly forgotten but still glowing with its own self-importance. The machine knows who Simon would rather be devouring.

* * *

Harry wanders down to The Arts Club in Dover Street. Max had made him join. The doorman nods as he passes through into the bar and orders a large glass of vintage cognac. He swipes idly through Tinder – the friendly smiles of the women blurring into one. He gets a lot of one-night stands out of Tinder. His profile picture with the expensive suit and promise of a free meal (he always pays and the women appreciate that) usually secures a date, and often more. One of them had even told him that he didn't look like the type of man to send pictures of his penis. No, agreed Harry, he wasn't.

He comes out of Tinder and scrolls down to 'r' in his phone's contacts list. Rachel is slow to pick up.

"Harry," she says in a drowsy voice. "I was asleep."

"Max is in Geneva… can I come over?"

"I've got an eight o'clock tomorrow," she says. "You sound

drunk. Don't phone me when you're drunk."

"Okay, sorry, speak tomorrow", says Harry, trying not to slur his words. He calls up Uber for the drive home. The doorman bids him goodnight as he steps out into the cold March night and Harry spots the car already drawing up to the kerb.

"Goodnight," replies Harry. "A very good night. Very good indeed."

CHAPTER THREE

Omar crosses the main concourse of Rome's Termini, towards the steps leading down to the Metro. He's wearing a dark brown suit that fits him surprisingly well, as do the shirt and the shoes that were also left in the closet of the hotel room in Syracuse. Inside the jacket pocket was a wallet with 500 euros in crisp new notes, and an ID card, Italian passport and driving licence in the name of Amal Abulafia. With the clothes was a pistol in a holster – a slate-grey Browning 9mm semi-auto, ex-French military.

They hadn't asked any questions at the reception desk, just handed the key as if expecting this ragged immigrant as their guest of honour. It was a mafia-owned hotel, recommended by the people traffickers in Tripoli.

The food was delicious and the bed comfortable enough and he decided it was safe enough to sleep, having first ascertained that the Browning was fully loaded. He slipped it under the pillow and was out cold for over twelve hours. No dreams, just a deep sense of replenishment. Reception told him that there was a ferry to the mainland leaving later that morning. He thanked them, checked out, and walked across the square. He'd wait and watch the morning ferry and then take the evening ferry, just in case anyone was double-crossing him.

Now he's finally in Rome, at Termini, where he's to catch the Metro to somewhere called Laurentina. He's bought a seven-day travel pass and a news magazine from a kiosk outside the station, noticing as he did two Arab boys of about twelve or thirteen sitting on a low wall, speaking to men as they passed. Occasionally a man would stop, and Omar noticed a tall, well-dressed man in his fifties walk away with one of the boys.

He waits for them to disappear down a side street and then Omar walks towards the other boy, who is now kicking his heels and nonchalantly chewing gum. He perks up when he sees Omar approaching, and then seems unsure, and looks away.

"Ahlan," says Omar casually by way of greeting. The boy steals a quick glance at him and doesn't seem to like what he sees.

"What's your name, kid?"

The boy kicks his heels and chews hard. Omar steps round in front of him and takes his chin in a forceful grip, wrenching the young head to face him.

"Hey!" he yelps. And then something about Omar's eyes, the way they don't seem to reflect any light, makes him stop. "What can I do for you, sir? I'm forty euros an hour, but twenty for a good Muslim man."

Omar's expression remains unreadable. "Where are you from, boy?"

"Syria, sir."

"Where are your parents?"

The boy shrugs.

"You sell yourself to the infidels?"

"I have to eat, sir." He's looking down the road, where a soft-faced middle-aged Italian in a baggy, ill-fitting suit is appraising him. When the man catches Omar's stare, he turns briskly and walks off.

"You like going with men?" he asks the boy.

"No, sir."

"You prefer girls?"

"Oh, yes sir. I love girls." And with his hands he moulds the shape of female breasts from out of his own concave chest.

"I might have a job for you then, one which gives you all the girls you want. The prettiest girls, all unblemished. And what's more it will put you right with God."

The boy looks away now. Omar notices that the pudgy businessman has not gone; he's hanging back at the end of the street.

"Look at me," says Omar, and the boy obliges.

"Will you recognise me again?" Omar watches as the boy's

eyes trace the scar down his cheek. It's a look he knows well of late.

"Yes, sir."

"And you're always here?"

"I've got nowhere else to go."

"Don't the cops hassle you?"

"Oh, no, sir, they can't be bothered with a little immigrant kid. Too much paperwork and anyway, it's not as if I'm stealing or anything."

Omar takes out the wallet from his inside jacket pocket and the boy catches a glimpse of the pistol butt. Omar knows he's seen it.

"You know how to keep your mouth shut?"

"Yes, sir."

He takes two crisp fifty-euro notes from the wallet and hands them to the boy.

"What's your name, kid?"

Adnan thinks of lying, but the man's blank eyes are so immoveable, so darkly penetrating, that he just stutters the truth.

"Adnan, sir."

The man nods. "Family name?"

"Ahmadi, sir"

"Good, and which town is your family from?"

The boy hesitates before naming a small town to the east of Deir al-Zour.

"That's good, Adnan," says the man. "I can help your family. Give them money, protection... even get them out if they want. Islamic State run your town now, don't they? Would your family like to get out? Maybe come to Italy, or even better to Germany. I can arrange this. I have connections."

"I don't know, sir," says Adnan, who starts looking down the street again, resuming the gum chewing. The pudgy Italian man is still there, pretending not to look.

"Listen, Adnan, your family will starve to death, or worse, if they stay there. The world has woken up to Islamic State, the Russians, the Americans, the French, the British... they're all bombing them now. What is your family's address – just give me the street name – and I'll make sure they're safe. Do you understand?"

"Yes, sir, it's Rammadi Street." And this was no lie.

CHAPTER FOUR

This they don't teach you at school – not even at the expensive public school that Max and Harry attended. They don't teach you that it is entirely possible to be paid a steady two per cent annual 'management fee' for just sitting on other people's money. Here's ten million dollars... take $200,000 for yourself... have a nice day. Why did his teachers not tell him that, instead of the subjunctive tense of the verb 'to be'? Be that as it may. Far be it for me to say. If truth be told.

Max was a 'star prop trader' with the right pedigree needed to go it alone and attract 'sticky' hedge fund investors – that's to say investors who will stay around for the long-term: institutions, pension funds and endowments. He earned his trading stripes on a proprietary trading desk at Goldman Sachs, that infamous spawning ground for the best of the best, and he had enough cash accumulated from bonuses to stump up the $2 million working capital needed to launch his own fund management firm, and the $10 million he needed to invest in it himself, a critical act to demonstrate his self-belief to savvy and demanding investors.

Star traders earned their reputation by making consistently strong returns, across all market conditions, whilst keeping to their investment strategy. Max was a high concentration short seller, spotting future price declines time after time and betting big. His investment strategy was fundamental equity long short, the most 'vanilla' of all but one that needs detailed research and analysis coupled with large and leveraged trades.

Max had the necessary steady hand, mentally and physically, for this. He sailed close to the wind but could never be proved to be an inside trader for any of his past or present trades. He knew and, more importantly, respected the rules – never would he be a cheat or be cheated. Did this extend into his personal life, Harry wondered time and time again as he slipped between the sheets with Rachel? It worried him that perhaps on some level he knew about their affair.

If truth be told, with assets under management, or 'AUM' in hedge speak, of $150 million (dollars… dollars… Harry only thinks in dollars now) that's $3 million a year earned for the business before they've even started to gamble with the investor's money. Naturally the business has costs: salaries, rent and so on, but many of the big costs get charged back to the fund – that's right – to the investors in the fund. Harry often thinks about some of these investors and knows that teachers, librarians and all the other *Guardian*-reading liberals that he used to count himself among, and how they had no idea that some – okay a tiny – percentage of their precious pension was being allocated to Max and his industry peers to play with at the biggest casino on the planet.

At which point twenty per cent of any winnings are theirs to keep. In a good year, and there's been a couple of rubbish years to factor in since they set up in 2010 but mostly they've been healthy thanks to Max's equity bias, fund performance has annualised at around five per cent. So that's $7.5 million profit on a year's investing, which makes $1.5 million for the firm. For many of the investors, their profit is tax efficient because although the investment manager is in London, the fund itself is domiciled in the Cayman Islands and they too are offshore 'sophisticated' investors. They'd taken a hit on Brexit – $12 million or so, but nothing that couldn't be recouped quickly enough.

And it's not like just going to the bookies and slapping a tenner on Lady Luck to win the two o'clock at Kempton Park, because they are constantly hedging their bets. "That's why they're called a hedge fund, dummy," Harry had once overheard Max telling some stranger in Tramp on Jermyn Street. Mind you, if you make a loss, it has to be recouped before you can earn more performance fee, that's why they call it the high water mark. But even if you don't, it's not like some goon in a cheap suit is going to come round and repossess your house. It's all very civilized and investors can always cut their losses and redeem with a month's notice. This they don't teach you at school.

*   *   *

Harry wakes at six, ten minutes before the alarm of his iPhone with its increasingly annoying ululating New Age medley supposed, he assumes, to gently lead the unconscious mind into the wakefulness, from whatever floaty spaced dreams you might be having.

Except that Harry had been having a sort of semi-nightmare – unsettling more than frightening – involving himself and Max and a frantic tube journey around London. Though this is nothing like the real London; it is a London that only exists in Harry's dreams, where the topography is all askew. Most of North London is countryside, for example. And the bit he always remembers – because this is a dream he has often – is that he finds himself on the wrong Circle Line train and missing the connection that will take him back. Except it's not the Circle Line. It's not even London, except it is and it isn't.

What fucking genius directs these crazy films we call dreams?

A slash of light above the curtains tells him it's a bright day outside, and for the next twenty minutes he runs on automatic. He showers, washing his hair with his prescription anti-dandruff shampoo before lathering in an expensive conditioner that claims to add thickness, and scrubs his body with the contents one of one of those small bottles he habitually picks up from hotels. Harry turns off the shower and, as is his ritual – a moment of pure being on a workday morning – he allows the water to fall from his body, feeling it ripple down his torso and legs, before stepping out of the cubicle and into his towelling dressing gown.

From the fitted wardrobe: a thin blue-striped shirt and navy silk cufflinks from Hackett, navy blue boxer shorts from Marks & Spencer (a Christmas present from his mother, bless her), charcoal-coloured cashmere socks to match his birdseye charcoal-coloured suit; off the peg but well-fitted. No tie: open-collar as usual.

He puts the kettle on and notices, through the expensive bi-folding patio doors courtesy of a previous owner, that it appears to be snowing, which is odd because he can only see a clear blue sky. And then he realises it's the blossom coming off the tree next door. Is it spring already?

A cup of peppermint tea, a brief scan of his unread e-mails, and he slips his wallet into his jacket pocket and is about to set the alarm when he catches sight of something out of the corner of his eye. He gives an involuntary cry, and steps back, the hairs rising on his scalp and the back of his neck. A mouse. At least he hopes it's a mouse.

Fuck, he hates old houses. Why did he allow Max to talk him into this three-stroke-four bedroom late Victorian terrace house in a leafy part of Hammersmith that an enterprising estate agent had once rebranded Brackenbury Village? But it really is like a village, thinks Harry; more 'villagey' perhaps than most villages in the countryside, like the one where his mum lives, which is basically just a bunch of houses plonked down in the middle of some fields, with their one pub full of bores.

Anyway Max insisted he buy here back in 2007 when mortgages were cheap and plentiful, especially when arranged through a broker Max had recommended.

Still £800,000 for three slash four bedrooms – the fourth bedroom barely big enough to house the exercise-bike that he never uses – seemed a lot at the time, and Harry had argued that he didn't need anything this big. But Max had gone on and on, like he was going to make something out of the deal. You've got to have a family home – that's where the market is around here. How did he know? Why did he care? Max just sees the trade in everything. Not to have done it would somehow have injured his sense of right and wrong.

Soon after he bought the place there was the crash, Harry losing his job, with six month's 'voluntary redundancy' pay-off to cushion the blow, and all sorts of dire prophecies about the property market. But interest rates were so low that no one needed to panic sell and anyway people were in a mood to sit tight. And then rich foreigners kept piling into London – a safe haven from the chaotic Eurozone, and for corrupt Russians and other criminals, and for newly enriched Asians with tax-free wealth to invest.

And on and on it went, and Harry's pretty but otherwise unremarkable Victorian house is now apparently worth at least £1.4 million, even with London prime's flattened, post-Brexit softness. But still, that's half a million pure profit – the tiny fourth bedroom where Harry stored suitcases alone adding at least £75K in value. "And that's a conservative estimate," said the agent who had sent about twenty postcards begging for Harry to allow him to value his home and was now, in his excitement, almost bursting out of his cheap suit. "If it goes to sealed bids... well, let's just say that we've been breaking records in this area every week."

He looks at his watch. Six thirty. The house is reasonably close to three underground stations – Shepherd's Bush on the Central Line, Hammersmith on the Piccadilly Line and Ravenscourt Park on the District Line. Harry prefers Ravenscourt Park – it's a shorter walk, and all he needs to do when changing at Hammersmith is to step across the platform and on to the Piccadilly Line, which is never too busy at this time of the morning.

He always gets into the last carriage because it stops nearest to the exit at Green Park. And when he reaches the station, at least a dozen freshly showered and spruced-up men dressed just like Harry in expensive suits and shirts, open at the collar, step out alongside him. If any of them found it amusing they never showed it.

His routine is to buy a croissant and an Americano with hot milk from the Starbucks on Berkeley Street. They always ask him his name so that they can write it on the cup. Harry must have told them that it was Harry hundreds of times, but of course they don't remember; that's not part of the job. So recently he has taken to calling himself Max, safe in the knowledge that Max never steps inside Starbucks; Max's morning routine is to drink a disgusting-looking smoothie containing beetroot, kale and whatever the latest 'superfood' happens to be, from the juice bar two doors along.

The office of Forward-Max Capital LLP is in an elegant redbrick town house on Farm Street. There is a small bank of buzzers in a tin box, each with anonymous, slightly tatty address cards – mostly for companies ending in the letters LLP. This is about as brazenly as hedge funds advertise themselves, although visible through the glass door, the marble staircase and oversized chandelier does all the promotion that is necessary.

Harry buzzes himself in, exchanges pleasantries with the porter, an old-style cockney – probably the last one left in Mayfair – and takes the lift up to the third floor. The building is leased by two other fund managers along with Harry's – although the firm is really Max's, the majority owner with a fifty-one per cent stake. Harry's holding is ten per cent.

Not that Forward-Max Capital LLP actually owns much in the way of assets. There's the furniture – glass and chrome inevitably – and the computers tirelessly parading banks of numbers and Bloomberg charts – six screens each for the portfolio managers, and three for Harry. But most of the tangible assets are hanging on the walls – quality artwork, not from some bespoke office-art website but all carefully sourced from local Cork Street galleries whose owners Max has schmoozed over the years. Modern stuff, semi-abstract landscapes mainly, and nothing too cutting edge.

"Leave that crap to Saatchi and the Russians," as Max once said.

"Good morning... lovely morning... spring has sprung," trills Fi, the latest receptionist-cum-office manager. She's only recently graduated from Exeter University with a degree in French. She's cheerful, presentably good-looking in a slightly bovine way and will no doubt be moving on soon enough, although, God knows, well-paid jobs like this for a twenty-three-year-old in London are hard enough to come by.

"What do we pay you, Fi?" asks Harry absently, almost surprising himself as much as Fi by saying this.

"Forty-five K base," she says, followed by a wary "Why?"

"Oh, sorry... no reason. Just trying to remind myself," he says briskly. "Keep up the good work." He thinks he hears her laugh as he walks through into the open-plan office, where James, Max's co-

CIO, or chief investment officer, is already at his desk.

"Morning," James says though a mouthful of pastry so it sounds more like, "Maw…maw."

The other three desks, usually occupied by Max and the two research analysts – Tim, who is American, and Cyril, who is French and the butt of Max's anti-French comments – are empty save for the banks of computer screens. On the wall, a huge TV screen hangs stuck on low volume and showing the Bloomberg news channel, a stock ticker along the bottom of the screen glowing red and green. James and the analysts continue their discussion and planning around Porsche and Volkswagen, two short positions Max had been looking to put on by borrowing the stock from their prime broker, who had a decent volume in their inventory. James had the authority to do the deals in Max's absence and would be pulling the trigger that day.

Harry is Chief Operating Officer, a 'glorified office manager' as he once heard Max describe the position, and therefore in charge of hiring and firing the likes of Fi. Finance, compliance and operations are also in his remit, although Max, who thinks that only portfolio managers should be taken seriously, likes to say: "There's not much to do once the trade has been made." In reality, given all the regulatory intervention since 2008, Harry had the most liability of them all and would be the one most likely to end up in jail, if it turned out there was any market abuse or other wrongdoing by any of the team. Even portfolio managers were starting to hear that penny drop.

Max had suggested Harry for the role after he lost his back-office job at an investment bank during the crash. His new firm was looking for a COO and Harry was available, and he seemed to have the right credentials. Max always had more confidence in Harry's worth than Harry ever had. More importantly, thinks Harry, he wanted a playmate. "I hate being on my own," Max has said on countless occasions. And now they were doing their personal account trades – the diamonds, the property, paintings, the watches – Harry was also a partner in crime. Except they weren't committing any crimes. More like a hobby really, or, as Max prefers to call it, the concierge game. Every business in Britain is in the same game, he likes to say: "We're concierges to the world."

CHAPTER FIVE

It's eight thirty in Geneva and Max hasn't slept a wink. It's neither early nor late; he doesn't feel refreshed or sleepy; he's living in the past, present and the future all at once, and it's making his head spin.

The plane landed just before three, local time, and then Simon had suggested they all go to a place he knew. It seemed ungrateful to refuse. The club contained an acquaintance, and after a brisk transaction, Simon and Genevieve took it in turns to visit the toilets, sniffing loudly on their return and looking very pleased with themselves. "No thanks," Max had said, on the five or six times he was offered the little paper wrap.

They drank coffee together in an all-night café on the Plaine de Plainpalais before Max took his leave of his by-now gabbling and limb-entwined companions and hailed a cab to his leased apartment in the Paquis – a lively and relatively scruffy but inexpensive district that he preferred to the smart bourgeois parts of town. He has no need for appearances in Geneva.

The two-bedroom flat is on the fifth floor and painted a uniform calico colour, and has a view from the living room of the lake. As he unlocks the front door and steps into the hallway he is hit by the silence. And when he gets used to that, all that he can hear is a ringing in his ears. Ringing… why do they say ringing? It's more like a high-pitched hum; white noise.

He goes over to the bedroom wardrobe, which contains an edited version of his wardrobe back in London: two suits, handmade by an independent tailor who used to visit him back in his investment banking days but which still fit beautifully even though Max has put on several pounds; several Ralph Lauren cashmere V-neck jumpers and a whole row of Turnbull & Asser shirts in varying single-colour shades, but the same monogrammed initials on the cuff: M-D.

There are also the casually expensive clothes, the smart/casual tapered trousers, designer jeans and Gucci loafers, the linen trousers for when it gets sticky in summer, and his running gear. This gives Max an idea and now he is pulling off his clothes as if in a race against time, and slipping into his shorts over black Nike dri-fit leggings and tying his trainer laces. He switches his watch for a complex digital GPS training device and walks briskly out of the apartment. It's a ten-minute jog to the shoreline of Lake Geneva, and now he sets off at a good pace. The early morning is overcast and grey and cold, but slowly he starts to feel better.

After a mile or so, he stops at a bench looking out over the lake, catches his breath and whips his phone out of his tracksuit pocket. The music from his earphones fades politely as he dials Dieter the gemologist, but only gets his answer-phone. "Dieter... Hi, it's Max... It's Tuesday... I'm over from London looking for a good stone. I was wondering whether I could pop over today... maybe this afternoon. Give me a ring. Bye." Then he adds as an afterthought. "Auf wiedersehen." Clocks by Coldplay resumes position and volume, and he continues running.

* * *

It's mid-morning in London, and most of the action on the European stock markets has already happened. There might be another burst of activity just before closing time, but for now a lull has descended and Harry finds himself at his desk and staring out of the elegant Georgian office window.

He'd already phoned the agent about the house on Charles Street and felt confident that the Arab's offer would be accepted by the end of play. Twenty two million with London prime going into reverse was not to be sneezed at.

Houses, and the store people put by them. His mum had only ever rented, and when the big farming estate almost doubled the rate a few years back – "to reflect market conditions" – Harry had stepped in to help out.

He had only ever visited Max's childhood home once, early on after they reconnected in their mid-twenties.

It had been a baking hot summer weekend and, feeling like a couple of swells, they had driven west out of London along the M3, roof down and music blaring, in a hired BMW convertible. "Never buy a car," was one of Max's aphorisms from that time. "One of the worst investments you can make."

He had since heard Rachel, who didn't get on with Max's family and never visited unless she had to, mock the house as 'suburban', but it seemed pretty impressive to Harry as they swung into the gravel drive that searing July Saturday; a detached building clad in red tiles with a steep, almost fairytale roof, and surrounded by close-cropped lawn browning in patches from a prolonged heatwave. "Perfect," said Harry, not for the first time that weekend, as Max cut the ignition.

Two dogs, English Setters Harry later learned, came lumbering out of the house to greet them, tails wagging furiously and the sides of their mouths turned up so they almost appeared to be grinning. A short way behind them came Max's mother, Sally, scrunching unsteadily on the gravel. Standing in the front doorway leaning up against one of the jams was a young woman – a female Max – honeyed skin, molten chocolate-brown eyes and a slightly sardonic smile on her lips.

Natasha was the sister's name and she was the most immediately welcoming of the family. Sally, the mother, was clearly besotted with her son, and seemed to view Harry as unfortunately necessary baggage. Max's father, Michael (or, as he insisted, Mike) was a semi-retired surveyor who had made his first fortune buying and then quickly reselling an office block on the Fulham waterfront back in the Eighties. They found him in the living room watching Test cricket on TV. He was wearing a sleeveless cricket jumper, Harry remembers, dirty old tennis shoes on feet that were up on a coffee table on which sat an open bottle of vintage white Burgundy. He didn't offer them a glass.

"How we doing?" asked Max.

"What do you think? Another sodding England batting collapse in the offing," said his father, before reaching up and giving Harry a perfunctory handshake. "Follow the cricket, Harry?"

It was the first of many such enquiries that weekend to which he could only give an apologetic "No." Do you play golf, Harry? No. Follow the rugby? No. Like skiing? No.

"Come on," said Max. "Let's go and find Tash."

Max's sister was lying on the lawn, propped up on her elbows and gently pushing away the two dogs who, tails thumping on the turf, were attempting to nuzzle into her. Harry could see the attraction. Long brown legs were topped by cropped white shorts, a white cotton shirt was open to reveal the top of her cleavage, the smooth tan broken up here with the faintest of freckles. With her sunglasses perched back on her honey-coloured hair, she looked a picture of health and vitality. But she also looked too disconcertingly like Max for Harry to find her immediately attractive.

To Harry's surprise, Max twisted her round, sat down on Tash's stomach and, straddling her, leant in and kissed his sister on the lips, before grabbing her shades and putting them on. "Get off," she said laughing, wriggling beneath his weight. Max jumped up and walked off, followed swiftly by Tash, who jumped on his back, Max grasping her legs piggyback style, and the two of them trotted off laughing towards the tennis court. Was this what they call horseplay, wondered Harry? He was an only child and had always found sibling relationships both mysterious and fascinating. He called her 'Moo' and she called him 'Squidge', and before his eyes, Max and Tash seemed to be quickly reverting to their younger selves.

"Do you play tennis, Harry?" Tash had turned, still smiling, walking backwards now, having slid off Max's back.

"A bit," replied Harry truthfully, grateful not to have to say 'no' again.

"Good, we can have a game later. The Buxtons are coming over. They're friends of my parents… neighbours."

The Buxtons duly came over. Pimms was drunk, as if no cliché of an English summer was going to be omitted this weekend, tennis balls smashed tipsily out of the court and into the shrubbery, and England's dismal batting performance bemoaned. Supper was a drunken affair, with everyone catching up on each other's lives in bellowing voices, while Harry, feeling excluded from their jovial banter, stroked the head of one of the Setters that had been lain on his lap, the dog's eyes staring dreamily up at him.

And not just excluded, but somehow meagre and unwholesome as they revealed the details of their lives: rounds of golf at Sunningdale, the debenture at Lords, upcoming summer holidays in villas in the Luberon and Tuscany, weekends here, there and everywhere, and underpinning it all, the sense of invincible wealth: of money earned and now stashed away in perpetuity, and their outlook as cloudless as the weather. He tried not to, but Harry couldn't help thinking of his mother in Norfolk, getting by on her cleaner's pay, and never going anywhere further than Cromer for her weekly shop.

It wasn't until the next day, sitting out under a huge parasol and eating a lunch (he still recalled) of coronation chicken, that Mike – perhaps because other avenues of conversation had dried up – started to take a personal interest in Harry, and in particular Harry's schooldays with Max. Had he been in any of the teams? No. Not even the house teams? No.

Harry couldn't see any common ground, and it seems that Mike, dressed in tennis shorts (he had played Natasha before lunch) and a slightly ludicrous sunhat, had come to the same conclusion. He poured another glass of wine and confined himself to remarking about the incredible weather they were having. Was Harry going anywhere for the summer? No.

"Harry's dad was killed in the Falklands," Max blurted out, as if he felt the need to make his new friend more interesting to his family.

"Gosh... oh how dreadful," said Sally, a ladle of coronation chicken now suspended halfway between the platter and her plate, as if to complete the operation would be somehow in bad taste. Harry was aware of a wasp hovering over his wine glass.

"Army? Navy?" said Mike, flushed from the wine and G&T, in a voice that suggested he was familiar with the services.

"Army," said Harry, batting the wasp away with his hand. "Special Forces."

This last one was a new lie. Up until now he had been comforted by the fact that it would take a lot of painstaking research for any of his friends – none of whom were given to painstaking research – to unearth a roll call of the Falklands casualties. Nowadays anyone could Google it. Harry hoped that his father being in Special Forces might mean his death was some sort of secret. But now, around this garden table amidst these tipsy strangers, that lie seemed preposterous. But instead of bursting out laughing at the mention of the words 'special forces', however, everyone nodded in unison and started eating the salad.

"Game of croquet after? Harry... Squidge?" said Tash, breaking the spell.

"Excellent idea, Moo," said Max.

Harry nodded enthusiastically. Weirdly croquet was one sport – if sport was what it was – that he was naturally quite good at. They'd played it at school and at friends' houses, usually while drunk or stoned. But that afternoon he allowed Max and Tash to take a commanding lead as he deliberately fluffed his shots. And when his ball was posted, he excused himself and went indoors. If they wanted to laugh about him now, Harry's dad in the Special Forces, it would be safe to do so.

He excused himself and went up to his room, a large sunny bedroom that overlooked the lawn, to pack. He could see them all bent over their mallets, seemingly absorbed in the game. Mike was sitting with his ridiculous straw hat pulled over his face, asleep by the look of it.

Max's room was across the landing, a strangely impersonal

43

space for what was a childhood bedroom, as if all the mementoes had been stripped out, the past erased – everything except three team photographs from school. The rugby first XV, with Max grinning on the far left of the back row. The cricket X1, Max again peripheral, but still part of the team. The hockey X1... ditto.

Natasha's room was further down the landing; Harry had already poked his nose in there the evening before. This was much more what a one-time teenager's room should look like: a chaotic mix of pop-star posters (there was a particularly large one of Damon Albarn), horse-riding rosettes and snapshots of Tash and her friends goofing around. There was even a teddy bear propped on a chair in the corner. But it was the room next door that interested Harry.

Where the rest of the woodwork on the landing had at some time in the recent past been given fresh coats of white paint, this door had been left alone, scuffed and yellowing, with two stickers on adjoining panels: 'Acid... Happy Mondays... E's the thing. He tried the handle. It was locked.

And then he remembered something – in fact he remembered something he had recalled before but then forgotten. He trotted downstairs and into the room where Mike had been watching cricket and where Harry recalled seeing a collection of family photographs in silver frames arranged across the top of a grand piano.

Recent ones of the family on holiday somewhere sunny. A wedding photograph of Max and Rachel – both looking extraordinarily glamorous but also wearing expressions that suggested that the whole thing was one big joke – or perhaps that was just Harry putting a retrospective gloss on what he now knew of their marriage. Rachel in her wedding dress with its plunging neckline, plunging to places he knew only too well. He suddenly felt intrusive, guilty in a way that he somehow didn't when rolling around in Max's bed with his wife.

Towards the back of the piano, records of further family holidays with Max and Tash now teenagers – Tash was perhaps thirteen, to judge by the not-long budded breasts barely justifying the bikini top. Max, Harry knew, was four years older, which would make him seventeen or thereabouts, a hairless, well-honed adolescent torso and an unruly mop where now it was carefully groomed. He was sitting at a table, lifting the lobster tail that was on his plate so that the camera could catch it, and grinning at the person taking the picture. Tash was at the far end of the table, looking at Max, and between them was another boy, a couple of years younger than Max perhaps, also topless and also looking at Max. He was finer boned, more feminine than his brother, with a sardonic twist to his lips – but definitely from the same stock.

Harry tried to remember his name. Funny how you know all the older children at school, but the younger ones barely registered. Nick was it? Why did he think it was Nick? And there, as further proof, was a double portrait of Max and his brother dressed in suits, as they would have done when travelling to school at the beginning of term. And right at the back, Max, his brother and Tash as children – Tash looked about four or five – posed in a row and smiling dutifully at the photographer.

Harry drove back to London so he couldn't see Max's face as he asked, "Don't you have a younger brother?"

"Had a younger brother. Nicky…" said Max.

"Nick… I thought so… Oh God, sorry. You mean…"

"He died when he was eighteen… drowned in his own puke the silly bugger…"

Harry had guessed that he was dead. When he had rejoined the family in the garden they suddenly seemed revealed to him in a new light. Mike was drinking too much, Sally seemed ineffably sad, the crows' feet around eyes and mouth not from smiling but from sobbing uncontrollably, alone in the endless afternoons. And Tash's gaiety and horseplay now seemed forced. Only Max seemed the same: unmovable, steady, unaffected.

"Oh Christ, sorry. Was it drugs?" asked Harry, moving over to the slow lane to allow the tailgaters to pass.

"Uppers, downers, e, speed, hash, but mainly alcohol. The toxicology report…" Max stopped and cleared his throat before continuing. "He was taking a holiday down in Cornwall after his A-levels, a week-long party by all accounts. They found him one morning…"

"Shit," said Harry, casting a glance at Max. He was looking stonily ahead.

"We don't really talk about it."

CHAPTER SIX

In Geneva, Max jogs back to his flat, showers, changes and, less than an hour later, is buzzed through a door of bullet-proof glass. Here he is eyeballed by a burly unsmiling man squeezed into a uniform that is supposed to suggest some sort of connection with the police.

The man nods at him, another glass door slides open and Max steps into a carpeted reception panelled with light oak, watched at each ceiling corner by a CCTV camera. To the right of the reception desk is a doorway to a corridor, but it's framed by a metal detector like the ones at airports, through which he must walk, having first divested himself of his watch, crammed money clip, keys and iPhone. A middle-aged receptionist asks him to wait a moment, gesturing to a leather couch in front of coffee table on which jewellery auction catalogues from Sotheby's and Christie's are neatly stacked.

He picks one up but almost at once a severe-looking woman in her thirties, with bunched strawberry blonde hair and a white smock rather like a dental nurse, steps into the room and holds out a small cold bony hand. Gretchen, remembers Max, that's the name of Dieter's assistant. The name seems so right for her. He follows her through an open solid steel door, which she closes after them and locks.

Dieter, no jacket and in rolled shirt sleeves, is standing stock still in front of a fluorescent lamp, staring intently at a small gem through his jeweller's loupe, thick lines spreading out from the corners of his eyes after decades of inspecting diamonds in this way. Maybe he was even born squinting into a magnifying glass. Gretchen simply stands in front of him until he notices her. He then looks up, and then at Max. "Mr Max. How are we?"

Dieter is a geeky geochemist at heart, overlain with a veneer of business acumen picked up while working in Antwerp and New York. Science rather than money is his driving force, and although Max is only a new and distinctly small-time downstream client, Dieter likes him because Max listens to him explain his love affair with diamonds, unlike those other grabby middlemen who beat a path to his cutting shop-cum-showroom in Geneva.

Max wants to learn about stones. He is genuinely fascinated and awestruck when Dieter speaks of some diamonds being almost as old as the earth, formed out of the immense heat and pressure of ancient eruptions or meteorite strikes.

And Max is genuinely interested. He admires people who know stuff.

"What is it?" he asks of the clear diamond that Dieter is now popping into a plastic pouch and handing to his white-coated assistant. Without a word she takes it into a back room, having first closed a solid-steel barred gate behind as quietly as it is possible to close a solid-steel barred gate.

"Oh, that's nothing much, part of a batch that came in this morning. But you, my friend, are in luck. Or maybe. How much do you have to spend?"

"Now that, my friend, is the eternal question."

He likes to call Dieter 'my friend' as if saying it will make it real, and gratifyingly Dieter seemed to have picked up the habit too. He reminds Max of the swots at school – the academic boys who would initially assume that Max was one of 'the lads' – a chancer hoping to steal their homework or pick their brains. Max wanted to do neither, just win them round by showing interest and erudition of his own. He knows how to be popular with all sorts of people; winning them round, that was the game.

It had been like that with Harry. When they had met up again by chance after school and university – it was a summer night outside a pub in Fulham – the 'Sloaney Pony' everybody called it – Harry was a raving leftie. It must have been after the Gulf War in 2003 because Harry was full of it – how Tony Blair was a liar who should be tried for war crimes, and so on. Max had been shocked by his opinions being uttered in a pub like this, where England's performance in the rugby or cricket was a more usual topic of conversation, but he was also intrigued. He didn't shout Harry down, like some of his party, but asked him questions.

Not that Harry could see past Max's expensive suit, not for a while anyway. Harry was a freelance journalist back then – writing interviews with visiting French film directors and selling them to the broadsheets for a pittance. He lived in Fulham with a bunch of other losers, whose main pastime seemed to be smoking spliffs and getting drunk. Wouldn't he like to earn some proper money, Max used to ask? And the message coming back from those small blue unhappy eyes was that, 'Yes… I really would like to. Show me the way.'

"Gretchen!" Dieter calls, raising his soft voice. Gretchen appears at the barred door. In her white coat and glasses, Max has an unwanted flashback to some porn video he has watched in the dim and distant past – one of the ones which actually bothered with a storyline. *Hot Dentists on the Job,* or *Horny Medical Examination* or something like that, a little light fiction before everyone is naked and getting down to the business. Meat and two veg, as Harry calls it. Harry's funny like that.

Rachel made him give up pornography. Or rather, about a month before their wedding – on a Saturday morning, he recalls – she appeared at his front door with a battered old suitcase from God knows where. She then went through the house picking up DVDs, old VHSs, magazines – even long-discarded copies of *Esquire and Loaded* – and piled them all into the suitcase.

"No more wanking off at photographs," she said. "Or videos." And she had driven Max and the suitcase down to the tip in Wandsworth, and chucked the whole lot into the skip marked 'household waste'. *Hot Dentists and Horny Nurses* were recycled, and Max has been as good as his word. He never watches the stuff unless he can't help it – which usually means Simon and his ever more freakish discoveries from the outer reaches of the Internet.

"Can you get me the New York pink?" Dieter asks Gretchen

and she walks off briskly. He can see that Dieter is excited by something, and it's not his assistant. Are they having a relationship? Dieter seems so asexual, it's hard to tell. Perhaps he's gay. Perhaps he fancies Max. Well, that can't be bad for business.

"While she's getting that one," says Dieter. "Let me show you something else."

He shakes the mouse across the desktop and starts clicking around on his computer screen until the picture he wants appears. It's of a massive, pink uncut diamond. "I bought this about two months ago," he says.

"It's huge," says Max peering at the pink rock with its sharp edges and uneven shape. "How many carats is she?"

"One hundred uncut."

Max duly whistles, but instead of looking proud, Dieter seems preoccupied, even a little worried. "We've been cutting and polishing it and so far so good, but large stones can be treacherous."

"Yes," says Max, who has heard about the risks of cutting large stones. "Remind me." The role of student is hard to shake off.

Dieter turns off the computer screen, and looks where his hand rests on the mouse. "Who knows what flaws lie beneath such beauty," he says dramatically, making it sound somehow tragic in his Germanic accent. But then it could be tragic. "Knots... fractures... we could be cutting and – kapow! – diamond dust. Shattered bits that might polish up into a cheap little engagement ring that you'd struggle to get 300 euros for." He shrugs.

"That's the risk – but upside is also great for the brave diamantaire. How much did you pay for it?"

"Ha... not so fast," says Dieter, taking off his glasses and polishing them with a cloth. "Anyway I have a good feeling about this one. I can't see any clouds or anything explosive, and if my hunch is correct, we are working our way towards a healthy octahedron, in which case there shouldn't be too much wastage." He pauses for effect. "When I do model it into a beautiful vivid fifty-carat pear-shaped pendant fit for the Sultan of Brunei, then we can talk about price. Perhaps I can give it a name – that has to be good for an extra half a million. Queen of the River perhaps – it's alluvial, you know. It was found in a river."

Max knows what an alluvial diamond is, because Dieter has also explained this to him before on several occasions. Most diamonds are mined, after tens of millions of dollars have been poured into geological surveys in some of the most inhospitable places on the planet – Siberia, the Barrens Sea, the Kalahari Desert. But sometimes... sometimes somebody out for a day's fishing on a river in somewhere sunny like Brazil sees something glinting beneath the surface of the water, and then they and their family never have to work again.

There is a clank, the gate opens and Gretchen appears with a cloth in her hand. Dieter takes it from her and unfolds a large orange stone. "We cut this just last week. It's 30.4 carats, from a seventy-carat rough. That's a lot of waste but it's a beautiful pure orange... a real 'fancy'. Here take a look... take a seat. Put it against one of these sheets of paper."

Max knows what to do. Dieter passes him the stone and his magnifying loupe and stands back. Max sits down at a desk that has padded elbow rests and whose surface is covered with sheets of white paper. He puts the loupe to his eye and finds himself being sucked into a kaleidoscopic universe of brilliant orange light so pure that it makes him want to gasp. He doesn't though because that would be bad for business.

"It's flawless," says Dieter, observing with a knowing smile Max's silent admiration. It is too, as far as Max can see at ten-times magnification. "If there had been any nasty surprises it would have come out in the cutting and polishing," says Dieter, unfolding the cloth that will soon re-encase the stone.

"Oranges aren't worth as much as pinks or whites, are they?"

"Oranges as clear and vivid as this one are. One hundred and fifty thousand dollars a carat."

Max calculates quickly. That's four and a half million bucks. "One hundred and twenty," he says. Dieter smiles as if he had been expecting this silly game. "One hundred and forty and that's my final offer. Isn't that what they say in films?"

"One hundred and thirty and I'll send my client round in a jiffy," says Max, holding the gem up to the loupe once more, as if reluctant to hand it back. It's true; the orange is utterly lovely.

"In a jiffy? One hundred and forty and I'll keep it exclusive."

"One three five and it's a deal," says Max. "And I want first dibs at that big pink one when it's ready. As long as you don't smash it to pieces in the meantime."

CHAPTER SEVEN

Harry gives it an hour after the key European exchanges have closed and the street's equity sales bankers have gone home, or off to the gym, bar or wherever they spend their evenings. Fi packed up at five thirty on the dot as she does every evening, yodelling a hearty *Goodnight!* from the reception area.

He now has the place to himself. Apart from the desks and the screens, the room looks like what it originally was – the drawing room of a Mayfair town house, complete with ornate fire-surround, elaborate cornicing and thick silk curtains. He re-reads Max's e-mail about the diamond, which sounds promising although he has reservations about the colour. Doesn't the Arab like pink? 'Don't worry – it's a beauty… a "fancy" as they say in the trade' Max e-mails back at once. And if he doesn't like it, we'll get another one for him. When will Max be back? Tomorrow night… Simon's invited him up for a day's skiing and they're leaving for his chalet in Verbier this evening. James the assistant can cover the portfolio.

Harry calls Rachel's mobile. She answers on the second ring. "How was the breakfast meeting?" he asks.

"So boring I've already forgotten what it was about. How was your day with your playmate away gadding on the ski slopes?"

"I kind of remember having sushi at lunch but apart from that I don't think I did very much work today," he says. "Oh, yes, I think I bought a house. Anyway Max has been buying a diamond for us."

"Aren't you the lucky one? I'll be fortunate to get a bottle of duty free."

"By the way, my tube will be rattling through Baron's Court in about twenty mins. I could bring a bottle myself… and something to eat."

"I'm not eating at the moment, but bring the bottle."

* * *

It's gone eleven by the time he gets back to his house in W6. The day had been blue and clear and full of early spring but now it is cold and the house feels cold. He switches off the alarm by punching in the four-digit code, and remembers the mouse. He'll get a trap at the weekend.

He turns up the central heating thermostat and, picking up the remote control from the coffee table, switches on the television. A harassed-looking politician is being grilled on *Question Time*. "I know how you feel," Harry says out loud, surprised to see condensation plume with his breath as he does so. He won't take his coat off just yet. He hasn't eaten but the fridge doesn't hold out much promise – although there is a pair of cold sausages that don't appear to have any mould on them. He sniffs the milk and miraculously it doesn't smell off, so he pours himself a bowl of Bran Flakes.

The evening with Rachel didn't unfold in the cheerfully uncomplicated manner he had anticipated. They'd drunk a couple of glasses each of the chilled Veuve Clicquot Champagne he had picked up in Fortnum's, before Rachel, still in her work clothes, says, "Come on, then," and started towards the bedroom. It seems so bloodless this exchange that Harry is taken aback. Christ, he thinks, Rachel is being the man and I'm the girl who needs wooing, who requires foreplay.

By the time he's undressed she's already naked under the duvet. Harry slips in and she pulls the duvet away and lies flat on her back with an impatient look on her face. There was a time when the sight of her naked would have been enough. The first two or three times the simple act of transgression – of being with his best friend's wife – had been enough. And Rachel has a great body, he thought. Lithe, a naturally honeyed skin, and long straight dark hair of the type Harry had always liked. He couldn't quite believe she would want to be fucked by him – she was, as the expression goes, out of his league.

But now, nothing. He dutifully licks her breasts, and runs his fingers down over her stomach and into her pubic hair, and she gives a little moan, but he feels strangely detached, going through the motions. She grabs for his flaccid cock, and he thinks she's about to say something when from nowhere comes the image of Mary, his friend from the old days – or his sort-of-not-exactly friend from his impoverished I-want-to-be-a-writer days – comes to mind and he starts to stiffen. Strange, he thinks, but goes with it, blocking out the reality of Rachel and thinking instead of Mary. What does she look like naked?

They see each other maybe twice a year – maybe once a year now – and have a drink in Soho. Mary is a freelance journalist, regular on a foreign desk last time he heard. They get on easily together and, as the conversation turns to films, novels and art – stuff that just doesn't figure in his life now – Harry feels himself sloughing off an alien skin, the one that's stitched together with equities, stop signals. He feels as if he has somehow come home.

He's inside Mary now, Rachel starting to writhe beneath his rhythmic pushing. He opens his eyes and sees Rachel watching him, so he locks his mouth on to hers to block out her gaze. He feels himself softening and thinks again of Mary – of Mary taking her clothes off. Where has this all come from? And as he empties himself into Rachel, who has not yet come, he thinks: I must give Mary a ring tomorrow. It's time we met up for a drink. And with the thought he starts to harden again, which Rachel takes as a signal to continue writhing beneath him, working herself up with moans and yelps to an orgasm. Or so he supposes, not particularly caring either way.

Afterwards they both have a bath – one after the other, Harry dipping into Rachel's oily water. He notices again all her expensive ointments and creams and candles. Back downstairs it's only half nine. She's wrapped in one of Max's dressing gowns as she pours him a glass of champagne. She doesn't join him on the sofa but takes the armchair facing him across the coffee table littered with glossy magazines – *Vogue, Harpers Bazaar, Tatler* – and untroubled books of photography, still in their wrappers.

"Don't you feel bad screwing your best friend's wife?" she asks followed quickly by "While the cat's away the mouse turns into a rat!"

He frowns. He's about to tell her about the mouse in his house, but it's not going to be that sort of conversation, he can see that. He's had countless scenes like this with girlfriends over the years, usually about his inability to commit. Anyway, there's an obvious riposte to that but he waits before replying, not entirely sure whether this is heading towards friendly banter or an argument. But then he realises he doesn't mind either way.

"Don't you feel bad screwing your husband's best mate?"

She doesn't flinch. She wants an argument. "Are you his best mate? Are you his mate at all?"

This takes Harry aback – as does his answer. "I love him like my father," he says. "I mean my brother... Freudian slip."

Rachel laughs, and then looks at him more softly than she has all evening. "You lost your father, didn't you? The Falklands War or something."

"Maybe Max is a father to me," he says, ignoring the question.

"How old were you?"

"I was three. I don't remember him and I don't remember him being killed."

"What can that be like?" Rachel asks herself, pouring champagne into her flute, ignoring Harry's glass and wrapping Max's dressing gown tighter around her. "I'm incredibly close to my father."

"I guess I'm incredibly close to my mother."

"She lives in Norfolk doesn't she?" says Rachel, imagining a Georgian rectory with a long gravel drive instead of the reality – a terrace of former farmworkers' houses on a main road. "I'll tell you what I think," she says. "And everybody thinks the same... Max's family, his other friends... the abominable Simon... they think you are a substitute for Max's dead younger brother..."

"Nicky? Nonsense..." The thought had crossed his mind.

"Wait a minute… listen." Her voice is thick with drink, and he can see her making an effort to arrange her thoughts. "Listen. They think that… they think that he thinks that if he can save you, then somehow he's making up for not saving Nicky."

"There may be a bit of that, I suppose."

"There's a bloody lot of that."

"What about you?" asks Harry, eager to change the subject. And then the question that he has always assumed he knew the answer to – the reason why he would have ever even considered having an affair with Rachel.

"Do you love Max?"

"Sometimes," she replies at once; it was a question she had obviously asked herself too. "He's a good man. And he used to be fun. You weren't around when we got married, were you?"

This is true. Harry and Max had been at school together, although not great friends. Not friends at all, if truth be told. They had different interests and they hung out with different groups of boys, although to be honest Harry could hardly remember Max at all. Biggish bloke who ran with the hearties – not particularly sporting himself but definitely not an intellectual. Still he'd gone to university, the same one as Harry – and with their shared schooldays it seemed inevitable that they would become acquaintances at least.

"No. You got married during my lost years," he says, using his favoured description of his early twenties, as if he were some sort of heroic alcoholic author, or a rock star with a heroin habit instead of a rather clueless young man sleeping on friends' floors in London, trying to get a foothold in journalism, spouting too much left-wing politics and smoking too much gear.

By the time they bumped into each other again in that pub in Fulham, Max was married. And obviously doing well for himself. Harry himself was hanging out with some underachieving druggie types from university, who were now all starting jobs in London with little or no enthusiasm.

"Fuck, for me those years were great," says Rachel, her voice thick, her eyes absent. "We fucking flew. High above the clouds… like gods, you know? Max was the best fucking trader, worked harder, played harder… we lived like gods, spending, spending, spending…"

"Masters of the universe," says Harry, trying to remember exactly what Rachel did for a living. Something high up in shopping, was the best he could come up with – some sort of buyer for a chain of luxury shops. He could imagine her and Max on an endless round of parties, holidays and nightclubs, their noses never far from a wrapper of cocaine.

"That's such a cliché, but yeah…" Rachel laughs. "We had the best fucking wedding – the reception was in the Lanesborough… everyone came… everybody… I think we were drunk for three days solid. Never out of bed for two of them."

She helps herself to the last of the champagne.

"Then we bought this place and just carried on as before. We worked hard, we got richer, we… but we weren't gods any more. Something changed. We'd come down from the clouds somehow… do you understand?"

"Married life, I guess; it's supposed to change you," says Harry. "I wouldn't know. Don't you want children?"

She looks at him for a moment. "Yes, I really do, now."

A thought crosses Harry's mind that Rachel is quick to read. "Don't worry, when I have babies it will be with Max."

"Better breeding stock, I suppose," says Harry. It was meant as a joke but sounds a bit pathetic, he thinks.

"Much better breeding stock." She's smiling. "What about you? Do you want children?"

"No," says Harry emphatically.

"That was strong. Why not?"

"I wouldn't inflict this world on anyone".

Harry looks so solemn that Rachel laughs despite herself.

"Has it been that bad? You know what I like about you? Emotional intelligence. It's like being with one of my girl friends."

"Thanks."

"Anyway it's a compliment. Cats and dogs..."

"Cats and dogs?"

"Yes, cats and dogs," says Rachel. "Most men are dogs –loyal, brave and a bit needy. But you're a cat... independent, selfish... you walk alone."

Harry doesn't say anything. Rachel just smiles a bit muzzily.

"Yes, you walk alone. But, look, on the baby front, time's running out, even for a goddess. You know what I think now? I think he was running away all that time, running away from what happened to Nicky. And I think weirdly you kind of saved him."

"Then we saved each other."

"Max says he saved you from scribbling for a living."

"I guess he did that," says Harry, and thinks again of Mary, who still scribbles for a living, and he felt protective of her.

"Should we stop doing this?" he asks suddenly, surprising himself.

Rachel gives a dry little chuckle and stands up, cocooned in Max's dressing gown as if it was a mink coat or the sanctity of marriage itself. "Too much baby talk, huh? It's been a good talk anyway; we should do this more often instead of fucking."

Harry is thinking: I agree. This is more pleasant.

"Well, I'm going on holiday on Saturday for a week," she announces, padding off to the kitchen and re-emerging with a fresh bottle of champagne, which she hands to Harry to open "Let's see what happens when I get back."

"A holiday?" he says, taking the bottle and planting it on the coffee table. "Where? Who with?"

She gives another dry little laugh. "Don't worry, it's with a girl friend from work…"

"I wasn't worrying…"

"Jess, do you know her? Anyway… Dubai. We're both dying for some bloody sun." Dubai sounds about right, thinks Harry, who has never had the desire to go there. Max has been, but from how he describes it – artificial beaches, air-conditioned shopping malls – it sounds dreadful.

"Let's see what happens," she says.

He takes this as his cue. Leaving the bottle of champagne unopened, he stands and walks into the hallway and picks up his coat from where he has left it folded over the arm of an antique wooden chair.

"You're not angry, are you?" she asks, following him into the hall.

"Does Max want children?" he asks, ignoring her question. He does feel a bit angry; perhaps very angry, and he isn't sure why.

"Yes, I think he does, or he would if…"

"If what?"

"It's like he's blocked. I don't think he's properly got over Nicky yet. His sister… Tash… she's surprisingly deep, you know. Do you know what she once said to me?"

"No."

"She was talking in therapy terms, of course, but she said Max would never get over Nicky until he had killed you."

*   *   *

Back at the house in Hammersmith – he can't bring himself to call it 'home' – he finds a letter on his doormat along with the advertising circulars. It's his mother's weirdly ornate handwriting on the envelope. De-activating the house alarm and looking around for any sign of small animals, he pulls open the envelope. Inside is a cutting, no more, the typeface he recognises instantly as being that of the only newspaper his mother ever buys: *The Eastern Daily Press*.

Norfolk businessman charged with child sex offences, reads the headline, before continuing: *A businessman from Norwich, Nicholas Mooreland, 63, has been charged with 15 offences of indecency between 1975 and 1987, against five boys aged between 10 and 14. The charges, authorised by the Crown Prosecution Service, result from an investigation by Norfolk Police specialist child protection detectives after information began to be received by Norfolk Constabulary in late 2014.*

There's more, but Harry folds the cutting and places it back into the envelope and places the envelope on the living room mantelpiece. He then picks it up again and slips the letter in between the pages of a road atlas lying on the coffee table.

On the kitchen table he opens his laptop and goes online, tapping the name Nicholas Mooreland into Google. Nothing. When he adds the word Norfolk, he is presented with the online version of the press cutting. He scrolls down.

There are no allegations of offending since 1987 and police stress there is no evidence to suggest that any children have been recently or are currently at risk.

Harry flips over to Facebook and looks up Mary. She doesn't post much stuff but she once told him she's 'a lurker' – always watching but never writing stuff. Maybe the world can be divided into posters and lurkers. Harry never touches social media – on Max's strictest instructions. "You can stop that at once," he'd told him when Harry said he'd opened a Twitter account. He still had his Facebook account though.

Mary's last message is a photograph of her with a girl friend taken in Budapest last summer. They're both posing with sunglasses in a larky way. 'Can't decide whether I prefer Buda or Pest' it says. Someone called Chris has written 'Is Pest full of pests?' and she has twelve 'likes' for the posting. Harry rests his cursor on the 'like' button but doesn't recognise any of the names that pop up. Suddenly he notices someone is messaging him directly. It's Mary.

CHAPTER EIGHT

Max traverses the foot of the black run and slides to a halt outside the bar-restaurant at the bottom. Simon, a far stronger skier, has already arrived and Max's recognises his skis and sticks poking up out of a mound of snow by the door. The slopes aren't busy this weekday in school term-time.

Releasing his own skis, he stomps inside the welcome fug and notices Simon already seated at a table with two small glasses of lager in front of him. "Got you a beer," he says without looking up from his phone.

"Thanks, I think I'll get a coffee too," says Max. "Fancy one?"

Simon grunts what Max takes to be a 'no' and continues to sullenly gaze at the numbers passing on his mobile. Max looks around for a waitress, and wonders once again about Simon's addiction to his screens. And then he notices that Simon is not alone – at least half the skiers in the restaurant are either thumbing text messages or intently reading one.

It's only eleven but they have been at it since eight, the bracing Alpine air shaking off a lingering sambucca hangover. They'd been driven up to Simon's chalet in Verbier yesterday evening, stopping off in the town itself for supper, before heading the last quarter mile up to the chalet, a traditional wooden affair up on the pistes, with access directly on to the slopes. Yours for fourteen million Swiss francs. Simon could have told him to the exact second what fourteen million Swiss francs would buy you in sterling, or euros or dollars or any other currency you fancy.

Max has a text from someone called Mahmoud Hakim Al-Wadhi to say that he has been authorised by the Saudi to inspect the diamond, and that he will be in Geneva tomorrow. Max phones Dieter to make sure the diamond can be at the safety deposit box by the end of today – the inspection will take place at the bank in

Geneva where Max has his personal trading account. The Arabs always pay into that account.

"How's the big pink coming along?" he asks.

"We're nearly there," says Dieter. "No problems anticipated."

"Is that your gay mate?" says Simon still looking at his mobile. "You know, Kimber."

"Harry, you mean," says Max, annoyed as always when Simon implied the Harry was gay. "No, it's my diamond-cutter in Geneva. Harry is holding the fort."

"Holding his dick, more like. Dad was a war hero or something?"

"Well, he was killed in the Falklands," says Max, glad to change the subject from Harry's alleged sexuality. Why did Simon think Harry was gay?

"Bit of a waste of space," continues Simon, still staring at his phone. The waitress places a café crème in front of Max, who picks up his beer and takes a big gulp. "Why do you hold on to him? Bum buddy?"

"Don't be objectionable, Simon, we were at school together, as it happens," says Max, before finishing off the rest of the beer in one. "He's good at what he does."

"And what's that?"

"Lots of things."

"You know what I think?" says Simon, finally looking at Max as he speaks. "I think you just don't like being on your own. And this Kimber, he's like having a dog with you all the time. Don't knock it; I had a lovely spaniel once, went everywhere with me – even to the pub. Bloody nuisance in the end though. Always driving it to kennels. Got run over on a shoot down in Sussex. Someone's Range Rover went over him. Bloody awful, had to give him both barrels, but can't say I was that sorry."

"Are you suggesting I shoot Harry?," says Max, wondering whether he ought to have another beer if they still had a few black runs to put in before lunch. "You could be right about me needing company though."

"Hor… hor… hor…" Simon, his lips pursed, has a look of glee on his red, sunburnt face. "Just made an absolute killing." He puts his phone down and looks around him, as if registering his surroundings for the first time.

"And I'm selling a pretty diamond," says Max. "Let's celebrate. Mine's a coffee with whipped cream."

* * *

Harry has arranged to meet Mary in a pub near Leicester Square, after which they are going to go for a meal in Chinatown. He decides to walk as it's a dry, if chilly, evening. From the office in Mayfair he slips through Dover Yard, past the shop where Max encouraged him to spend five thousand on his watch, and advised him that he carefully keep its original box and UK-stamped perforated certificate for future part exchange, which Harry has since kept locked in his small bedroom safe. He glances at the Rolex now. Just before seven: no need to hurry.

He exchanges nods with the doorman outside The Arts Club in Dover Street, before swinging round on to New Bond Street with its flags of a hundred different luxury brands. He passes Asprey, Bulgari, Boucheron, Tiffany, Cartier and Boodles, stopping behind an Italian couple volubly admiring a white diamond necklace set in platinum. Their clients don't shop here. The Arabs prefer Max's discreet concierge service, believing – rightly – that they are getting a better bargain and a better product.

He strides up Cork Street, glimpsing at the latest exhibitions as he goes. The paintings speak of expensive good taste rather than creative innovation. A tall, gaunt young man in a long, fur-trimmed coat is gazing in at one of the windows – his hairline severely shaved while his beard makes him look like a Tsarist monk as designed by Jean-Paul Gautier; in Mayfair even the freaks look a million dollars.

Actually quite a few of the rich people around here look freakish, Harry often thinks. It's as if too much money – like religious people say it does – has actually warped their souls. he thinks, poverty can have the same effect, as he finds him; Burlington Street. Burlington Street, Burlington Arcade, Burlington Bertie. For some reason Harry thinks of Max when he thinks of Burlington Bertie – unfairly, he acknowledges, because Max isn't really like that at all. Max is anything but a foppish idler.

And then he reaches Regent Street, the great river of humanity – shopping bags in hand, eyes determinedly in front of them – that divides Mayfair and Soho; two completely different worlds separated by wealth and this unceasing torrent of shoppers and tourists. Stepping into Beak Street, and therefore into Soho, is for Harry also like stepping back into his past. His early twenties in viewing theatres – De Lane Lea, the Soho Screening Rooms, MPC on Wardour Street – catching previews before interviewing German starlets or visiting American directors – and selling his features to all-comers. Fifty pence a word, if he was lucky.

He met Mary at *The Guardian* – at the paper's old office in Farringdon. They'd both been called in to do holiday cover on the arts desk, subbing copy by other freelancers or stuff knocked out by big-name critics who got shirty if you changed a comma.

After a while Harry realised that Mary fancied him, although their regular meetings after they had finished the stint at *The Guardian* and gone their separate ways didn't seem like dates. Not to Harry anyway: perhaps Mary hoped for more. Perhaps she thought they were creeping towards a romance.

"Stop leading her on," had been Max's blunt advice when he once spoke about Mary.

He had had other relationships – six months here, a year there – but nothing that stuck. As he got wealthier, he started to attract another type of woman, ones that saw him as a prospect; a nice big home in Fulham or Wandsworth, regular holidays, private school for the children and, of course, the need never again to have to work. Endless lunching and shopping. These relationships had a predictable shelf life of about four to six months, enough for the woman to realise that Harry was not going to be a simple meal ticket, and for Harry to sense a lack of proper compatibility.

In the meantime he met up with Mary less and less; the last time must have been over two years ago now. She had moved into news journalism early on, he recalls. There was a long stint as a London stringer for Agence France-Presse, and she might have been at *The Independent* for a while. Yes, that's right. They had met for a drink at Canary Wharf when both *The Independent* and Harry's bank had been in Docklands. She had been more amused than impressed by Harry's newfound affluence.

He heads down Lexington Street, jinks along Brewer Street and on to Old Compton Street, with its Italian delis, French patisseries, Portuguese cafes and sushi bars, gay shops and bars. Men seated outside on even this chill early spring evening eye him appraisingly, and he realises how odd he must seem here in his beautifully cut suit, dodging in between men in skinny jeans and fat headphones.

An overweight man pouring out of a bad suit, shirt half untucked and waving a cigarette around is shouting into his phone outside the entrance to the Groucho Club. What he is really shouting is: 'Look at me... I belong to the Groucho Club'. He too gives Harry an appraising look, but this one is not carnal. Perhaps, he thinks Harry is famous. Or a commissioning editor.

But Harry pulls a right, away from Groucho's and down Dean Street and past a louche hangout from an earlier age of the Soho myth, The French House, across Shaftesbury Avenue and into Chinatown, the air thick with the smell of five-spice and with red-orange glazed ducks hanging in every window.

The pub is on the corner, and Mary is already sitting at a small table, reading a copy of the *Evening Standard*. She smiles at Harry as he navigates through the throng of drinkers, and he feels a warmth, he realises, like he hasn't felt in a long time. He squeezes his way to the bar and returns to their table with a glass of sauvignon blanc and a pint of lager.

"You look more expensive every time I see you," says Mary cheerfully.

"As soon as I leave Mayfair I feel like some sort of freak."

"Freaks of Mayfair," says Mary, fingering the lapel of his suit jacket. Mary herself is wearing a denim jacket and a scarf wrapped around her neck. "It's a book. *The Freaks of Mayfair* by E. F. Benson.

"Never read it," says Harry. "But I will now."

"So what's new?"

"Apart from selling a house to a rich Arab?"

"Ooh… listen to you," says Mary, gently mocking, and taking a sip of her wine. "How many rich Arabs are there?"

"I don't think anyone knows… thousands."

"What a kleptocracy… their royal family, I mean," says Mary. "How they let that family just endlessly line their pockets with the oil money is beyond me. The Saudis seriously need to kick out their royal family for a starter – and I think they will now that America has its own oil and doesn't need those crooks."

"And what would they replace them with? An ayatollah who does worse things to women than not allowing them to drive? Anyway, you know what… what I've come to realise in the last few years? I don't care… I really don't care. I wish I could, but I've got to be honest."

"Nonsense."

"It's true… I'm just like everybody else… I live in my own little bubble."

"You've changed then," says Mary.

"Or maybe I was always like this deep down. Or maybe not deep down because I think I'm probably quite shallow…"

"That's not true," says Mary, with an indulgent chuckle.

"No, I am… shallow and rather selfish. Very selfish. None of it really matters."

"Maybe not to you…"

"Exactly. None of it matters to me. I just want to be rich, and you know why?"

Mary doesn't answer, just looks at him steadily, a little pityingly.

"Because money is power and I don't want anybody to ever

have power over me ever again."

"Blimey. Where did that come from?"

"Can't you see?" Harry fears he might be sounding too earnest. His relationship with Mary wasn't like that. Honest, yes, but not earnest.

"Max has power over you," she says.

"That's different." Harry realises he's almost been shouting; a couple propped up by the bar are looking at him.

"Is it?" says Mary. "Sorry, but it seems to me that you're like his butler or something."

"His concierge," says Harry with a grin. "Max is always talking about how we are concierges to the super-rich. Well, I guess I am concierge to Max. And I don't care because Max is making me rich – no one ever did anything like that for me before. They wanted to change my politics, maybe, or make me a better person. But Max, he's making me stinking rich and that, Mary, is true empowerment. And anyway…"

"Anyway what?"

"Max thinks he has me at his beck and call, but not really."

She shakes her head and says, "Maybe you're right, but I'm sad to see you like this all the same. I won't pretend."

"Why though?"

"I don't know, but mainly because you don't look happy."

"Who is happy?"

"Well, I think I am," says Mary, and Harry realises that he's been talking about himself for too long. "How's journalism?" he asks, deliberately modulating his voice which, he realises, had become overexcited.

"Okay. Badly paid."

"It was ever thus."

"No, it wasn't," says Mary, suddenly annoyed. "And just to think I'm marrying another bloody journalist. We'll be skint forever and a day."

"Marrying?" says Harry, sobering up quickly and barely able to get the word out of his mouth. He feels like the bottom has just fallen out of their evening together.

"Yes, to Ben. Christ, when did we last meet? Didn't I tell you about him?" She is looking at Harry curiously.

"No," says Harry. Words feel dusty and awkwardly shaped, but he feels he must say something. "How long...?"

"Oh, about two years or so. He was on the foreign desk with me. We're thinking of going abroad somewhere. Either that or buy a house in some shit-hole. Can't afford anywhere decent in London anymore."

"I see," says Harry. Mary is looking at him in silence, right into his eyes.

"Harry," she asks at length. "Did you invite me here on some sort of date? I thought we were, you know, friends."

"No... I thought... we..." This is useless, he thinks. "I don't know. I guess I just don't know who I am anymore." How pathetic that sounded. He takes a swig of lager.

She almost laughs at this, but looks at him instead with a good-humoured frown. Now she rubs his upper arm. "I didn't think you fancied me." And then: "We've known each other so long, it... it seems weird talking like this."

But not unpleasant, he thinks. "I know... I'm sorry... I just... don't let's spoil anything. When is the wedding?"

"In August. Will you come? Registry office, I'm afraid."

He sinks the rest of his pint in a hurry. "Don't tell Ben about this, please."

"No, of course not. No..."

Mary buys a round and they try and speak of normal things, but it seems false and Harry is glad when she announces that she has to go. They kiss cheeks on the street, and he's about to turn away when she pulls him and lands a soft kiss on his lips.

"Harry... I would have once. In fact I fancied you rotten when we first met. Don't be a stranger."

Now he's walking blindly down Shaftesbury Avenue, past all the theatres with their lights and enlarged newspaper notices claiming they are masterpieces... five stars... brilliantly staged and acted.

"Shit... how stupid can you get?" he asks himself, out loud. Eventually he finds himself on Piccadilly, and the crowds are thinning. The homeless girl and the dog are sitting there – but he doesn't notice, walking blindly by.

* * *

Mary also heads for Green Park underground, to take her on the Victoria Line to Brixton, and then a bus up Brixton Hill to Streatham. She feels both angry and a bit sad – fuming at Harry for making a pass at her like that. Was he so lonely and fucked up? What had happened to all those pretty gold diggers he used to date when Mary quietly hoped that she might be the one? All those girls at Corney & Barrow who could size up the cut of his suit at twenty paces? So long ago now. So long ago. Desire had eroded and a friendship had grown up in its place – and now he suddenly wants to sleep with her. Too fucking late, mate.

Deeper than her anger is a sadness, a recognition that she doesn't want to see him again. It's the money thing. Once they would have talked about films they'd seen, or TV shows or books or politics even – now it was the diamonds he was flogging to Arabs, and the houses in Mayfair he was shifting as if life was a game of Monopoly.

And his hedge fund management business, which Mary doesn't really start to understand. Ask her anything to do with international affairs, from the precise makeup of the warring factions within Syria or the details of the EU's Lisbon Treaty, and Mary was your woman. European equities? No idea.

The Brixton train pulls in and Mary is relieved to see there are plenty of seats – she doesn't have to squeeze in next to some fat bastard spreading his legs out to show how entitled he is. She stares up at an advert for an online dating service, an unshaven, good-looking young man with long hair grinning at a grinning blonde. So young and so in love.

That's the trouble with the rich – they can't imagine what it's like not to have money. Mary and Ben know because they once had money – or at least well paid staff jobs when newspapers used to dish those out, complete with expenses. She never really thought about what she spent. That for her is now the definition of luxury. Not to have to give money a second thought.

If she'd been clever she'd have got a mortgage back then, but then she was out of the country so much, and now it was out of the question. She and Ben rent in Streatham, a first floor flat on a quiet side road, with (thank goodness) quiet neighbours. That chunky watch Harry was wearing would have covered six months' rent.

She and Ben had been made redundant by their respective newspapers within six months of each other – sacked and then rehired for shift work. They'd moved jobs many times over the years so there wasn't much of a pay-off – enough to put a deposit on the rented flat and pay for the first three months. God, how depressing. And hurtling towards forty the pair of them.

Stockwell Station comes and goes. They had started looking to buy somewhere – but London, even the grotty bits that no one would have considered five or ten years ago – they're now beyond their reach. Who would have imagined Peckham would become trendy? Or Hoxton? Somebody must have imagined it – and made a killing in the process.

As for Mary and Ben. Self-employed, no deposit, forget it. They'd go abroad. A two-bed in Beirut with views of the Mediterranean; there must be some bargains to pick up in Kabul now the Americans have gone. The rapidly decelerating train rattles in to Brixton Station rattled. End of the line.

CHAPTER NINE

Max leaves Verbier while it's still dark, and reaches Geneva as a sunny morning emerges from behind the shadow of the mountains. The roads into town are all billboards for private banks and expensive watches – Max's kind of products.

Mahmoud Hakim Al-Wadhi turns out to be a young man barely in his twenties, Max guesses. He has a patchy, fledgling moustache, perhaps to try and make him seem older. With him is a tall, silver-haired man and a short bobbed, blonde woman in her thirties. He, it transpires as he whips out his loupe to inspect the stone, is an Egyptian gemologist; she is a Swiss lawyer.

The lawyer looks at the paperwork – certificates from the Gemological Institute of America and the European Gemological Laboratory, as well as a Kimberley certificate to certify that the diamond is 'conflict-free'.

"It's from Botswana," says Dieter, who is also present at the bank with Gretchen, who's wearing a beige business suit today.

"The certificate of provenance, I see, was signed in Guinea," says the lawyer.

"That's normal," says Dieter. "It just means it was processed in Guinea." The lawyer nods.

"Well, it's a nice stone," says the gemologist.

"Isn't it just," agrees Max, who has not spoken until now.

* * *

Harry opens his front door, flicks the hall light switch and begins to stride towards the beeping alarm box. Then he notices the animal, scuttling quickly but unhurriedly along the length of the hallway skirting board, dragging its tail behind it. A rat. So, it was a rat. "Shoo," he says involuntarily, the hairs rising on the back of his neck. Surprising the things that come out of mouths at times like these.

Where has it gone to? The alarm beeps are becoming urgent now, so he taps in his code. Then he switches on the living room lights and looks around, and then the kitchen lights. Nothing. His breakfast things still lie on the table – a dirty cereal bowl, a plate off which he'd eaten his toast. Crumbs and smears of butter and jam. Christ, no wonder he has rats. He needs a cleaner; Max had always said so. But hiring cleaners is not something that comes easily to Harry. After all, his mother is one.

He picks up the bowl and plate and places them in the dishwasher. He is wiping down the oilcloth when his phone rings.

"Harry… buddy boy, we're on a roll," announces Max in a thick voice. He sounds drunk, and Harry can hear someone, a man, in the background and some music. Simon?

"The Saudi… he's agreed to buy the diamond. Five million dollars. Once we've paid off the dealers our cut's just under half a million… four and half hundred thou'. I've done the maths: it's just over three for me, and a little over one for you. Not bad, eh?"

Three-to-one was their agreed share on all their side-dealings, and Harry thought that was pretty generous in the circumstances. After all, when all is said and done, he is always just tagging along for the ride. Somehow Max thinks his contribution amounts to more than this, when all Max really ever wants is some company.

"Fantastic… fucking brilliant," says Harry, trying to match Max's enthusiasm. One hundred thousand pounds. For what? What worried Harry was what was coming next.

"And what's more Dieter has an absolute beauty lined up. Could be worth more like six million," says Max.

"Right. Strike while the iron is hot…" he says without enthusiasm.

"Exactly," says Max, slurring the word so it sounds more like 'ecshactly'. "And this time we're going it alone. No backing – just us. Time for some serious money. We'll sell our houses, sell our bodies for sex, do whatever it fucking takes so we don't need financing, and buy the bloody thing ourselves. And then we'll keep all the profits. A million each, easily. And then we'll take it from there. Two or three deals like that each year, sell the company to some dimwit German and we fucking retire by the time we're forty. Fuck it all."

Simon, or whoever was in room with Max, echoes with a shout: "Fuck it all!" Harry realises the song they're listening to over there in Switzerland is 'Brothers in Arms' by Dire Straits. Harry always teases Max about his cheesy taste in music, and Max being Max, instead of getting defensive, takes an interest in the music Harry likes: Pulp and Oasis from his uni days, jazz and even classical. Not that Harry listens to music much these days.

Simon is singing along, badly.

"Gotta go buddy," Max is saying. "I'll be back tomorrow. Did you speak to Rachel?"

"Yes, she's gone shopping… with her mate Jess… in Dubai."

"Ha! Fuck it all," says Max.

"Yes, fuck it all," says Harry.

CHAPTER TEN

For nearly two weeks nothing seems to happen. Outside every day has been the same – an unbroken grey sky occasionally grows even darker and threatens to rain, but mostly it just remains a pale, implacable grey. A cold wind too: everyone has stopped talking animatedly about spring, and what their plans are for Easter. In fact they don't discuss the weather any more at all; they have returned to winter mode, sullen and grimly determined.

The trees, just starting to burst their buds earlier in the month, are now in suspended animation, waiting for further orders. Harry overheard Fiona at the office the other morning telling the trader Cyril that she'd heard on the radio that it is going to stay like this until July. Cyril shrugged his French shoulders and in that French way said, "I never go outside anyway."

European mid-cap equities seem to be taking their cue from the weather; they too are stuck. The markets everywhere seemed to have stalled, unsure of what direction to take. The uncertainty over Brexit isn't helping. They might as well all go home.

In fact the only thing that seems to be shifting is Harry's house. On Max's instruction he told the eager man from the estate agency that he wanted cash buyers only and a quick completion, for which he'd price the house at fifty grand cheaper than similar houses in the area. The man said he had someone perfect lined up, an older couple who were downsizing from Notting Hill, and that he'd get them round as soon as possible. In the meantime Harry phoned a pest-control company.

He hasn't seen his rat, although he can hear it. The creature seems to have taken up residence in the ceiling space above the kitchen, and is gnawing on something. Perhaps it's the electrical wires and it will burn itself to a frazzle. It stops when Harry bangs on the ceiling with a broom.

He hasn't heard from Rachel since she went to Dubai, and that, he thinks, is probably for the best. And there's been no wedding invitation from Mary, but he texts her anyway to thank her for the other night and to apologise that he seemed so out of sorts. She texts back almost immediately with a smiley emoticon and a kiss. Harry starts to get a hard-on.

"Is Rachel okay about selling up?" he asks Max when they slip out for some sushi at lunchtime.

"She hates that flat… hates Baron's Court. She wants to move to Notting Hill. A few of these trades, and we'll be able to afford Notting Hill."

Max's estate agent had arranged an open day the previous Saturday and seven offers came streaming in before the end of play – all of them for more than the asking price. He selected the four cash buyers who were ready to move and told the agent to choose the one who could complete the quickest. Two of the prospective purchasers say they can complete by the end of the month – that's little over a week away. Max's solicitor seems doubtful whether that's possible, so Max phoned Simon's solicitor who said it was perfectly possible. He got the business.

The reason for their haste is the diamond. The diamond. The big pink one that is going to be his and Max's first solo deal, without investors. Their own money was going to buy this gem, and they were then going to reap all the profit when the soft, big-lipped Saudi took out his camel-skin purse and bought the thing.

And they were going to stay liquid – pump the cash into another stone, and then another, and then another. And when they'd exhausted all of that, then they would stand back and look at their mountains of cash and decide what to spend it on. A new-build penthouse beside the Thames, thinks Harry, with no mortgage and no rats. And a place in Barbados for the winters.

For now they are all going to Switzerland. Max, Harry and Simon – in Simon's jet. Harry offers to take a scheduled flight, but Max insists they stay together. Simon doesn't like Harry and thinks there's something fishy about him, and there will be bullying questions on the flight over, unless Harry can extricate himself.

Simon isn't someone who just thinks things, he says them too, which, as long as you aren't the one he is saying things about, can be quite funny. Simon is fun, but he is also dangerous. Fuck it, a few deals like the big pink one and it wouldn't matter what Simon, or anyone else, thinks of him. Fuck them all, as Max liked to say.

Still, he feels uneasy. Harry never expected to be in the slightest bit wealthy. Just having some money left over at the end of the week for a few drinks would have been his idea of being rich before he bumped into Max at that fateful night in the Sloaney Pony.

He had accumulated wealth just by being Max's friend and – okay, he had to face it – paid companion. Money by osmosis. But now he was expected to start playing the game for real, become one of the big boys, put his balls on the table, or whatever it was that Simon liked to say. Simon didn't think Harry had any balls.

They are going to fly out to Simon's chalet in Verbier to ski for a couple of days. Harry can slip and slide down the nursery slopes – he never really got into skiing, or any other sport for that matter – while the other two exhausted themselves on the black runs, hopefully not breaking anything because on the Thursday they had a rendezvous at a small luxury hotel in the centre of Geneva. The Arab is in town and wants to see this diamond Max is so full of. Max has even taken to calling it the Queen of the River – as Dieter had joked.

Two days skiing, mountain air, and then a million dollars in the bank. Life is sweet, thinks Harry, who has just returned from a meeting with a nervous Japanese industrialist who insisted they drink saki. There had been much smiling and frantic nodding and drinking of saki, and now Harry doesn't feel good for anything. Just scrolling through contacts on his phone, and feeling a little horny when he reaches r for Rachel. But that last time had been such a disaster.

He gets up suddenly and walks into reception. "I've got to go home; I've got an estate agent coming round," he lies to Fi on reception.

"How exciting," she says, and sounds as if she genuinely thinks that it is. In what universe is meeting an estate agent exciting, he thinks. Max is also out with a client, and Tim and Cyril are both identically posed, leaning back in their chairs with their hands behind their heads.

"Tell Max I've got some house business to sort out. I'll be back in tomorrow morning."

"Yes, of course, Harry," says Fi brightly. "See you tomorrow."

Harry decides to let the train pass Baron's Court. Rachel won't be there anyway, she'll be at work, but in Harry's current muzzy state of mind, the compulsion remains. He changes at Hammersmith and gets off at Ravenscourt Park, and as he starts walking back to his house he realises he hasn't been back from work this early in a long time.

It's a lovely afternoon; the weather that had been grey and cold for weeks on end has now suddenly switched, and markedly for the better; spring had recommenced. He can smell it as he walks up along the side of the park, he can see it in the pink blossom on the trees planted on the pavement – trees which annoy him whenever it's raining and he has to navigate past them with his umbrella.

He passes a primary school playground where children are yelping and screaming in the unaccustomed warm sunshine. A small boy with a mop of sandy hair has his face pressed against the bars of the playground fence and as Harry passes he asks him to throw back his tennis ball, which has evidently been thrown or hit over the top and now rested by the back wheel of a parked car. Harry picks up the ball and throws it up high over the fence. "Thank you" the boy says and rushes back to his game.

As he puts his key into the lock of his soon-to-be-no-longer front door he notices a neighbour – a woman in her seventies perhaps, with a green cardigan and hair in a bun, putting something in the bin in her front garden. "Oh, hello," she says. "Lovely day isn't it." Has he met her before? Should he know her name?

"Beautiful isn't it?" he agrees.

"There was a man here earlier looking for you – from the

police," says the woman, obviously happy to have this important news to deliver. "He left you a letter."

Slipping into the hallway and heading off the alarm, which has begun its beeping sequence, Harry notices the card on his doormat. It's from a DC Andrews of Norfolk Constabulary, asking for Harry to get in touch.

*   *   *

Rachel is in the kitchen, wearing black jogging bottoms and a black vest, her bare shoulders damp with sweat, and drizzling wasabi dressing into the box of quinoa, artichoke and pomegranate salad she has bought from the food hall at Selfridges. She takes a deep gulp from a large glass of red wine just as Max steps behind and spreads a hand across one of her bottom cheeks, and then up round her waist and towards her breasts.

"You can forget that," she says.

"Not fair," he says in a mock petulant child's voice, keeping his hand where it is, running his fingers along the hard base of her sports bra. Rachel doesn't move, merely lifts a fork full of salad towards her mouth.

"God, I hate quinoa", says Max, screwing up his face. "When is someone going to blow the whistle on that stuff and admit that it's disgusting?"

"When's the last time we went out for a nice meal together? When was the last time we did the River Cafe?" says Rachel, squirming and brushing away his hand. "You and Harry have all these lovely lunches at Scott's, Nobu and places like that and I always have to eat on the hoof like this."

Max removes his hand with a sigh.

"Well?" she asks, sitting down cross-legged on the sofa by the TV.

"You're right," he says, pouring himself a glass of red.

"It's like you two are the lovers. Or the old married couple."

79

"I know… I know… the trouble is I just don't fancy old Harry. Shame I've got to spend three days in Switzerland with the old bugger."

"Old bugger… you said it. Switzerland? Is this the diamond? Any news on the flat?"

"We'll get a sale all right and when I've sold off this diamond we can move to Notting Hill. Promise. I can order sushi, if you like. Or an Indian?"

"Too late… I'm eating it now. Seriously, why don't you just stick to what you're good at – swindling investors with your fees? Anyway, that Saudi. Do you even know his name?"

"Bin something"

"Bin Laden?"

Max slips beside his wife on the sofa, who shuffles along to make room. "Do you like him? Harry, I mean…"

"No," says Rachel without missing a beat.

"No, nobody seems to like him except me."

*   *   *

The evening is still warm and full of the promise of spring, but Harry is glad of the roaring fire in the Abergavenny Arms, his local pub – or rather a popular and much-garlanded gastro-pub that attracts visitors from all over London. They come from far and wide but Harry, who only lives two streets away, has only been here once before, when he and Max had been house-hunting back in 2007.

"Brilliant," said Max. "A great neighbourhood pub like this is worth at least a hundred grand on the price of local houses. That posh butcher should help as well." Harry hadn't noticed the posh butcher.

A lot of people are standing outside, smoking, laughing and enjoying the unseasonable mildness, which means that there are tables to choose from inside. Harry selects one of the array of colourfully named draft bitters, and takes a table near to the fire. He feels very strange and he doesn't like it.

Nicholas Mooreland has been locked safely in Harry's past for a long time now – the key memories have been re-played so often that they had come to seem like scenes from a film that he has seen so many times that he knows it off by heart; they have taken on the qualities of a story, and settled into Harry's own private mythology. He can deal with it.

The smell of cigar smoke can still take him by surprise, though, in the way that smells can – bypassing all the defences that the mind can deploy and plunging him straight back into Mooreland's proximity. Mooreland and his big fat cigars, plumes of smoke filling the house with their residual stink.

He knew it for what it was. For a time at least it meant good things – sweets, chocolates, bottles of cider consumed without his mother's knowledge. The close, friendly attention of this high-spirited man, with his muzzy chuckle, leg-pinching and funny nicknames for everybody. His nickname for Harry was 'Kimbo'. Legs akimbo. Ha-ha-ha-ha.

And now here it was, in black and white, in the *Eastern Daily Press*, which was as good as the Bible for his mum.

"Excuse me…" A couple in their thirties, she wearing a Barbour coat, he holding a dog on a lead, as if this was genuinely a country pub, ask if they could share his table. Drinkers are coming back inside now, the pub filling up. Instinctively Harry drains the last of his pint. "No, please. I'm just off anyway."

CHAPTER ELEVEN

It's an early start for Switzerland. Max orders an Uber to pick him up at five, leaving Rachel sleeping on her front and gently snoring, her naked back visible from where the duvet has been pulled aside.

There hadn't been any sex last night, despite Max's kneadling, caressing and insistent good humour, but in the end he was just glad to not be exiled to the spare room. This is the way it should be. He makes a mental note to get Fi to book a really romantic restaurant for them for when he gets back from Geneva. It could be a double celebration.

The car arrives on time and makes good progress through the almost empty London streets; up over the Westway, down the Marylebone Road and through Whitechapel towards Canary Wharf. Simon texts to say he's 'lashed' and that he hasn't been to bed, but looking forward to a full afternoon on the slopes. He has a 'doxie' with him. Harry also texts to say he's en route. The plane takes off at seven.

In the small executive departure lounge Simon looks wired, a skinny red-headed girl dressed in party clothes looks thoroughly bemused – as if she'd taken Simon's talk of taking his private jet to Switzerland as a mere boast, whereas the plentiful lines of Charlie had been enough to string her along for the night.

"We really flying then?" she says in an estuarine accent. Max thinks she looks like a small frightened rabbit.

"Yes, my dear, we're really flying. Why else did we go all the way to Edmonton and fetch your passport?" Simon is squinting into his mobile as he says this. "Let's hope my trades work so we can afford this little jolly."

The girl looks non-plussed, but politely proffers a hand to Max.

"I'm Rhiannon by the way," she says.

"Thank God you said that – I knew it began with an R," says

Simon, but the girl shows no sign of being offended.

"You're a one," she says.

Thankfully Simon remains fully engaged with Rhiannon during the entire flight to Geneva. The Saudi has emailed to bring forward their meeting, so it's going to be business before pleasure and from the airport they are to take a taxi straight to the bank where their pink baby is sitting, all snug and secure in a safety-deposit box.

The Saudi wants to meet at the hotel at seven, and they are to bring the diamond with them. "He's not going to come to the bank… that's not how these people work," says Max, when Harry objects. "It'll be fine. I've arranged to take the diamond out at five, and we put it in this." Max lifts the briefcase with a handcuff dangling from its side. He'd bought it from a specialist shop in Mayfair one day last week, particularly attracted by the biometric lock that meant it could only be opened using Max's fingerprint. Simon had burst out laughing when he saw it, much to Max's annoyance.

"Put it this way, anyone wants the diamond they're going to have to hack my arm off to get it," he says.

"Better not make it your wanking arm," guffaws Simon. "Or at the very least they'll have to chop off your finger to use as a key."

Max looks out of the window as Lyon passes somewhere down below. He looks happier than he has in weeks, thinks Harry. He can sense a deal – the deal – the one that is going to set them on their way.

"What if it's another no-show," says Harry. "We can't keep going to and fro from the bank to the hotel. Someone will take notice and follow us. Especially with that bloody suitcase. Wouldn't it be less conspicuous if you just put it in your coat pocket?"

"Don't worry, Harry. You worry too much." This is true, thinks Harry. Every night this week he has woken up in his hotel room just off the Hammersmith roundabout and lain awake worrying about what he has now done. The house sale went through in a moment, thanks to something Max knew about called an attended exchange, and he had liquidated everything he owned and invested it in this tiny piece of pink carbon.

He never thought he'd have a million pounds sitting in his bank, and sure enough it didn't sit there for long, being wired to Dieter's bank just two days later. Now it was a case of waiting, and by the end of the week he should have doubled his money.

The manager who takes them down to the safety deposit room eyes Max's suitcase with alarm, thinks Harry, or maybe he's just projecting his own doubts. They look at the stone, which looks disappointingly small now, perhaps because they each know how much of them is invested in it. Max slips it in a leather pouch, pulls the drawstring and places it in the briefcase.

"Can everyone please verify that the diamond is in the briefcase," says Max solemnly.

Harry wants to laugh, but the manager says, "Of course, monsieur. I can verify that the diamond is in the briefcase."

* * *

The taxi ride to the hotel takes ten minutes but it feels like hours. At one point a motorcyclist overtakes the cab and pulls in sharply, causing the taxi driver to brake, before speeding off.

"Thank God for that," says Harry. "I thought we were being carjacked."

They've decided to take a room in the hotel rather than hang around in the lobby. Harry needs somewhere to stay, and Max's flat is too small. Tomorrow, twice as rich as they are today, they will head off to Verbier, where Simon and Rhiannon will be waiting for them.

"I have a message for you," says the receptionist as Max and Harry sign in. It's in a heavy cream envelope, expensively embossed and smelling of perfume. A woman's perfume? Max opens it. *Room 102 at 7pm* is all that is written on it.

"Can you tell me who has booked Room 102?" Max asks the receptionist, showing him the letter.

"The whole of the first floor has been booked out," the man

says. "I am afraid I cannot tell you in whose name."

"Then that's our man all right," says Max.

They have an hour to kill. Max orders a hamburger and chips from room service, but Harry feels too sick to eat. What if the Arab doesn't like the diamond, or doesn't want to pay the price that Max is setting? What if he only wants to pay three million instead of five million?

Max is obviously agitated too, because he's pacing the room. "I wish Rachel was here now," he says. "We'd spend this hour having sex, and no offence, Harry, but you're not my type."

"Nor you mine," says Harry. Are they still having sex, he wonders? They have such a strange relationship. There's a knock at the door and he jumps. It's room service. He wants to phone Mary, involve her in his crazy adventure – how she would laugh, and be amazed. Outside their third-floor window, Geneva twinkles in the darkness. Two floors beneath are the people who will make them or break them. I am being over-dramatic, thinks Harry, as he watches Max eat his hamburger as if he was fucking Rachel. Greedily, blindly. Only twenty minutes has passed.

* * *

The first floor is quiet. They expected to be met by security as they got out of the lift, but no one is about. Max knocks on the door of room 102. Moments later it's opened by a man with an earpiece and a suit that can hardly contain his muscles. The security guard looks at them stonily and ushers them into a living room in pink damask.

A huge bouquet of flowers sits on the sideboard, with the compliments of the hotel. A pair of double doors open and a young woman – the woman they had met in London – softly enters the room and offers her hand. Max takes it and bows, and Harry follows suit, trying not to remember the woman's sardonic gaze when we first met.

"My father is next door with my mother," she says. "I am to show them the diamond. Please."

"Errr…" Max is looking at Harry, who instinctively shakes his head. The woman frowns. "The diamond… please. I am to show them."

"This is most irregular," says Max. "We can show him ourselves."

"My father is with my mother," the woman says again, as if that explained everything. She puts out her hand.

"Well, I don't know," says Max, but he has already laid the briefcase on the back of a sofa, and is pressing his fingertip against the biometric lock. The woman, Harry realises, is staring at him.

"How are you?" she asks.

"I'm, ah, well," he manages to say. Max hands her the pouch with the diamond in it.

"One moment," she says, and steps through the double-doors that lead into the adjoining room.

Their hearts are both beating hard. They look around. The security guard is gone, they are alone.

"What the fuck?" says Harry.

"I know, most irregular," is all that Max can say. They wait, standing where the woman had left them, in the middle of the room, which Harry realises smells of the same perfume as the letter.

"How long do we give them?" he asks.

"We can't just barge in there," says Max, who is reddening from his neck upwards. Harry too feels flushed. "It might scupper the whole deal. Just wait."

More minutes pass. Max goes over to the front door, opens and peers down the corridor. No one is there, not even the security guard. Where did he go?

"I don't like this," says Max, whose face is puce now.

Harry goes over to the double doors and knocks gently. No reply. He waits and then again, more loudly this time. He puts his ear to the door, and hears voices. He listens, and realises that it's coming from a television. He opens the door. The room is empty. He opens another door, which leads on to a bedroom, which is also empty. The bedroom door to what turns out to be room 103 is unlocked. The lights are on but it's as room service left it that morning, with another enormous bouquet of flowers on the central table. Room 104 and Room 105 are the same.

"Shit... shit... shit," says Harry. "We've been robbed."

CHAPTER TWELVE

"So, you're saying that you went to the room of this Arab woman to sell her a diamond and she stole it." The female police inspector is probably in her late forties , with deep lines etched around hazel eyes that have seen too much. This is the fourth stranger to whom Max has unfolded his story in the past – he looks at his watch again – four hours and twenty three minutes, and he has to admit that it becomes ever more fabulous and unlikely each time he repeats it.

"That's correct – correct and totally true," he says. "Except our arrangement was with her father with whom I have had several dealings in the past, and it was his daughter – who I have met once before – who opened the door and took the diamond, supposedly to show her father, who was in the next door room."

The inspector's eyebrows rise up involuntarily, not for the first time while she has been taking his statement. He can see what she's thinking – that he's just a fool who's been very irresponsible with a valuable possession; she must see it ten times a day. "Is the diamond insured?" she asks, without looking up from her computer keyboard.

"Yes, but no," says Max, a note of despair entering his voice for the first time since the theft. "We won't be covered for taking the diamond out of the vault and giving it to a stranger in a hotel room, let's put it that way." He has another thought. "And, no, this is not an insurance scam."

The inspector's mouth moves fractionally into a half-smile. "The thought never crossed my mind." She speaks perfect, French-accented English, far more fluent that the harassed male colleague who had originally interviewed them after they were escorted to the gendarmerie HQ. He didn't seem to be able to make head nor tail of their story, and eventually stomped off muttering to himself, in search of someone who spoke better English.

Harry had continued opening all the doors on the first floor of the hotel, shouting and swearing like a drunk on his third bottle of vodka, but Max could already see that they had been the victims of a beautifully – yes, he has to admire it – simple sting. With a strange calm, he called the lift and descended to the lobby. The receptionist quickly called the duty manager, whose face seemed to retreat into itself as Max told him what had happened.

He kept jabbing on the computer keyboard and saying, "The Saudi party is booked for two more nights." He then phoned upstairs, but received no answer.

"The Saudi party," he kept repeating, like a spell to ward off evil spirits. He pulled himself together. "They must have gone out."

Max had slapped his own forehead in exasperation. "What are you talking about? They were never there. Did you actually see them check in?"

"Please, one moment, monsieur," the man said, returning to the computer. "I have only been on duty for two hours. Gregoire!" he had called to a young man who has been checking in another guest. *"Venez ici."* The manager had a rapid word in Gregoire's ear. "My colleague is going to check the rooms."

"Don't bother, I've already done it." Harry had appeared at his side at this moment, his sweat-covered face a blotchy pink.

"The whole floor is completely empty," he said. "It was a set-up. Get them to call the police at once, Max. Fucking hell..."

"And you don't know the name of this woman," says the female inspector back at the police station. She looks like she wants to smile again – never give a sucker an even break, she is probably thinking.

"Like I said, I wasn't dealing with her, but her father."

"Ah, yes." Just a moment. The woman stands up and opens the door, putting her around the opening to talk with a colleague in rapid-fire French. Max recognises the word *embassy*. She returns, holding a sheet of paper.

"We have been in touch with the embassy here in Geneva and they say that the Saudi's e-mail account has been hacked. Neither he, nor anyone in his employ, booked those rooms at the hotel."

"Ha! Brilliant!" Max shouts. "Then it must be his daughter who is hacking his e-mails. His password is probably even her name. It seems to me that you are bound to bring her in for questioning."

"Ah, yes, that is the other thing," the woman says. "The lady in question goes by the name of Aafia…"

"Brilliant, she has a name," shouts Max.

"Yes, but she also has diplomatic immunity."

*   *   *

They return to London in a daze, Harry with a hole in the pit of his stomach as he realises that he has returned to square one in life. How could they have been so stupid, or greedy? Simon has lent them his plane and a floor at his house in Islington for Max and Rachel to stay. Harry books into a hotel near Victoria Station using the company credit card.

The British police duly take their statements, and the insurance company agrees to a meeting, while not offering any hope of recompense after they had acted so rashly with the diamond. And, yes, Aafia has diplomatic immunity.

The only lead that comes their way in these dismal days, which they spend in the offices of Forward-Max Capital LLP, comes when, on a whim, Harry e-mails Mary to tell her what's happened. Perhaps there might be a story in it. Mary phones him almost at once, and they arrange to meet in the pub. A different pub this time. She'll come to Harry's office. She's interested to see it, she says.

The Market Tavern on Shepherd's Market is large enough not to be too crowded on a Wednesday evening after work. In the upstairs room they find a corner where it's quiet enough to talk, Harry having ordered a pint of Kronenberg for himself and a large sauvignon blanc for Mary.

"God, Harry, I'm so sorry… no, really," she says as they settle in. Mary seems friendly and concerned enough, but he senses she's being a little guarded. Or is that just him, now that he knows she's not interested? Outside it's still light just about, the clocks go forward that weekend.

"We've been idiots," he says. "Tell me all about the Saudis."

"God, where do you want me to start?"

"Where do you want to start?"

A great gale of laughter comes from across the room where five or six young men and women are seated – office workers by the look of them.

"Do you know anything about our Saudi gentleman and his daughter?"

"Quite a lot actually, or at least about the father, and it's all quite interesting," says Mary, taking a thirsty gulp of her wine. "Ooh, that's nice.

"Go on," says Harry, taking a nervous swig of his pint, and leaning in so that can better hear what Mary is saying, the group of office workers having steadily turned up their volume.

"Well, in many ways he's like your Donald Trump"

"*My* Donald Trump?"

"Sorry... I only assumed..." says Mary with a mischievous half-smile. "Anyway, he made his second fortune buying and selling real estate in 1980s America. His first fortune was as a sub-contractor for the Bin Ladens..."

"The Bin Ladens? Now you're really confusing me. He was some sort of terrorist?"

"You're thinking of Osama Bin Laden... Osama was the black sheep of the family. The Bin Ladens were a family-run construction firm who built most of Saudi Arabia – its roads, cities and royal palaces. They even rebuilt Mecca. So your man was a sub-contractor for the Bin Ladens during the 1970s oil boom, and then decided to move to America and try his luck there. And like President Trump, he dealt in real estate – anything from golf courses and shopping malls to Manhattan tower blocks."

"I see," says Harry, taking a long gulp of lager.

"It then gets a bit murkier," says Mary, leaning in, so that her hair falls down near to his own face. In another life he would have stroked it. "It's then that he became some sort of middle man between American arms manufacturers and the Saudi government. This is where he made his real money, possibly billions, although a lot of this is hearsay and circumstantial evidence. He certainly crops up in enough photographs alongside Congressmen with strong links to the military-industrial complex."

"Brilliant," says Harry, smacking the edge of the table. He's beginning to feel a bit tipsy. "He's a concierge... just like Max and me."

"Slightly bigger league," chuckles Mary. "Anyway, he left America after 9/11, for whatever reason, and settled here in London."

"What about the diplomatic immunity... why does he have that?"

"No idea, or why his daughter has it either. Possibly to facilitate arms deals... he's certainly never held any official ambassadorial role. And there's another strong possibility – in fact, I'd wager, a probability."

"Which is?"

"He's some sort of spook or political fixer... a behind-the-scenes, sort of dark-arts type. Not someone you should be messing with in any event."

Harry is silent, unlike the party of office workers which is getting ever more noisy and raucous. "I see," he says at length.

"But..." says Mary, looking at him intently.

"Yes?"

"If you should want to go looking for his daughter then I know where the family home is. It's in Oxfordshire. A big stately home they bought when they moved here in 2002 and where the daughter spends her down time."

*   *   *

"You're nuts," says Rachel as Max explains the plan of action. "You'll get arrested. Why don't you just go round there and ring on the front doorbell?"

"Because we won't get anywhere near the front door," says Max. He's stuffing a raincoat into a rucksack.

"E-mail him then; it's much easier than breaking and entering."

"My e-mails just ping back."

"I still think you're crazy. It's Harry's idea I take it?"

"It's Harry's idea," says Max taking the raincoat out of the rucksack and this time folding it into a tight ball. "But I wholeheartedly agree with him."

CHAPTER THIRTEEN

"What a truly classic English pub," says Max, pushing another forkful of steak into his mouth. As he chews, his eyes seem to film over. It's true, thinks Harry, taking in the horse brasses, hunting scenes, snoozing Labrador by the crackling fire. The landlord's, it seems, and it's called Basil, which makes Max laugh.

"Bas-il," he repeats.

The landlord of the Golden Lion in Luddeston – the nearest pub to Luddeston Hall – is the type Harry likes; late middle-aged, fat, polite and efficient but not nosey. He worked in a pub in Norfolk one summer holiday after he left school, and the landlord, Terry, was just like this one. "I haven't seen my cock in over thirty years," was one of Terry's favourite sayings. He kept a water pistol behind the bar and used to squirt drinkers who were slow to leave at closing time.

They had taken a train to Oxford and then a taxi for the forty-minute drive to Luddeston. There's only one other customer here today, a bearded man of about their age, with lank long hair and a look of private amusement on his face as he sits at the bar nursing a pint of bitter. Part of the fixtures and fittings, thinks Harry, who has known the type over the years. Perhaps he's a farm worker contemplating an eternity of ploughing straight furrows, of harrowing and harvesting and driving up and down fields as he listens to *Steve Wright in the Afternoon* on the tractor radio.

Max is having steak and chips and salad and Harry is eating lasagne and chips, with sticky toffee pudding – they have decided that they needed to get as much fuel inside them as possible, given the uncertainties of the coming afternoon.

A pinched and harassed-looking middle-aged woman – the landlord's wife presumably – bustles out of the kitchens to serve them: two hikers, with boots, chunky sweaters and rucksacks under the table.

"Off for a walk then?" she asks, chirpy but, like her husband, not really interested in their answer.

"Yup," says Max, looking greedily at his plate of food as it's placed in front of him.

"Would you like mustard or ketchup with that?" says the woman, firing on automatic. Fine dining thinks Harry. But then what he really wants to ask the woman comes blurting out of his mouth.

"Who owns the big house? Luddeston Hall is it? Anyone famous?" He can feel Max tense beside him.

"Oh, an Arab. Bin something," says the woman. "Not that we ever see him. They don't drink, see… Muslims." Max laughs rather too loudly.

"Good one," he says. "Not very good for business those Muslims."

"No, and we need all the business we can get nowadays. Mustard, did you say?" They hadn't said.

The pub returns to its previous pleasant torpor, the gentle crackling of the log fire joined by the energetic clinking of their knives and forks as they demolish the food. Microwaved, bland, but then hunger is the best chef, as Harry had read somewhere.

"Bin shopping." It's the bearded man at the bar.

"Sorry," says Max.

"Bin shopping," repeats this joker. That's his name. Bin… shopping." He chuckles to himself. "He's there now, Bin Shopping… the A-rab."

"Oh, yes?" says Max, feigning indifference through a mouthful of chips.

"Know how I know?" continues Beardie. "His helicopter comes in right over my back garden. Bloody racket, it is."

"Can't be good when you have the washing out," says Harry.

Beardie doesn't smile. "Oh, no, too high up for that," he says. "Noisy mind. He arrives on a Friday and leaves on a Sunday… not every Friday or Sunday mind… but when he's here, those are his days." The man seems satisfied to have got that off his chest and returns to staring into his pint.

"They don't mix with the village then?" says Harry, who knows the sort of things that annoy villagers. Not mixing is the cardinal sin.

"Not in the slightest." It's the landlord who takes the bait. He puts down the glass he seems to have been drying since Max and Harry turned up half an hour ago and now joins in the conversation. "He did buy the cricket club a new pavilion, mind."

"Wow," says Max. "That's not too bad then. Always good to keep the cricket club on side. How long has he lived here?"

"Let me see. I took over this place in 2001 – it was after the millennium because the previous owners had a big party for the village on Millennium Eve."

"It was 2003," chips in Beardie. "I remember the fuss. The Cobhams – that's the family that was there before – had been there for 500 years or something, and they sold up to an Arab. It was in all the papers. His daughter came in here once – remember that, Stu?"

"Don't I just," says the landlord with a chuckle. "She came in and ordered a coke… all on her own… the whole place went hush, you could hear a pin drop. Pretty little thing. That was about ten years ago."

"Did you ask to see her ID?" asks Max.

"No I did not. Between you and me I never ask anyone for ID unless they arrive in a pram with a dummy in their mouth. We need all the business we can get, and that's no lie."

"She took a load of photos with her phone," says Beardie. "We'd never even known you could take photos with your phone back then. Not embarrassed at all, just photos of the bar, the walls, the tables and the rest."

"I asked her what she wanted them for," says the landlord, taking up the story. "Know what she said?"

Harry and Max shake their heads, electrified by even this faint contact with the woman who had stolen the diamond from them.

"She said she was doing a school project on English pubs because back in her country they don't have pubs. Then her minder came in – a big brute – and she left. A pretty little thing. Quite cheeky I think."

"She was fucking gorgeous, hope she don't wear no veil," says Beardie, proffering his empty glass to the landlord, who takes it and pumps in a refill. "She's living it up in London now, so I've heard." He watches his glass of bitter being placed in front of him and with that he lowers his mouth on the glass's rim, and sucks in the froth.

"There's a path that goes along the side of the estate... we won't get any trouble from any security guards, will we?" asks Max. His plate, which he pushed away from him, is wiped clean.

"Er, no, it's a public right of way," says the landlord. "It's mostly fenced off with a high wooden fence... isn't that right Robert?" Beardie, whose name it seems is Robert, shrugs. "Where you headed anyway?"

"Landport," says Max. "I reckon a good two hours from here. What do you think?"

"I wouldn't know," says the landlord, "I don't walk anywhere if I can help it."

"Me neither", says Robert.

*   *   *

Max sits beneath a tree and unfolds the Ordnance Survey map they have brought with them. He creases it until he has the relevant section that includes Luddeston Hall and its grounds. The footpath comes off the village street just along from the pub.

He had tried to talk Harry out of this escapade; it seemed undignified. He had tried all the clichés – there are other fish in the sea, don't cry over spilt milk, learn from your mistakes, and (his favourite one) it's only business, but he can see that Harry is obsessed with this damned diamond.

Harry feels cheated and he wants to have his revenge. Max, who has never borne a grudge in his life, can't understand this, but he quietly admires it. Perhaps he was too lenient with people – Tash always said he let people walk all over him. The truth was he didn't like arguments and confrontations, it just wasn't his style. Simon once said that his generosity was a mask for weakness, and that had struck home.

But people liked Max, and the fact that he wasn't guarded or stingy or inquisitive. His handshake was respected as the handshake of a gentleman. The Saudis – many of them Bedouin after all, Harry had discovered during his manic online research since the theft of the diamond – liked that in him. And if that trust is abused?

"We have to put this behind us," he says, one last stab at halting this desperate course of action. "We can build up again – you know, in this life, it's possible to make and lose several fortunes."

Harry peels off his rucksack and lets it lie on the mossy bank, next to where Max is sitting.

"You can do that perhaps. Nothing has come easy to me," he says. "To own a house and part of a thriving business was more than I could have dreamed of. And now look – I've got a room in a cheap hotel and you're sleeping on your best mate's spare bed and not a bean to our names. What have the last ten years been about?"

Max nods, and looks at his friend. He wants to reassure him, but part of him also thinks it's time they took up arms, it's time they became men. He had liked to believe that Harry's dad had been a brave soldier killed in action. He always felt his own generation had been cheated of the opportunity of going to war. He has never had to test his mettle.

Some guys at the bank had taken up boxing. At the end of a day's trading they'd take the DLR from Canary Wharf to these old East End gyms, where they'd learn to spar with broken-nosed pros. And they'd have real fights. Max went to one once and watched a trader he knew called Josh punch the shit out of some guy from derivatives.

The ref had to step in, but not after Josh had pummelled this poor bloke so his face was no longer recognisable. Everyone from the trading floor had been cheering like crazy, and all these old

Cockney types were grinning. War must be like that, thought Max, class distinctions dissolved in the heat of battle.

"Into battle!" shouts Max.

Harry looks up from the map, and smiles for the first time in a long time.

"Into battle!"

CHAPTER FOURTEEN

The Ordnance Survey map shows the footpath starting at the end of a lane that had a line of houses to its right, with their back to the estate – one of them presumably belonging to bearded Robert. Delineated in a broken green line, the footpath hugs the edge of Luddeston Hall for about 100 metres before veering off at ten o'clock and away from the estate.

On the train to Oxford that morning Max had outlined his plan of attack – his belief being that the stretch where the footpath abutted the estate would be heavily fenced and possibly guarded and that their best bet was to walk on for about a mile, to where he had noticed a copse that led back to the far end of the estate. This would provide cover as well as potentially being less fortified.

"You've got military blood in you, what do you think?" he had asked as they left the last dregs of London behind them.

"Sounds like a good plan," Harry had said, over-enthusiastically, thankful that Max had even considered this course of action, which seemed full of risk and more futile with each passing minute.

And yet he couldn't bring himself to do nothing, to let the bitch – or whoever was behind the robbery – get away with it. The anger drives him forwards now. He needs to rid himself of the feeling of hopelessness that threatens to envelope him as they trudge down the lane, and onwards on to a muddy track that is flanked on one side by a well-maintained two-metre high wooden lap fence topped with a double strand of taut, well-maintained barbed wire.

They expect there to be guard dogs of some kind, and Max has brought along various cuts of meat, some which have been wrapped in cling film. These are the ones that have been soaked in Rohypnol that he says Simon gave to him. He doesn't want to think what Simon uses it for.

"How much does Simon know?" Harry asks.

"Oh everything," says Max. "He's a good bloke Simon… solid. You know he once saved my life?"

"How so?" Harry realises how much he hates Simon. How much he fears him. They are nearing the end of the high fence, which takes a sharp right as the footpath starts veering off to the left.

"We were in some dodgy pub in Fulham… God this was years ago… and outside a couple of hard-nuts started giving us some lip. Pissed both of us… and the rest. Anyway, one of them pulled a knife on me, but Simon hit him from behind with a bottle of wine he'd nicked on his way out. Right on the head… the bloke dropped like a stone."

"Was he all right?"

"I've often wondered."

The memory dissolves as Max takes in the thick, tall unpassable evergreen hedge that forms the boundary once the slatted wooden fence runs out, stretching off at a sharp angle to the footpath. It reminds him of the yew hedge at his parents' place, hundreds of years old and shaped like a cloud, except this is that faster-growing variety that his parents despise for some reason. Leylandii. How does he remember that?

The copse on the ridge of the low hill sweeps round to almost touch the far end of the hedge, just as the map says it should. They'll find a way through, or over. Dusk is when they will attack – just two hours from now. Attack. Max is enjoying the martial aspect of this operation – in fact he hasn't felt this alive for a long time. He feels like a spy, like Matt Damon in *The Bourne Identity*. At the same time he knows this is completely crazy, and they'll end up in police custody by the end of the day. At least someone will have to sit and take notice then. Perhaps the Saudi himself, whoever he is.

This particular Saudi he has finished with – no worries there. Plenty more super-rich fish in the sea. But even if they manage to get into the house undetected what do they expect to find? A handy map leading the way to the daughter's bedroom, and there, sitting on top of a chest of drawers alongside pony club cups, what? Their diamond?

Harry is desperate though; Max can see that. He doesn't realise that fortunes can be made over and over again once you know how. But this is the last shot Max is going to give at getting back this diamond. After that they'd have to take it on the chin and get back to making money. If you deal in shares for long enough – even boring European mid-cap equities – you soon learn that you win some and you lose some. There's absolutely no point in obsessing; you just end up chasing your losses.

Learn your lesson and move on. Fuck, the crash of 2008 had taught him that if nothing else. Almost wiped out one minute, then making the sort of percentages that ought to be outlawed – it was so criminal. On Barclays alone he had tripled his bet in six months. They don't advertise those returns on their website.

"We're early," he shouts to Harry, who is making a ferocious pace and is now a good twenty metres ahead of him. "Let's get to the copse and wait up, take the lie of the land."

At the point where the footpath comes closest to the copse, just as it starts to veer away, there is a gate with a sign attached *Private property – no public right of way*. Below is another sign: *Danger – keep out. Shooting in season.*

"What season?" asks Max.

"Pheasants probably," answers Harry, who used to be paid twenty pounds a day to beat for a farmers' shoot in Norfolk. Twenty pounds and all the beer and whisky you could drink. He remembers being fifteen years old, sitting on a straw bale with the blow heater blasting out in the barn, exhausted gundogs panting out great gusts of condensation, while Harry was sick-drunk on lager and scotch.

None of his schoolmates had holiday jobs as far as he could tell. It was skiing at Christmas and Easter, and their parents' place in Umbria or the Dordogne for the summer. He was invited along a couple of times but had to refuse. He couldn't afford it, and that was soon understood about Harry. He was hard up. No one seemed to mind. His dad was a hero.

"Shooting season ends the end of February I seem to remember," he says.

"No, you're right," says Max, recalling the crazily expensive shoots he used to go on with Simon and the others back when that's what you did as young City bloods. "Can you imagine – caught breaking into an Arab's home with intent to steal…"

"Take back what is rightfully ours," corrects Harry.

"As you say, but, caught breaking into some Arab's home and all anyone cares about is whether we trespassed during the pheasant-shooting season. Let's hope the magistrate sees it that way."

*　*　*

There's a clear path through the copse, and to judge by the number of spent orange shotgun cartridges they pass, this is where the guns stand, although, says Harry, they'd usually be out in the field, waiting for the birds to be put up.

"You're a funny guy," says Max. "Do you remember your dad?"

"No," says Harry, wrong-footed by the question, but not having to lie, which is a relief.

"A hero though," says Max. "You know, Harry, that's why I'm doing this for you. If it was me I'd just write this diamond off… you know that don't you? A fucking shit thing to happen, but then shit things happen. You've always got to move on, in my world. But you – and I think there must be a part of you that's your dad – you don't want to move on, forget what's happened, you want to fucking hit back. I can see that… I can really see that."

Max is getting quite exercised by this speech, but Harry can't feel anything. In fact he's thinking how little he really knows Max. There's a chance he might actually be mad. That explains why he's going along with him on the hare-brained venture. He suddenly feels responsible and wants to tell Max to turn back. Let's get back to equities and screwing our clients. He's right. They can fight another day – fuck this A-rab, as Beardie in the pub put it.

Five million quid.

Five million quid.

No, they must go on.

Max lifts a hand, as if he's an Indian tracker in the Wild West and has scented danger. He's crouching. "This looks a good spot," he says, tugging his rucksack from his shoulders. Harry looks at what Max can see – the second and third floors of a magnificent – there is no other word for it – building emerging from the top of the leylandii. They've chosen a good spot.

Harry rummages around in his rucksack. The jemmy clanks next to the thermos, which he removes, but what he's looking for is a book, a tatty, well-thumbed, second-hand book he bought from Amazon. Printed in 1974, it's a guide book to Luddeston Hall, produced in the years between when the Cobhams realised that they needed to open up to the general public – the "grockles" as they no doubt would have called them – and when they realised that cream teas and guided tours weren't going to keep them afloat. That's when they sold up to the Arabs and moved to a chateau in France.

Harry takes the book and starts reading aloud. "The main portion of the house is Elizabethan with Jacobean additions, etc."

"This is crazy," says Harry, putting the guidebook down.

"No it's not, Harry, we're doing the right thing."

"Then we're crazy."

Max looks at him. There's a slight suggestion of disappointment in his eyes. So, thinks Harry, he's doing this for him – Harry, the son of the dead war hero. This is going to be our Goose Green, and the Arabs are the Argentinians. Too late now to tell him that the war hero wasn't a war hero. That he never existed. That this mythical figure was the big lie that he carried all the way through their schooldays together and university and into adult life.

Except that it didn't feel like a lie any more, and the only person who ever asked directly about it is Simon. It's one of the reason he hates Simon – that and the fact that Simon had always disliked him, smelt him out like a farm terrier sniffs a rat.

"What time shall we attack?" asks Harry. A smile spreads across Max's face. He looks across at the house, where lights have been turned on against the gathering dusk. They are acclimatised to the dimming light and so it only feels marginally darker.

"Looks like they're gathered in that end of the house to judge by the lights. Can't see any outside lights but safe to assume that there are some and that they will be motion activated."

"I've been watching it get dark for the last week," says Harry. "I know London's different, but I reckon it will be fully dark in just over an hour's time."

"Let's set our watches for twenty minutes then," says Max, yanking his woollen balaclava from his rucksack. He's fully into the role now.

CHAPTER FIFTEEN

They run in short bursts, bodies bent forward to make themselves smaller, not because they've seen people do this in films – cops and the like – but because it feels entirely natural to do so. Max is holding the drugged meat in case they meet any dogs, and Harry has the cutters. They find a section of hedge that appears diseased and has died back to a brittle brown and start wriggling through, only to meet metal-link fencing.

Harry snips the latticework of wire, aware that the fence was likely to be rigged up to an alarm system. But there's no commotion as he completes his ragged circle and pushes all the loose wire away from them. They squeeze though and find themselves on bare earth. It's a long stretch of border, lined with freshly pruned roses. It seems a good point to wait and see whether they've triggered any alarms.

Max twists the binoculars from where they've become entangled around his neck, and scans the house. There appear to be no lights on at all on the ground floor, except from one window in the middle of the house, where a faint light glows. On the floor above nearly all the windows are blazing, and on the floor above that, three windows are illuminated. As Max watches, the curtains are drawn on one of these rooms.

"Let's make for that bush over there," says Max pointing to what in fact is a patch of tall ornamental grass – ghostly in the twilight – close to the only illuminated downstairs window. The lawn is soft and springy and noiseless, unlike the clanking in their rucksacks. "We'd better leave these here and just take what we need," says Max. What did they need? Harry couldn't think clearly.

Max is pointing to the downstairs window with the faint light emanating from it, and Harry suddenly realises he's being ordered to go and take a look. In the same second it hits Harry that Max is a leader, the sort of man other men would follow into battle.

Harry steps as lightly as he can across the gravel that surrounds the house and crouches beneath the window. Slowly he raises himself up, ready at any moment to flee. The light is coming from a television set. Sitting sideways on to him on a sofa is a man in chef's whites watching a football match. Another man, also in chef's whites, is standing doing something on a sideboard, with his back to him. He walks out of the room to Harry's right.

"Seems to be the servants' quarters," he reports to Max after crunching his way across the gravel.

"Good," says Max. "I wonder where they go out to have a cigarette… that would be our best bet of a way in. Let's take the meat, a torch and the jemmy. Leave the rest here."

"Is that wise?" asks Harry.

"Don't question, just do it," says Max, and Harry wants to laugh. Is leadership akin to madness? He takes his torch, a small pair of binoculars and the jemmy from the rucksack and pushes the bag into the middle of the grass. Max nods, and does the same with his rucksack. They creep around the edge of the lawn so as not to have to walk on the gravel, spotting a gateway that seems to lead into an inner courtyard, a suspicion confirmed when they make out a lighted doorway. Max looks through his binoculars.

"That looks like a staff entrance… there's a crate of Coca-Cola and a wheelie bin. Come on."

The courtyard is presumably where the carriages drew up in the olden days, thinks Max. He keeps to the shadows, close in to the wall, waving his hand to make Harry do the same. They are about twenty paces from the lighted door when it swings open, and the chef they'd seen earlier watching football announces himself with a rasping smoker's cough, and lights up a cigarette.

Fortunately his full attention is taken with whatever he is looking at on his phone. Max and Harry remain stock still, Max looking around for any other signs of life. All the windows looking in on the courtyard are dark. Dragging deeply on his cigarette the chef finally finishes, flicking its lighted butt towards them. With that he turns and returns inside, without locking the door behind him. Max creeps on until he's right beside the door, slowly turning himself so that he can reach the handle.

He beckons Harry urgently with his hand, and Harry trots over. He takes another look, and then opens the door and they're inside. They move away from the light and the sounds of football, and down a darkened corridor that leads to a narrow staircase, no doubt the servants' staircase once. Harry becomes aware of his racing heartbeat and takes a deep breath.

The stairs lead to a choice of corridor. Right, though the fire door, looks as if it might lead to staff bedrooms. The left hand corridor looks more promising. They reach another fire door and Max stops to peer through the small square window. He nods, and slowly pushes open the door, which leads out onto a landing, surrounding what looks like the main staircase. There are large paintings in dark frames along these walls, men on horseback and large naked women – the sort of stuff you find in museums, thinks Max.

The carpet feels softer, plusher underfoot, and there's a smell of expensive room scent of the kind that is soaked up and emitted along sticks. They have something similar in the office. Faintly they can hear music, pop music, and it seems to be coming from a room at the far end of the landing. Someone's bedroom? Aafia's? That would be too lucky. Max nods in that direction.

Outside the door they stop and listen. It's Billy Joel, *Uptown Girl*. Harry shrugs his shoulders. Too late. Someone is coming up the staircase, and fast. Max turns the door handle and they step into the room.

"Good evening, gentlemen, and what can I get you?"

At first Max thinks it's the landlord from the pub standing behind the bar and somehow they've arrived back at the Golden Lion. And then he realises that the room has been mocked up to look like the Golden Lion, right down to the hunting prints and horse brasses. But the Golden Lion with a million pounds spent on it. The man who has addressed them from behind the polished mahogany bar is also fat and middle-aged, but the face is sleeker, less careworn. Ironic eyes stare out of it.

"A pint each of best, perhaps?"

CHAPTER SIXTEEN

The pair of them nod dumbly in unison.

"You don't seem surprised to see us," says Max, managing to verbalise what he and Harry are thinking. .

The man nods towards a CCTV monitor in the corner of the room. A selection of views show the main doors as well as the courtyard and the lawns where they had been hiding. Infrared presumably.

"Not that you didn't announce yourself earlier," says the man. "The pub has strict instructions to ring the boss if any strangers turn up asking about the house and who lives there. Stu rang ahead with your names – or the name on the credit card you paid with. The boss says he's very happy to see you, Max."

Max laughs. "In that case I'll have a pint of your best, landlord."

"And you, sir?"

"I'll have the same," says Harry, just as the door swings open and the Arab guy with tight white jeans and thick, long greasy hair steps into the room – unsmiling just as he had been when they first saw him in Mayfair hotel lobby. The barman makes himself busy.

"His excellency," the man announces, and steps aside as the Saudi waddles into the room, in full Arab dress, and with a benign smile on his pudgy face.

"Max. Max," he says coming over to the bar and clapping Max on the shoulder. "And Harry, isn't it?" Harry nods. "You have been served?"

The barman comes over with the pints and places them on mats – the very same mats used in the Golden Lion, notices Harry. "Always in finest condition, the bitter," says the Arab. "Never drink it myself."

"Your usual, your excellency?"

The Saudi nods and beckons his guests towards a table, a dark wooden table with four chairs just like the one that they had eaten their lunch from.

"Amazing," says Max. "I bet the food's better here than down the road though."

The barman places a chunky crystal tumbler in front of the Arab and fills it with twelve-year-old single malt Islay whisky.

"Cheers," says the Arab raising his tumbler.

"Cheers," says Max and Harry.

"Now, what brings you here trespassing on my property? It's not theft when you break into someone's house, is it… it's burglary. Have you found anything?"

The greaseball in the white jeans steps forward and drops both their rucksacks on to the floor. Harry can see a silver candelabra poking out of the top of his.

"Hey…" he says.

"It would be too easy," says the Saudi. "But tell me, what did you really come for?"

Max sups his pint and looks the Arab in the eye. "We want our diamond back."

"Your diamond?"

"Yes, the one your daughter stole from us in Geneva."

"My daughter?"

The Saudi leans forward, his rheumy, dark brown eyes staring hard at Max.

"If you mean Aafia – I disowned my daughter a long time ago."

"What about at the hotel?" asks Harry. "She didn't look very disowned then."

The Saudi takes a dainty sip of his whisky, and gives a little shiver.

"I was hoping to bring her back into the flock, but I fear that it's… too… late."

"So you're not involved in stealing our diamond… it was your daughter working on her own?" asks Max. Harry decides to leave the talking to Max.

"Precisely."

"But you knew about it?"

"Of course. The moment you reported your suspicions to the police. They did the courtesy of phoning the embassy in Geneva who phoned me and I told them exactly what I'm telling you. The theft – if such a thing actually occurred and it wasn't just an insurance job – was nothing whatsoever to do with me."

"The insurance was null and void because we took it out of the back vault."

"That was foolish."

"You had requested that we bring it to the hotel. You e-mailed us."

"My e-mail was hacked. I requested nothing. If you don't believe me ask the Swiss police, they could see that my e-mail had been hacked."

"By your own daughter…"

"Or her associates."

Perhaps it was the long afternoon in the cold, or the effects of the alcohol, but Harry suddenly feels tired. He stands up.

"I've had enough of this. Your daughter stole our diamond and we want it back."

"Sit down." It's the greaseball in the white jeans and he has a gun in his hand – a stubby but lethal-looking revolver. The barman is nowhere to be seen. Harry sits down.

The Saudi leans in again. "There are things in this world you do not understand," he says.

"Enlighten us," says Harry, softening the sarcasm in his voice as he watches the greaseball slip the revolver into his jacket pocket.

"My daughter, Aafia, she has your diamond, no?"

"That's the last time we saw it," says Harry.

"She does have our diamond, your excellency," says Max, emolliently. "She asked to show it to you and that's the last we saw of it."

The Saudi waves his hand airily as if the theft of a £5 million gem was spoiling an evening in the pub with friends, and then looks at them thoughtfully. Max notices, not for the first time, how the whites of his eyes are yellowing. Is that a kidney problem? The Arab starts nodding to himself, as if he has made up his mind about something.

"Aafia has always been trouble to me. She is very wilful, like her mother. And now…"

Harry and Max lean in.

"And now she has run off with a fucking useless playboy." Max and Harry are both taken aback to hear this usually measured man swear. "Excuse my language, but this man is the worst type. A user. He doesn't have any money so she supports him. She gives him everything, it hurts to see her waste her money, but more importantly, her youth on this man. She is of an age to make a good marriage, and he is… what?"

"What is he?" asks Harry and the Saudi looks at him fully for the first time through those dark brown eyes afloat in those yellowing globes.

"Who knows what he, or who he is. Not a Sunni anyway. He is a Libyan." The Saudi almost spits the words out.

Max and Harry frown at each other, not really understanding the nuances of what he is saying.

"He is a poor Shia boy and he lives in Italy like he's a billionaire, but really he's just a thief. He steals from my daughter, and now, it would seem, she is stealing for him. But now…"

The Saudi takes another dainty sip of whisky.

"Now I have a little job for you."

* * *

"And what if we refuse?" says Max. The Saudi has laid out the details and terms of his 'little job'. They are to travel to Italy immediately, on his private jet, all expenses paid. They are to hire a suitable vehicle – arrangements to be made by his office – and to track his daughter down to her address on the outskirts of Rome. He didn't have an exact address, but knows of a café that she frequents.

At this point cowboy boots returns with a box folder, from which he took a pile of black and white photographs. They are of Aafia, several of her sitting at a table on the pavement terrace, sunglasses on top of her head, and speaking into a mobile phone. Others showed her entering and leaving the café, whose name was emblazoned across the glass frontage and sun awnings. Café Paolo.

"Well, of course you can refuse, but then you will have certain problems."

"Such as?" says Harry.

"Well, apart from the undeniable evidence of breaking and entering – perhaps you wanted to get your own back on my daughter… a few priceless artefacts to make up for your loss…"

"But hold on…" Harry again.

"More harmful I think will be the harassment order that my lawyers will take out. You will not be allowed within fifty miles of my presence, and since I spend my weeks in London that might be inconvenient for your business…"

Harry looks at Max. "Can he do that?"

Max shrugs.

"Let me assure you that I can," says the Saudi, draining what is left of his whisky. "And there are a hundred other ways that I can make your life difficult. Your government goes to great efforts to make sure our life in your country is as comfortable as possible.

"More importantly, I think for you," says the Saudi, pointing his tumbler at Harry. "Is the five million. No?"

Harry nods.

"Here's the deal. You find my daughter, and take a picture with her to prove it, and I'll drop all charges and leave you alone. Get her to leave with you and away from Rome and I'll pay you the money you're owed. I don't mind how you do it… just do it."

*   *   *

"What do you think?" asks Harry as the chauffeur-driven Mercedes glides them back towards London.

114

"I don't think we have a choice," says Max, after a pause. "In for a penny…"

"In for five million quid."

CHAPTER SEVENTEEN

As they'd been led to expect, a man is waiting for them as they emerge through customs and into Arrivals at Rome's Fiumicino airport. Short, balding, middle-aged and, as far as Max and Harry could tell, Italian, he is jigging his name card absently, like a mother rocking a baby, as if the movement might sooner catch the attention of Kimber and Draycott – although he seems to instantly recognise them as they wheel their cabin-sized suitcases out onto the concourse. Had he been sent a photograph of them? Who took the photograph and when? Harry's paranoia, Max is coming to realise, is contagious.

"Buongiorno, signori," he says. "Passports please."

Max and Harry exchange a glance, Max nods and they hand over their passports. Unsmiling, the man flips on to their photo ID, nods, and hands them back. "Follow me please."

He strides surprisingly purposively for such an unassuming-looking man, leading them down an escalator, through some sliding doors and past taxi queues. A small car park houses the various hire companies – Avis, Hertz and so on – but in an unmarked area behind these is their transport, a black van that manages to look fairly innocuous despite the blacked-out windows.

"A Mercedes Viano," says Max, who, despite his disdain at the investment returns on ever actually buying a car, seems to know his vehicles. He's been ferried around London in one of these, usually with Simon.

The Italian nods. "Mercedes, si," he echoes, as he blips open the vehicle, and reaches on to the front passenger seat, emerging with the hire documents and a plastic shopping bag, which he hands to Harry. It's full of mobile phones.

"Use it once then throw away," he says, brandishing one of the phones and mimicking the act of throwing. His eyes are on Harry, intense and serious. "Now… *aspetta*… please wait a moment."

He presses a number and waits, and almost immediately a text message bleeps in return. The man takes the mobile, climbs into the passenger seat of the vehicle, and starts inputting some coordinates into the satnav. He waits a moment, checks that he has entered the correct destination, and slides out of the seat again. He looks comically tiny for such a large van.

"This," he says. "This now finished." Max notices that it's an old model iPhone – an iPhone 4 – before the man extracts the Sim card, slips it into the breast pocket of his jacket, puts the phone on the ground, before repeatedly stamping on its with his heel, and turning to them with a dramatic flourish. "Remember; use once and then chuck," he repeats. "They are all prepaid with cash. Now your own phones please…"

"You what?" says Harry.

"You want our phones?" echoes Max. He looks as if he's been asked to hand over one of his kidneys.

"It is essential," says the man. "They will be posted to your office in London."

"But what about using the Internet?"

"Don't use the Internet." They stand staring at the man. "Please, your phones."

"Oh well, in for a penny," says Max, who fully intends buying a new one as soon as possible.

"The Internet on these has been permanently disabled," says the man, pointing at the bag of phones in Harry's hand. Everything is paid for," he says, handing Max the key. "*Arrivederci*."

With that, he turns and marches off, Max and Harry watching him stop at some lifts, and then vanish behind their sliding doors.

"O… kay," says Harry. But Max has opened the back door of the Mercedes and is appraising the interior. The inside has been reconfigured so that it looks like a tiny sitting room, with four deep individual leather seats, the rear two divided by a table. The ones he'd ridden in London had had TV screens between the rear and the driver, but this one is interconnected.

"Well, which phone shall we start with?" asks Harry.

"You choose," says Max settling himself down in the driver's seat and trying out the position of the gear stick and rear-view mirror. He takes out a wad of euros, slips them into the plastic folder with the hire documents, and puts the folder underneath the sun visor.

"You never know", he says.

As always when they share a car anywhere together, the assumption is that Max will drive. Not that Max is a particularly expert driver – he is safe enough and not easily distracted – the assumption merely seems to reflect the rest of their lives. Max takes control; Harry goes along for the ride.

The satnav soon leads them on an autostrada that leads them to a ring-road circling Rome, the A90. Eventually Max is prompted to take an exit, which seems to be taking them away from Rome.

Harry notices with pleasure the tall cypress trees that line an otherwise anonymous dual carriageway through an industrial suburb of warehouses and car dealerships. The temperature, according to a red neon sign outside a chemist shop, is 22 degrees. The time is 10.32, but it feels so much later.

At traffic lights no one seems to give the black Mercedes with blacked-out windows a second glance, which reassures Harry. They take a right down a narrower road, the scrubby spaces between buildings becoming larger, until they reach what feels like a town centre with smaller shops. Twenty metres and on their left they have reached their destination, the satnav announces.

"There it is," Max almost shouts, looking across to Harry and out of the offside window.

"What is?" asks Harry, who has been trying to figure out why a wealthy Saudi woman and her playboy lover would choose to hole up in such an anonymous, working-class suburb as this.

"The cafe… the one in the photograph."

The Cafe Paolo has a white facade that also advertises ice creams and pizza, above a pavement terrace – the terrace where Aafia and her boyfriend were photographed – that is demarcated by four or five plant pots with nothing growing in them. An old man is the only customer on the terrace, stirring a cup of espresso, before unfolding a newspaper and disappearing behind it. Another old man in serge trousers is shuffling his way past, shopping basket in hand. A van is unloading vegetables – boxes of lettuce and cucumbers – to a greengrocer next door. A boy on a noisy moped breaks the torpor of the scene, which then folds back on itself as he disappears round the corner, the sharp racket of his machine growing steadily less ear-splitting.

"What now?" asks Harry.

"Fancy a coffee?"

"Good idea."

There are three men seated at a table playing cards, and they look up briefly as Max and Harry – suddenly very aware of the expensive cuts of their chinos and tailored shirts – make their way to the bar.

"*Si signori?*" says an old woman, rinsing glasses and not looking at them

"*Duo cafes,*" says Harry, who on the flight has been reading a tourist Italian phrasebook he bought at the airport.

They had barely retired to a table three along from the card players when Harry jumps out of his seat and dashes round next to where Max is sitting with his back to the window.

"I don't believe it," he hisses. "Don't look… it's them."

Max turns and looks all the same. Aafia and her boyfriend have settled at a table on the terrace and are sitting there, looking absently out into the road – the man with a packet of cigarettes and a lighter stacked in front of him, just as they had been in the photographs that Aafia's father had shown them.

The old woman notices them too. She emerges from behind the bar and shuffles over to the door. Max takes up position in Harry's old chair and puts on his sunglasses, making him look twice as conspicuous as before. The card players obviously think Max's choice of indoor eyewear is odd, because two of them are now staring at him. They must look like a couple of plainclothes

119

policemen, thinks Harry. No, too well-dressed for policemen. Gangsters?

The old woman is having a long conversation with Aafia and her boyfriend. What are they talking about? The unbelievably hot spring weather? Global warming? The price of coffee? The two strangers inside? Not once do they glance in the direction of the interior, Max is relieved to note. But what to do now?

The old woman decides for them. She shuffles back into the cafe and over to their table.

"The signor and signora ask if you would like to join them on the terrace," she announces in remarkably clear English. "Two more coffees?"

CHAPTER EIGHTEEN

Aafia has that amused turn to her mouth that Harry had noticed on first seeing her in London. The man has an unreadable expression behind his dark glasses. He has several days growth of stubble and a strong, beak-like nose: Libyan, Aafia's father had said.

"We meet again," says Max, scraping back a white plastic chair to join them. "Can we have our diamond back? Or do you plan to pay for it now?"

The man laughs, a rumbling smoker's laugh. He taps out a cigarette from his packet of Marlboro Reds, puts it between his lips and lights it. "Tariq is my name," he says emitting a plume of smoke.

"Daddy told you where to find us then?" says Aafia, cutting sharply across Tariq. "What a kind man. So caring. He must really like you."

"Daddy wants you to come home," says Harry.

"Is he worried about me?" says Aafia in a mock childish voice, turning to him. "I doubt it. He's just using you to get at me."

"I don't care about that," puts in Max, suddenly business-like. "Fact. You have our diamond and you haven't paid for it. We would like it back or we'd like paying for it."

The man lets out a long deliberate plume of smoke, and shares a silent conversation with Aafia.

"Come on then – come with us," she says. "Leave your car here, we only live a couple of blocks away."

The next part has the logic of a dream, or a nightmare. They follow two paces behind Aafia and her boyfriend, who's wearing white jeans, a short-sleeved white cotton or polyester shirt, and dusty old battered loafers. Aafia is wearing an expensive cut of blue jeans that show off her beautiful round bottom and long legs. Harry can't help but notice. Neither would appear to be carrying a gun or a weapon of any sort.

No one speaks, they just trudge along, Harry and Max both feeling that they are doing something dangerous and stupid, but, despite the feeling in their stomachs that they are looking over a great precipice, both men feel compelled to continue as if in a trance. Harry had read a book once in which prisoners were taken out to be shot by a firing squad and he had often wondered what it must be like to be drawn to your certain extinction. Now he thinks he has a rough idea.

The sense of being led meekly into a trap intensifies when they reach a door in a long white wall. The boyfriend opens it, peeks in to check something, and then opens it wide, beckoning them to enter.

Inside is a large yard to what looks like a compound of several huts and sheds. The boyfriend takes out his key ring and presses a fob button, which in turn activates a door on one of the breeze-block garages at the end of the yard. Max and Harry walk helplessly towards this as if resigned to their doom, on legs that seem to have lost all feeling.

Inside the garage is a car – a shiny new navy blue Audi A6 – while various cans line the walls. The shelves are stacked with the usual sort of things you might find in a garage: spanner sets, foot-pumps, a big can of WD 40… but the boyfriend is now unlocking an inner door at the far end that Max notices with dread contains steps down into some sort of basement or cellar.

Down they go, towards a dim light at the end that Max sees is a table. Two men, burly and mute, are standing against the walls, but seated around the table are three – what Max's father used to refer to (usually in the context of a derogatory remark) as 'Middle Eastern gentlemen'. Two are about Max and Harry's age, but between them is an athletic dark-skinned man who is younger. He has a black scarf draped around his shoulders and a scar running down one of his cheeks. Max looks into the man's eyes and it's like running into a brick wall.

"Take your jackets off."

It's the man to the left of this unsettling youth who has spoken – and his accent is northern. Max thinks it might be a Yorkshire accent, although he is very sketchy about England north of the Cotswolds. He spent three years at Edinburgh University, but even there had mixed mostly with public schoolboys like himself.

"Your jackets," the man repeats.

Harry realises that his shirt is soaked in sweat. Max's, he notices, is still dry, as Max peels off his jacket, and neatly folds it over the back of one of the chairs. A man steps forward from against the wall, pulls the jacket roughly from the back of the chair, and starts checking the pockets. Having extracted Max's wallet and passport, which he throws on to the table, he chucks the jacket on to the floor, and gives it a kick for good measure. Harry hands his jacket to the man, who gives it a similar treatment.

"Watches… and that," orders the Englishman, pointing at the fitness-tracker on Max's wrist. Harry wonders what sleep patterns it would register in the coming days. Max's pulse rate is presumably off the scale, although he notices an oddly detached look on his friend's face. Perhaps he's in shock.

And then a powerful force is wrenching his hands behind his back, and they are being bound. Harry lets out a yelp as rope or cord seems to cut through his wrists. He tries to wiggle his fingers but that just makes the stinging worse.

"Not so tight," shouts Max, as if this was a game of make-believe, as both he and Max are pressed down into the vacant chairs.

The northern-accented man opens and shakes Max's wallet, depositing bank cards and driving licence and a wad of euros, pristine from the cash point at the airport, on the table. He picks up Max's fitness tracker and looks at it in bemusement.

"This have GPS in it?" he asks the man with the scar, who nods, takes the fitness tracker from him and grinds it under his booted heel.

"What are your names?" asks the northerner.

"Max and Harry," says Max, as just then a door opens and another man brings in their overnight bags and the plastic bag

123

containing the mobile phones. So they've broken into the van. Max still has the keys in his trouser pockets.

The two older men at the table lean in and exchange something in Arabic. The younger man nods, and looks at Harry. "What are you doing here?" he asks in good if heavily accented English. Harry can only stare dumbly back. What is he doing here in a cellar somewhere outside Rome?

"Your friend Aafia stole our diamond," says Max, in a cool, clear voice, and looking around for Aafia, but she has vanished, along with her boyfriend. "And we are trying to get it back. Aafia's father, told us where to find her. It's that simple."

"There is no diamond," the man says. "I don't believe you... you are spies. British spies."

CHAPTER NINETEEN

Max and Harry find themselves being lifted from behind and pushed towards a door, which leads into another inner sanctum, this one with its walls lined in mattresses. In the middle of a room a video camera sits on a stand and the two of them are prodded towards the front of the lens. A painful kick to the back of their knees finds them sprawled on the floor.

"On your knees," says the young man with the scar. "Pray that your god will save you." With that, he leaves the room and Max and Harry are left on their own.

"Fucking shit," says Harry.

"Fuck, fuck, fuck…" says Max.

A minute passes, or maybe five – it's impossible to tell. Max sits himself on his bottom and Harry follows suit.

"They're going to kill us for a gawping internet audience of millions. Something to watch between the kitten videos," says Max. "Poor Rachel… and Mum and Dad…"

At that moment one of the security heavies comes into the room, and walks over to where the camera still stands, and to Max and Harry's astonishment he picks up the camera and throws it on to the concrete floor. He then does likewise with the laptop that sits on a small wicker table in the corner.

They say nothing but watch him walk round behind them. Harry gives an involuntary shudder, and feels something tugging at his wrists. Suddenly the sharp, burning pain has gone and he can move his hands.

"Move your fingers… get the circulation going," the man says to Harry, before cutting Max free as well. They can finally see the cords that have been causing them so much agony; it looks like strimmer wire.

"Who are you?" asks Max.

"Saudi secret service," says the man quietly. "Take these guns. That door leads to a staircase. Go up the staircase and you will find the woman and your diamond. Be quick. The others are in conference, deciding what to say on your beheading video."

Max and Harry find themselves holding pistols, the closest either has come to a gun other than a hunting shotgun; they smell of oil.

"The staircase now… quick," the man says, as if sensing their bewilderment. "The diamond is in a safe above the bed. The number to open the safe is 1438… that's the date in the Islamic calendar…"

Harry, who has imagined the world watching his death on the Internet – perhaps 'favouriting' it and forwarding it to friends – wastes no more time.

"Come on," he says to Max, and trots up the staircase. If he is going to die, it's going to be like a lion rather than a sheep.

He pushes open a door at the top and finds himself in a bedroom. There's a low double bed, on one side of which is sitting Aafia's boyfriend – and two single mattresses. The safe is, as their saviour had indicated, above the bed, but it's open and, as far as Harry can tell, empty. The younger man with the scar, his would-be executioner, is standing by the window, seemingly sending a text on his mobile. He stops and throws the phone on to the double bed.

"Don't move… put up your hands," says Harry, just as Max arrives in the doorway. Max points his gun at the boyfriend.

"Where's Aafia?" asks Harry, scooping up the mobile from the bed. The man with the scar scowls, the first expression he's seen on his face "Where's the fucking diamond? I give you five seconds… one… two…three…" Neither men speak or move.

"Four… five… Right you cunt… you're the first to die," says Harry levelling the tip of his gun with the scarred youth's torso. He starts squeezing the trigger.

"Stop, Harry… stop. Stop!"

It's Aafia, who has appeared just behind Max at the top of the staircase. She has in her hand their passports, the bag with their mobile phones and, looking as beautiful and orange and otherworldly as they remember it – their diamond.

"Follow me."

*　*　*

They charge down a staircase behind Aafia, and through a door that leads on to the street – their faces bathed in a sunlight neither man expected to see or feel again.

Tariq is standing by the door with his back pressed up against the wall. Harry instinctively raises his gun, but Aafia shouts for him to put it down. Aafia and Tariq exchange some words in Arabic. Tariq brushes the top of Aafia's arm and heads off.

"This way," she says calmly to Max and Harry, and now Aafia is rushing up the street, her haste alarming enough for Max and Harry to run as hard as they can. Behind them they hear shouting, and several gunshots in quick succession.

"Hide your guns," Aafia shouts as she turns another corner, recognising the cafe frontage where a small crowd is gathered around the black Mercedes. The car alarm is going off with a piercing ululation. Both men push their guns warily down the front of their trousers, Harry keeping his cupped so it doesn't slip down a trouser leg. Christ, he thinks, I hope it doesn't go off.

The crowd, mainly youngsters, part as Aafia arrives and then Max and finally Harry. The blacked-out driver's window has been smashed and a policeman has his head thrust inside. He withdraws it as Aafia approaches and starts talking animatedly to him in Italian.

There follows a conversation that neither of the Englishmen can follow, but is apparently fascinating to the crowd gathered round the car. From time to time Aafia points to Max and Harry, and the crowd's eyes swivel as one in their direction. Is she telling the cop that she's been kidnapped and that he needs his help? Max looks at the gun in the policeman's holster.

Max appears to cup his balls, whereas in fact he's trying not to let his own pistol fall down his trousers. Harry keeps an anxious lookout in the direction from where they have just come, but nobody seems to be following.

Finally the policeman starts nodding vigorously, saying, *"Si, signora, si, si..."* and Aafia beckons Max and Harry over.

"Get in and drive," she says. "I've told him that nothing has been stolen and I've reported it to the car hire people and that we're returning there straight away. Now, just drive."

CHAPTER TWENTY

Omar pulls aside the bedroom curtain. The Saudi woman is talking to her Libyan boyfriend, the British men standing back looking shit scared. She gives the Libyan's arm a quick squeeze and they are off in opposite directions. Omar knows instinctively whom he has to follow, and charges down the staircase with demonic speed. Behind him, from inside the compound, there is shouting and some gunfire.

The Libyan is walking fast, but turning and spotting Omar he breaks into a run. But Omar is fast and fit and soon makes up ground. He never trusted the woman or the boyfriend, they just didn't smell right. And he knows the Libyan followed him into Rome the other day, when he went to visit the kid in the hotel.

Omar shoulder-barges Tariq against the wall and, as the Libyan stumbles, he hammers the side of his fist into his temple. The Libyan's eyes go blank, his mouth opens as if to say something, and then he drops like a sack of wheat onto the dusty yard floor.

Omar looks around for a weapon but can't see anything to hand, so he lifts Tariq by the armpits, sizes up his lolling head, and puts all his strength into another hammer blow to the temple. He recalls his unarmed combat instructor, a Chechen who had been in Spetsnaz, the Russian Special Forces, teaching him that a blow like this to the temple could easily kill a man.

The Libyan doesn't make a sound as he hits him, and there is more shouting inside the compound, so Omar decides it's time to make his departure. He jogs to the side door that leads into the garage. Everything he needs is in the Audi.

The keys are hanging where he left them, and with a click of the button the garage doors start to lift as Omar secures his seatbelt. As he noses the car forward one of his men, Sabir, staggers across the courtyard holding his stomach. Blood is seeping across his shirt and he is waving his gun erratically. Omar jogs over to the wooden double doors that lead on to the street, unbolts them and pulls them wide, and jumps back into the Audi. He pulls into the street with a screech of acceleration.

He drives quickly for several streets and then slows down and takes a steady pace towards the ring road. No time to think right now – he'll work out what's gone wrong later.

Just before the ring road there's a heavily shaded rest area, and Omar pulls in, stops the engine and gets out. In the boot are several pairs of number plates, one of which he selects. These are the car's real ones.

Back in the driver's seat he pulls up his phone, calls up the GPS tracking device he has placed in the Englishmen's Mercedes and logs on. After a short delay he sees where they're headed. Due north.

CHAPTER TWENTY-ONE

They've been driving for just over four hours – four hours in which Aafia has sat motionless on the back seat, her long black hair dancing in the wind that's coming in through the smashed driver's window, while she stares blindly out of her side window, not uttering a word.

Harry has her covered with the gun, while Max drives, occasionally picking fragments of shattered glass from the window frame. The exit signs for Florence have long ago stopped and now a sign on the autostrada says it is 250 kilometres to Milan, and the satnav agrees. Max glances at his watch.

"We'll take the Como route into Switzerland," he says. "Best avoid France; France is officially at war, or something, or a state of emergency because of all the terrorist attacks. And apparently the French borders are tough these days anyway because of all the migrant boat people coming into Italy. The Frogs don't want them."

"The Swiss won't either, surely?" says Harry. "They're not even in the EU."

"According to Google, they're signed up to whatever that 'open border' agreement is called."

"Yes, but nobody has open borders any more... not since Paris," says Max.

Now Aafia turns and looks Harry in the eye.

"I won't give you any trouble," she says with a softness that belies the fierceness of her stare, and then looks away out of the window again. Harry's arm is aching and he lowers the gun for a moment. "Why would I have given you the diamond and the way out? I could easily have reported you to that cop."

"Why should we trust you?" he asks. "You were happy to see someone chop off our heads earlier today."

Aafia makes a clicking noise with her tongue. "No one was

going to chop off your head," she mutters as if to herself, still looking out of the window. "Well, perhaps Omar wanted to, but we wouldn't have let it get that far."

"Who's Omar?"

"He's the cunt with the scar."

Max lets out a laugh, and Harry joins in. "Did you just call him a cunt?"

"And he is," says Aafia.

Harry levels the gun again. Now the immediate fear has passed – the survival instinct – would he use it? Could he? He tries to re-ignite his anger.

"I thought we were going to die," he hisses with a vehemence that surprises him.

"Please put the gun down," says Aafia.

"Er... no, I won't," says Harry.

"Put it down," says Max. "Let's hear what she has to say."

Aafia gives a little nod. Harry lowers the pistol.

"I'm sorry if you were frightened, but you were never in any danger."

"Sure looked like a fuck of a lot of danger to me," says Harry, who feels that his survival somehow depends on remaining angry.

"We wouldn't have let them kill you."

"Who's we...? Who's them...?"

"Can I have some water?"

Max nods and Harry passes her a small water bottle he had fortunately bought at the airport, taking a firmer grip on the gun at the same time.

"What do you think this is all about?" asks Aafia, before gulping greedily.

"I haven't got a fucking clue," says Harry. "You're a spoilt little rich girl who's got mixed up with a bad lot and you stole our diamond to fund them."

Aafia gives a little laugh. "If only it was so easy."

"Enlighten us."

"You know about my father... you know he is a powerful man.

Let me tell you about me."

Max and Harry say nothing and Aafia continues.

"I have two brothers and six sisters, or rather two brothers and six half-sisters. I'm the oldest girl and my father's favourite. You know you can tell, can't you?"

"Yes," says Max emphatically. It's suddenly like they are three young friends talking freely, perhaps the morning after a party or a wedding.

"Except it's the other brothers and sisters who can usually tell," continues Max. "Nicky was my mother's favourite."

Harry tries not to look at Max. Aafia is still watching the passing verges of the autostrada.

"Anyway, he always kept me close. My half-sisters were all sent home and had a strict upbringing, but me and my brothers we went to America with him – I lived just outside Washington for the first eight years of my life. Then we came to Europe – an international school in Brussels for two years, then Switzerland for a year, and then when I was eleven I was sent to a jolly old British boarding school for girls."

She was staring out of the window all the time as she said all this, as if recalling a dream.

"Which one? Do I know it?" asks Max. Harry can't take in the weird normality of the conversation. Max sounds like he's chatting in the pub rather than driving for his life with a suspected terrorist in the back of the car.

"Firle Manor? You might have heard of Wycombe Abbey – we played them at netball and lacrosse."

"My sister Tash considered Wycombe Abbey," says Max.

"Anyway, there were lots of foreign girls at Firle – I think we kept it afloat. There were other Arab girls too, but I was too westernised for them and used to hang out with a bunch of Russian and Italian girls, and one or two English. A naughty crowd. When I was fifteen I was caught drinking and that was the end of that."

"What happened then?" Max is really enjoying this story, thinks Harry, while he looks for inconsistencies.

"My father took me away, and I was sent to Jeddah in Saudi for the next three years. My God… ha—" She stops.

"A bit of a shock to the system, eh?" says Max.

"You don't know how much. I went to live with my half-sisters and my father's second wife in a compound on the edge of town. It was like a prison. I had to wear a headscarf around the home, and the hijab when I went out. Not that I went out very often, and never alone. My sisters and I and even my stepmother had to have a male to accompany us anywhere – to the shops even; it was usually one of my stepmother's many brothers. Do you know what *hijab* means? It means barrier or partition – like you weren't wanted, like you were separated off."

"We see it every day in Mayfair," says Harry. It seemed like another life now, the hedge fund, the days of sitting at his desk while the money rolled in; one that might never have really happened.

"My half-sisters were all right, but rather limited; they knew nothing but this weird captive life. I tried to make the most of it and actually even felt a bit relieved not to always have the latest fashions. I even did quite well at college. But it was so restricting. I remember when I was seventeen I wanted driving lessons and was told I could forget that idea at once. And if I took the bus I had to run the risk of being groped – even when my uncle was sitting there, just across the aisle. Mind you, I think given half a chance…"

"Go on," says Harry. Aafia turns to look at him, with that amused, half-mocking look he had first noticed in the restaurant in London.

"You want to hear more about me being groped by my uncle?"

Harry tries not to blush, but can feel his cheeks redden. "No. We want to know how you got from there to here." She turns back to the window, speaking towards the blackened pane as if towards the grill in a priest's confessional.

"I wanted to go to university and I wanted to do it in Europe or America, not in some Muslim country. And I knew my father missed me… you could tell in the tone of his phone-calls and letters… and since he lived in England, I applied to colleges in

London and got offered a place at the LSE."

"The London School of Economics," says Max, once again engaged with the story. What a jolly drive they are having across Italy. Harry instinctively looks out of the back window to see if he recognises any of the cars following them.

"Yes, the London School of Economics. I studied politics and economics – my father let me do it, which surprised me at the time. Perhaps not now. I think he had plans for me; I think he still has plans for me.

"You know the first thing I did when I got to London? I went shopping at Selfridges and booked some driving lessons. But I kept my headscarf for a while; it seemed to make people interested in me at college, I'm not too vain to admit. And I met some pretty cool people – radical feminist Muslims, can you believe; and Islamic fundamentalists – the eradicate Israel, drive out Christians, reclaim the eternal truth of the Quran types – all varieties in between.

"In the holidays I lived with my father in the country house that you broke into." This was accompanied by another amused look at Harry. He felt himself becoming aroused. "A weird double life. My father used to like hearing about all my friends at university, and then I realised…"

"You were spying for him," says Harry.

"I think so," says Aafia, this time looking at him without mockery. "Not in any specific way, you understand; he just wanted to know current waves of opinion amongst westernised Muslims – Saudis in particular. But then something happened, the political became personal; I became involved with a bunch of feminists – men too. What's that: a 'meninist'?"

It was first time Max or Harry had heard her attempt to crack a joke.

"My father had bought me a large flat in Kensington and we started to use it as a safe house for female Muslim students who were being abused in some way. And so it grew. I came to realise that the whole Islamic fundamentalist thing… the interpretation of Islam known as Wahhabism, and that means Saudi Arabia and Isis

135

in Syria, Iraq and Libya, is sending women back to the Stone Age."

"You're not Isis then?"

"No, fuck, we're the very opposite of Isis."

"You're trying to tell us you're some sort of radical feminist do-gooders," says Harry. Max glances across at him; Harry isn't sure whether he has understood.

"No, no," laughs Aafia. "We've gone way beyond that now."

"And what about your boyfriend? Your father doesn't seem very keen to call him his son-in-law."

"He's not my boyfriend. My father knows that."

There is a silence. "What is he then?" says Harry.

"Tariq and I met at the LSE. His father was in Gaddafi's government for a while, but became a dissident... moved to London when Tariq was about fourteen. He was my first proper boyfriend – we became lovers in my first year."

She looks at Harry and Harry finds he can't return her stare. He glances over at the satnav. Two hundred and thirty kilometres to Milan.

"His one dream was for Gaddafi to be overthrown and for him to return home and help turn Libya into a social democracy," says Aafia, turning to stare out of the window again. "So when what you call the Arab Spring happened in Libya in 2011 we both went over to try and see what we could do. With all the country's oil reserves and only six million people we thought we'd create the new Dubai – a Dubai with equal rights for women." She gives a dry little laugh.

"What's happening in Libya?" shouts Max. He might be his father enquiring about the Test score.

"A mess," says Harry, who followed the news more than Max.

"NATO should have followed up," says Aafia. "But as always it never does. It destroys but can't build in its place. Now Libya is not the new Dubai, it's the new Iraq. The new Syria. Only..."

"Only what?" asks Harry softly. She looks at him; this time he holds her eyes with his.

"Only it's just there – over the Mediterranean – near enough to jump on a rickety old boat and hope for the best. Do you know the distance between Tripoli and Sicily? Three hundred miles... something like that."

"Which is why you're based in Italy?" Harry's neck feels stiff from staring over the seat at Aafia.

"We were pretending to be a safe house," she says.

"A safe house for who?" shouts Max.

"For terrorists coming over from Libya and pretending to be migrants. People like Omar."

"Why?" Max again.

"So we could keep an eye on them."

"Who's we?"

"Some people you will meet soon enough." Max and Harry exchange a glance.

"What fucking people?" Harry sounds almost shrill, and Aafia smiles.

"Let's just get wherever we're going."

They're silent for a while, and Harry wonders why he's finding it so hard to ask the next question.

"So Tariq is no longer your boyfriend," he says eventually.

She's giving him that sardonic smile again. "No, we split up. Happens all the time I gather. He now works for my father."

"For your father?" splutters Max from the driver's seat.

"Yes, didn't he tell you?"

"No, he told us he was a no-good Libyan playboy sponging off you," says Max.

"Will he be all right?" asks Harry.

"He'll be all right." She smiles. "He knows how to look after himself."

CHAPTER TWENTY-TWO

An enormous locust is crawling up Tariq's forearm. He is back in Libya and he is so happy, his dead mother is even there, alive and well and laughing at Tariq's stories. But the locust is annoying him. He tries to swipe it away, and he can hear voices telling him not to. The voices sound Italian.

He opens his eyes, breaking though what feels like a crust gluing his eyelids together, and, blinking the fog away, he focuses on a square of light to his right. A window. It is covered in vertical strips of curtain. There is someone sitting by his bed – a uniformed policewoman. He can feel nothing.

"Bon giorno, bella," he says. Or does he yell it? She is very pretty, with her hair scraped back into a bun and her almond eyes and pert little nose. He feels euphoric and would like to ask her on a date.

"What brings you to Libya, my sweet?" he asks. But he realises he's speaking Arabic and she doesn't understand. Never mind, I will serenade her all the same. "You remind me of a girl I once loved," he says. "What was her name?"

But the policewoman has gone, and instead a man in a white coat, a doctor, is looking at him with concern.

"I'm not in Libya, am I?" he says in Italian this time, and tries to sit up. This makes him feel queasy, and he slumps back against the pillow. Except he can't feel the pillow against the back of his head. It must be a very soft pillow. Is this a luxury hotel? He can see a heart monitor however, and for some reasons it makes him laugh.

"No, signore, you are in Rome. You've had a very bad fall."

"A fall? I don't remember."

"We're not sure how it happened, but you were found in the street. You say you don't remember what happened?"

But Tariq can't remember. Suddenly he wants to cry. Perhaps he is crying. He can't feel anything.

"There was something important," he says. "But I can't remember."

"Never mind, signore," the doctor says, his eyes examining the side of Tariq's head. "A detective will be here soon and you can talk to him."

"Yes, a boy. A little prostitute."

The doctor's expression hardens.

"Very good, signore. You can tell the detective."

CHAPTER TWENTY-THREE

The boy, Adnan, sits on the edge of the hotel bed, which has not been made up, and on which lies an open tourist street map of Rome. He has strict instructions not to bother anyone; not to ring the reception or ask for room service. Not that there is any room service at this hotel.

The door of the wardrobe is open revealing its contents – a canvas holdall and a coat that's two sizes too large for Adnan. Inside the holdall, he knows, is a sort of corset packed with explosives and ball bearings. The man showed him how to put it on and it weighed a ton. He also showed him how to detonate it.

Today is Friday. Just before midday on Sunday he must walk to St Peter's Square, and squirm his way into the middle of the crowd that will apparently be there to listen to an important Christian holy man, and he must…

"I must die," Adnan says disconsolately to himself.

He had refused and wept when the man first told him about the mission, and begged for mercy, but then the man had handed him his phone. On it was a video, shaky at first, but then Adnan had recognised the people in it.

His mother was sitting on the floor holding their baby brother. His younger sisters, Amena and Layal were there too, as was his younger brother, Sami. They seemed to have been crying, their eyes red, and none of them was smiling, which was unusual for them because they were usually so happy – even with the war and everything.

The camera panned out and he could see his uncles and aunties – Auntie Nooda who was always so nice to him – and her husband, his mother's brother, Sayid. And Auntie Zeinah, his father's sister, and her husband, Mohammed. And there was grandpa Hounan, with his enormous nose, and grandma Rasha, who was crying and waving her hands. It upset Adnan to see her crying. Why was she crying?

And then he saw the barrel of a rifle, and as the camera zoomed out he saw that along the walls of the room where the family was sitting stood men dressed in black and holding rifles. The faces were masked, except for the eyes. Adnan felt frozen to the core.

He thinks of his father, with whom he made the crossing to Italy. By the time they had reached the island called Lampedusa, his father was very sick and he had to be taken to hospital. Adnan had been taken to the immigration reception centre, which had mostly been full of Africans, but there had been a Syrian boy there, Yaman, who was two years older than Adnan and they had become friends.

His father didn't get better. He died. Adnan was alone now in this strange new world, alone except for Yaman.

Yaman turned out to be adventurous and brave – in fact he had made the journey from Syria all on his own. When they were finally taken to the mainland, to an old school on the outskirts of Rome – their bus being hit by stones thrown by local residents who were shouting and giving them the finger – Adnan and Yaman decided they needed to escape. They spent a week doing nothing but sitting around with this huge group of strange adults and a few kids, and then they just walked out one morning. It was so simple. At first it was simple.

They made their way to the central station in Rome because that's where a lot of other Syrian kids were hanging out. But they didn't have any food or money, and then one of the other kids showed them how to make some money. They just had to go with the men.

He hadn't seen Yaman for days, not since the man with the scar put him up at the hotel, and he missed him. Especially now.

The video on the man's phone suddenly went blurry and there was a commotion, his family shouting and screaming. When the camera focused he could see his uncle Sayid being dragged from the room, the men in black pushing back his relatives with their rifle butts.

The camera followed Uncle Sayid outside where he was made to kneel. A blindfold was put over his eyes, and a man told him to beg Allah for forgiveness. Adnan pushed away the phone and told the man he didn't want to see any more. The phone lay on the bed and Adnan could hear the shot.

CHAPTER TWENTY-FOUR

By the time they are approaching Milan, Max and Harry are feeling hungry and pull over at a service station. Aafia, who had seemed to be dozing, rouses herself and squints out of the window.

"I need a pee," she says.

"Ah," says Harry.

"I need a pee," she repeats firmly.

Max is drumming his fingers on the steering wheel, thinking hard. What if she was to do a runner, or barricades herself inside the toilet cubicle and refuses to come out? Or screams at the nearest attendant that she's been abducted? They're not going to shoot her anyway. They have no leverage and she must know it.

"Don't worry, I won't run away or make a scene," says Aafia. "In a funny way I'm looking forward to our trip to Switzerland. I don't think you know what you're getting into."

Harry, with his memories of the hotel room in Geneva, and Aafia's barefaced trickery, can't bring himself to believe her.

"Okay Max, you get us something to eat – a ham sandwich or something – and I will follow her to the toilets. I swear..." he says this last bit while staring ferociously at Aafia, but can't bring himself to finish his sentence.

She returns his gaze steadily, without expression. "Can I have something with cheese," she says, her eyes still on Harry; her dark brown, unreadable eyes appear to be enjoying a private joke. "And a Coke." She smiles at Harry.

"We need petrol as well," says Max. "And just as well that I hid these" he says with a note of triumph, taking the plastic folder with the hire documents from behind the sun visor and picking out the euros he had stashed there.

"Come on then, let's go," says Harry, folding his jacket over the gun. She has the upper hand and knows it, he thinks; all Harry has is his desperation. Would twenty years in an Italian jail be so bad? It's one way of ending it all.

"I can't get out," she says.

Max opens his door, gets out and opens Aafia's door. She steps out onto the forecourt and stretches, her arms up above her head, and starts walking towards the service area where the shop, a restaurant and rest rooms are situated. As he follows two paces behind, Harry can't help but notice her great arse that is accentuated by the tight jeans. She half turns as if she can sense his admiration.

There is a queue of two outside the 'signore' – an old woman dressed in black with hair sprouting from a mole on her chin, and a teenage girl. They both stare at Harry as he stands behind Aafia. Eventually it is her turn.

"Don't be long," he says. She doesn't reply, but disappears inside.

While he's waiting, Harry steps over to a road map of Italy that is on the opposite wall. He finds Milan and then searches out Lake Como – it doesn't look too far. The map also shows a part of southern Switzerland, and he manages to find Verbier. It would have been quicker to head towards Geneva by crossing the border at Chamonix, but that would have meant crossing two sets of borders, the French followed by the Swiss. And the French, from the first-hand accounts he has found online, are being extra vigilant because of the ongoing state of emergency after Paris and Nice. So much for open borders. He hopes that the Swiss won't be so attentive.

He looks at his watch – five minutes have passed – and becomes aware of an alarm going off – a high-pitched oscillating sound. The old woman comes out, followed a minute later by the teenager, both of them looking at Harry as they pass. The old woman shakes her head and mutters. A young woman who has gone in after Aafia also comes out. The alarm continues to sound.

"Aafia!" Harry shouts from the doorway. No answer. He pokes his head round the corner and notices a fire door at the far end, beyond a row of sinks, has been opened. A light is flashing in tune to the alarm.

"Shit!" he says turning, pushing past a surprised woman leading a toddler into the ladies. *"Scusi, signore."*

Charging outside he comes to an abrupt halt. Aafia is standing leaning against the Mercedes, her head towards the sun, her eyes closed. Max is marching from the payment kiosk, carrying two laden plastic bags. She lowers her head as they approach.

"Amateurs," she mutters.

* * *

They barely speak for the next hour or so until signs start appearing for Como and 'Svizzera' and the satnav tells them they are nearing the Swiss border.

"What are we going to do with you Aafia – hide you somehow?" says Max, speaking over his shoulder. It's the first time either of them have addressed her by name, thinks Harry.

Aafia, who has been lying slumped with eyes closed, opens them uncertainly, as if she has been dozing.

"It's all right," she says, starting to pull up the front of her shirt. Harry grips the gun and raises it to just below seat height. She's wearing a black money belt, which she starts to unzip.

"What's in there?" Harry almost shouts, but she doesn't reply – tugging out a passport which she hands in Harry's direction. He takes it and looks at the cover which is green and covered in Arabic script.

"It's my get-out-of-jail-free card," she says, reading his thoughts. "I take it everywhere."

"Okay," says Max. "So what's our story?"

"We're going to your chalet in Verbier," says Aafia. "That's what rich people do. At least that's what we're doing now, isn't it?"

"How do you know about Verbier?" says Max, addressing her through the rear-view mirror.

"I heard you talking about it."

Harry laughs, despite himself. "You're a cool chick, Aafia," he

145

says. He likes using her name. Max glances over at him. "What do you think will happen when we get to Verbier?"

"I dunno," says Aafia. "Perhaps we can go skiing."

This time Max laughs. "I'm not sure there'll be any snow left."

"You will reach your destination in twenty miles," cuts in the satnav. The destination that they'd punched in is Lugarno, just over the border in Switzerland.

"Okay, we're going to the chalet for the weekend," says Max. "What day is it?"

"Friday," says Harry, after some thought.

"Okay, we're going for the week. A holiday."

"A happy little threesome," says Aafia. Is there something teasing in her voice, thinks Harry? Is Max interested in her as well?

"How about the truth?" she continues. "You've abducted me at gunpoint and are taking me against my will into their country."

"What about the bit about stealing our diamond and threatening to behead us for YouTube?" says Harry.

"I think they'll be more interested in your gun."

Talk of the diamond has Max once again feeling for the reassuring lump in his breast pocket. He wonders where best to put it while they pass through Swiss customs.

"What will your father do once we tell him that we have you?" asks Harry.

She waves her hand as if the batting away the question. "I've already told you, it's not my father you have to worry about."

"But what will your father do?" says Max.

"He's my daddy, he just wants me safe and by his side."

"He won't harm you?" continues Max.

"Harm? Harm is what these fucking so-called Islamic State bastards do," she says, suddenly vehement. "Sexual slavery – do you know what sexual slavery actually means? It means that you can be raped at will – over and over and over again. It means you are owned by your rapist."

"And you and your gang are fighting this under the guise of being Islamic State?"

"That's right Mr Harry," she says, leaning forward and giving him both barrels with her dark brown eyes. "That's exactly what we're doing." She slumps back into her seat, and begins staring out of the window again.

"What else have got in that money belt?" asks Harry.

"Just my mobile phone... and these..."

She opens her palm to reveal five or six bullets.

"You may want to load your gun now, or perhaps it's safer if you don't."

CHAPTER TWENTY-FIVE

The Italian customs post is in the middle of a Chiasso, a compact town with utilitarian concrete apartment blocks in its centre and chalets dotted up the surrounding hillsides. They join a line of cars that slowly trundles under a sign announcing 'Valico Turistico di Brogeda', and past a customs officer in sunglasses sitting in a kiosk who doesn't look up as the drivers roll past, some with passports proffered from the car window. So far so good, thinks Harry.

He has hidden the gun under his seat and is trying to look as nonchalant as possible. He glances back at Aafia, who is still staring out of her window. Cars seem to be passing smoothly through the Swiss customs barrier.

It's now their turn and Max hands the three passports to the Swiss customs officer.

"What happened to the window?" the customs man asks.

"Someone tried to break in when we were in Rome", says Max. "Nothing was stolen. We've reported it to the Italian police and the car-hire company"

The man nods as if to say of course a fancy car like this would be broken into in Rome, and then he bows his head to look in at the back but can't see through the tinted windows.

"Descendez la fenetre, si'il vous plait," he says. "Open the window, please."

Max fumbles around for the button, eventually finding the right one for the rear window. Aafia sits up and looks neutrally at the customs man, who nods, and starts tapping in their passport numbers. He looks long and hard at Aafia's. *"Corps diplomatique?"* he asks through her window. She nods.

"What is your reason for visiting Switzerland?" he asks.

"Holiday," says Max. "Vacances."

"Ou?"

"Verbier"

The man nods. "Okay, if you could pull over on your left, where that white car is just leaving. Merci."

"Shit," thinks Harry. Max does as he is told, and pulls up by a uniformed man and woman, who place an orange plastic bollard in front of them. They have a dog with them, a spaniel of sorts. "Explosives or drugs?" mutters Max softly.

"We're about to find out," says Harry.

The woman steps forward. *"Bonjour, monsieur."*

The dog is being led around the car and sniffing energetically. *"Bonjour, madame,"* she says noticing Aafia.

The dog completes its tour of the car. The woman pulls the bollard away, and with a sweep of her arm, signals that they may go.

"Fuck, fuck, fuck, fucking hell," says Max, with mounting glee.

"Must have been looking for drugs," says Harry.

But now they're being flagged down by another official, this one in a hi-vis yellow jacket, who gesticulates for Max to pull in by his side.

"Bonjour monsieur," the man says, before tapping the windscreen. "You will need to buy a vignette to drive on the motorways. You can buy one over there for forty francs."

* * *

It's dark by the time the satnav guides them to Simon's chalet in Verbier. They had pulled in at the Co-op Supermarket in town, and filled an enormous shopping trolley full of food and wine. Above the cashier's counter Harry noticed a sign in French and English informing the clientele that the Co-op would be open as usual on Easter Sunday.

"What day is today?" he had asked Max.

"Friday… Good Friday," said Max darkly. "Tell me one thing that's been good about it."

"Well, we didn't get killed."

"Yet."

Harry lets it ride. Probably a reaction to the hell of a day they'd had, but Harry for one feels elated that they've made it to Switzerland, with Aafia, in one piece. She is scanning the newspapers sitting on a rack near the checkout, having informed the men that, no, she didn't have particular dietary requirements. Finding what she's after, a copy of that day's *Tribune du Geneve*, she places it in the trolley.

Although snow clings to the trees and mountains, the road up to the chalet is clear, as is Simon's driveway. Max knows that Simon hires people to keep the place ready for use at all times during the season, and he may even have stocked the fridge, but Max doesn't want to risk it. The short exchange of texts that they had had was to say, yes, it was fine to use the chalet for as long as they liked, and that the combination for the alarm is 1976, Simon's year of birth presumably – Max recalling that Simon was a few years older than him. A typically thoughtless code was Harry's silent reaction when Max told him.

The heating is on when they arrive – either by remote or courtesy of the same people who cleared the driveway of snow. Now they are here in these familiar surroundings, scenes of so many fun-filled days and nights, Max can feel the tension draining from his body.

Harry has been excitable and talkative ever since they made it through Swiss customs, but Max has kept on his guard, trying not to let his mind flash back to that cellar, and that video camera waiting to record his death for the whole world to see. It seems incredible that this was only this morning.

Aafia stands in the hallway and looks around. She's been to chalets like this before, when she was a boarder in England and a friend's parents took her skiing with them. It was a Russian girl she quite liked for her rudeness – Sofia. This one is even furnished the same – with faded Persian rugs, paintings of Alpine scenes and framed photographs of someone skiing. It's a large bloke wrapped in skiwear so that he looks like the Michelin man. Simon presumably.

As he unpacks the bottles of Côtes du Rhône and Chablis on the kitchen sideboard, Max realises with a jolt that their ordeal is not over. They can't simply kick back with a few drinks and a nice supper, and discuss the day's adventure as if it was a particularly hairy descent of a black run.

"Right... we need to eat and then sleep," he says, resuming his role as leader. But he sounds tired. "I think we need to take turns."

"You go first... I'm not in the slightest bit sleepy," says Harry. "More like wired if anything."

"Me too," says Aafia. "I'll stay up with Harry."

Max nods slowly. "Okay, but first we need to load Harry's gun."

"I can show you if you like." And before they can think of the possible consequences, they let her pick up the gun, clip the bullets into the magazine and then slip the magazine into the gun. It's done crisply. If she wanted to, Aafia could now be the captor, and Max and Harry her captives. She could even have killed them. Max's gun is on the sideboard at the other end of the kitchen. They say nothing, but the realisation is there.

Aafia hands the pistol to Harry with that sardonic smile of hers. "There is one other thing we've forgotten. The selfie... for my father." Should they smile?

"Press in more closely," says Aafia. Harry's cheek brushes Aafia's hair.

"Wait," she says, picking up the copy of *La Tribune de Geneve* from the table. "Hold this up, Harry." He holds it in front of her; a bit closer and they would be in an embrace.

She takes four of five photographs. And then a close-up of the date on the newspaper.

"Who are you sending it to?" asks Max.

"My father, of course; as you said, this will release you from your obligations."

"And who will your father send it to?"

"Everyone who needs to see it."

"Do you think we're safe here?" Harry asks Max. He shrugs, and starts unpacking the food – pasta and some jars of pasta sauce – from one of the shopping bags. Aafia picks up a bottle of Chablis and reads the label.

"I think we'd better leave for Geneva in the morning," he says.

CHAPTER TWENTY-SIX

The Swiss customs officer has taken Omar's Italian passport in the name of Amal Abulafia and is tapping the information into his computer. Omar, who has told the woman that he is travelling to Geneva on business, gently drums the steering wheel and tries to look unconcerned. The woman hands the passport back and suggests that Omar buy a vignette for the motorway. He thanks her and drives over to where they're selling the vignettes. He can pay in euros.

He also buys a coffee and scans his phone. The Britons' car has come to a halt in Verbier, and has been there for an hour now. Is it safe to assume that's where they're staying, or have they just stopped for a meal?

Omar Googles the distance from Chiasso to Verbier, and it tells him 286.1 kilometres, which will take him three hours and twenty minutes, but that route takes him back into Italy. He tries a longer route through Switzerland is told that this will be thirty-four minutes slower.

"That's fine," he says to himself, and guns up the Audi again.

* * *

Aafia stares at her phone for the best part of a minute, and then stands up and heads to the kitchen sink. Looking around she finds a glass jug and fills it with hot water. She then drops the phone in.

"What are you doing?" asks Harry, who has been watching her through the kitchen door, from the living room sofa in front of the wood burner, which he has managed to get going. Max has gone to bed with his alarm set for two in the morning – still four hours from now.

"Someone sent me a message pretending to be Tariq," she says, returning to the room and sitting down next to Harry.

"Who?"

"I don't know, but it's not Tariq."

"Omar perhaps?"

"I don't think so. Tariq got away… you saw him."

"Where did he go?"

"To warn the Italian security services."

"To warn them about what?"

She looks at him, the firelight reflecting on her chestnut brown eyes. Then she seems to come to a decision and shakes her head.

"I will tell you," she says. "But tell me about yourself first."

Harry sits back and stares into the flames of the wood burner. He's had two glasses of red, and is wondering whether it might be safe to have just one more. The pistol is on the table by his side, along with one of the iPhones from that bag that they were given by the man at the airport – just this morning – and which is now charging. The wine is making him feel warm and relaxed. Surely they'll be safe here for one night.

"What do you want to know?"

"Everything," says Aafia. She is sitting with one knee up on the sofa, pointing towards Harry, with her hand sweeping her hair back on one side.

"Well, I was born in Norfolk. I never knew my father – he was in the army and was killed in the Falklands War with Argentina. I was two."

She doesn't utter any of the usual platitudes. 'Oh, I'm so sorry', or anything like that. She just carries on staring at him, expressionless.

"You've told that story many times before," she says eventually. "Now tell me something you've never told anyone before – ever."

He pours himself a glass of wine now. He nearly died today; he nearly went to his grave without telling anyone.

"Okay. So this I've never told another soul. I was sexually abused when I was a boy."

She sits back, not in recoil, but suddenly interested. "Go on. By who?"

"By my mother's boyfriend. Except I don't think he ever loved my mother, he was just using her to get at me."

"Yes," is all Aafia says. Not 'No', but 'Yes'.

"His name was – is – Nicholas Mooreland. He was a local businessman... very popular. Everyone loved Nick. My mother worked as a cleaner in her village... she'd never had any money until Nick came along. She used to clean for him and he soon swept her off his feet. This was when I was ten.

"He smoked cigars and drank cider and whisky and I remember when I was first introduced to him, over Sunday lunch at our place, he said I ought to try cider, I was old enough now. I was thrilled. Cider, wow...

"And I got a bit tipsy – the first time in my life. And he was looking at me with an amused look on his face. He had these weird bulbous eyes and thick specs that made them seem even more so. And fleshy lips where his cigar would be most of the time. He made me feel special. No one made me feel like that at home or my school – the village school, a really crap school.

"Anyway, Nick, as he asked me to call him, was always round at ours. I'd come back from school and know he was there because of the smell of cigar smoke. We'd eat together and watch TV, but weirdly he never stayed over. I don't know whether he and my mum ever had sex, I didn't want to think about it... still don't really... or whether she just liked the romance and the way he made her feel special. I can't think that they did – after all, his thing was for boys – prepubescent boys.

"And of course the money came in handy. He was loaded and he lived alone in this huge house on the edge of the village. He had one of the first Game Boys and said I could go over after school, if I wanted, and play Super Mario, and Sonic Hedgehog... Mortal Kombat... God, I remember them all.

"We used to play each other, and there would always be sweets and loads of chocolate to eat. And he'd bring out the cider and I'd swig it out of cans and get quite drunk. He was always nudging me and squeezing my knee, and one day he started rubbing my thigh and, God, I'm so ashamed…" She doesn't say anything, for which Harry is grateful, just puts out a hand and touches his arm.

"How long did it carry on for?"

"Two years, maybe more. Until my voice broke anyway. He didn't like boys when they reached puberty, or so I realised afterwards."

"What happened then?"

"He paid for me to go away to boarding school. That's how I met Max. He paid for me right up till I was eighteen… I never really saw him again. I think he dumped my mum pretty smartish and presumably moved on to another boy, or perhaps he had several on the go at the same time. I don't know. My mum wouldn't have said boo to a goose, and I guess she would just be grateful he paid the school fees. I was just glad to be away, and I was able to reinvent myself – and the whole story about being there on an Army scholarship because of my father being killed in the Falklands and all that."

"So that's not true, about your dad being killed."

"I never knew my dad," says Harry, wanting to reach for his wine glass, but not wanting to be released from Aafia's touch. "He was in the military, but in the US Air Force, I believe. There's an American air base near us and I think it was a one-night stand."

"You never asked?"

"It doesn't matter who he is. I don't care."

"And what happened to this Nicholas…?"

"Mooreland. Actually he's recently been arrested. I've been asked to give evidence."

"And will you?"

"Let's get out of this one alive first."

She drops her hand and smiles at him, but says nothing. He feels liberated, as if for the first time in his life he's been able to be truly himself. It's like a skin, or several skins, have fallen away. He reaches for his wine glass and drains it. He feels strangely tired, as if he could sleep for years.

"One question to you," he says. "Why did you give me the unloaded gun and Max the loaded one?"

Aafia smiles and reaches for her own wine glass.

"I didn't think Max could ever kill somebody," she says. "But I thought you could. And now I understand."

There is a silence, in which anything could have happened. He might have reached across and kissed her. Instead headlights shine though the gaps in the curtains and a car can be heard pulling up into the driveway.

CHAPTER TWENTY-SEVEN

Aafia is up from the sofa and across to the window before Harry can even sit up straight. She holds the edge of the curtain slightly aside and peers outside.

"Turn out the light," she says without looking at Harry, who stumbles across to a standard lamp in the corner and switches it off. The gun, loaded now, is on the coffee table, and he picks it up, plays with the safety catch as Aafia had shown him, and then takes up position where the living room leads on to the front hall.

"Leave the light on in the hallway and stay where you are," hisses Aafia. "It'll make you harder to spot that way."

"Should I wake Max?"

"No time," says Aafia. "If he comes in the front door be prepared to shoot."

"Who is it?"

"I don't know."

But she suspects, or fears, who it might be. Omar was scary, but not because he would kill without compunction – although he would – but because he knew exactly what he was doing. He's professional through and through, unlike some of the amateur jihadis with their newfound doctrines and power.

The security light is on in the driveway and she can just make out the car parked right behind the Mercedes. The headlights are turned off but the figure behind the steering wheel doesn't move. He's talking to someone on his phone. Back up? And Aafia can just make out another figure in the passenger seat.

"He's making a phone call... and there's two of them," Aafia says, briskly matter of fact. There is no note of panic in her voice.

"Are you sure I shouldn't wake Max?" says Harry, who's crouching now, practising looking through the gun sights. The front door is bolted from the inside, he is reassured to see.

"No, stay there. You're perfectly placed. Right, he's getting out."

The figure goes round the back of the car and out of sight. Nothing happens for perhaps a minute, just Harry repeatedly bringing his eyes up in line with the gun sights. Aafia comes over to where he's crouching and drops on her haunches beside him. The door handle starts to turn, once, gently, and then more forcibly, three or four times. Then silence.

"He's going round the back," says Aafia, who has seen a shadow pass the curtained window.

"Fuck... I don't really know the layout here," says Harry. "Let's think..."

"Quick, this way," says Aafia, as she starts to move in the same direction as the shadow. It takes them through a sort of formal dining room and into the kitchen. They can hear a door being pushed open just off the kitchen.

"What's through there?"

"A sort of utility room, I think," says Harry, training the pistol on to the door between the utility room and the kitchen. The handle turns and it starts to open. A man's voice says something.

A plastic shopping bag emerges first, followed by Simon, followed by a girl wrapped in a thick, long ski coat.

"What the fuck!?" says Simon, staring at Harry, who has his pistol aimed at Simon's chest. Simon puts down the carrier bag with a chink, it's full of bottles, and stands there gawping at Harry.

"What the fuck? Is that a gun? Where's Max, you haven't shot him have you? I always said you'd end up murdering him."

The girl in the long ski coat screams as she realises Harry is indeed holding a gun, which he now lowers.

"Oh, hello..." says Simon, noticing Aafia. "Welcome to my humble abode." A looker, he thinks. Well done, Harry.

"Let me look at that gun. Where did you get it? Is it loaded?" He takes the pistol from Harry, who hasn't said anything. His throat is parched, he realises. He's not sure whether he can speak.

Aafia doesn't say anything either, just stands there appraising

Simon. The girl seems reassured by her presence and gives a little giggle, nervously extending her hand.

"I'm Kylie... pleased to meet you," she says with a strong Liverpool accent.

Aafia doesn't take the proffered hand. "Oh, shit," she says instead, and starts walking out of the room, only to be met in the doorway by Max, who's holding his phone.

"Si... hi... just got your message," he says sleepily. "Why didn't you guys wake me up?"

"Max... thank God you're alive. What are you doing with guns? Is it loaded?"

And with that Simon takes aim at the kitchen window and pulls the trigger. His hands buck upwards as a loud retort fills the silence of the kitchen and the spent cartridge tinkles on the floor.

"Shit, that hit me in the face," says Simon, kicking the case across the other side of the room, and walking over to inspect the small hole surrounded by a web of cracked glass.

"Idiot," mutters Aafia, her ears ringing.

CHAPTER TWENTY-EIGHT

Omar has never seen snow like this. Only in the movies. Of course it snowed in Afghanistan when he was there, but never settled on the trees and the big sloping rooftops like this, like in the Hollywood films he enjoyed as a kid, watching on bootlegged videos from the market. *Home Alone*, that was his favourite. America – the Great Satan as the Iranians called it – looked such a magical place then.

He parks in front of a large supermarket and enters his password into the GPS app. They haven't moved. They're here in Verbier, for the night at least. He goes on Tripadvisor to look for a hotel – he'd prefer to sit in the car all night, but he'd be too conspicuous. He finds one that looks impersonal enough, logs in the coordinates, and pulls off.

* * *

The detective went hours ago, to be replaced by a different sort of policeman – security services, thinks Tariq. This man spoke in English and wanted to know more about his upbringing in Libya and what he had been doing in London and his relationship with the Saudi woman. Were they really married? When?

Tariq was able to speak lucidly about all this – almost ebulliently thanks to the opiates rushing around his body – but the more recent past, the last few weeks, remained a blank. The man kept talking about a compound out by the airport, near where Tariq had been found lying unconscious, and where they'd also discovered assault rifles, Kalashnikovs, automatic pistols and an MP5 submachine gun. When did he come to Rome? What was the plan? A Paris-style attack? All the signs were there, said the man.

And all Tariq could recall were a cafe where he'd spend his days with Aafia, like lovers idling their way through a long holiday, and a man with a scar. A truly frightening man. Did he remember his name? Omar, that's right, Omar.

The man said he'd be back in the morning. Three guards were posted outside his room, and another, discreetly in the corner of the room, in case he started to talk in his sleep, or whatever. This man, Tariq noticed now, was fast asleep. He wondered what time it was. Who was this young boy who kept impinging on the edge of his consciousness?

CHAPTER TWENTY-NINE

"You mean to say you were nearly the stars in your own execution video?"

They're sitting around the kitchen table, having explained the happenings of this extraordinarily long day.

"Shouldn't we go to the police?" says Kylie, not for the first time.

"She has a point," says Max.

"No, not the police… not here," says Aafia. "Maybe tomorrow in Geneva, or better still, in London. But we don't give ourselves over to the village cops – this is far too big for them."

"But I'd feel safer," says Kylie.

"The cops are probably on their way anyway after Simon fired the gun," says Harry, still smarting at Simon's remark about always thinking that he was going to murder Max. "What's out there anyway? You could have killed a neighbour."

"There are no neighbours," he says. "That's the attraction – a party house."

With that he reaches up on a shelf and pulls down an orange Le Creuset casserole dish and opens the lid. Inside is an old school black plastic film canister, which he opens. He tips three of four anti-moisture bags on to the table, along with a similar number of paper wraps, one of which he starts to open. Then reaching behind him he places a small mirror and a razor blade alongside.

"I'm going to bed," says Aafia. "Where can I sleep?"

"Come on, the night is still young," says Simon, chopping out some lines of powder.

"Don't worry, I'll find somewhere," says Aafia, standing up and walking off. Simon is looking at her bottom.

"Hey, you," says Kylie, following his eyes. "I still think we should call the police."

"Too late now," says Simon, pushing the mirror in her direction, along with a snipped length of drinking straw.

Harry finds Simon's insouciance strangely reassuring, and he feels safer now that at least there are five of them. But he also feels desperately tired all of a sudden, while his ears are still ringing from the noise of the gunshot.

"I might turn in too," he says.

Simon guffaws. "You and the Saudi woman have something going on? I reckon she likes you."

"I need some coffee," says Max when Simon pushes the mirror in his direction. "We'd better head into Geneva first thing. How long you staying, Si? Could we borrow your plane?"

"I'm coming with you, mate. You're not leaving us here on our own."

Kylie giggles, and then sniffs. Harry stands up, takes the pistol, slips on the safety catch and walks out of the room. A staircase leads upstairs to the bedrooms. The first one has an enormous double bed, and a weight-lifting bench in one corner. There's an en suite, with what looks like Simon's toiletries all over the place.

The next room is dark. He switches on the light and sees the shape of Aafia underneath a duvet. She doesn't stir, and he turns off the light again. Next door is an unmade bed, presumably where Max had been sleeping. He doesn't bother to undress, just kicks off his shoes and pulls the duvet over him. Within two minutes he's fast asleep.

*   *   *

Nadia Pizzuto of the 'Antiterrorismo Pronto Impiego' sits in the glass-walled cubicle that serves as her office and ponders the long meeting that has just concluded, leaving used disposable coffee cups cluttering her usually neat and tidy desk. Part of the Guardia di Finanza that historically investigated financial crime and smuggling, the ATPI was the main anti-terrorist department in Italy, and Nadia is its rising star.

It's a quarter past midnight when she phones her husband, Alessio, on the secure line and tells him that she won't be home tonight. He's watching football highlights and sounds a little drunk. Their daughters went to bed at ten on the dot, he says, before emitting one of those groans that football fans are prone to give when some player has a near miss on goal. Nadia says goodnight, hangs up and leaves him to it.

The call to Europol in The Hague can wait until morning; she doubts they can help anyway. She stands up and walks over to the corner of her little office, picks up the bin and then sweeps all the coffee cups into the container. The action helps clear her mind.

Approximately twelve hours ago they had received reports from the state police of shooting in the Fiumicino district of Rome, and the discovery of four bodies – all of them men of Arab appearance – and a significant cache of weapons – assault pistols, rifles, automatic pistols, grenades and even a sword. One of the victims, the report stated, appeared to be still alive. He had been taken to the Ospedale San Camillo, where he had been put straight into intensive care.

The location of this massacre was a large compound of workshops, garages and sheds that was rented from a local businessman. Two Arabs, a man and a woman, had said they were looking for storage for their new online shopping site, selling carpets and other homeware. They could use it for manufacturing an atom bomb, for all he cared, said the businessman, considering the crazy rent they were willing to pay.

He had only visited once in the six months they'd been there, said the businessman when questioned that afternoon. The Arabs hadn't exactly made him welcome, so he hadn't been able to check out what they were actually up to. There hadn't been any complaints, the money was excellent, and his other businesses hadn't been doing brilliantly since the financial crisis.

The Arabs hadn't been completely mendacious, thinks Nadia; after all one of the cellars was being used for online business – the online business of decapitating enemies of Daesh and, posting the results on the Internet. That at least seemed to be the purpose of the installation they discovered, complete with camera on a tripod and a laptop, which had been found smashed upon the floor, and the black robes, along with a series of placards in which short sentences had had been written in black marker, like cue cards:

We are spies from our govement in Britain – pathetic slave of the White House and mule of the Jews.

We say to our small insificant island – give up the fight against the might of Islamic State. Only a fool would wage war with a land where the law of Allah reigns supreme.

Our govement and our people must understand how foolish we are to fight a people who love death the way we love our life.

The IS is here to stay and they will continue to wage jihad until the whole world will be ruled by Shariah.

Nadia, who spent three years posted to Washington, where she perfected her university-level English, notices spelling mistakes on the placards. The lack of any blood suggested that a video had yet to be filmed here. Had someone or something interrupted this latest piece of Isis propaganda theatre? The way that the laptop had seemingly been thrown on the floor suggested some sort of struggle.

The reading material found on site, several copies of the Quran and tourist guidebooks on Rome, strongly suggested some kind of Paris-style attack, but where and when?

Initial forensic reports stated that the three dead Arab men had been killed with two separate guns – two of them shot at close range with a Glock 26, the third at a longer distance using an MP5 submachine gun, which also appeared to have sprayed the walls of the compound. The identity of the weapons didn't take long in coming, because both were found next to the bodies of the dead men and matched the calibre of the discharged bullets.

The fourth man had no gunshot wounds – instead he had trauma to both sides of the head indicative of being hit by a blunt instrument. He had regained consciousness at approximately five o'clock this evening, and on being interviewed, claimed to be suffering from memory loss, but had otherwise been cooperative.

His name, it is quickly established, is Tariq Fakroun, a Libyan granted political asylum in the UK in 1999, along with his family. He was granted full UK citizenship in 2011, and he lives in London. He is married, he claims, to a Saudi national named Aafia. They belong to a group that fights Islamic extremism in all its forms, and is especially dedicated to countering IS, or Daesh as they preferred to call them. They came to Italy in order to set up a fake safe house for terrorists posing as immigrants – something that was remarkably easy once they had found the right contacts inside Syria.

This all sounds like an elaborate double bluff, thinks Nadia – a phony back-story if ever she heard one. Her trusted deputy, Fabrizio, who had conducted the interview, was however prone to believe the man, and Fabrizio was as cynical as they come. She will make an appointment to interview him herself tomorrow morning.

Tomorrow is Saturday, she notices with a quick glance at her desk diary. She is due to take her daughters to a party in the afternoon, the first time she will have spent meaningful time with them for nearly two weeks. Sighing, she scribbles a question mark next to this item, and then her eye drops to the Sunday. Easter Sunday.

CHAPTER THIRTY

Harry is having his London dream again – the one where London bears only a passing semblance to the real city. Once again he's having problems making the right connection on the Circle Line – a Circle Line unlike the real one – this Circle Line more like a rural overland railway, in Kent or Essex or somewhere like that.

Usually in this dream he's on his own, but Rachel is with him this time. She's leaving Max, she explains, and going to live with her friend Jess in Dubai. Harry doesn't feel unhappy at this news, just friendly towards Rachel. She puts her arm around his shoulder and starts to squeeze. Now she's shaking him, quite roughly.

"Hey!"

"Harry… Harry!"

He can just make out Max by the light of the open door, looming over him.

"Wake up, Harry, we need to make a move soon."

"What time is it?" is all Harry can think to say. He remembers where they are now and sits bolt upright.

"A little after six," says Max. "I think we all need to leave at first light. I've already emailed Dieter to expect us with the diamond."

Dieter? Who is Dieter? Oh, yes, the gemologist in Geneva.

"Shit! Where is the diamond?" he says.

"You have it," says Max. And Harry stretches for the jacket that he had pushed under one of the pillows last night, next to the gun. The hard lump is there where he left it, in the inside pocket. Harry sighs and fights the temptation to drop back on the mattress and return to his dream, or at least the oblivion of sleep.

Max meanwhile looks in on Aafia, who is curled up asleep on one edge of an enormous bed, and he decides to leave her for the moment. He kind of trusts her now, but doesn't at the same time.

He doesn't really understand her story about fighting IS, but he can't argue with the fact that she helped them escape a horrible and very public death. Not that he can think about that. He tries not to.

He also decides to leave Simon and the girl for now, and goes down to the kitchen and puts another capsule into the coffee maker – his fifth or sixth cup of the morning. It's about two hours to Geneva and there shouldn't be too much traffic if they set off in good time.

He's arranged to meet Dieter at midday, and he's booked three economy tickets to London Heathrow, just in case Simon didn't want them to use the private jet. He couldn't think why he wouldn't, but Simon is an unpredictable beast and perhaps he might decide to stay on and ski, or party with this latest girl (what was her name?) despite everything. Max wouldn't put it completely past him.

Pulling aside the curtain, he can't see any evidence of dawn, just white snow illuminated by the light from the chalet. He drains his coffee, and goes back upstairs, knocking gently on Simon's door. No answer. He knocks again and hears a girl's drowsy voice.

"Who is it?"

"Max. Can I come in?"

"Just a minute."

Max can hear the rustling of bedclothes and assumes the girl – Kylie, that's right – is making her way into the en-suite. Instead she appears at a crack in the doorway.

"Hi-ya," she says.

"Hi. Is Simon awake yet?"

"Simon? Isn't he downstairs? He's not here."

"Are you sure? I've been downstairs all night and I haven't seen him."

"Of course I'm sure," says Kylie. "He went down to get something from the car, he said. I don't think 'e came back. I fell asleep anyway."

"Oh Christ," says Max and turns and rushes down the staircase. The front door is bolted from the inside. He goes through to the kitchen and into the utility room. The door there is closed but it's unlocked. Max opens it and is hit by a frigid blast of air, his breath condensing in great plumes.

He can't have come out this way, thinks Max. He has been in the kitchen all night. Except he did move into the dining room for an hour at around one o'clock and tried to resuscitate the fire in the wood burner. He'd almost dozed off on the sofa after failing in that task, and had moved back to the kitchen to make the first of several coffees.

There is a skiing jacket hanging on a hook in the utility room and a pair of lined gumboots. The boots are too large for him, as is the coat, but he puts them on anyway and steps out into what seems like a back alley. Past a bin, the alley opens out on to small lawn, which is blanketed in thick snow. A mess of footprints, lightly dusted in fresh snow, goes along the side of the house in both directions, and Max follows these round, past a hedge and on to the driveway. Simon is sitting on the ground, propped up against his car door.

"Fuck, Simon, are you okay?" says Max, although he is clearly not okay. Max walks closer to the body, his feet crumping on the snow. Simon's face stares inertly ahead, an expression of peevish annoyance set on skin that is greyish looking compared to the pristine snow. As Max approaches he can see that the front of his shirt is stained a brownish red.

CHAPTER THIRTY-ONE

Omar had chosen a hotel that looked large enough to be anonymous but not so luxurious as to attract any fuss – and booked a room at the four-star establishment that was reasonably central. Amal Abulafia had a single room for one night, breakfast included.

He stared at his passport after the receptionist handed it back to him with a professional smile. Amal. At least it began with the same letter as his real name, Ahmed. Ahmed the Victorious. Ahmed the Forgotten One, his history shed like a skin in self-defence.

When did Ahmed die, to be replaced by Omar? Certainly not in 2003, as the Americans invaded and Baghdad fell. Unlike most Iraqis, who waited to be rid of Saddam with a sullen cynicism, Ahmed was a true believer. He had met the great man once, a seventeen-year-old proudly saluting the president as he inspected the cadet force lined up in his honour. He was sure Saddam had smiled at him as he passed.

He also met Uday Hussein, Saddam's eldest son, on two occasions – once when he volunteered for the Fedayeen, Uday's ultra-loyal paramilitary force, and once – after his father had persuaded him to join him in the Republican Guard instead – when he had helped train some Fedayeen recruits. These young men, Ahmed was disillusioned to discover, were more interested in access to new cars, private hospital care and kickbacks from minor officials than loyalty to the Ba'athist regime.

Ahmed himself was born in Tikrit, 140 kilometres north of the Iraqi capital of Baghdad and famous for being the birthplace of Saddam Hussein. In fact Ahmed's family were related by marriage to the same tribe as Saddam, the Al-Bu Nasir, kinsmen especially favoured by the dictator for the supposed loyalty of their blood ties.

Ahmed's father was a tank commander in the Medina Division of the Republican Guard who had fought in both the long war with

Iran and against American troops in Kuwait. By the time the Americans and British invaded in 2003, Ahmed had celebrated his eighteenth birthday by joining his father in the Guard, attached to the Nebuchadnezzar Division and donning the same celebrated red beret of this elite corps just two days before the first US Tomahawk missiles landed on Baghdad.

Nebuchadnezzar was stationed just outside the capital, ready to meet the American spearhead, but already Ahmed knew there would be no fighting. Men had laughed when the Americans first dropped their leaflets telling Iraqi soldiers how to surrender, and they'd burned them in their braziers. But he could see that they were receptive, even if they knew that if Saddam survived, like he did after the Persian Gulf War of 1991, that they would probably be killed if they deserted.

But after the first air strikes, they openly discussed surrender, and when the Americans appeared on the horizon, most simply jumped down and abandoned their tanks. Omar pulled off his red beret and threw it into a thorn bush in disgust.

Meanwhile his father's Medina Division was ordered south to the defence of Najaf, a strategic town on the main highway into Baghdad, hiding under palm trees to thwart the Americans' drones and spy satellites. Amazingly this ancient tactic worked.

On the first night, as the Americans attacked in Apache helicopters, it looked like the defenders had got the better of them, sending many of the choppers back to where they had come from, either on fire or badly shot up. The following day the Americans changed tactics however, the helicopters not stopping to hover this time, but acting like attack aircraft. Ahmed's father's tank was destroyed where it stood on Highway 9, his body incinerated in the cockpit.

Ahmed only found this out months later. For now he made his way into Baghdad in time to witness Saddam's statue in Firdos Square being pulled down by a US tank, as enthusiastic Iraqis waved sledgehammers for the cameras of the world's press and cheered the Americans. It was all staged and, noticed Ahmed with surprise and alarm, many of them were actually cheering not for their foreign liberators, but for a slain Shia cleric, Mohammed Sadiq al-Sadr. The Shia, it seemed, hoped to inherit Iraq from Saddam and the Sunnis.

Ahmed made his way to an uncle's apartment in Mansour, a well-to-do neighbourhood in Baghdad, passing discarded uniforms on every street, and the first drifts of looters, the sound of shattering shop front windows accompanying his lonely journey. He saw one cluster of American soldiers, looking huge under their weight of body armour, but for the most part it was just excited groups of Iraqis, desperate for the spoils of war, even if meant stealing from a neighbour.

His uncle, Farid, was something of an intellectual and therefore distrusted by Saddam, despite Farid's loyalty to the Ba'ath party and to the army that he spent his youth fighting alongside. There were a group of senior Sunni military men gathered in his apartment when Ahmed showed up, the old soldiers greeting him warmly and shaking their heads in despair when Ahmed told them of the mass surrender that he had witnessed.

They already had a plan – to reach out to as many Sunni officers in the regime as possible and persuade them not to waste their time fighting for the lost cause of Saddam, but to stockpile weapons for the bigger war to come. It was about this time that Ahmed first heard someone suggest that they create an Islamic state led by an emir.

As the weeks passed and the looting got worse, a decision was made to send Ahmed and five other young men to visit the leaders of the gangs that were organising a lot of the plunder. Ahmed demanded half of all they had taken, 'for the cause'. The gang leaders, little more than jumped-up street hoodlums, knew that Ahmed was serious, and they agreed.

But Ahmed was getting impatient for some real action, and decided to form a guerrilla group with the men with whom he'd approached the looting gangs. Their first idea was to detonate a roadside bomb near a newly built American base on Canal Street, and one of his new comrades brought along someone from al-

Qaeda, a much older Egyptian guy recently arrived from Afghanistan, a veteran mujahid. Like an addict for holy war, he had travelled to Iraq for the jihad after the Americans invaded.

One of Ahmed's guerrilla group was an engineer in an artillery regiment and, in between long and rather boring anecdotes about Osama bin Laden, the Egyptian taught him how to take an old artillery shell and bore very slowly into the casing with a hand drill to reach the explosive material. Then, once you have a nice hole, you put in some C-4 plastic explosive and finally a blasting cap. The funny thing was that they built this bomb in a local mosque, everyone knowing what they were doing but saying nothing.

They carried the bomb to Canal Street and planted it on the edge of the road, running a wire from the road to their hiding place in the shrub. It was a busy highway and they didn't need to wait long, detonating when a lone Humvee passed. The explosion flipped the vehicle on its side, a crowd quickly gathering around to gawp at what happened.

The little band of guerrillas didn't run, but remained to watch as stretchers carried away the Humvee's occupants. There was no fear among Ahmed's group, only a sense of elation. A sense of liberation. It was to be the first of nine such roadside bombs, only one of them not detonating. But after the first three or four attacks, Ahmed's band noticed that the Americans were starting to move around in armed convoys, sweeping the hinterland with mounted machine guns.

Ahmed was arrested in November of 2003, not for anything in particular, it just seemed that the Americans were sweeping up every young Iraqi male. And it was at Abu Ghraib that Ahmed became Omar.

The American guards called everyone Omar or Ali Baba, or 'fucking ragheads' as in 'Come here you fucking raghead'. Ahmed decided that Omar would be his name when he got out of this hellhole and started killing the fucking Americans again.

He wasn't subjected to the worst humiliations that Abu Ghraid had to offer. He didn't have to masturbate in front of the female

American soldiers – butch-looking dykes Omar thought – or pile up, naked except for a sack over his head, on top of other naked prisoners. He didn't have electrodes clipped to his genitals or receive the cold-water treatment. He was threatened once with a snarling dog, but when he didn't flinch, the guards got bored and moved on to someone more easily bullied. They had a lot to pick from.

Omar, as he now proudly called himself, was released from Abu Ghraib in May of 2004, to make room for fresh inmates for the guards to humiliate. He had made some useful contacts while inside, including a small group of freedom fighters who had been sent to Iran for training, receiving lessons in detonating charges, magnetic circuits and laser circuits. It's bloody cold in Iran, they all agreed, but Omar was never going to that Shia-dominated country.

Instead he fell in with a group of Sunnis newly arrived from Fallujah in Anbar province, seventy miles to the west of Baghdad, and not far from Abu Ghraib. Apparently the Iraqi army had abandoned huge amounts of military equipment when they deserted their posts and this was now all in the hands of the insurgents.

These men had been arrested in the aftermath of the ambush of private military contractors from Blackwater, whose charred corpses were dragged through the streets of Fallujuah before being strung up on the bridge spanning the Euphrates. They said that the city was full of foreign fighters – Yemenis, Saudis, Moroccans, Palestinians, Syrians and Lebanese – who virtually ran the place.

These foreigners had weird religious practices, Omar's new friends told him, like forbidding smoking. Anyone caught with a cigarette would have his fingers chopped off. And they wouldn't allow vegetable sellers to display cucumbers and tomatoes next to each other because this was deemed too suggestive and erotic. Weird, agreed Omar.

What was good, however, was that most of these foreigners were Sunni. The Shi'ites were being pushed out of Fallujah, killed if they didn't take the hint and leave of their own accord. It made life easier if you knew who to trust, without having to worry about

Shi'ites spying for the Americans. And when Omar walked out of Abu Ghraib on a beautifully fresh late spring morning, he jumped on the first bus that was making the thirty-minute trip to Fallujah, feeling that his new life had finally begun.

CHAPTER THIRTY-TWO

It was midnight in Verbier and Omar sat at the desk in his hotel room staring at the screen of his laptop, reflexively loading and unloading the magazine of his Browning Hi-Power. It was the very make of pistol that Saddam Hussein personally carried, knew Omar, and the mafia giving him this particular make, despite there being more up-to-date models available, seemed like a good omen.

The car hadn't moved, parked along a cul-de-sac at the far end of town. He made a note of the coordinates, clicked the magazine back into the pistol, and went over to lie on the bed.

He never trusted the Saudi woman. What was a woman doing involved in a job like this anyway?

The Saudi woman had the money, of course, but a job like this didn't need money, just careful planning, thinks Omar. He had argued for an anonymous flat in the immigrant areas of Rome – Piazza Vittorio had been suggested – but the commander said that he had to go to the safe house organised by the woman. The commander was getting greedy, but Omar could see why; the Saudi woman had recently handed him 100,000 euros in used 100-euro notes, to do with as he saw fit. It was a nice touch, but he wasn't moved. As for the commander, Omar would deal with the commander when he got back to Syria.

No, he never trusted the girl, or her Libyan so-called husband either. Omar made sure she remained veiled within the compound, but outside she flaunted herself in tight jeans and tops, visiting that cafe where they'd sit all day drinking coffee and behaving like young lovers. That was part of the plan, showing themselves as the occupiers of the compound, the young married couple opening an Internet furnishing business, but they seemed to enjoy the role too much for Omar's liking.

He followed them one day and just watched. One reason why

they went to the cafe was to talk openly, he suspected, and sure enough they did a lot of talking – her especially. She pretended to be modest and submissive in the house, but here he could tell she was anything but.

Anyway there will be no more talking after tonight. Omar has decided that he can't wait until morning; his guess is that they will take off first thing, so he's going up to the house to have a look around. He knows it's the right one because an Internet search shows it belongs to a British subject called Mr Simon Fellowes. Mr Simon Fellowes would seem to be some sort of forex trader – very rich obviously.

The receptionist looks up and smiles impersonally as Omar trudges across the lobby. He's not carrying a suitcase or any other bag with him, the Browning nestling out of sight underneath his jacket. It's snowing very gently in the car park out front.

The Audi swings out on to the main road through Verbier, heading towards the outskirts. In five minutes he slows down and passes the end of the cul-de-sac, deciding he will park here, hidden by a long hedge. He gives it ten minutes then quietly opens and closes the car door and trudges softly up the lane towards the house. It's a quarter to one.

The driveway has an electronic gate but no CCTV camera that Omar can see. There's a pedestrian side gate that has a simple latch on it, which Omar opens, slowly swinging the gate towards him. He stops dead. There's someone standing the other side of a bush, about three metres from where Omar is now poised stock-still.

Whoever it is, he is pissing into the hedge. Omar tries to get a fix on him and sees quite a large man standing profile on, letting out a long stream of piss, a cigarette or a spliff or something in his mouth. The man gives a loud belch, zips up his flies and lets out a long stream of smoke. Omar can smell it now; it's hashish.

The man turns, a fatuous smile on his face dropping like a brick as he spots Omar standing in front of him. "What the..." says the man before Omar peppers his heart with silenced automatic pistol shots. The man manages to stagger to his car where he drops, sitting upright but stone dead against the driver's door. Omar lets out a sigh of relief that he didn't set off the car alarm.

CHAPTER THIRTY-THREE

Tariq has no idea what time it is. It's dark as far as he can tell through the strip blinds of the hospital window, the faint sounds of the Roman night – car horns, sirens, the constant traffic – muffled by the double-glazing. The light is on in the corridor, enough to softly illuminate his room, where a man sits staring into space. As he watches, the man yawns, and leans down to pick up a pink newspaper from the floor: *La Gazzetta dello Sport*.

The immediate past seems so important but Tariq simply can't grasp it. A slightly painful orange mush is how he described these memories to the doctor yesterday, or today. The doctor suggested that he wind back his thoughts as far back as he can remember and then to start telling himself the story of his life, like he was the subject of a novel. "And like a good novelist," the doctor had smiled, "leave out the boring bits."

Well, he remembered the rushed arrival in Britain in 2001, when he was eleven. His father had been released from prison four months earlier after another short stretch inside on the orders of Muammar Gaddafi. The dawn flight to Tunis and then from Tunis to London, on a plane full of British tourists, sunburnt and tucking into the duty-free booze at such an early hour.

He remembered how cold Britain was – even in June, when they arrived and took a house in Muswell Hill with the help of other Libyan exiles. It was a big house but they were a big family and Tariq shared a room with his brother Hisham, four years older than him. He also had three younger sisters and a younger brother. How they used to huddle round the central heating in those first days.

And he remembered 9/11, watching the attacks on the Twin Towers on television, the whole family absorbed by the unfolding events. His parents were horrified, but he remembers Hisham looking at him and giving him the thumbs-up signal.

He'd like to forget all about school, especially the early days before rich relatives intervened and paid for him to go private. The classes were huge and anarchy and bad behaviour ruled. The teachers seemed so ineffective. There was some name calling, especially in the two years after the September attacks and in the run-up to the invasion of Iraq. A bunch of white kids decided that Tariq was Iraqi and started bullying him a bit. Hisham and some of his big mates intervened and sorted that one out.

He managed good grades at A-level and got into university in London to study engineering and maths, which is when his life truly started. And it really began towards the end of the first year when he met Aafia.

It was through friends, mostly white liberals with a good sense of humour, the types he seemed to gravitate towards. All his girlfriends until then had been English girls – he was attracted to the blonde, blue-eyed ones, the stereotypical northern Europeans – and it was mostly about the sex. He wasn't sure he was that interested in them as people, and vice versa, although one girl declared her undying love for him. But she was very needy and Tariq couldn't cope with the histrionics.

With Aafia it was different. It was quiet, it was unspoken, and it was both physical and intellectual. When did they first meet? It must have been through friends. That's right, she was studying philosophy, politics and economics with Holly, a good friend of Tariq's and one of his flatmates.

Neither of them pushed it, although they both knew. To be honest, it was a new experience for him – love. It was an unnervingly powerful force, and Tariq wasn't entirely sure what to do with it.

The guard noisily leafs through the pages of his newspaper, snorting loudly, like a pig, as he does so. He then sniffs hard twice, like he is trying to unblock his nose, and he glances over at Tariq, whose eyes are half closed. Remembering.

Tariq wasn't at all religious. Growing up he and his brother listened to rap and house music, smoked spliffs and drank alcohol, although Hisham suddenly gave up drink and drugs and started reading the Quran one day, and the brothers started drifting apart.

At university, Tariq had been shocked by the hard-line Muslim students, with their talk of 'dirty kuffars' and establishing Sharia law. Some of the worst were the women – still girls really – willingly submitting to this nonsense. Tariq was so glad that Aafia was angrily opposed to these so-called radicals, and was lobbying the Students' Union to ban the hate preachers they were inviting to speak.

All she got back was a bland statement about 'freedom of speech' and going on about equality and diversity guidelines. Freedom of speech, equality and diversity – fat chance of that in these bastards' utopias. Aafia and Tariq decided to start an underground group to oppose the fanatics.

Luckily she was well off, to put it mildly. With a generous allowance from her father they were able to open a small office off-campus, the same office that they would use during the Libyan uprising of 2011 to disseminate reports from Tripoli, Benghazi, Darnah and other cities. They'd speak to contacts on the ground in Libya, men and women that Tariq's father had put them in touch with, and pass these reports onto media outlets in Britain and America.

Tariq had wanted to go to Libya himself as soon as it looked like Gaddafi was going to be toppled, but his father persuaded him that it would be too dangerous and that he'd be more usefully employed telling the western media what was actually happening in the country. Foreign journalists were no longer being granted visas at the time, and Gaddafi had had all the Libyan journalists arrested at the start of the uprising.

He finally returned to the country of his birth and early childhood when the elections for a new General National Congress were announced for the summer of 2012. Despite arguments about how to run the election, and some violence, Tripoli was full of optimism as Tariq campaigned for a candidate for the liberal National Force Alliance under Mahmoud Jibril.

The noise, the excitement, the familiar yet unfamiliar smells, the green, black and red flags of pre-Gaddafi Libya everywhere – Tariq never felt more alive. He purposefully didn't wash the blue ink from his forefinger, the ink that recorded that he had cast his vote. Aged twenty-two, in love and returned to his homeland, those heady months probably marked the zenith of Tariq's happiness.

It all went to pot, of course. The militias wouldn't put down their arms and started competing with each other in murderous turf wars. The Islamists and their allies rebelled after being defeated fairly and squarely in the 2014 elections, a plebiscite overseen by the United Nations. Their so-called Libya Dawn coalition seized Tripoli and the new government fled to the eastern city of Tobruk, shielded by their allies in Egypt. And into this power vacuum stepped Islamic State.

There's a tap on the door. It's the changing of the guard. The belching sports lover stands up wearily, pats down his crumpled suit, and without a word exchanges place with a younger man dressed in tracksuit bottoms and a white tennis shirt. The replacement has a trim moustache and watchful, intelligent eyes.

"Bon giorno," he says. *"Come stai?"*

CHAPTER THIRTY-FOUR

"We shoulda rung the police… we shoulda rung the police… we shoulda rung the police…" Kylie's voice is as shrill and insistent as a car alarm. Harry sits with his face in his hands, while Aafia stands expressionless by the kitchen doorway. Max feels strangely calm, detached even. Perhaps it's the lack of sleep.

"Anyone know the Swiss for 999?" he asks.

"Fer fuck's sake, your mate's dead. Call the fucking police."

"Not helpful," murmurs Aafia as she steps over to the window and pulls the edge of the curtain slightly to one side. It still looks like night out there.

Harry stands up, pushing his chair screeching back on the floor tiles. Without a word he walks out of the room.

"Where are you going, Harry?" shouts Max.

"I'll follow him," says Aafia, and slips out after Harry.

"We gotta phone the police… we gotta phone the police… we gotta phone the police…" Kylie is looking at Max through mascara-smeared eyes.

"Kylie, do me a favour," says Max, trying to keep his voice even. "Shut the fuck up."

She stares at him for a second or two, picks up her coffee mug and smashes it on to the floor tiles. The door opens, and Aafia's head pokes round.

"What was that?"

No one answers.

"Harry's gone outside," Aafia continues, holding up the pistol by its trigger guard. "And he left this."

Max nods in acknowledgement and picks up his phone.

"Fuck… why can't I get a signal? There was a signal last night."

"Me neither," says Kylie, who seems to have composed herself now that she's smashed some crockery.

"I'll try upstairs," says Max.

"No use," says Aafia. "I've tried that already. I've tried everywhere."

*   *   *

Max is no longer afraid. In fact he feels exhilarated. He isn't sure how long this sensation will last, but that isn't something he's asking himself at the moment. Yesterday, less than twenty-four hours ago, he had faced extinction and he found to his surprise that he wasn't thinking about himself, or the people he would be leaving behind – Rachel or his sister or his parents.

Max's thoughts were for a person he would be joining on the other side. He found himself thinking about his brother Nicky.

Joining Nicky in death, in the forever – oblivion not an afterlife – suddenly seemed like an attractive option, compelling even. Perhaps this was what he had always wanted since that day during his final year at university when his father had telephoned to tell him to come home at once. Something terrible had happened.

Max had been cruising to a mediocre law degree at the time – a third or a 2.2 if he got lucky. Law bored him but his father said it would be a key to all sorts of more interesting jobs. But for now university was more about the social life, the girlfriends, the drinking buddies and playing five-a-side football and cricket in the summer. Pimms in the sun. Two in the morning listening to the latest sounds, spliff smoking lazily in the ashtray. Those were the days, my friend, we thought they'd never end.

He was in love for the first time, with a girl from Sunderland, who had been raised in a terrace house, whose dad worked in a car factory making Nissan Micras. She seemed incredibly exotic. The Pulp song *Common People* was still quite popular at the time, and the lyrics struck a chord.

Her name was Sarah and he liked her accent, and despite her

constant teasing about Max being 'posh', she quite liked it that he was what she called upper class.

"Upper middle really," he used to tell her. "Daddy's only a surveyor."

"Daddy's only a surveyor," she would mimic him.

"It's true," Max would reply. "He just got lucky. One little office block in the right place at the right time." But Max and Sarah got it on in the sack, where it really mattered. And Max thought he loved her.

It ended that afternoon in April. Not straight away, there were phone calls and letters and stuff, but Max never went back to university. Sarah came to the funeral, which was incredibly intense, and stayed at the house for a couple of days afterwards, but it was kind of awkward. Max was all over the shop – his mother was completely in pieces, and she viewed Sarah with undisguised hostility. Who, or rather what, had he dragged into the house at this incredibly difficult time?

Sarah was quite sweet about it all really, but he could see that their worlds would never really come together. Not in these circumstances anyway. He drove her to the station and promised to write when his head was in a better place. Neither of them wrote, though, and he heard years later that she had shacked up with a friend of his. He didn't think anything came of it though.

He jacked in his stupid law degree; he never saw any of his uni friends again – except Harry, of course, but then he didn't really count Harry as a uni friend. They had never hung out, just silently acknowledged each other's presence, or exchanged a few memories about school.

Max had gone travelling for a couple of months – to Thailand and India – got sick, came back, and watched a lot of telly. His mother was shot to pieces at this time, drinking like a fish and hardly ever sober. Some of the things she said. But then maybe she always had them in her mind and now, in her grief, it was all coming out.

"I told you to look after Nicky," she would berate him, which was true. "It's your fault."

It was his fucking fault? How so?

She had actually confided in him a year earlier that Nicky was always getting drunk or worse. "Keep an eye on him, won't you, Max? Be the big brother."

He had said "Yes, of course," but then he was away at Uni and anyway, seventeen-year-olds like Nicky get drunk, and worse. That's what they do.

Anyway, it became clearer than it ever had been before that Nicky was the love of her life, and that Max was not, in any way, shape or form. His sister, Tash, was the apple of his father's eye, so that just left poor old Max. Fuck them all.

Then he remembered something that his godfather, Mark, who worked in the City, had said to him at Nicky's funeral. He hadn't really taken it in at the time, but it suddenly felt very appealing. "Come and work in the City," Mark had purred over the rim of a glass of funeral wine. He looked the part, sleek and expensively dressed, a belly fattened by a thousand business lunches. "That's where the real money is to be made. I've got the contacts... just come and see me when you're ready." And, boy, was Max ready.

CHAPTER THIRTY-FIVE

Harry steps outside, his breath immediately exploding into tendrils of water vapour illuminated by the light above the doorway. He instinctively sidles into the shadows and waits, listening. Anything is better than waiting in that house, like rats in a trap.

He's acting instinctively now. All he knows is that he has to get away from that chalet, and that he has to take the diamond with him. He can hear Aafia calling his name from inside the house, but otherwise there is only the muffled quiet you get with thick snow. He has pulled some of Simon's skiing salopettes over his trousers – too short they ride above his ankles, exposing his inadequate city shoes, and grab at his crotch, but they are better than nothing. Simon's skiing jacket is likewise too small, scrunching his shoulders and leaving his wrists open to the cold.

Now his eyes are acclimatising to the darkness, Harry realises that dawn is slowly emerging and the dark outlines of the mountains are beginning to make themselves known. Satisfied that there is no one in the immediate vicinity he slowly and stealthily begins to follow the mess of footprints – Max's he assumes – around the side of the house and towards the front, halting in the shadow cast by the driveway security light.

Simon's body is still sitting propped up by the driver's door of his 4x4, a dusting of fresh snow along the tops of his legs, on his shoulders and on the top of his head. Harry emerges silently into the light and moves closer. The face seems grey, the mouth partly open and a distant – a very distant – look in the glassy eyes. The front of his torso is just one enormous stain of what looks like, in this light, chocolate brown, almost black, and his hands lie uselessly, palms upwards, by his sides. It's the first dead person he has ever seen.

Harry hadn't liked Simon – feared him really – but that seems irrelevant now. The man's life has gone, and his stiffened shell is all that remains. Harry feels something he had never expected to feel towards Simon. Pity.

Why had he come outside? For a spliff before bedtime? That didn't make sense; Simon was never one for smoking outside. Had the cocaine made him restless? Harry's eyes rest on some dark drops on the snow near the bush, where they had been shielded from any fresh falls. Near them he can just make out a melted, yellowed circle where Simon must have taken his last piss.

Harry stands up from where he is crouching and gingerly makes his way over to the little pedestrian gate next to the electronically activated driveway barrier. Poking his head out so that he can see further down the road, he freezes at the sight of the rear end of a car, the hairs rising on his scalp. It's an Audi. The Audi A6 he had seen in the garage in Rome? It could be.

"Fuck," he exclaims involuntarily, pulling himself back into the camouflage of the hedge. He waits, suddenly aware that his bladder is bursting. There is no way that Harry is going to have a pee though, not after Simon's example. He isn't going to die with his cock out. He thinks about letting it run down his leg, but decides against pissing himself. He'll wait.

Silence. Once again he pushes his head out around the hedge so that he can get a better view of the car. It is definitely an Audi A6 and it has Italian number plates, and a man is sitting in the kerbside passenger seat – some sort of thick antennae poking out of the driver's window. Or is it a rifle barrel?

Just then the man's head turns suddenly, so that he is in profile. It's as if he has sensed Harry's presence, or perhaps heard him. Harry doesn't wait, but he turns and runs back past Simon's body, round the side of the house, and into the shadow by the back door. He stops, waits and tries to hear anything above his rapid breathing.

Dawn is taking a firmer grip now, and Harry can see that the garden runs up a slope, abutting onto the garden of the neighbouring chalet. There's only a low meshed fence dividing the two, even more scalable after snow has drifted up against it.

There's a sort of evergreen shrub near the top of the slope and

Harry makes his way towards that, his legs sinking in the soft virgin snow up to his knees. He's leaving a trail that even a novice hunter could follow with the utmost ease – he just hopes that the man in the car has more important things on his mind.

It's surprisingly hard going and Harry rests behind the shrub to survey the scene. There appears to be no movement from around the house, which is now revealing itself in the strengthening dawn light. Harry feels safe enough to lower his salopettes, unbutton his flies and let out a steaming stream of piss.

The last splash is just cutting into the snow when he spots the figure walking purposefully around the back of the house. Harry's not sure but the figure seems to have some sort of rifle strung across his shoulder.

The figure appears to be making an inspection of the doors and windows, and Harry hopes that he doesn't turn and spot the churned snow leading to his hiding place. With a rifle he'd be able to pick off Harry with ease. Fuck! Why hadn't he taken the gun?

Fuck Max and his stupid fucking plans to sell diamonds to the super-rich. "We'll be proper rich… proper rich, Harry, do you know what that means?" he used to say of their concierge operation. Proper dead, more like.

But Harry knows what proper poor means – proper poor like his mum stuck in that god-awful village in Norfolk where nobody but a few local inbred landowners had any money. And the odd businessman like Nick Mooreland. The odd paedophile businessman like Nick Mooreland. There. He could say it now. He felt strangely liberated after his talk with Aafia last night, and he didn't want to die now that he had tasted freedom.

Instinctively Harry pats the inside pocket where the diamond is nestled. He has his wallet with his credit cards, he has his passport. The gun was his parting gift to the others, a better chance of defending themselves against whoever killed Simon – that Omar character presumably. But if they are rats in a trap, then Harry will be the rat that survives.

His plan, such as it is, is to make his way into the centre of

Verbier. He must catch the first train to Geneva, but when to contact the police? He can't be caught up in any investigation – he has to get to Geneva and to get the diamond safely stored somewhere. He doesn't want to lose the diamond again. Anyway, the others have phones so they can contact the police. Surely they've done it already. He pulls out his phone, the last of the ones that they were given by that man at the airport in Rome. God, that was only yesterday – only twenty-four hours ago. It has a healthy signal. The others will be all right.

The man has disappeared from sight. Shit! Where did he go? Harry looks over at the fence and reckons it's about ten or fifteen metres, and there's another, similar shrub to this one about another ten metres on the other side. He could laugh. This is the sort of situation he had painted for his school friends of his imaginary father, scrambling across Mount Tumbledown in the Falklands under Argentinian sniper fire.

Concentrate.

He's running now. Or rather he's crashing through the thick snow, stumbling, crawling and almost swimming at one point. The fence is easy enough to get over and he is almost at the shrub-hiding place when he hears a sharp crack in the snow about a metre or so behind him. Then another. The figure down below is firing at him. He can see the flash.

The shrub won't afford much protection from bullets, and he passes it and he throws himself down beside a low structure half submerged in the snow. It's a log store. Another bullet thumps into the earth beside him, and Harry squeezes himself against the wooden structure, trying to make himself as small as possible. Another round, this one smacking into a wooden upright less than a metre from Harry's head.

And then it goes quiet. Harry can't bring himself to stand up and take a look – Omar, or whoever it is down there, is probably waiting for him to do just that. It's properly light now, but Harry's view is restricted to the path he has forged along the slope. He can't see the house.

His shoes offer no protection against the cold and wet, and his socks are soaked, his feet freezing. But the adrenaline is pumping and he can't think about that now.

The neighbour's house looks impossibly far off. A better bet would be to make for the next garden along, which is protected by a low stone wall. Without thinking too hard about it, he sets off at a furious ungainly waddle, expecting bullets to rain down on him at any second.

He makes the wall in no time, throwing himself over and landing in the top of a rose bush, which snags his salopettes and the arm of his jacket. There must be a flower bed underneath all this snow. He pulls himself free, ripping both top and trousers in the process.

There are no shots this time as far as he can tell, but Harry's presence has set a dog barking. He can see it now, chained up at the back of another identikit wooden ski chalet. The back door opens and the figure of an old woman appears, swiftly joined by a man. They stand there staring at Harry as he crouches behind their garden wall. Call the police, he finds himself muttering – don't just stand there.

He waves idiotically and they go back inside, closing the door behind them. Thank God they didn't let the dog off its chain, it's an ugly great brute. Hopefully now they'll call the police.

To the left of the house is a driveway that opens on the main road into the centre of Verbier. Keeping close to the wall, Harry makes his way down towards the house, towards the cage where the dog is going crazy now, yanking on its chain and slavering. Crouching low he runs across the back of the house towards the drive and then on to the main road.

An old-style VW camper van, pale orange and white, is making its way slowly – weirdly slowly, thinks Harry – in the direction of the town centre, and Harry sticks up a thumb, hitchhiker style. He used to hitch a lot as a teenager – it wasn't something people seemed to do any more. If you don't own a car then you're a loser, and if you're a loser why the hell would I give you a lift?

Sometimes he would even hitch back to Norfolk for the school holidays, as his classmates' parents arrived in their Range Rovers and Mercedes. He'd save the train fare money that his mother had sent (God, how many hours of drudgery had that cost her?) and use it in the pub later.

Back for the hols. But at least Mooreland had lost interest by then. He had lost interest pretty much as soon as Harry's voice broke. And the oddest thing? The thing Harry could still not reconcile in himself, and yet another reason to hate himself? A small part of him felt rejected.

The camper van grinds to a slow-motion halt and Harry can just make out three young blokes inside, with beanie hats and, despite the still weak early morning light, mirrored aviator sunglasses. The driver unwinds his window.

"Where you going mate?" he says in an expensively educated accent aiming at something street and that sounds half-cut on weed or something. Harry's reflection stares back at him from the guy's shades.

"Into town," he says.

"Cool, jump in," says the driver, his mirrored eyes dropping down Harry's ripped salopettes to his saturated city shoes. Harry opens the back door before they can decide that he's some sort of desperado, and slips on to the back seat, where a bundle of jumpers has been hastily thrown into the back to make room for him, joining a whole load of other rubbish and a stack of snowboards. Harry was right: they are stoned, the van's interior reeking of spliff.

"Can you drop me at the train station?" says Harry, noticing a top note of alcohol amidst the cannabis residue.

The guy beside him grins through a few days' worth of beard and nods, like Harry has made an amusing observation.

"There's no train station in Verbier," the driver shouts over his shoulder. "We can drop you at the telecabine, which will take you down to the station at Le Chable."

"Okay, great – that will do," says Harry.

"Where are you headed?" asks the driver.

"Wherever the wind takes me," says Harry.

The guy beside him is grinning and nodding wildly now.

"Cool," he says.

"Wow!" exclaims the driver, as a police car shoots past going in the opposite direction. It's going fast, but probably not as fast as these stoners think, and its lights aren't flashing. Harry can see the driver appraising him afresh through the rear-view mirror.

"Don't worry, they're not looking for me," says Harry.

The driver breaks into a grin.

"Don't care if they are, mate," he says. "Don't care if they are."

CHAPTER THIRTY-SIX

Omar, when he sensed the movement that made his head turn, had been sitting in the car thinking that the Saudi bitch was good for one thing. Her money.

The hundred thousand euros she had given him in cash went a long way in the black market, and among various toys he had bought this radio-frequency jammer from a Serbian guy in Rome. One of the mafia links.

The jammer was American-made, one of the tens of thousands of such devices developed by defence contractors during the Iraq insurgency to counter the massive problem of roadside bombs.

Under al-Qaeda tutelage, Omar had quickly graduated from his simple IEDs to more sophisticated weapons involving radio frequency receivers and digital signal decoders crammed into the bases of fluorescent lamps. These would link to firing circuits and then the weapon itself. The Americans called these bombs 'Spiders', and Spiders were carrying away American lives at an alarming rate. One year after President George W Bush declared the end of major combat operations, improvised bombs had killed more than 2,000 American troops in Iraq – a small proportion blown up by Omar and his little team.

At first Omar used simple trigger switches, like key fobs and the little plastic devices used to open garage doors, to detonate their roadside bombs, but the Americans eventually found a way of jamming these, driving around with so-called Warlock jammers in their Humvees and so Omar's men moved on to more sophisticated triggers, latterly cell phones. Mobiles were designed to overcome the reflected signals and therefore weren't fooled into being triggered by the jammer.

The Americans spent billions on developing these devices, and ultimately money talks, and their more advanced jammers could block anything from a key fob to a mobile phone, and it was one of these state of the art devices, with its four antennas, that Omar had pointing towards the ski chalet. It was effective to a range of about fifty metres and he was pretty confident nobody in that house would be able to get a signal on their phone. Thank you America!

By 2007, remote controlled IEDs were becoming next to useless, but by then Omar had been invited to join a training camp, not in Afghanistan as he'd assumed – most of these had all been obliterated by the Americans – but just over the border in the Waziristan region of Pakistan. He flew to Islamabad by way of Turkey, and was met at the airport by a man he later learned to be a member of the Pakistani intelligence services, and who drove him deep into the mountains of Waziristan – an eight-hour journey in an off-roader in which the two men exchanged barely one word.

The first camp was tiny, just a couple of huts really, and he was only there for under a week. Omar got the feeling that he was being carefully scrutinised. Spies were a constant threat. The people who ran it weren't al-Qaeda as such, but a Pakistani outfit called Tehrik-e-Taliban Pakistan, or TTP for short – the training had been outsourced it seemed.

He moved to a succession of similar camps over the next two months, but wherever he went the routine remained the same. Morning prayers followed by a lecture on the significance of jihad, before some weapons training and physical drills. Omar was bored by the lessons on how to handle AK-47s and PK machine guns, and how to plant mines and construct IEDs – he already knew all that. So after a while the veteran jihadists, some of them gnarled and really old mujahideens dating back to the Soviet occupation of Afghanistan, suggested he help train the raw recruits, Pakistanis and Afghans mostly, but also one or two foreigners. Omar remembered one in particular because he stood out so much – a blond, blue-eyed Australian whose requisite beard was laughably wispy.

In the evening came the interminable videos of atrocities committed against Muslims, from Bosnia to Chechnya and Palestine to India, along with lectures about the Crusades and other historical crimes. Omar again quickly became bored by these – he had enough reasons to hate the Americans without this stuff – but what electrified him was something totally unexpected. Religion.

Raised in a largely secular Ba'athist military family where religious observance was outward at best, Omar was initially sceptical when a middle-aged cleric from Saudi Arabia, who acted as the camp's travelling religious adviser, seemed to single him out for special attention. Perhaps he sensed Omar's lack of faith, but this guy started to work on him, gently at first.

He'd ask him about the Prophet and what he knew about Muhammad, and then he'd get him to read aloud passages from the Quran. He'd then encourage Omar to memorise devotions and say them several times a day, whenever he felt his attention straying from what he called 'the cause'. The cleric won over Omar by exempting him from the evening's repetitive video horror show so that they could discuss the holy book and its relevance for today's Muslims.

They had deep and, for Omar, very meaningful discussions. Suddenly it all seemed to make sense, and he felt ashamed of his irreligious upbringing, and he could see how Iraq had allowed itself to be weakened from within by its lack of absolute devotion.

"We have all been asleep for hundreds of years," the cleric said. "But now it is our strict duty to emulate the Prophet in every way."

This included the complete imposition of Sharia law – not the watered-down version that they had in the Kingdom, said the Saudi – the complete submission of women, and absolute opposition to heretics and apostates, not just Jews and Christians, but to Shia and Sufi Muslims as well.

Omar started to see apostates everywhere, even in the camp. He caught a young recruit smoking and hauled him in front of the camp's leader, a burly ex-Taliban fighter. The veteran laughed it off, but he caught the cleric's eye and saw that he approved. He was becoming teacher's pet.

*   *   *

Sensing the movement behind him, Omar quietly but purposively opens the door and slides out. His Browning is already poised to shoot. Listening he can hear the sounds of salopettes rubbing noisily as someone makes a run for it.

He goes round to the back of the Audi, holsters the Browning, opens the boot and takes out the silenced Kalashnikov, and heads after the sound of the retreating salopettes. Whoever is wearing them seems to have stopped. Omar waits too, controlling his breathing as taught by the Australian jihadi in Afghanistan. It turned out that he had actually been in the Australian Special Task Group occupying the country when he saw the light and converted.

And then the salopettes start up again, and Omar can tell that he's breaking up the hill away from the house. Without even glancing at Simon's body slumped against the car, Omar jogs round the side of the house, and round to a back door bathed in light. He can see the figure heading for a large shrub at the top of the sloping garden.

Omar hasn't fixed the sights on the rifle, and cursing his stupidity he takes as good an aim as he is able at the figure wading through the drifts, and squeezes the trigger. A miss, and another – the man was moving just too quickly. He would wait for him to stumble, which, judging by his wild movements, he would do at any moment.

But the figure clears a fence with some ease, so Omar takes another pot shot – this one closer. The man is making for some sort of low shelter in the next-door garden, which gives Omar something larger to aim for. This shot hits something solid, to judge by the thwack as the bullet lands. He can see the man's head clearly now, and it's stock-still. He obviously thinks he can't be seen. And as Omar draws his sights onto the man's head, there is a sound to his left. Someone is opening the back door.

CHAPTER THIRTY-SEVEN

"My name is Maurilio Marcone and I am an officer with the Polizia di Stato based here in Rome," says the pleasant young man, somehow managing to look professional in his tennis shirt and tracksuit bottoms. He has pulled up a chair to Tariq's bed and is surveying him in a friendly manner. What he hasn't revealed is that he is one of the foremost Italian specialists in enhanced cognitive interview technique that aims to retrieve as much accurate information as possible from witnesses to a crime.

Nadia Pizzuto of the 'Antiterrorismo Pronto Impiego' had phoned him at home yesterday evening as he unwound over supper, looking forward to spending a long Easter weekend with his family. Anybody but Nadia and he would have refused the request to attend the hospital first thing in the morning, but he respected this tenacious detective as someone as dedicated as himself to the craft of policing. He had also always quite fancied her.

"How are you this morning?" he says, leaning in slightly towards Tariq. "Have you had any breakfast?"

"What time is it?" Tariq asks.

"It's half past seven," says Maurilio. "Have you managed to sleep?"

It's a good question thinks Tariq. Has he slept? Yes, for a while during the night, and he could drift off now, given half a chance.

"I know, I'll order some coffee and rolls," says Maurilio. "Are you allowed to eat or is it 'nil by mouth'?"

The man is looking at the end of the bed for some doctor's notes, but there aren't any. Tariq doesn't know why, but he likes this man. He doesn't seem like the police.

"I was going to take my family to the coast this morning," he is saying. "Maybe I still will. It's a gorgeous day outside." And he lifts a couple of the strip blinds over the window, but the view of the backs of other buildings is in shadow. "Well, you'll have to take my word for it."

Maurilio is conducting a textbook cognitive interview, indeed Maurilio Marcone has written the textbook – the one used by every budding interrogator in the Italian police force. Step one: greet and personalise the interview and establish rapport. Step two: explain the aims of the interview.

"Okay Tariq," he says. "So I need to know as much as you can remember about the last few weeks. Now I understand that the blow to your head has made this difficult, but I'm going to help you. Is that all right?"

"Perfectly," says Tariq, who suddenly now feels quite hungry. "Perhaps we could have a pastry and a coffee, if I'm allowed."

Maurilio smiles. "I'm so glad."

* * *

Once the bolts have been slid back, the door of the chalet swings open wildly and a young woman with very long bare legs and a too-large ski jacket around her shoulders stumbles out on to the path.

"Kylie, for fuck's sake, you can't leave," says a man's voice that Omar recognises from Rome. One of the British spies. He shrinks himself into the wall, props the Kalashnikov beside him and reaches for the Browning .

"I don't care… I'm leaving," she announces dramatically. "I can't just sit in that house with Simon dead outside."

"Kylie, whoever killed Simon is probably still out there. For pity's sake come back." This is a woman's voice, also one that Omar recognised. The Saudi whore.

"No, no, no… I'm going to fetch the police."

"You'll freeze," the whore says. "Come on, Kylie – we'll keep the doors bolted and he won't be able to get in. We've both got guns."

"Come back, Kylie, please. Simon's dead… there's nothing that can be done about," the man cajoles. "Harry's already gone to fetch the police."

So that was Harry, thinks Omar. He estimates it will probably take him at least fifteen minutes to get into town. Let the idiot girl go, he's thinking, and Allah grants him his wish.

"You'll have to suit yourself," the man says. "But for God's sake be careful." And with that the door pulls shut, and the bolts are slammed tight. The girl stands there for a while looking at the door, pulling the ski jacket more tightly round her shoulders. And then she notices Omar standing there, and jumps out of her skin. Omar puts a finger to his lips.

"Police," he mouths at her.

She looks at him petrified, and begins to step forward.

"Thank fuck," she says.

"What's happening?" he mouths again. "We got a call from someone called Harry."

"Oh, thank Christ," says the girl. "Me friend... he's been shot. I say 'me friend', but I don't know him really. We met at a nightclub in London. But he's dead."

"Okay... okay..." hisses Omar, wanting to keep her quiet. "Come closer... I have a plan."

The girl hesitates, and Omar can see her looking at his scar. Then she steps nearer anyway, near enough. He grabs the lapels of her ski jacket and swings her round so that he has his left forearm across her throat. He then places the barrel of his pistol against her right temple.

"Right, this is what you do if you want to live. Got it?"

The girl nods vigorously and squeaks her assent.

"You bang on the door and say you want to come back in. You've changed your mind. You want to come back in." Omar tightens his forearm around her throat and she nods again.

"Let's go then."

*   *   *

Tariq is regretting the coffee. It's gone straight to his head and he's having difficulties not tripping over his tongue as he relates his story to this Maurilio Marcone with the easy manner and sympathetic intelligent face.

"It's all right, slow down," Maurilio is saying in accented but faultless English honed during three years studying for a psychology MSc in Manchester. "Start at the beginning."

"How about starting in Sirte?" says Tariq, draining the last of the coffee and lying back against the bank of pillows that Maurilio has arranged for him.

"Sirte," says Maurilio, spelling out the word. "In Libya?"

"My birthplace. And the birthplace of Muammar Gaddafi, although that, as every Libyan schoolchild knows, was in a tent just outside the city. Gaddafi turned Sirte into the seat of government after he took power and transformed the place, my father told me. Parliament was moved there from Tripoli, and all the ministries. My father worked in the oil ministry – he was quite high up and knew Gaddafi personally.

"Gaddafi was crazy, everybody knew that – but crazy like a fox. You know he wanted to turn Sirte into the capital of a United States of Africa?"

"Really? I didn't know that," says Maurilio. "I did, however, know that it was the administrative capital under Italian occupation during the Second World War." And then he holds up the phone he has by his side. "Google."

Both men laugh.

"What was it like growing up there?"

"Idyllic, in a word," says Tariq, sinking back into his pillows. "My father was important, we had a good income, although you don't know any different as a child, do you?"

Maurilio shakes his head.

"The streets were clean, there were always new buildings going up, the sun always shone and we had the Mediterranean on our doorstep. It was a happy time. I couldn't believe it when I came back in 2011. The place was completely devastated.

"Near the end of the civil war Gaddafi declared that Sirte was the new capital of the Great Socialist People's Libyan Arab Jamahiriya – Jamahiriya was Gaddafi's own word he made up, it means the 'republic of the masses'. Gaddafi was always changing Libya's official name."

"Tell me about your father. Why did he flee to the UK?"

"He was loyal to Gaddafi up to a point, but he was more loyal to Libya. He was well travelled as part of his job with the ministry, and he knew that with the country's small population – we're only six million – and huge oil reserves, that the country could be really prosperous. Tourism too – Libya has beautiful beaches and climate, and many archaeological sites, although Daesh are starting to do their worst there."

"By Daesh you mean Islamic State?"

"Yes, but we don't use those words", says Tariq. "They are not truly Islamic and not a state. But, anyway, Gaddafi kept needling the West. I think my father's disenchantment really started with the bombing of the Pan Am flight over Scotland. He knew Gaddafi was openly supporting groups like the PLO, the Red Brigade and the IRA – he had become in America's words 'a state sponsor of terrorism'. Daddy just thought it was craziness. You know that there is a theory that Libya wasn't behind the Pan Am bombing at all – that it was Syria?"

"No, I didn't know that", says Maurilio.

"Anyway, whether it was Gaddafi or not, it almost doesn't matter. The thing is that he let himself be portrayed as this almost comic-book ogre, and that was enough for America. The oil embargo imposed by the United Nations after the Pan Am bombings really hurt the country, at a time when it should have been booming.

"They fell out in the Nineties. My father was always lobbying for Gaddafi to somehow get the oil sanctions lifted, and they started arguing openly – a very dangerous state of affairs. My father arranged for us to all go on holiday to Tunisia in 1999, and that was the last I saw of my home and of Sirte as it was.

"Of course Gaddafi had us followed to Tunisia, but my dad was an old hand at all this cloak-and-dagger stuff and we shook them off. So then we flew from Tunis to London and gained political asylum. The British government was only too happy to welcome an enemy of Gaddafi. And then what? Within weeks Gaddafi did exactly what my father had been urging all along – he handed over the bombers."

"So you really grew up in London?" says Maurilio softly, managing to make it sound like a question, although he had already read the case files overnight.

"Yes, and we were well off. Clever Papa had been sending money out of the country to Switzerland for years before we left. We lived in a suburb called Muswell Hill, and then later to Hampstead which is a wealthy liberal neighbourhood in north London. It's famous for its exiles. Did you know that General de Gaulle lived there, and Jinah, the founder of Pakistan?"

"That, I didn't. Do you like history?"

"Very much. And politics. That's one reason I can't abide these Daesh fanatics – the way they want to destroy the past."

"Imagine what they would do in Rome…"

Tariq sits bolt upright.

"What is it?" asks Maurilio, intrigued.

Tariq can't answer, but the suggestion that Daesh might attack Rome sparked some neural activity in the orange blob that was his memory of the recent past. Luckily Maurilio was skilled enough to let it pass.

"Anyway, you were saying. About London."

"Oh, yes," says Tariq, sinking back against the stacked pillows. "So I went to school – a private day school eventually after a god-awful time at a state school. And then university, where I met Aafia."

Ah, yes, Aafia, thinks Maurilio, but he doesn't say anything.

"She's Saudi – her dad's some sort of diplomat. Very wealthy anyway. She's her father's pet, and he allowed her an independent upbringing in the UK, where he was based in some sort of ambassadorial role – linked to the arms trade, I think. Every door in Whitehall was open to him, as you can imagine."

Maurilio wasn't sure what or where Whitehall was, but he let it ride.

"We both had an interest in left-wing politics… I was into the whole Palestinian thing and she was big on women's rights in the Arab world. I used to think that feminism was a diversion from the main issue, which was Israel's occupation of Palestine, but she persuaded me that the two were linked. Or rather, I let her persuade me, because I fancied her like crazy."

Maurilio chuckled. Tariq would have made a good Italian man.

"Anyway, we became a couple, and a team, organising protests and meetings. Our phones were tapped and my flat was broken into twice, but this just seemed like confirmation that we were doing the right thing. I began to take an interest in my homeland, in Libya, and the Arab Spring erupted bang on my twenty-first birthday. I remember watching the TV reports of the first anti-Gaddafi protests in Tripoli while dressing to go out to dinner with Aafia and my parents to celebrate my twenty-first. It turned into a double celebration."

Tariq told Maurilio about his helping disseminate information to UK journalists during the uprising and about his helping with the 2012 elections, and how Libya fell apart in the following years, and how he watched in horror as IS started taking a foothold in his beloved country.

"Sirte – my home town, or what is left of it – is now the main Daesh stronghold in Libya. It is part of the caliphate. They want to build a naval base there in order to attack shipping in the Mediterranean, and to launch God knows how many fighters across the seas. IS leaders from Syria and Iraq are flocking there, because those countries are becoming too dangerous for them. They won't admit it to the poor bastards they're sending to their deaths every day, but the caliphate is finished in Iraq and Syria. Libya will be there new home. . It's a disaster. This is happening on your doorstep… Italy's doorstep."

"So tell me why you came to Rome?" says Maurilio calmly.

"Because of that. In 2015 I went back to Sirte to help with the uprising there against Daesh, but it was hopeless and we were outnumbered. Before I was able to escape in a convoy of trucks belonging to Gaddafi loyalists – how ironic is that? – I witnessed three crucifixions. Crucifixions!

"I did however make contact with most of the leading anti-IS elements in the city and learned about plans to send foreign fighters to Italy to create terrorist cells for future attacks. And I learned about one attack in particular – one aimed at Rome."

Tariq is sitting up again. It's important that he doesn't get too excited, thinks Maurilio. He's doing very well, but it must flow naturally. The policeman remains silent, and Tariq sinks back into the pillows.

"Do you know the significance of Rome to the so-called

Islamic State?" asks Tariq.

"No, I really don't know," says Maurilio, slightly worried that they are getting sidetracked, but eager to keep the flow going between them.

"These people believe in the apocalypse… the end of days… and it will be ushered in when the armies of Islam meets the armies of Rome in battle in Syria. But who are the 'armies of Rome'? Some believe it means the Americans, others the Turks, because the Rome of the Prophet was the Eastern Roman Empire based in what is now Istanbul. But others think more literally. Rome is Rome, and Italy must be encouraged to join the war against IS, just as the attacks on Paris led to French involvement."

"So it's going to be a Paris-style attack?"

"Oh, no, much worse."

"Worse?"

"I believe so."

CHAPTER THIRTY-EIGHT

Max unbolts the door and slowly pulls it back, only to suddenly feel an overpowering weight thrusting back at him, rocking him back on his heels and unbalancing him. The door flies back on its hinges to reveal the petrified face of Kylie framed by an arm around her neck and a pistol pointing at her head. Above and around her looms Omar.

"Throw your guns on the floor!" shouts Omar, taking in Aafia, who now has Harry's gun in her hand. It's pointed at Kylie, Omar's shield.

"Please… please…" Kylie is whimpering.

"He'll kill us all anyway," says Aafia, taking aim just above Kylie's head.

"I'll count to three," says Omar. "One…"

Max looks at Kylie's wildly beseeching eyes, and then the stream of urine running down her leg and onto the tiled floor.

"Okay," he says, bending slowly at the knees and lying his pistol on the floor.

"Kick it away from you," says Omar, and Max flicks the gun with his toecap so that slides across the tiles to the far side of the room.

"Now you," says Omar to Aafia.

She is looking at the Arab with pure hatred and, to give her her due, thinks Max, an absolute absence of fear. And then she seems to sigh, nods and throws her gun on the floor, where it clatters to a halt beside Max's.

Omar shoves Kylie hard so that she staggers and falls to the ground, immediately burying her head in her arms and starting to sob.

Omar aims straight at her and fires, the first shot sending her sprawling on her side. It seems to have done its job because the second bullet merely evinces a sharp spasm, as Kylie's wretched face registers the shock that she must have felt a second ago.

"Noooo…." screams Max, rushing at Omar, only for Omar's gun to smack him on the cheekbone with a crack. He can actually see stars for a moment. Recovering, he sees Omar pointing the gun at him.

"And now you," he says.

"Omar…! Wait." It's Aafia. And she starts talking urgently in Arabic and whatever she is saying seems to be staying his hand. He's still looking intently at Max, but he's listening. The predatory gaze softens as Aafia continues talking. And then he starts asking questions – short, sharp questions by the sound of them.

Max steals a glance at Kylie. Poor Kylie, who chose the wrong night to go on a whimsical jaunt with a loaded forex trader. It must have seemed so exotic – the midnight flit to Switzerland, the skiing chalet, the endless cocaine. A pool of a dark blood is slowly seeping from beneath her torso. The long legs that would have first attracted Simon's attention are folded beneath her. She has returned to the foetal position.

Aafia is still talking, and whatever she is saying is registering with Omar, who gives a slight nod. He still has the gun pointed at Max, but Max relaxes slightly as he senses a deal being brokered. This was his territory and he recognises the signs.

And then Omar is alert again. He's looking out of the window towards the slope behind the house. Max follows his gaze and notices the two figures – policemen – walking slowly across the garden, looking at the ground in front of them. They seem to be following some tracks in the snow, and the tracks appear to be heading towards Simon's chalet.

Sweeping his pistol to and fro across the kitchen, so that Max and Aafia are both covered, Omar steps back and retrieves the guns from the floor. Max watches as he secures both safety catches and slips them in his coat pockets.

"Stand back from the window so they can't see you," he says to Max, who takes a last glance outside and sees that the policeman are now only about metres from the house. They are definitely following footprints in the snow. Harry's?

Aafia says something in Arabic, which earns a sharp rebuke

from Omar. "Shut up, both of you!" he says, turning off the kitchen light. It's now far brighter outside than in, the effect doubled by the intense white of the snow.

One of the policemen, a young man whose beard does little to disguise his age, presses his face to the window. Omar doesn't waste any time. Stepping forward he fires twice in quick succession, the second shot clean in the centre of the man's forehead.

Bursting out of the door he finds the second policeman still fumbling with his own standard issue SIG P225. Two shots finish him off, and Omar steps over and takes the gun from the dead man and slips lightly back into the chalet as calmly as if he had been letting the cat out.

He throws his Browning on to the sideboard, and checks the SIG's magazine. It's fully loaded. He extracts the gun that Aafia had been holding, the one that Harry had left behind.

"It's empty." His voice is almost amused.

Max can't speak, he's still trying to take in what has happened. Kylie and now these two policemen. He seems to have stepped into a different world with different rules, where it's okay to kill people and carry on as if nothing abnormal has taken place. A world where you murder without compunction.

"So this is war," he finds himself saying aloud.

Omar and Aafia look at each other and then back at Max, and for the first time Max notices a shred of humanity in his scar-faced adversary. It's nothing as obvious as a smile, perhaps just a slackening of the face muscles or a dilation of his pupils.

"Yes, this is war," he says. "And now we must go."

He's talking sharply in Arabic now.

"He's asking 'Do you have your passport?' and 'Can you drive?' translates Aafia.

"Yes to both questions."

"Naam," says Aafia, or something like that. Max recognises it from his dealings with her father. It was the word he always wanted to hear from him. *Naam*... Yes'.

"Now we go," says Omar. "Back to Rome."

* * *

The stoned ski-boarders in the VW camper van set Harry down by the cable car, and drive very slowly away. They'd wished him luck and had even leant him some Swiss francs just in case he needs it for the ride.

It's not yet eight o'clock and the telecabine doesn't start running for another half an hour, so he trudges into the centre of town looking for a clothes shop. They only seem to stock ridiculously expensive designer ski-wear and anyway none of them is open until half past nine, so Harry withdraws some cash from an ATM and walks back to the telecabine.

He doesn't like heights, but he hardly notices as he's swept down the mountainside on the first lift of the day, most of the traffic, skiers newly arrived the Easter weekend, travelling in the opposite direction. His feet are so cold he can't feel them, and he doesn't try to stamp them because the cable car already seems rocky enough. Perhaps there's a washroom with hot water at the station. After all, this is Switzerland.

In the event he doesn't have time to find a washroom because the next train for Geneva is due in five minutes. He buys a one-way ticket and heads on to the platform of the chalet-style building, just in time as a red-and-white train bearing the legend Saint-Bernard Express glides to a halt.

Watching the excited, freshly-slept skiers descend from the train, he has that trippy, up-all-night sensation that he used to get in his twenties when, going to raves in Waterloo or Dalston, he used to meet commuters on their way to work.

He needs to change trains at Martigny he was told by the woman in the ticket office, where there would be a ten-minute wait, and the train would arrive in Geneva at 11:57. Probably to the minute, thinks Harry.

Luckily the train is heated, and Harry finds an unoccupied bank of seats and peels his socks off. His feet are as white as he has ever seen them, except the ends of his toes which appear a little blue. God, don't say he has frostbite. He thrusts the socks and shoes right up against the radiator grid and takes out his phone. There's no reception. He'll try again in Martigny.

They'll ask why he didn't contact the police in Verbier, of course. He panicked? Unlikely. He was in shock? More plausible, but still redolent of cowardice. That he didn't want to end up in a police cell with a priceless diamond in his pocket? Closer to the truth. That he left Max and Aafia to their almost certain deaths? He can't think about that now.

He'll be ostracised, of course. But who by? He assumes he will never see Max again. Rachel ditto. Simon is dead. Max for all he knows might be dead. Probably is dead. The company will maybe close, and he will leave London. He'll go up to Norfolk, sort his mother out financially and then he'll go and live somewhere cheap and hot. Greece or Thailand, where no one knows his name.

There's a respectable looking middle-aged, balding man reading a Kindle at the end of the carriage. Harry walks towards him, aware that he's in bare feet and what he's about to ask won't improve on this first impression.

"Excusez moi, monsieur. Parlez vous anglais?"

"A little bit," the man replies in English.

Holding up his phone as a sort of guide to translation, he asks, "Do you know the number to ring the police in an emergency?"

The man stares at him for a moment, and Harry thinks he doesn't understand.

"Police? *Urgence?*" he answers at last.

"Oui. Police… *urgence."*

"It's 117, monsieur. One… one… seven."

"Merci monsieur," says Harry, padding back to his seat. He's sure the man will remember the strange barefoot Englishman on the train who wanted the emergency number for the police. He stands within sight, playing with his phone, making a great show of trying to get a signal. And then what he doesn't want – the man is getting up to help him.

"You just dial 117, monsieur, and your phone will find the right network."

"Oh, I see thanks."

"You have an emergency now?"

"My passport has been stolen," he lies.

"Look… we'll be in Martigny in less than ten minutes. Wait

until we arrive and look for a policeman."

"You're right," says Harry, grateful for the let out. He has to change at Martigny anyway. "I'll do that."

He pulls his socks off the radiator grill: they are still slightly damp but at least they are hot. Wisps of steam are rising from the soles of his shoes, but the uppers are still saturated. He'll have to find a clothes shop in Martigny. He can also phone the police – he can always cite the man on the train as a witness; it's not much, but it does show some willingness.

The train is in a tunnel as he does up his shoelaces, his feet unhappily returned to their moist prison.

"Monsieur...." The man is leaning over the seat in front of Harry. "Martigny is after this tunnel."

"Ah... *merci monsieur.*" He has an idea, and extends his hand. "Monsieur?"

"Monsieur Remy," the man says.

"Monsieur Kimber," says Harry, pointing at himself.

"Bonne route," says Monsieur Remy. *"Et bonne chance."*

* * *

Omar hustles them out of the door, past the dead bearded policeman lying on his back and looking even younger now, staring sightlessly into the heavens. Max notices a figure standing at the top of the garden. It's an old woman with an apron round her dress, like she has been interrupted in the midst of baking a cake. Omar notices her too, but thankfully doesn't seem perturbed. Instead he ushers them down the side alley, past Simon, who now looks almost unreal, his face drained of any colour. Max finds himself breathing hard.

"Wait," says Omar, opening the boot of the Audi with one hand while pointing his pistol at them with the other. He rummages about and extracts a short black crowbar with a yellow rubber handle. Max has something like it at home.

"Come," he says, the two of them trudge after him, to where the hired Mercedes is where they parked it yesterday.

"You," he says, looking at Max and throwing the crowbar on the ground at the back of the Mercedes. "Get rid of the number

211

plates."

Max prizes the sharp end of the crowbar in behind the number plate and it snaps in two. He yanks each half off and moves round to attack the front plate, which comes off in one.

"I could get good at this," he says to try and cheer himself up.

"Bring," says Omar, pointing to the plates. Max picks them up and they trudge back to the Audi.

"You, in the front seat," he says to Aafia. "You," he says pointing his gun at Max's head with one hand, the key to the Audi proffered in the other. "You drive."

Whatever deal Aafia has struck with Omar, and Max feels sure that any bargain with Omar comes at a high price, it feels sensible to simply act his part for now. For the moment it feels like a reprieve.

As they drive to the end of the road, they see the police car parked outside a house two along from Simon's. An old man, presumably the old woman's husband, is standing by the open doorway. Max can see Omar through the rear-view mirror, sizing him up. Would he know enough about cars to report the make and model?

Omar winds down his window, and fires a warning shot that has the man scuttling inside.

"Right," comes the voice from the back seat. "Faster now."

With his pistol in his left hand, Omar re-sets the satnav with his right. Rome, Italy. The device finds its coordinates and a blue route emerges.

"Turn left in fifty metres and then keep right for nought point seven kilometres," a neutral woman's voice commands. Arrival time 16:40, the screen informed him. It is enough.

"Passports," barks Omar, with an impatient clicking of his fingers.

Aafia looks at Max, who slips a hand into his inside jacket pocket and produces his battered, burgundy-coloured booklet and hands it to her without a word. Aafia retrieves her own from her money belt, and hands both to Omar, who nods, apparently engrossed in putting a battery back into his phone.

"In two hundred metres, turn left on to Place Centrale," the satnav voice says, and then more insistently. "Turn left on Place

Centrale."

They are passing the hotel where Omar had spent two or three hours with his eyes closed, unable to sleep, after killing the British man. He had checked out of the hotel at four that morning, saying that he had to be at a meeting in Geneva at eight. The receptionist didn't seem remotely interested, but asked if he wanted to take some pastries for the journey. They now sit on the back seat next to Omar.

"Keep right and continue onto Rue de Medran."

He now turns his attention to the passports. The whore's is black with the palm tree emerging from the crossed swords. Kingdom of Saudi Arabia is written in gold script, beneath the same words in Arabic. 'Diplomatic Passport' is inscribed below in English and Arabic in the same gold script.

One day soon there will be no immunity for the House of Saud, thinks Omar with satisfaction. Their reward for helping the crusaders invade his homeland in 1990 and 2003 is at hand, and the caliphate will reach soon into the Arabian Peninsula. The apostates will be removed and true Sharia will govern the people.

He now turns his attention to the British passport. Maximilian Charles St John Draycott. Date of birth 25th December 1979. The date stirs something in his memory.

"Twenty-fifth December 1979," he reads aloud.

"My date of birth," shouts Max over his shoulder. "Christmas Day."

No, that's not it, thinks Omar. Christmas Day! The pagan festival of Santa Claus and turkey. No, of course. It was the day that the Soviet Union invaded Afghanistan. It was when the first airborne Soviet paratroopers landed in Kabul. It was the start of all this.

"At the roundabout, take the second exit onto Rue de la Poste."

Omar reads on. Place of birth: Stockbridge, Hampshire.

"Stock-bridge… Stock… bridge…" he says.

"Stockbridge," says Max. "My place of birth."

"Do you still live there?" asks Omar.

"No, but my parents do." At once he feels uneasy. Why had he said that? But Omar is already on his phone, and now he's talking quickly in Arabic. Aafia looks concerned.

"What's he saying?" asks Max, but he can understand the words 'Draycott' and 'Stockbridge' and 'Hampshire' because Omar is spelling them out.

"Who's he talking to?" Max shouts. "Who's he talking to?"

"Turn right and stay on the Route de Verbier"

"I don't know," says Aafia. "He's telling someone to find your parents."

"Turn right and stay on the Route de Verbier"

"Omar, who were you talking to?"

"Silence now and drive," he says raising his pistol.

"Turn right here," says Aafia.

They continue in silence, except that Omar is muttering something under his breath, almost chanting. Aafia listens intently and can finally make out what he it is that he keeps repeating to himself.

"We will conquer your Rome, break your crosses, and enslave your women," he is intoning. "We will conquer your Rome, break your crosses, and enslave your women. We will conquer your Rome…"

CHAPTER THIRTY-NINE

Martigny, spread out along the Rhone valley, is slightly bigger than Harry imagined, and so is the station. He gives a final wave to Monsieur Remy, who is also preparing to leave the train, and steps down onto the platform, making a great show of looking around, and then strides off purposefully in the direction of an exit sign.

He desperately needs some new clothes. He may not have looked too odd in his salopettes and city shoes in Verbier, but here he is beginning to attract curious glances from people waiting for their trains. First though he finds a timetable and looks for the next train to Geneva, and is relieved to see that they seem to be pretty regular, every half hour or so, the journey taking just over ninety minutes.

In the station cafeteria he asks the whereabouts of a nearby supermarket and is told that there is a large Co-op about five minutes away, down the Avenue de la Gare, and then turn left. On his way he passes a clothes boutique that seems to sell everything that he needs, and he goes in and makes the owner's morning by buying a new shirt, pullover, trousers, pants and socks as well as a pair of decent trainers. The company credit card is accepted.

With many salutations, Harry makes his leave of the overjoyed owner, an unshaven, middle-aged Middle Eastern man with an enormous paunch, and makes his way back to the station, stopping at a bench to pull out his phone. There are no messages and no missed calls. He remembers that they couldn't get a signal in the chalet. Perhaps no news is good news.

He goes into his contacts, and taps the number that he had Googled on the drive up from Rome – a private vault in the centre of Geneva. Yes, *monsieur,* they were open on a Saturday. The smallest of their safety deposit boxes measure 60mm by 250mm by 350mm and would be sufficient to store one diamond, unless the diamond is very big – ha, ha.

And it would cost 200 Swiss francs for a year… very reasonable, I'm sure you will agree… with a 400-franc refundable deposit. And would *monsieur* require his own key? Then that would be a further refundable 800 francs. Very good. We close at five p.m.

He then searches for flights to London, finding an EasyJet departure at four p.m. with available seats. He books one, and downloads the boarding card to his phone.

He pauses to think before he makes the second call. What should he say, or, rather, what should he not say? He looks at his Rolex. It's ten minutes past ten. There's a train for Geneva leaving in twelve minutes. He taps in the numbers 117.

"Police. *Puis-je vous aider?"* It's a woman's voice.

"Hello… do you speak English?"

"*Oui Monsieur.* Where are you calling from?"

"I'm in Verbier."

"Verbier"

"Yes. Please go quickly. There's been a shooting."

"What address?"

"I don't know the address."

"When did this happen?"

"About two hours ago."

"What is your name?"

"Harry Kimber. Harry, like Prince Harry. Kimber. K – I – M…"

"That's all right, Mr Kimber, we have your details. Where can we find you?"

"Hello… Hello… Hello? I seem to have lost you. Hello?"

After that unconvincing pantomime, Harry ends the call, and opens the back of the phone, extracting the battery and putting it in the inside pocket of his brand new jacket, and walks back to the station. The train leaves in five minutes. What did she mean 'We have your details'?

* * *

"Daesh is finished in Syria now that Russia has entered the war on the side of Assad."

Tariq has just been seen to by a doctor, who checked his pulse and examined the various instruments connected to his body. He feels tired now, but wants to continue talking to this intelligent man with the sympathetic demeanour.

"And when the caliphate starts shrinking, then just watch the foreigners and adventurers disappear as quickly as they arrived. The people are terrified of them – the women especially – but they won't openly rebel. Daesh won't have much popular support on the ground, though; the people can't wait to see the back of them. Have you heard about a thing called a 'biter'?"

"No, no, I haven't," says Maurilio, who had allowed himself to drift off a little during this little speech about Islamic State's prospects. He has to let the conversation drift wherever Tariq wants it to go, but he hopes it will return soon to Rome.

"A biter? No. What is that?"

"It's a tool that these so-called fighters carry – it's like a pair of tongs with sharp claws – and when they see a woman who they think is showing too much flesh they clip off pieces of their flesh. It's agonising apparently, and really just sadistic, and they're using them more and more. Women have to be fully veiled, wear loose or baggy trousers, gloves and socks, and be accompanied by a male relative, if they don't want to be at risk of being clipped like this. My friends in Sirte say it's being used there now."

"That's just sadistic, like you say."

"Anyway, they're finished in Syria, and possibly, after that in Iraq. I'm not so sure. It's why so many of the top leadership have gone to Libya. They think they're safe there. But the caliphate needs a real showstopper soon to encourage more recruits."

"And that's going to happen in Rome, you think?"

"I know."

Maurilio hesitates. He's at a vital moment, but how best to approach? He must help Tariq build a narrative.

"When did you and Aafia first arrive in Italy?"

"About six months ago," says Tariq, looking round for a glass of water.

"Here," says Maurilio, standing up and handing him the glass that's on the bedside cabinet.

"We hired the compound as a workshop and storage for our

supposed online import-export business with North Africa – carpets and ceramics and stuff like that. We've got a lovely website that actually works, although the stuff is so deliberately expensive that we don't get that many orders. But when we do, we send out stuff. It's amazing how stupid some people are."

"My wife wants a nice old Moroccan rug. Remind me to avoid your website."

"All our stuff is from Tunisia, and that's the point," says Tariq. "The Tunisian government has been building a barrier along its border with Libya since the attacks on tourists in 2015, and are proud about how effective it is at keeping out terrorists, which makes everybody think that the country is safe from infiltration. But that's rubbish – apart from the many Tunisian Daesh fighters, the border is easy to broach, especially at its southern end."

"So, what, I don't follow. How does this benefit your import-export business?"

"Italy's a big trading partner with Tunisia and freight between the two countries is common and unexceptional. Boats come in all the time from Tunis to Civitavecchia."

"And there's a ferry crossing to Civitavecchia," says Maurilio, who knows the port well from the spell in which he was seconded to the DCSA, the Direzione Centrale per i servizi Antidroga – the Italian drugs squad.

"And Civitavecchia is only forty minutes from the compound. We've used the ferry three or four times… bringing back carpets and stuff," says Tariq. "But mainly we've used freight companies."

"Yes, but why?"

"So that customs get used to us and our company."

"But why?"

"Because that's how we attract Daesh to work with us."

"Why, what do Daesh, as you call them, want to import? Drugs? Guns? Semtex?"

"No. Sarin."

* * *

The mountain roads are becoming progressively less full of hairpins as they approach the Italian border. There's quite a bit of traffic now, and Max has to overtake a slow-moving caravan, and an old couple crammed into a tiny car. Nobody is speaking, the only voice that of the satnav and that has gone quiet for the past ten minutes as their route stretches unbroken before them.

Max is beginning to feel desperately tired as the adrenalin deserts his brain to re-group somewhere deeper in his body. A couple of times now, he has realised that he has forgotten that he was driving, his mind so distracted that for ten-minute stretches he has been on auto-pilot.

He looks in the rear-view mirror, hoping and fearing that he will see the flashing lights of a chasing police car. Instead he meets Omar's implacable gaze and returns to his thoughts.

What will happen at the Italian border? Will they have traced the hire car back to Rome and therefore have Max's name? Will the old man – the neighbour in Verbier – have noted the Audi's number plate before he scuttled back inside his house? Perhaps he was a car enthusiast and knew his Audi A6 from his Audi A3. Surely news must have been broadcast now of the massacre at the chalet, the murder of two policemen and two English people – a man and a girl? What a story for the Sunday newspapers.

Omar is having similar thoughts, but he's drawing rather different conclusions. The old man, he presumes, will ring the police straight away, reporting that a man in a car pointed a gun at him. He will be told that two policemen are already at the scene, and then his wife will hurry back into the house to say that she can't be sure but she thinks one of the policemen might have been shot. She thinks she saw a body by the back door. The old man rings back.

This spurs the police into action, but they are already two men unaccounted for. The local police stations are only manned on weekday mornings and afternoons, and backup must come from the town of Sion, nearly an hour away. Omar, who has meanwhile Googled for police stations in Verbier, is encouraged by scanning an accompanying Wikipedia article that discusses the way in which the Swiss police operate in their separate cantons, and jealously guard their independence. The federal police become involved in such matters as money laundering and terrorism, but how long will it take those local cops in Verbier to piece together the bigger picture?

He imagines them now, staking out the chalet and waiting for the tactical assault unit to arrive from down in the valley. It will be a while, he feels, until they charge into that house of death.

The Great St Bernard Tunnel is one point five kilometres away, the satnav announces as they pass petrol stations and hotels and restaurants, and finally enter a roofed section of road, with concrete slabs on the left where the road clings to the mountainside, and a concrete colonnade on the right with views of the mountains beyond. Max is finding the strobe effect of the columns hypnotic and slows down.

"Why are you slowing?" barks Omar, the first thing he's said for about an hour.

"I'm tired, these pillars are mesmerising me. I'm scared I'll crash."

"Why don't I take over?" says Aafia, a suggestion that elicits a rasping sound from Omar.

"Women must not drive," he says.

There follows a sharp exchange in Arabic, which at least breaks up the monotony of this endless hypnotic colonnade.

"Stop at the Tunnel of Great St Bernard in 800 metres," interrupts the satnav, as they pass a sign saying the same thing. Max wonders what he will do if they are asked to stop and get out of the car. Will he run? Will he be shot before he can run?

Instead they pull up at a tollbooth, where a grumpy middle-aged woman tells Aafia that the rate for a car is 27.90 euros or 29.30 Swiss francs, Aafia handing her a fifty-euro note from her money bag. The change is handed over without a word. They move on.

There seems to be some sort of customs facilities and a couple of cars have been pulled over. Or perhaps they're just parked there. Nobody is about. A vortex of lights and white lines swallows Max as he enters the tunnel, and he clears his throat loudly as if this will pull him back from the abyss.

"Holy fuck," is all he manages to say.

CHAPTER FORTY

Professor Luca Guardiano of the Chemical Research Centre in Naples was eating breakfast at home with his two teenage daughters – a rare treat these days – when the call comes through. His wife, Carmelinda, brings him his phone, which has been ringing insistently on the kitchen sideboard for the past ten minutes – each time it went to the messaging service, whoever it was would call again without leaving a message.

"Twenty missed calls," she says, picking up the side plate on which are the remains of a bread roll and replacing it with his phone. Almost immediately it begins to ring again.

Anybody else and he would have given them short shrift for interrupting the start of a long-awaited Easter holiday break, but Nadia Pizzuto of the anti-terrorist police wasn't just anybody. He had worked with her before, in 2014, when chemical weapons surrendered by the Assad regime in Syria had arrived at the port of Giola Tauro in Calabria.

Pizzuto had been sent to check on the security arrangements at the port, which was heavily infiltrated by the Calabrese Ndrangheta mafia, who used it as a hub for importing cocaine. Guardiano led the small team of Italian experts to monitor the destruction of the 130 tonnes of mustard gas and sarin.

Having been transported to Italy on a Danish freighter, the chemicals were transferred to an American ship, which would take them out to sea and neutralise the toxins in a titanium reactor. Guardino was on board to witness the event.

"So how dangerous is sarin?" Pizzutto asks him twenty-five minutes later over Skype on the laptop that arrived at his apartment ten minutes earlier, carried by two men who claimed that the computer had been 'vetted and was uncompromised'.

"Well that depends," says Guardino, and Pizzutto remembered the calm and clear manner in which he explained complex scientific matters. She appreciated him for it.

"It's most effective in vapour form, which is how we think Saddam used it, along with sulphur mustard, against the Kurds when he killed 5,000 of them in Halahbja in 1988, and how Japanese religious cultists used it on the Japanese subway in 1995. As a gas it quickly enters the lungs, and starts attacking the neurotransmitters in the nerves – making them go a little crazy."

"How does that manifest itself physically?" asks Pizzutto, who is scribbling on a jotting pad.

"Okay, so sarin is colourless and odourless and so the first thing that a victim will notice is that their nose is running like crazy and their eyes watering. Then the mouth drools and vomits, and bowels and bladder evacuates. It's not dignified. After that the chest tightens, the vision goes blurred and, if the exposure is great enough, convulsions, paralysis and death occur in anything from one to ten minutes. A single drop of sarin the size of a pinhead can be enough to kill an adult."

"And the good news?" asks Pizzutto, joking to give herself some space as she continues to furiously note down Guardino's words.

"Hold on one second," she says, finding the voice-recorder app on her phone. "Carry on."

"Well, since you ask, the good news is that if the person doesn't die then recovery is relatively quick and complete. They won't be left blind or infertile or prone to cancer. And most people exposed to sarin don't die. Plus, there is a lotion that can be applied to the skin immediately after exposure that works well. The US military used to stockpile it. When are you expecting this attack?"

Pizzutto can't help herself – she laughs at the professor's assumption, so neutrally inserted at the end of his spiel.

"We are not, professor, and this conversation never took place."

"Understood, Nadia. Now can I return to my holiday?"

"One thing," Pizzuto thinks carefully how to phrase the next question. "Were there to be an attack, in the centre of a major city, say, how would it likely be carried out?"

"I presume you mean a terrorist attack?"

Pizzuto makes no reply. The fact that she heads the anti-terrorist police should speak for itself.

"Well, sarin dissolves very easily in water, and the Tokyo attackers carried their's in plastic bags, diluted in water. They then boarded trains, dropped the bags and punctured them, before getting smartly off the trains. They weren't suicidal, like some of these Islamic groups we have now.

"The thing with sarin is that it not only dissolves easily in water, it also vaporises very easily. It's a very volatile nerve agent, so that once released in liquid form it vaporises and enters the environment. There is a plus side to this: sarin evaporates so rapidly that the threat is short-lived. So if I was a terrorist I would do it somewhere confined, like the metro. Or in an office building."

"And where would they get the sarin from?"

"Right now? Multiple sources. We suspect the various mafias took their slice of Assad's WMD – the stuff that Assard didn't hold back for his own use, of course. That's why you were in Calabria in 2014, isn't it? But more worrying at the moment is Libya. Islamic State is known to have got their hands on stockpiles of sarin and mustard gas from the Gadaffi era, and they've already used chlorine in Iraq."

"Okay, so how would they transport it from Libya to Italy?"

"Well, like I said, it's odourless and colourless and dissolves in water. In bottled water? In a ship's hull? I don't know. How do they get cocaine and heroin into Italy?"

* * * *

"Okay, two hours, then you drive," Omar says to Aafia.

"Miracles never cease," says Aafia under her breath, before twisting around on her side, slipping down the seat so that her head is resting against its back, and closing her eyes.

Omar settles back into his seat. There is nothing they can do now. All is in the hands of Allah and his mercy.

He remembers the lessons taught to him by the Saudi cleric in Pakistan. The man's view of the world was different to most of the al-Qaeda leaders he had met. He referred to Osama bin Laden respectfully enough, calling him 'Sheikh Osama', but Omar could tell that he believed al-Qaeda's approach was past its sell-by date.

And though he was a Saudi like Bin Laden, the cleric adhered to Wahhabism, the purest form of Islam that demands the strict adherence to sharia law, the demotion of women to their rightful place beneath men, and that Shia Muslims are heretics and apostates to be persecuted along with Christians and Jews. And above all he believes in a caliphate. Not in some distant future, but now.

Omar sat at his feet, completely spellbound as he spoke of returning to the sacred texts and the example of Muhammad himself, following them absolutely and without deviation – what the cleric called 'the Prophetic methodology' – and this was why the Shia were heretics, because what they believed in was an innovation, and to innovate on the Quran is to deny its initial perfection. And so all 200 million Shia are marked for death.

This new understanding suddenly became a blinding reality when Omar finally returned to Iraq in the autumn of 2010. In the three years since his departure, al-Qaeda had all but been defeated by the Americans, their leaders and top fighters jailed, and the government of Prime Minister Maliki was leading a Shia-dominated one-man state in Baghdad. The Sunni minority – top dogs under Saddam – were now second-class citizens, denied jobs and subject to random arrest. Malaki's supposed government of national unity had turned into a Shia dictatorship, riven with cronyism and corruption.

Omar had decided to station himself in Mosul in the far north of Iraq, and about as far from the government of the Shia heretics in Baghdad as he could manage. From there he made discreet contact with his former comrades in the resistance to the American invaders and discovered that most were either dead or in jail. However one of them, an old Saddam loyalist called Abu with whom Omar had blown up Humvees during the early days of the occupation, introduced him to a man who was going to change his life.

Camp Bucca in southern Iraq had originally been called Camp Freddy by the British who stored their prisoners of war there. When the Americans took it over in 2003, they re-named it after Ronald Bucca, a New York fire marshal who died in the 9/11 attacks on

New York. Bucca, an experienced marathon runner, had made it to the seventy-eighth floor of the South Tower of the World Trade Center – pretty much exactly where the second of the hijackers' plane struck.

Anyway, Camp Bucca was where Abu got to know another Abu – Abu Bakr al-Baghdadi, who had also been a prisoner of the Americans. By the time Omar was introduced to him, one day in late October, after an all-day car journey during which Omar had been blindfolded, al-Baghdadi had recently become the leader of al-Qaeda in Iraq following an American attack that had killed the previous commanders.

Al-Baghdadi impressed Omar from the start – a quiet, purposeful, organised man in his early forties, he reminded him of his former mentor in Pakistan, the Saudi cleric. Al-Baghdadi was understandably extremely security conscious and had been whisked away by his bodyguards after less than fifteen minutes of their meeting, but Omar had felt the force of his intelligent gaze and had come away with the feeling that he had passed some sort of test.

It was less than a year later, immediately following the murder of Osama bin Laden in Pakistan, that he met al-Baghdadi again. He wanted help in organising a response – a suicide attack on a police station to the south of Baghdad that they had been scouting as a possible target.

Omar's phone wakes him from his reverie. It was a simple text: 'Draycott family located'.

CHAPTER FORTY-ONE

Harry allows the moving walkway to carry him past the endless advertisements for private banks and luxury watches, and feels like laughing. He is now officially part of this world, he thinks, glancing at his Rolex. Forty minutes till his flight and he has no luggage – not even a diamond which now sits snugly in its safety deposit box in Geneva.

The process could hardly have been any easier. His passport was photocopied and a deposit taken, along with a year's rental in advance – all on the company credit card. A neat, nondescript man, with a manner just the right side of obsequious, took him through the whole process, handed him the key and wished him good day. Out into the bright crisp sunshine of Geneva.

It's only as he approaches the departure gate that he begins to feel uneasy. If Max has been killed, then it wouldn't be long before they traced the hire car. But hold on, they hadn't hired the car, it had been the Saudi who had arranged the Merc.

Then if Max had been rescued, he would have notified the police of Harry's absence and they would be on the lookout for him. He slips the battery back into his phone, which tells him that he has twenty-three missed calls.

The woman at the departure gate scans the boarding card on his phone, and lets him through. Passport control is in a glass booth on the way to the security area, and Harry nonchalantly hands his to the young man, who gives it a perfunctory glance and passes it back. "Merci," says Harry and the man nods, his attention already moved onto the next traveller.

In the duty-free area, Harry heads straight for a shop selling books, magazines and sweets, with a rack of newspapers by the checkout. He scans the local Swiss newspapers, but they're full of yesterday's news. He Googles 'Swiss news' and receives an eight-hour-old BBC news item about a new initiative to expel foreigners found guilty of minor crimes. He takes the battery back out of his phone. A departure screen above his head tells him that his flight will be boarding in twenty minutes. It's now just after twenty past three.

He finds a snack bar, places a ham and salad roll and a bottle of sparkling water on a plastic tray, and finds a corner seat with a view of a TV screen. It's some sort of news magazine programme with a smartly dressed man and woman by turns addressing the camera and each other. Harry can't hear what they're saying because the sound is turned down.

He's just unwrapping the cellophane from his roll when an aerial shot of Simon's chalet fills the TV screen. The next shot is of bodies, draped in blankets, being wheeled out of the driveway on trolleys. A caption beneath simply says *Verbier*. Harry fights the urge to be sick.

A uniformed policeman is being interviewed now. Microphones thrust under his nose. And then two mug shots fill the screen – God knows where they were taken. On the left is Max and on the right is Harry.

Harry shoots to his feet. Luckily he is the only customer, and the server has his back to him, rubbing the spout on a coffee machine with a cloth. Leaving his sandwich and drink, he stumbles out into the concourse – the server saying *"Merci, monsieur"* to his retreating back. He searches for a toilet sign, and sees that there's a gents nearby.

Seated in a toilet cubicle he takes some deep breaths and tries not to be sick. Why Max and Harry's photographs? Were they murder suspects? And does that mean Max is still alive? Then where is he?

He puts the battery back in his phone, but there doesn't seem to be any signal here. There's less than ten minutes to boarding. Should he just give himself up? Why was he trying to leave the country when he knew there was one dead person at the chalet, and others in mortal danger? Could he say that he was in shock? Isn't he in shock? Taking another deep breath, he tells himself that he's in the hands of the gods now, and with that he feels strangely serene.

* * *

"We're running short of petrol," says Aafia, who has been driving for the past half-hour. Max opens his eyes. He hasn't been asleep; it's just been a relief not to have to watch the road any more. He was getting dangerously spaced out going through the tunnel back there on the Swiss border.

Omar has decided to cut down past Genoa instead of taking the more direct route by way of Milan, because of roadworks on that route. They will re-join the E35 south of Bologna. The satnav is suggesting a 17:03 arrival time, but they can always put their foot down.

"And I need to go to the bathroom," says Aafia.

"Me too," says Max, remembering Aafia's vanishing act on the way up to Switzerland. God... when? Yesterday... could it really have only been yesterday?

Omar is silent for a while.

"Okay, stop at the next service station," he says. "But you can piss in your pants."

"That's disgusting," says Aafia, followed by something in Arabic. "You can't expect us to do that."

"You don't seriously think I'm going to let you go in a women's toilet on your own, do you? How stupid do you think I am?"

Less stupid than he and Harry, thinks Max. "At least can't we go in a bush... maybe in some picnic area?" he suggests.

"Maybe," says Omar absently, his thoughts returning to his homeland, the caliphate. After the attack on the police station, Omar had become one of al-Baghdadi's most trusted fighters, and with his knowledge of bomb-making he was sent to the Iraqi capital to coordinate a spate of IEDs and car bombs across the city, just days after the final American troops left the country.

Then things began to change, and the Sunni minority began to protest at Prime Minister Maliki's sectarian policies. The protests were peaceful at first, but not the government's response, and after the massacre at the Hawijah peace camp in April 2013, armed resistance became the order of the day.

By then the so-called Arab Spring had reached Syria, and Assad was in serious trouble from various armed rebel groups. Where others saw nothing but anarchy, al-Baghdadi spotted opportunity, and he, Omar, was one of the experienced fighters that was sent to Syria to set up Jabhat al-Nusra as the al Qaeda affiliate in Syria.

"Petrol ten kilometres," announces Aafia, breaking into Omar's thoughts.

"Okay, we'll pull in there," he says.

Aafia puts her foot down, and before too long they're turning off and drawing up next to a pump.

"The key," demands Omar when Aafia turns off the engine, and she passes it back to him.

"Okay... everybody out. You," he says looking at Max. "You do the petrol."

With stiff legs and a bursting bladder, Max steps down on to the forecourt. All around, oblivious to his plight, normal life continues. A Dutch motorhome owner is filling up in the space in front of the Audi. Across the forecourt, a fat middle-aged man yawns expansively on the way back to a Fiat that looks too small to take his weight. The sun shines and the breeze is warm. Max is sure he can smell the sea.

Omar has corralled Aafia around to the side of the car where Max is standing with the pump. She bends and stretches and jogs on the spot. "I need a pee," she says. Omar, watchful, one hand inside his coat opening, and no doubt attached to his pistol, ignores her.

A sharp click tells Max that the tank is full, and he returns the handle to the pump. "Come, we go together," says Omar. "You two in front." They walk over to the pay station.

"Tell me, Aafia," says Max, suddenly feeling liberated from Omar's immediate command. "Why did you steal the diamond? What did you want the money for?"

"A new life," she says smiling. "After all this is over... a new life. A life without my father, and without Tariq."

"Without Tariq?"

"We're not lovers, you know. Not any more."

229

They're in the shop now. There's a short queue, and up and to the left of the till is a screen. Looking back at Max is a slightly blurred facial photograph of himself, next to one of Harry. The image changes to a notice advising of motorway roadworks, and Max wonders whether he imagined it.

"Did you see that?" says Aafia, handing over a 100-euro note. Max nods.

"Okay, back to the car," says Omar.

"I need a pee," says Aafia.

Max senses the hand tense under Omar's coat. Would he shoot them here? Max wouldn't put it past him.

"Come on," he says, and they return to the Audi. The Dutch motor home has gone, as well as the overladen Fiat. Aafia climbs back in to the driver's seat.

"We'll find a place. Drive round to where those trucks are parked," says Omar, pointing towards a sort of lay-by beyond the shop, where three freight lorries are pulled up. There is a bank running along its side, with bushes growing up its slope. Aafia pulls up behind the last of the trucks.

"You go first," he says to Max, lowering his window and pulling the Swiss policeman's gun from inside his coat. "Stay where I can see you."

Max goes behind a bush and, with his back to the car, empties his bladder to the accompaniment of a long sigh. He buttons up and returns to the car.

"Now you, pass me the key first," says Omar, as Aafia starts to open the driver's door. She passes him the ignition key, and steps down out of the Audi. She goes further into the bushes than Max, causing Omar to tell her to stay in sight. She pulls down her trousers and squats with her back to the car. Omar has his gun trained on where he can just about see the top of her arse.

And then she stands, pulling up her trousers. And she's off, crashing through the bushes and up the slope.

"Bitch... whore." Omar is struggling with his door handle. "You stay here!" he barks at Max, who has just noticed a lorry driver standing by the side of his truck, smoking a cigarette. Omar spots him too and stops, returning to the car.

"Never mind, it doesn't matter," he says, looking more angry than flustered. "Take the key. Drive."

CHAPTER FORTY-TWO

Harry is in the departure lounge waiting to be called, his back to the other passengers who have already started a queue, and looking out of a window past the runways and across at the Alps. The mountains are bathed in the afternoon light. Next to him a young man is simultaneously reading a Kindle and listening to music through earphones, while on his other side a woman is speaking on her phone in French. There don't seem to be any uniformed police around.

Rows one to fourteen are called, and that includes Harry, so he stands up and joins a shorter queue that is forming alongside the other one. There's a short, fit-looking man in jeans and T-shirt talking animatedly with the girl at the departure desk and she seems to be checking down her list. Harry has a sinking sensation as the man nods and steps to one side, looking carefully at Harry's queue. Nothing for it but to meet his fate.

As he approaches the desk the man seems to take no interest in him. The girl takes his passport and the scans the boarding pass on his phone, and wishes Harry a 'good flight'. Relieved but slightly perplexed, he makes his way towards the plane, looking back at the man who he thought had been a plain-clothes cop. The man isn't returning his gaze.

Harry is relieved to find that he has his bank of three seats to himself and, only ten minutes later than scheduled, the plane starts taxiing down the runway. "The flight time this afternoon will be approximately one hour and thirty minutes," announces the captain, "and the weather at Gatwick is overcast, with a temperature of twelve degrees." Someone groans on a seat behind him.

They're gaining speed now, and with a thrust the plane is airborne, with Lake Geneva below them, and banking away. Down there lie Simon and Kylie. Harry feels badly about Kylie. And somewhere down there are Max and Aafia... the lovely Aafia... and

Omar with his scars. The nightmare is receding fast.

Harry buys a copy of *The Times* and an overpriced sandwich that is so chilled that it doesn't taste of anything. He decides against having a small bottle of wine, not so much because it would go straight to his enervated, sleep-deprived head, but because he wants to postpone celebrating his deliverance until he is safely back in London.

As they pass over France, Harry tries to make out landmarks. Is that river the Gironde or the Loire? He likes looking at maps. And he likes France, where he had his first foreign holiday, when the school arranged a trip to Paris. Perhaps he'll live there for a while – buy a nice, rundown old cottage in the middle of nowhere and with a nice climate, and grow his own food.

And then as the northern coast of France starts to pass by the window, the captain announces that they are beginning their descent into London Gatwick. Almost immediately they run into a bank of dirty grey cloud, and the plane starts shaking in the turbulence, the seatbelt signs pinging into life. Harry checks his Rolex, which is saying a quarter past five Swiss time.

Heading low over the patchwork fields of Sussex, Harry can see that the trees are starting to green up. But the fields look bleached and worn out after the long winter, more so under the leaden skies. Rain streaks the window.

The landing is smoothly executed, and the captain asks everyone to stay seated until they reach their gate. He has no luggage, and, Harry suddenly remembers, he has no home. He'll find a hotel near to work in Mayfair and charge it to the company. And then he must try and locate Max.

The plane finally comes to a stop, a fuel truck making its way across the tarmac for the quick turnaround back to Geneva. And then Harry notices the three black Range Rovers parked in front of the departure gate, and the men, compact-looking blokes wearing trainers, their T-shirts tucked into their jeans, standing arms crossed next to their vehicles.

There's a chorus of unbuckling seatbelts as the passengers start to stand up and rummage in the overhead lockers, but Harry remains seated and watches the men walk purposefully into the terminal building. Perhaps he's imagining things, like with the man at Geneva airport.

Being fairly close to the front, Harry is soon making his way past the smiling cabin crew with their phony farewells, and onto the walkway connecting the plane and the terminal. There seems to be some sort of hold up at the top of the walkway. "They're checking passports," a man in front of Harry tells his travelling companion. "Why here?" People immediately start patting pockets and looking for theirs.

As he emerges out of the walkway Harry sees the burly looking men he had spotted from the plane, and all them are now looking straight at him. Behind them stand two uniformed policemen with machine guns.

They don't wait, but push their way through the handful of people in front of Harry, and take him by the arms.

"Harry Kimber?" asks one of them.

"Yes?" says Harry, trying to make himself sound surprised. The other passengers are looking at him horrified.

"Can you come with us?"

* * *

On the other side of the embankment, Aafia finds herself in open country. She crosses a dirt path, and a narrow drainage ditch, and leaps into field that is already sprouting whatever crops have been planted here. There's a line of trees about a hundred metres in front of her, at the far end of the field, but the going is muddy and she almost slips and falls.

Aafia is fit, however, and although she gave up jogging with Tariq after they split up, she still goes for a long run twice a week. There was a sort of canal near the compound in Rome which was suitable, if you didn't mind the whistles and remarks from the Italian men. Actually they came as almost a light relief from what she had left behind in the compound.

The first fighter to turn up from Libya was genuinely horrified to find himself in a position of equality with a woman. He couldn't understand what Aafia was doing there, and wouldn't eat with her, or even stay in the same room, despite Tariq explaining that she was financing the whole operation.

The second guy to turn up at the compound was only posing as a fighter. He was one of the two undercover agents from the Saudi secret services, Al Mukhabarat Al A'amah. He was a good actor, and pretended to despise Aafia too, and told her to wear a veil when she was in the compound and to cover hands arms and legs. But mostly he played at being aloof and generally grumpy. Aafia quite liked him, but it still added to the tense atmosphere.

And then Omar arrived and things became ten times worse. He was actively belligerent and questioned her every move. He didn't seem to understand why she and Tariq had to keep up this pretence at being loved up and running a legitimate business. Any Muslim is a suspect in the West, was his attitude, but Aafia questioned to herself whether he had ever been to Europe before, and even remotely understood it.

He was so indoctrinated – all this stuff about purifying the world by killing millions of people, and how slavery, crucifixion and beheadings were a legitimate form of conquest, as laid down by the Prophet himself. He quoted endlessly from the Quran. Aafia didn't argue. She just pretended to agree with each of his insane, and insanely boring, utterances.

He didn't seem to be pursuing her now. She was half way to the trees and she hadn't heard any shots. She had calculated that Max was more valuable to him, and that he couldn't leave him to chase her. She wasn't sure how much Max understood, but it seemed likely that his family in England were about to receive a visit soon. Maybe today. Some sort of coercion was about to be enacted. There was something Omar wanted Max to do. Where did that fit in with the boy? She must keep running.

Aafia reaches the tree line, and slumps down behind the trunk of one of the poplars, panting hard. No bullets are whistling into the undergrowth and surely she must be out of range here. She swivels round to look at the ground she's just crossed and Omar doesn't appear to be chasing her. This doesn't surprise her.

Omar still has her passport, but in her money belt is a wad of 100-euro notes, and an ultra slim Vivo X5 Max mobile. The number is in her contacts, under the word 'gym'.

"*Pronto,*" says a gruff man's voice, within two rings.

"Is this the gymnasium?" she asks; the agreed code.

"*Si, signorina.* How can I help?"

"I would like to renew my membership."

CHAPTER FORTY-THREE

Tariq had been left alone for a couple hours, Maurilio promising to return after a while. Perhaps he should rest.

But the memory of the sarin had prompted associated memories. Omar was the leader of the three fighters who had arrived, one by one, from Libya. Tariq knew that Omar had taken to tailing them when he and Aafia went on their daily visits to the cafe, behaving like the love birds that they no longer were, and one day he decided to tail Omar in return.

He had followed him to Rome Termini, and then to a cheap nearby hotel. What's the name of the hotel?

"There's a hotel… near the central station," he says as soon as Maurilio steps back into the room.

"A hotel? Go on."

"I followed him one day, to this hotel."

"Followed who?" asks Maurilio, putting down the paper bag that contains his lunch – a salami roll.

"Omar… his name's Omar. He's an Iraqi and he's a veteran Isis fighter."

"Can you remember the name of the hotel?"

Tariq shakes his head in frustration. "No… no… I can't. I can sort of visualise it."

"You keep doing that," says Maurilio. "I'm going to have a word with your doctor… see if you're fit enough to go on a car ride."

* * *

They arrive at Fiumicino airport twenty-five minutes ahead of the satnav's original estimate. Despite his tiredness, Aafia's dash for freedom had given Max a new burst of adrenalin, and the last six hours of the drive had sped by in silence. He couldn't quite believe that the dots hadn't been joined up yet, and the Italian authorities hadn't been alerted to the existence of the Audi. And surely Aafia would have phoned the police by now.

He had tried to engage Omar in conversation but each question was met by the same response of "Quiet now," like he was trying to calm a nervous beast, which just made Max feel even more uneasy.

A few kilometres from Fiumicino, the satnav guides them into a trading estate, with huge furniture stores, shuttered today, and several half-built warehouses. After a few more lefts and rights, they turn into a row of brick buildings, some of them in the process of demolition, and the satnav announces without any suggestion of satisfaction at a job well done, that they had arrived at their destination.

"That one there," says Omar, pointing his pistol at a low brick edifice with a huge blue roller-shutter door.

"Park round the side," he says.

"Turn off the engine and give me the key," he tells Max, who complies, his uneasiness beginning to build in the pit of his stomach. He doesn't know what else he can do; just carry on and see what fresh hell this leads to.

Omar unlocks a side door painted the same blue as the loading bay shutters, and gestures for Max to go inside. It's a plain office, with a table, a swivel chair, and a notice board, pinned to which are what look like health-and-safety notices, and a small frosted window probably too narrow to climb through. He unlocks another door and beckons Max over. This windowless, bare-bricked space is obviously some sort of store room.

Omar wheels in a swivel chair and tells Max to sit down. Is this going to be another attempt at a filmed execution? More recruitment propaganda for would-be jihadists?

Omar returns with a pair of handcuffs. He tells Max to put his arms behind his back and the cuffs are snapped tightly on to wrists. He winces at the pain and tries to move his hands. They had been cuffed to the back of the chair.

He then returns with a length of nylon rope, which he uses to tie Max's ankles together, looping them round the back of the chair and tightening them so that Max now feels completely trussed.

Lastly the blindfold, a strip of cotton material that might have

237

been an old shirt, is wrapped around Max's eyes, and knotted at the back with a couple of sharp tugs.

"And you can yell as much as you like... there's absolutely no one around to hear you," says Omar, followed a second later by the sound of the door closing and the lock turning, and then the faint sound of the desk drawer being opened, and then closed. Slightly louder is the noise of the side door to the outside world closing and being locked.

*   *   *

Omar retrieves a new passport and driving licence, these ones British and in the name of Tahmid Ahmed from Leicester, and locks the outer door. He knows that his is the only occupied building in this part of the trading estate, the others in the course of demolition. He had to be out by the end of April the agent had told him when he rented it. The end of April is fine, he assured the man. Would he like to be paid in advance in cash?

He drives the eight or so kilometres to the airport and enters the long-stay car park. From the boot he retrieves the long bag containing an assault rifle and two handguns – each individually wrapped in woollen blankets – and ammunition. This bag he carries to the shuttle stop to the airport. The afternoon is warm with only the faintest of breezes. Omar hopes that the fine weather will continue until at least tomorrow.

The bus eventually arrives, and he joins a smattering of other passengers, and the stop-start journey continues to the terminal building. A pretty girl is looking at him, and she looks away as he returns her stare. It was the scar again. Perhaps he needs some sort of plastic surgery.

At the terminal he makes for the car hire desk, and books a Fiat Panda in the name of Tahmid Ahmed, to be returned the same time tomorrow afternoon. The paperwork completed, he walks to where the car is located in the short-stay multi-storey car park and drives off in the direction of Rome.

CHAPTER FORTY-FOUR

"You do not have to say anything. But, it may harm your defence if you do not mention when questioned something which you later rely on in court. Anything you do say may be given in evidence."

Harry has been driven at high speed to a police station, having been informed that he is being detained under the Terrorism Act. Searched, photographed, fingerprinted and swabbed, he is now sitting in a room on his own in front of a table where a recording device has been placed, just like he's seen in countless films and TV dramas. Only it's him, Harry Kimber, sitting here this time.

A man and a woman enter the room – both middle-aged and stressed looking, their clothes crumpled as if they'd slept in them.

"You'll be pleased to hear that you've made news headlines all around the world," the man says in an unpleasant voice, having introduced himself as belonging to the South East Counter Terrorism Unit. "Massacre at the Swiss ski chalet. Would you care to tell us all about it? We've got all the time in the world."

"I will... willingly. But shouldn't I have a lawyer present?" says Harry.

"You can make that request," the man says. "Would you like to make that request?"

"I would," says Harry.

"It may take up to forty-eight hours, but that's up to you."

"Forty-eight hours?"

"In terrorism cases, yes."

A muddled rush of all those famous miscarriage of justice cases pass through Harry's mind – the Guildford Four... the Birmingham Six. For some reason he has always mistrusted the police. Oh, fuck it...

"I have nothing to hide," he says. "Where shall I start?"

"How about with these?" says the woman with a smirk, carefully placing two plastic bags on the table in front of them.

Harry can see at once that they contain the key to the safety deposit box and the accompanying paperwork.

*   *   *

The doctors are initially reluctant to let Tariq leave the hospital. Phone calls are made, meetings are called, and it's eventually after five when a medical team accompanied by Maurilio and Nadia Pizzuto arrive by Tariq's bedside.

"Do you want to see if you can walk?" asks one of the doctors, having detached him from the various drips and monitors.

Tariq sits up and swings his legs over the side of the bed. A rush of nausea hits him but then subsides. Gingerly he puts his feet on to the vinyl-matted floor, and equally carefully he puts his weight on them.

"So far, so good," he says to Maurilio, who smiles.

They have parked a wheelchair for him by the door, and as Tariq pads towards it he begins to feel light-headed. One of the doctors sees him hesitate and puts a supportive arm around the small of his back.

"I'm okay now," says Tariq, and walks more steadily towards the chair. Nevertheless he is glad to sit down again.

"Okay," says Maurilio. "The doctor here is going to come with us as we take an ambulance down to the central station. We'll drive around and see if you recognise which hotel that you saw Omar go into. Do you think you are up to that?"

"Yes," answers Tariq unequivocally.

"Good," says Maurilio. "Let's go."

As he is wheeled down the corridor and into a lift, Tariq breathes heavily to ward off spasms of nausea. These are weakening though, and he starts to get used to this upright position.

"What actually happened to me?" he asks the doctor who is accompanying them. He looks at Nadia Pizzuto and she nods.

"Well, it looks like your attacker used the sides of his fists to hammer your temples – an extraordinarily effective way of killing someone, if you ask me. You were lucky."

"Straight out of the manual of Krav Maga," says Pizzuto. "It's a type of street fighting developed by the Israelis, brutal and effective. We were given lessons once. All I remember is to kick a man in the balls at the first opportunity."

"Like in Butch Cassidy and the Sundance Kid," says Maurilio.

"Never seen it," says Pizzuto.

"Paul Newman... Robert Redford? Oh never mind."

They are through the sliding doors at the hospital entrance now, and the sunlight feels fierce to Tariq. A pair of dark glasses are put on his face by one of the doctors, as he is wheeled towards the back doors of a white and orange ambulance.

Tariq is lifted up on the tailgate and pushed gently into a space big enough to take a wheelchair. A doctor takes a small seat next to him, while Pizzuto and Maurilio pile into seats in front. A police car parked in front starts with the flashing lights and they're off.

"Are you okay? How are you feeling?" asks Maurilio, leaning back.

"I'm okay, I think," says Tariq, although the sudden return to the busy streets of central Rome does feel unsettling. "Do you have a bag, in case I feel sick? Otherwise I'm fine."

Pizzuto radios ahead to the police car to tell him not to drive so fast, as they head down the Via Solferino and the Via Marsala, and pull up by the central station.

"Tariq, what do you remember of the hotel?" asks Maurilio.

"Erm, well, it was cheap looking... a bit tatty," he replies. "Brown... why do I think it was brown?"

"Main road or side street?"

"Side street... definitely a side street."

"Far from the station?"

"Not too far, I don't think."

Pizzuto is scrolling down her iPad, while talking to someone through a headset. Maurilio is studying a street map. The doctor puts a hand on the underside of Tariq's wrist and feels his pulse.

"I reckon we're looking at about twenty hotels," says Pizzuto into her mouthpiece. "Most of them are on the west side. Let's start with Via Giolotti, and sweep up and down, nice and slowly, each of the streets… go with the one-way traffic obviously…"

"A flag," says Tariq. "A German flag. I remember thinking it odd that it had a big German flag…"

"We're looking for a German flag," Pizzuto repeats at once to the police car ahead. "Do you know what that looks like?"

"Black, red and yellow," says Maurilio. "It's black, red and yellow."

"Black, red and yellow," relays Pizzuto.

"But faded," says Tariq. "Like I say… tatty."

They set off, zigzagging along the side streets nearest to the central station. And there it is. A big faded German flag outside a tall, narrow and dirty brown building.

"Two stars…" says Maurilio, peering out of his window and then back at Tariq. "Is this the one?"

"I'm pretty sure," he says.

Pizzuto is talking to someone on her phone in an Italian too rapid-fire for Tariq to understand. *"Si… si… Si…"* she repeats now.

"Well, this may or may not be relevant," she says when she finally hangs up. "But this hotel has links to the Mafia."

"The Cosa Nostra?" asks Maurilio.

"No, the Calabrese… the same mob we checked out for chemical weapons in 2014. Okay, let's pay them a visit."

Maurilio, Pizzuto and two armed police from the advance car pile out on to the pavement and into the hotel. Tariq leans back and takes several deep breaths, causing the doctor to feel his pulse again.

"Did I have a mobile phone on my person when I was brought in?" he asks the doctor.

"The police already asked us about that several times. No, you didn't."

"Did they search for one near where I was found?"

"I don't know, you'll have to ask them that," says the doctor.

The two uniformed police emerge from the hotel, with a short, middle-aged man handcuffed to one of them, followed immediately by Pizzuto and Maurilio. They make their way over to the ambulance, deep in conversation.

"Okay, well, your Omar was here," says Pizutto. "In fact he was here about an hour ago. He left with a boy who he's been putting up here for the past two weeks, a rent boy according to the manager. He says he hears the boy crying himself to sleep every night, but luckily they don't have many other customers."

"I bet they don't," says the doctor, surveying the shabby exterior of the hotel. "Especially German ones."

"He's been crying himself to sleep and whimpering sometimes during the day," continues Pizzuto. "Obviously a deeply unhappy lad – an Arab, the manager said. But after Omar called today, the boy seems ecstatic – almost jumping with joy."

"He must be the first person who has ever been happy to see Omar," says Tariq.

"Right, we need all the street CCTV from this whole area," says Pizzuto. "And while that's being arranged, I have a meeting at the Palazzo del Viminale to explain to the Minister of the Interior why we allowed a terrorist cell to operate on the outskirts of Rome, completely undetected for six months."

CHAPTER FORTY-FIVE

The boy is happy to be out of the hotel, but even happier for the man to tell him that the suicide-vest was only a test. He wanted to see how brave and loyal the boy is and that his devotion to his family and to his Sunni faith will be rewarded.

The boy wants to ask about his family, but doesn't dare in case something horrible has happened to them. But then the man starts asking him questions. Does he like video games?

Yes, the boy says that in the old days in Syria, before the war, he shared an Xbox with his two brothers, and also he played on his uncle's old PlayStation.

"I have a video game for you," he says. "It's great fun."

They are driving through an area with large buildings selling furniture and things, except there's no one about. After a few turns they enter a place where everything seems to be demolished, or in the process of being demolished. There's rubble everywhere, and bits of twisted steel emerging from the ground. At the far end is an intact building, low and made of brick with big blue doors.

The man parks alongside this building, by a side-door that's hidden from the road by scrubby bushes. He unlocks the door and beckons the boy inside.

"Hey, hey, is anybody there?"

It's a man's voice speaking in English from behind an inner door.

"Don't worry about the *kuffar*, I've locked him in there for his own protection. You want to see my cool truck?"

The boy nods, and with a different key, the man opens another door which leads into a huge warehouse space, in the middle of which is parked a very cool truck indeed. It is a dark olive green and armour plated, with a sort of V-shaped steel contraption on the front, like the snowploughs the boy had seen in movies. He looks up on top of the cabin roof. Yes, sure enough, there is the nozzle.

He had seen one of these machines in action five or so years ago, when the uprising against Assad had spread to his home town. The police had two of these trucks that had fired water at the protesters. The boy had been far enough away not to get soaked, but he knew someone whose brother had been in the way of the stream; you couldn't believe how powerful it was, he said. It just pushed him into the ground like he was nothing, he said.

The police had two of these trucks and had fired water at the protesters. The boy had been far enough away not to get soaked, but he knew someone whose brother had been in the way of the stream; you couldn't believe how powerful it was, he had said. It just pushed him to the ground like he was nothing, he said.

"It's a water cannon," the boy says.

"Very good," says the man. "You want a go?"

The boy nods, excited but nervous at the same time. He's happy to be spared the suicide bomb but he's still wary. He so wants to ask after his family.

"Come on then, jump in."

The passenger door is open and he clambers inside, the man pressing a button on the wall which activates the big roller door. He joins him in the cabin and starts the engine, and the truck – a noisy, vibrating brute – edges out into the daylight. The windscreen is covered in a steel mesh that makes it hard to see clearly, but the man flicks a switch and a sort of TV screen comes to life. The screen is split into four views – front, back and sides.

The man steers the truck round the far side of the building, and comes to a halt facing a field, and puts it into neutral.

"Okay, this is the fun bit," he says. "Here are the controls."

The man rests his hand on a silver aluminium box that sits between them, and which has three buttons on it.

"So listen carefully… it's quite simple when you have practised it. This button here turns the water cannon power on."

The man presses. He then moves to the bottom switch. "Press to the right, idle speed low for low pressure. It's important you do this first."

"Okay," says the boy without conviction. He likes cars and machines generally, but the man's quietly intense manner is intimidating.

"Okay, now open our valve," he says, clicking a switch that sits behind a joystick, "and start the water engine."

He presses the middle button on the aluminium box and an engine somewhere at the back of the truck rumbles into life, and a jet of water starts pouring from the cannon. He can see it clearly on the CCTV.

"Finally, switch to high pressure," the man says, flicking the bottom switch in the opposite direction.

The water is powering out now, and by moving the joystick, the man can direct it where he wants. This bit looks fun, thinks the boy, as the man starts to reverse the process, turning off the hose. He then repeats the process just as before, and the boy thinks he can remember the order in which he needs to flick and press buttons.

"Okay, I'm going to leave you to play with this now. Think you'll manage?"

"Yes, sir."

"Good boy," and the man gives his shoulder a squeeze. The boy feels proud. He wants to ask about his family again, but thinks it had better wait. The man gets out of the truck and the boy watches him walk round the side and away from the back and out of sight.

CHAPTER FORTY-SIX

After Max heard Omar speaking Arabic to someone else, he stopped his shouting. It was only on the off-chance that somebody other than his captor had for some reason visited the building that prompted him to call out. The police perhaps? They must have identified the Audi by now.

Then the loud engine noise had started up on the other side of the wall, and after a few moments, the sound of something like a lorry being driven off, but not far, because Max could still hear it idling, but through a different wall this time. His hearing is becoming quite acute now; this is what it must be like for blind people, he thinks.

There's another noise, a grinding mechanical churning and behind it a whooshing like water – a garden hose, but far stronger. That stops abruptly, and now Max can hear footsteps approaching, a door opening, and then another. His blindfold is yanked off and he finds himself blinking up at Omar, who appears to be scrolling through his phone.

"Here," he says, holding the phone up in front of Max's face. It's a video, and, with a horrible lurching sensation in his guts, he recognises the television room from home, the one where his father likes to watch sport and get quietly sozzled on expensive claret. And there is his father looking aggrieved, and his mother and then Tash.

"What is this?" he says.

"You don't know?" Omar says. "It's your family. Listen…"

Tash is talking to the camera.

"These men say they will kill us if you don't do what you're told. But you must do what you think right," she is saying.

This provokes an outburst from whoever is holding the camera, and Max can hear his mother off camera shouting, "Don't you dare touch her!"

The camera is now pointed at his father. He's wearing that old cricket jumper he puts on every time he watches sport on TV. How can this be happening? How can this be going on in their home in a village in the middle of Hampshire? It's just too weird.

His mother is on the screen now.

"We don't know what to do," she is saying. "The Buxtons are coming round to play tennis any minute now and we don't want to get them involved…"

"Mummy, please…" It's Tash's voice. Max can hear the desperation in her voice.

The lens swings round again to Max's father. A man in a black balaclava is holding a pistol to his head.

"Maxy… do what you think is right. Do what you think is right," his father says.

The screen goes blank. Max lets out a long sigh, like he has been holding his breath. He is horrified but at the same time he has never felt more proud of his family.

*   *   *

Mary doesn't usually mind working the Saturday shift on a Sunday paper; she prefers it to working Mondays for a daily. You no longer got paid time and a half, like in the old days, but the atmosphere is usually less intense that on a weekday.

It presents its own problems, of course. People are harder to contact at the weekend, or less willing to spend time speaking to a journalist. And if she had to check a spelling or a meaning, the writers themselves don't like being disturbed on a Saturday. They're out doing things that ordinary people do on a Saturday – shopping or going to a football game.

The foreign desk is uncomfortably close to the sports desk however, and on a Saturday afternoon that means the sports subs congregating around the television screens, and groaning or cheering in response to the ebb and flow of the match they're watching. They won't really knuckle down until nearer to full-time when the first match reports start coming in from around the grounds.

Mary herself is tidying up a report from their correspondent in Moscow, about an oligarch who has been charged with assaulting his girlfriend. The man apparently punched and slapped her in public view in one of Moscow's top restaurants. She'll push the subbed copy back to the editor, but wouldn't be surprised if it was dropped at afternoon conference.

She makes herself a cup of tea with the kettle that is kept on the floor at the corner of the news desk and settles down for a few minutes of surfing the property websites. Sidcup in Kent is the area that she and Ben are now looking at, the sort of leafy suburbia they would have mocked just two years ago as being a fate worse than death. But even here a two-bedroom flat, which is what they want, costs around £300,000 – and they are shooting up in price with each passing month. Sidcup as a house-price hot spot. How depressing.

She closes Rightmove and returns to the Press Association wire, scanning for any late-breaking foreign news stories that need to be included in tomorrow's edition. The foreign news editor, Charlotte, goes into conference in half an hour, so she needs to be up to the minute.

"This might be interesting," she calls across to Charlotte. "Shooting at a Swiss ski chalet belonging to a British national. Four dead. Two policemen. This looks like a big one."

They simultaneously turn to look at the bank of televisions that run at ceiling level across the length of the news desk. Charlotte is already flicking through the twenty-four-hour news channels when she stops at one showing an aerial shot of a snowbound ski chalet. The caption reads *Verbier*. She turns up the volume.

"The victims are being described as a British man, an unknown woman and two Swiss policemen," the reporter is saying.

"British... okay... this could be interesting," says Charlotte.

But it's what happens next that has Mary reeling. Photographs of two men are shown side by side as the reporter says that two British men are wanted for questioning. She doesn't need the reporter to say their names. She can see who they are.

"Jesus... fucking hell..."

"What is it?" asks Charlotte.

"I know that man. In fact I sort of know the other one too."

Charlotte walks round to where Mary is standing, looking at the screen with her mouth open. But the pictures have gone.

"Who is he?"

"Harry Kimber... I know him from way back... we both started out in journalism together."

"He's a journo?"

"Not any more, no. He's in the hedge fund industry."

"Wise man," says Charlotte. The news report is showing bodies being wheeled out on trolleys under blankets. "Oh, God, is he one of those, do you think?"

"I don't think so," says Mary. "I think they're saying he and Max are wanted in connection with the killings."

"Who's Max?" asks Charlotte.

"Oh my God... Oh my God... Max... It's a long story," starts Mary, and then remembers she's talking to her editor. "He's the banker who got Harry out of journalism and into hedge funds. They're inseparable... Tweedle Dee and Tweedle Dum...

"I saw Harry for a drink just a couple of weeks ago; it seems they'd started acting as middle-men... 'concierges' he called it... for a Saudi billionaire. They'd just purchased this huge diamond worth millions and were going to sell it on to the Saudi at a vast profit. Only the Saudi's daughter set up a sting in a Geneva hotel..."

"Hold on... hold on," says Charlotte, who is struggling to keep up. "They're trading in diamond rings?"

"Hence why they're in Switzerland," continues Mary. "She stole the diamond basically, and vanished using diplomatic immunity. He was in a right state when I saw him, saying that he'd sold his house and liquidated all his assets in order to buy the diamond and was now left with nothing. He was pretty angry, but..."

"Okay, slow down," says Charlotte. "We need to talk to the

editor."

The editor, Tom Rivington, a slim, neat-looking man in his late thirties, is discovered over by the production desk, leaning over one of the subs and staring into his screen. Charlotte and Mary park themselves by his left shoulder.

"Hellooo," he says. "What's new?"

"A big one. Have you got a minute?" asks Charlotte.

"Of course," says Tom. "Shall we go to my office?"

His 'office' is Tom's sarcastic term for his desk in the corner of the open plan office. It's separate from the other desks, which is the only indication that it belongs to someone of importance at the newspaper, most of the other journalists elbow to elbow on long tables.

He perches on the edge of his desk, Mary noticing an incipient paunch beneath Tom's tight white shirt, as she and Charlotte relay the story between them.

"What do you think we ought to do?" he asks eventually.

"Well, shall I write up everything I know about the case so far?" says Mary. "Harry and Max's backgrounds and all that, and how they got themselves mixed up with the Saudis."

"Better get that all legalled if the Saudis are involved," says Charlotte.

"Good… yes… do we have anyone in Switzerland?" says Tom, but before he can get an answer, they notice another of the subs from the foreign desk approaching.

"Sorry to interrupt," says the young man, another shift-sub whose name Mary has forgotten. "I thought you ought to know. Harry Kimber's just been arrested at Gatwick. Lots of witnesses to the arrest apparently, and some mobile phone footage that's already on Sky and online. He's being done under the Terrorism Act."

CHAPTER FORTY-SEVEN

The man known to the Romans who worked at the port as 'the Calabrese', stands staring out of his office window. Even on the Saturday before Easter there is much activity on the wharves, as freighters dock and warehouses are stacked and emptied again.

He is in his late sixties, with thick, lustrous grey hair swept back to reveal a handsome face, spoilt only by pockmarked cheeks that are a legacy of teenage acne. But it was his natural self-confidence that had always won him the ladies, starting with his wife back in Calabria, and continuing with a string of mistresses as long as Italy itself, he likes to joke.

He first met the Saudi girl six months ago and she had appealed to him at once; she was a looker all right, but it was more than just that. Word had reached him, as all words at the port eventually did, that a Saudi woman was looking into freight transport from Tunisia, and Domenico had been immediately intrigued. What was a member of this wealthy elite doing sniffing around these dirty old docks? There had to be money in it.

One of his main men, Gianni, made contact and told the Saudi that his boss would be able to help with all her requirements, and although initially suspicious, Aafia soon found a perfect ally in this flirtatious but obviously highly intelligent businessman.

Domenico, for his part, liked Aafia at once. She seemed shrewd and hard working, and nothing like his own layabout sons who were spoilt rotten by their mother. In fact, Aafia – as she soon sensed as he talked about his family – was the daughter he never had.

She was only interested in the odd container here and there, but Domenico enjoyed her company so much that, unusually for him, he didn't allow this paucity of business to dismiss this cool-headed girl. He too had good instincts, and sensed that there was another, deeper story behind these modest shipments of carpets and vases and arak – the aniseed drink so beloved of Arabs. And let's face it, he thought, the Arabic taste in hard liquor was a growing market in Europe right now.

And Aafia had understood early on that Domenico was some sort of mafioso and had a hand in most of the port's activity. It was only later that she understood that he was not the Sicilian variety of mafiosi, but belonged instead to the Calabrian 'Ndrangheta.

From there, a spot of online research revealed that the 'Ndrangheta were considered more powerful than both the Cosa Nostra of Sicily and the Camorra of Naples, and their drug smuggling and other nefarious business interests represented three per cent of Italy's entire GDP. They were always on the lookout for legal businesses that could be used for money laundering, and this seemed like a useful avenue to explore.

Things had changed for Domenico as soon as the Arab man turned up – this Omar, with the scar and the dead eyes. He could tell that Aafia didn't like the man one little bit, but for some reason she had to tolerate him. He made his own enquiries and learned that Omar was being helped in his passage by the 'Ndrangheta family back in Reggio that was involved in the people-smuggling business.

He told Gianni to see what Omar wanted and, if possible, to help him. Gianni reported back various strange requests, including a water cannon. Gianni said he'd passed the request onto his Serbian contacts in Rome, who knew more about how to get their hands on this sort of stuff. The Serbians had been the ones, back in the 1990s, to supply the 'Ndrangheta with so many of their firearms – including, Gianni remembered, bazookas, and they were now well established in the arms trade.

Domenico owned a gym in Civitavecchia, which was part legitimate and part used for money laundering. One of the gym's phone numbers – rarely given out – was routed directly through to him, with a pre-ordained code. Anyone not using the exact form of words was brusquely told to contact the main reception – that this was the private number of the gym's owner.

Which is how he found himself talking to a breathless sounding

Aafia, who had escaped from Omar at a petrol station somewhere near Genoa. Once she had calmed down she was able to check her phone's GPS and give him the exact location. She then told him exactly what Omar intended to do with his water cannon. Domenico was shocked.

He had no love of the present Pope, who in 2014 had visited Calabria and excommunicated the 'Ndrangheta. "The adoration of evil and contempt of the common good," Pope Francis had said of the organisation, as if this Argentinian understood life in southern Italy. Domenico himself went to church-led religious festivals in the village of his birth, and even had a father confessor, who once explained to him that there was a difference between a sin and a crime. The sin of 'Mafia' doesn't exist, he told Domenico. Where is it written in the Bible?

All the same, Domenico understood how deeply religious are the people of Calabria. If an Islamic terrorist were to unleash a sarin attack on St Peter's Square on the holiest day in the church's calendar, and it was later revealed that the attacker had received the help of the 'Ndrangheta, the implications would be unthinkable. He phones Gianni.

"A matter of utmost urgency," he says without introductory pleasantries, so that Gianni knows it's important. "Drop everything. Get in touch with your Serbian contact at once and find out what happened to that riot water-cannon truck. We have to find it... today."

CHAPTER FORTY-EIGHT

Omar walks round the back of the building to discover the boy still happily spraying water into the field, and is glad to see him experimenting, alternating between a thin, hard jet and a diffuse spray, and moving the nozzle up and down, left to right, and back again.

He opens the passenger door, clambers up and slips in beside the boy, who grins proudly.

"Do you think you have the hang of it?" he shouts over the noise of water cannon engine.

The boy nods enthusiastically.

"Tomorrow we're going to have some fun with this, and nobody is going to get hurt. We're going to spray some kuffars. We're going to soak the infidel. A bit of a prank. You up for that?"

The boy nods again, grinning ear to ear.

"You proved your faith and your bravery and your devotion to your family by being willing to sacrifice yourself," he shouts some more. "Your reward will be this bit of fun. They won't like it and they'll be angry, but the worst they can do is lock you up for a few weeks. At least you'll get regular meals for a while. Do you like Italian food?"

The boy shrugs, then laughs.

"You do this for me and your family will welcome you back with open arms, the day you decide to return, or when they come to join you in Europe. You'll be a hero in every true-believing Muslim heart for making fools of the pagans."

The boy seems to celebrate this remark by shooting a high arc of water that splashes down into the field – uncultivated scrubland, for Omar didn't want a nosy farmer asking about his business – and giving Omar the thumbs up sign.

"I spoke to your mother this morning and she is happy that you are doing this, and not getting yourself killed," Omar lies. Well, it's a sort of lie. The boy's mother was murdered this morning, along with his father, sisters and uncles. The boy himself would be dead by this time tomorrow, so in that sense he would be joining his family.

Of course the truck itself is packed with explosives, which Omar will detonate using his mobile, just like the old days in Iraq. But this time he will have taken the fight to the heart of the enemy, to Rome on Christianity's most holy day. He will wait till the police and soldiers are swarming over it, having arrested the boy and the British spy. Then… boom! The icing on the cake, as the Australian jihadi used to say.

For now, the boy is happy – happy that he isn't going to have to die, and that he has the approval of the man with the scarred face. He wants to impress the man – he is like a second father to him.

"Now, I want you to use up all the water," says Omar, tapping a gauge on the control box, which shows that the tank is three-quarters empty. "I'm going to make us some supper."

Omar mimes eating, and then opens the cab door and jumps down. The boy watches him on the CCTV screen, striding off round the front of the building.

Lining the back wall of the warehouse are several dozen plain brown cardboard boxes, some of which are marked with a small black tick. Omar opens one of these and pulls out a bottle of colourless liquid, the label showing a brand of arak popular across the Middle East. Omar puts it back in the box, and counts the containers that have the black tick. There are eighteen in total, each containing twelve litres of sarin. That's just over 200 litres in total, a gift from the late Muammar Gaddafi.

In a grey, stainless steel cupboard in the corner hangs his yellow biohazard suit, which was priced at just over $4,000 on the Internet, he noted, but cost him just 500 euros from the Serbian who had supplied the water cannon. Apparently they had a job lot from when Syrian chemical weapons were transported to Italy a few years back, before an American warship had destroyed the chemicals at sea. He had tried on the suit several times, and although a size too small for him, it was possible to carry out quite fiddly operations while wearing it.

He would mix the sarin and water while the others slept tonight, which they would do soundly thanks to the barbiturates he was about to mix in with their last supper. The last supper, he repeated out loud, smiling. He knows enough about the prophet Jesus Christ to know that before he was crucified he shared a last meal with his disciples.

And on Easter Sunday Jesus rose from the dead, or so the Christians believe. This Easter Sunday, some of the most devout of these believers will die a horrible death, drooling, vomiting and shitting themselves in one of the holiest places in Christendom. TV cameras and countless mobile phones will be there to catch the moment. The Internet will broadcast his great victory.

And Omar himself will be there to witness it in person. He will stand at the back of the crowd, well out of reach of the water cannon and upwind, just in case any vapour was to blow in his direction. But the weather forecast for tomorrow is set to continue cloudless and without much breeze, just as it is today. Beautiful weather in which to receive the Pope's blessing.

At the back of the building next to the office is a small kitchen. Omar unpacks the two plastic shopping bags that are sitting on the sideboard. In one there are four potatoes, two large onions, two red peppers, two large cans of tomatoes, a head of garlic, a loaf of bread and a bunch of now rather wan and wilted coriander. The other bag contains three cans of iced tea and a bottle of temazepam.

CHAPTER FORTY-NINE

Harry has been in this cell for about an hour now – he can't tell exactly how long it's been because his phone and his Rolex have been confiscated, along with his belt and trainers. He has been alternately sitting and lying on the hard blue plastic mattress with its one folded blanket, and pacing up and down the room, trying to make sense of the police's questioning.

The detectives wouldn't answer any of his own questions, but to judge by their repeatedly asking about Max, Harry formed the opinion that Max was no longer at the chalet and isn't among the victims.

"Where is your friend now, Harry?" the woman had asked. She kept emphasising the word 'friend', like she was insinuating the opposite. "Where have you agreed to meet up?"

The residue from the gun he'd been handling for most of yesterday had shown up, of course, leading to the detectives accusing him of shooting Simon and his girlfriend. Why had Harry done that, the woman had asked? Was it because Simon had surprised them at the chalet? Did he like Simon? Did he perhaps owe him some money?

And then there was the business with the stolen diamond. Okay, the male detective had said, you kidnapped the Saudi woman and took her to Switzerland. What then? Did Simon object to what you had done? Did an argument ensue?

"No one kidnapped anybody," he kept repeating, keen to nip this one in the bud. The policewoman's smirk just got stronger.

Harry kept asking about whether they had checked with the Italian police about the terrorist hideout near Rome. Surely that would confirm his story.

But if that was true, the female detective put in, why hadn't they just gone to the Italian police and handed themselves in? Why drive all the way to Switzerland?

Harry kept explaining about the deal with Aafia's father, and suggesting that they contacted him directly. Was Aafia safe, he wanted to know? As with Harry's other questions, the detectives just ignored him.

"We can see that you reported the stolen diamond three weeks ago, but that the matter wasn't taken any further... was that because there was no stolen diamond? Were you laying the groundwork for a long con? Does this diamond you say is sitting in a bank vault – does it in fact belong to Aafia? Or to Simon? He's a rich man, able to run a private jet. Was the diamond intended for his girlfriend, who's also been murdered?

"Kylie... Kylie was murdered too?" blurts Harry. The two detectives don't reply, merely exchange glances.

Why didn't Harry contact the police as soon as he escaped from the chalet? What will they find, once the warrant has been issued, in the Swiss safety-deposit box? Why didn't he give himself up to the police in Geneva? Why had he attempted to flee to Britain? Was he a Muslim convert? Did he believe in jihad? Did he know they could keep him here for another twenty-eight days?

All Harry could think about was the diamond. Could they confiscate it, maybe as proceeds of a crime? Or perhaps as suspected funding for terrorism?

Max had escaped, he was sure of that or they wouldn't be asking Harry about his whereabouts. He thinks Aafia might have got away too. But then there were four bodies on the news item he had seen at Geneva airport, which would suggest that Max and Aafia had been killed by Omar. Maybe this was a double bluff to see whether or not Harry was surprised that Max and Aafia had escaped.

It suddenly made horrible sense that he would be the prime suspect. His motive was to steal the diamond, and killing the others would get rid of witnesses, and, in Max's case, the diamond's co-owner. The way he had coolly deposited the gem in a Swiss bank vault and then made good his escape to London. He was, in their eyes, doing a runner.

"I need to see a lawyer now," he says to the detectives.

"Sorry, no can do," the man replies. "Not yet. You're not being held on suspicion of shoplifting, you know. This is a multiple murder with possible terrorist involvement. By the way, I see you attended a 'Stop the War' rally in March 2003. Care to tell us about that?"

*　　*　　*

Max can no longer feel his feet or his hands, but the discomfort has been superseded for a while now by the sounds and smells of cooking. He hasn't eaten since yesterday evening and is now ravenous. He can hear Omar – he thinks it's Omar – chanting as he stirs the cook-pot and. From time to time he taps the wooden spoon on the pot's rim, like Max does when he cooks, which is rarely and ostentatiously.

His thoughts until now have been with his family, and his father and his sister telling him 'to do what he thinks is right', and his mother babbling on about the Buxtons coming over to play tennis. It was too weird, this collision of the mundane family life in Hampshire, the blamelessness of it… fuck, his childhood home… and the situation he finds himself in here, held captive by this fanatical terrorist for God knows what end.

And Max feels guilty for dragging them all into this mess with his deals and his moneymaking. And he blames Harry – Harry and his greed, his inability to let go when a deal goes bad. Where the fuck did Harry get to anyway? Why didn't he watch his back? That's what mates do. That's what Simon did outside that pub in Fulham.

The door is unlocked and opens. Max can sense rather than see the light from next door, and he hears Omar speaking in Arabic. There is someone with him, an accomplice.

The smell of the food is intense now. He hears something, a plate perhaps, being placed on a table, and some cutlery. More talking in Arabic. Are they going to eat in front of him? Is this a new form of torture?

And then he senses someone step behind him and can feel their hands on the back of his head. The blindfold is tugged off and Max finds himself staring at the scared face of a boy, an Arab boy of about twelve or thirteen. Omar is standing against the far wall with his arms folded and staring at Max – his eyes unreadable but a faint smirk on his lips.

He barks something at the boy, who picks up the bowl from the table and a spoon.

"He's going to feed you," says Omar. "It's not hot."

The boy scoops a spoonful of what looks like potato and tomato and draws it towards Max's mouth, but his hand is trembling. Omar says something encouraging to the boy, as if he were trying to calm a nervous animal, and he nods.

Max brings his mouth to meet the spoon and sucks up the contents which are warm and blissfully tasty. He chews but finds it hard to swallow.

"Water?" he asks.

Omar leaves the room and Max and the boy look at each other. The boy is obviously petrified of Max.

"My name's Max," he says, but the boy just shakes his head. He doesn't seem to speak English.

Omar returns, pulling the ring-top on a can of some sort of drink. Not Coca Cola, that's for sure, which is what Max is craving at the moment. It's a blue tin with *Brisk* written on the side in large cartoonish writing. Iced lemon tea. Omar motions for the boy to take the can and he brings it to Max's mouth. It tastes tepid and sweet, neither iced nor tea-like, but there's a hint of synthetic lemon.

"Shukran," says Max, having learned the Arabic for 'thank you' from his dealings with the Saudis.

"Al'afw," responds the boy. Omar barks something in Arabic, and the boy resumes spoon-feeding Max the vegetable stew. Max makes the same sort of greedily appreciative noises that he emits while having sex with Rachel.

CHAPTER FIFTY

"Tariq... we believe there will be a sarin attack on Rome, but where? In the metro, like in Tokyo?"

Tariq has been taken back to the hospital and allowed to sleep for three hours. But now Maurilio is back, accompanied by a handsome woman in her forties, with dark hair tied back to reveal a forcefully intelligent face. Maurilio had introduced her as Nadia Pizzuto of the anti-terrorist police.

"I've been lying here trying to think," says Tariq. "I can't remember where they were going to let off the sarin, or if I even knew. Perhaps I wasn't in on that secret. The boy I thought was maybe some sort of suicide bomber."

"He was," says the woman, Nadia Pizzuto. "We found a vest packed with explosives in his hotel wardrobe."

Tariq nods slowly. "Okay... of course... but there must have been a change of plan."

"My thoughts entirely," says Nadia Pizzuto. "We've identified all the dead men at the compound, by the way. One Libyan, one Iraqi and a Saudi national. The Saudi, it appears, might have been an agent for Al Mukhabarat, their secret service. Any idea about him?"

"Yes, he was our minder," says Tariq. Pizzuto's eyebrows shoot heavenwards.

"Well, he was there to look after the Saudi woman," says Tariq. "He's the one who helped her escape – her and the British men."

Maurilio and Pizzuto are looking at each other. They turn and say in unison: "The British men?"

*   *   *

A little under two weeks ago – it was a Tuesday evening, and an old friend had phoned me in a state of some distress. So I agreed to see him for a drink in our usual meeting place, a pub in Soho.

His name is Harry Kimber and when I first knew him, about fifteen years ago, we were both struggling to get a foothold in journalism. Movies were Harry's thing at the time, and we were both freelancers attending movie junkets and film festivals and picking up interviews with obscure directors and up-and-coming actors to sell to the nationals. We had a laugh together, and used to socialise some of the time, and I remember a funny, slightly shy bloke and I admit I quite fancied him at the time.

I soon got tired of all those self-absorbed actors, lecherous directors and obstructive PRs and found my real metier with foreign news. I started subbing shifts on various national papers, before I took the plunge and worked as a stringer in Cairo and then Istanbul for a couple of years, returning to London and getting a full-time job on the foreign news desk of this newspaper. But that's a different story. It certainly fucking is, Mary thinks angrily, to be made redundant and then hired back as a casual.

Harry and I used to meet up every six months, or whenever I was in town, by which time he'd ditched journalism and become a banker.

He began dressing very smartly and wearing expensive watches and generally looking completely out of place in our favourite Soho pub, but also on a deeper level he seemed to have changed. Our conversations became about money and property and stuff like that, whereas before money was never a topic because neither of us ever had any.

We met up about month ago and Harry told me how he and his partner in a Mayfair hedge fund had started servicing rich Arabs – one wealthy Saudi in particular – choosing property and diamonds for him and creaming off the profit. He called it 'concierge' work, and said that he and Max, his friend and co-partner at the hedge fund, were going to start self-financing these deals instead of piggy-backing on other people's money, but frankly I wasn't that interested. Sadly, I decided that the friendship had run its course and that we had nothing in common any more. I felt that Harry sensed that too, and that would be the last I heard of him.

And then I received this distressed phone call. It turned out that Harry had sold his house and liquidated most of his other assets so that he and Max could buy a beautiful diamond from a dealer in Geneva. They were going to sell it on to the Saudi, pocket a million pounds profit each, which would finance the next 'concierge' deal. And so on and so on until they were filthy rich and never had to work again.

But then it had all gone horribly wrong, he told me. They bought the diamond for several million pounds – I can't remember how much exactly now, but it was a lot of money. They were then summoned to a hotel in Geneva, ostensibly by the Saudi. Invited upstairs to a suite of rooms that his party had apparently booked out, and were allegedly met by his daughter who asked for the diamond to show her father.

Already behaving unconventionally and somewhat recklessly – they would never usually show a diamond off like this, it was usually in the ultra-secure offices of their gem dealer in the centre of Geneva – Harry and Max had grave misgivings at handing the diamond over to the daughter, a woman in her twenties who they knew only by sight. She had accompanied her father to a meal to celebrate a house purchase in Mayfair that Harry and Max had brokered.

This woman had insisted that she would show the diamond to her father, who was in the next room, and, despite their unease, Harry and Max had handed her the gem and, in effect, their whole worldly wealth. In fact the whole operation was, he said, an elaborate sting, and she had vanished with their diamond.

The police weren't interested once it was established that the Saudi woman enjoyed diplomatic immunity. And this was the situation when I agreed to meet Harry for a drink.

The only practical advice I was able to give Harry was the information that the father – some sort of diplomat or spy – had a country home in the UK, where he spent most weekends. His *daughter, whose name I had by this stage learned, supposedly lived in the house with him there…*

It wasn't going to win the Pulitzer Prize, but as a first draft of the situation, plainly stated, it wasn't bad. She could spruce it up later. Charlotte had told her to write a thousand words, but to let it run over if necessary. Mary glanced up at the clock on the pillar by the foreign desk, and continued to write.

I can't say what happened in the eleven days since I met up with Harry, but this afternoon the news broke that he had been arrested as he flew back to London Gatwick from Geneva. He's currently being held in Sussex under the Terrorism Act. His friend and diamond co-owner is on the run and wanted by Swiss police in connection with a multiple murder at a ski chalet in Verbier belonging to a British foreign exchange dealer by the name of Simon Fellowes, who is one of the victims.

The other victims are an unnamed British woman of about twenty years of age and two Swiss policemen. The truth of what happened in that chalet will no doubt emerge in the coming days and weeks, not least if and when Harry is released from custody and is able to tell his side of the story. My guess is that it will involve a Saudi woman and a missing diamond.

Not the most elegant report she has ever written, but Mary emails this draft to Charlotte, who picks it up at once and starts to read.

"Lovely, Mary," she says without removing her eyes from her screen. "That'll do nicely. I'm going to send this over to the lawyer as it is, and then I'm going to tighten it up in a couple of places. But, thanks, darling, that's great. Do you think we can find any pictures of Harry anywhere? What about his company website?"

CHAPTER FIFTY-ONE

Max wakes from a dreamless sleep and can't tell whether the low drumming sound is in his head or on the outside. The light in the room is on, a strip light that hurts his eyes. He's still handcuffed with his arms behind his back, but his legs have been untied, so he sits up and immediately wishes he hadn't.

A powerful ache in his forehead spreads down behind his eyes, a wave of nausea passes and returns, and Max throws up all over the thin mattress that he has been laid down on. By Omar presumably. Lumps of potato and red pepper – last night's stew – are spread out in front of him like evidence of some sort of obscure crime he can't remember committing.

The vomiting helps ease the headache, but now his neck feels painfully stiff from where he has been lying with hands behind his back. His right shoulder has seized up as well, and hurts when he tries to sit upright. He props himself up against the wall, neck bent like the Hunchback of Notre Dame, and remains still with his eyes closed.

There is definitely a rumbling noise, and it seems to be coming from the other side of the wall, which he can now feel vibrating slightly. He opens his eyes and notices the boy with his back to him, fast asleep on a similar mattress to the one Max has just been sick on.

Max doesn't remember falling asleep. The boy had fed him the rest of the stew, and Omar had taken the empty bowl and left, leaving Max and the boy staring helplessly at each other, unable to communicate in each other's language. He remembers feeling suddenly tired and fighting to keep his eyes open. And now this. What time is it? Is it night or day? How long has he been asleep?

The rumbling noise stops, and Max can just make out the sound of Omar clumping about next door. Something is being dragged across the floor, a scraping noise, and then the rumbling noise resumes. Another wave of nausea hits him, but he manages not to throw up this time.

God, he hasn't felt this bad since the morning after his stag do all those years ago, a twenty-four-hour drink and drugs extravaganza that featured the usual dangerous sports and strippers. Had Simon arranged it? God, Simon. Poor Simon. His best mate probably. A truer mate than Harry.

Max spits out a chunk of vegetable.

Rachel hadn't shown him any mercy with his hangover. She insisted he take her out to lunch at the Wolsey, and Max had been sick in the toilets. She laughed when he told her and said it served him right. He thinks she went to Ibiza for her hen weekend; he can't remember now.

The rumbling stops again, and Max tries to work out how Omar managed to untie him from the chair, untether the ropes from his legs, and lie him down on a mattress without waking him. The stew must have been drugged. That must be the slightly chemical aftertaste he has in his mouth now. Oh, well, probably for the best. He wouldn't have slept otherwise.

There is a key turning in the lock and the door opens, and Omar is standing there, his shirt patched with sweat and his face puce. He looks at Max, impossible to read as always, except that one time in the chalet when Max had said 'So this is war', and Max had felt something akin to fellowship. Omar frowns and Max sees that he's looking at the vomit-covered mattress.

He walks over to the boy and kicks him hard in the bottom. The boy jerks up and looks around blearily with half-closed eyes, unable to shake off the drugged sleep.

"Come… it's morning," he says, followed by something in Arabic, and the boy, re-orientated, gets to his feet and follows Omar out of the room. By pressing his back and shoulders in the wall, Max also manages to writhe up to his feet, which he stamps on the ground to try and get some feeling into them. His forehead starts throbbing again, so he stands with his eyes closed. Another wave of nausea comes and goes.

The boy returns and he's holding a red enamel mug out in front of him and a hunk of bread, nervously like he's feeding a wild beast. The mug, Max can smell, contains coffee. Black coffee. He brings his lips to it and drinks, and then spits the scalding liquid back into the cup.

The boy backs away, but Max motions to him that it's okay, and mimes the fact that the drink is too hot by making blowing noises. The boy seems to understand, and offers him the bread instead. Max nods and clamps his teeth into it. It's hard and stale. His mouth still tastes metallic.

In this fashion he manages to drink the coffee and eat some of the bread, but more importantly, he feels, to build some trust and understanding with the boy. By the time he's finished this paltry breakfast, a bond of sorts has been created.

Omar reappears. He's been splashing water on his face, his hair is combed back and he has a fresh shirt on. He wouldn't exactly gain entry to the smarter restaurants in Mayfair, but he looks a good deal better than he did a few minutes ago. He also has his gun once more to hand.

"Okay, let's go," he says, indicating the direction of travel with the muzzle. Max follows him through the office he remembers from yesterday, through another door, through which he notices a small kitchen where Omar must have cooked his narcotic stew, and into a huge space where is parked a large olive green truck.

"You drive this?" Omar asks.

He has once, something similar, but a long time ago. A friend at school had been a farmer's son and one summer when he was sixteen Max had helped with the corn harvest. This involved driving an old lorry, he remembered, although he can't now remember why.

"I think so," he says. "Bit like driving a car, only slower."

"Good," says Omar. "You drive."

"Drive where?" Max asks, and Omar holds up a satnav in reply. "This tell you where. I follow. You follow instructions." And to emphasise the point, he waves his pistol.

"I might need these taking off," says Max, holding up his wrists. He's feeling weirdly cocky.

Omar walks up to him and strikes Max across the cheek with the back of the pistol. Max falls to his knees and thinks he can taste his own bone. Something weird anyway, cartilage from his nose perhaps? Then Omar's boot lands in his stomach, winding Max, who rolls onto his back, wondering where the next blow will land.

It doesn't arrive. Instead Omar is leaning over him and unlocking the handcuff from one wrist. Max's hands, newly liberated, feel alien to him. He shakes his arms as if they belong to someone else, the handcuffs jiggling from the end of his right arm.

"Stand up," says Omar, and Max rolls over on his side, and using the hand that is his but not his, he pushes himself into an upright position. He notices the boy looking at him. Scared.

"It's all right," he says to the boy. "We're going for a drive. That's all. A drive." The boy stares back at him dumbly.

Once Max is standing Omar shoves him in the small of the back towards the truck.

"Get in," he says.

Max clambers up into the driver's seat.

"Put your hands on the wheel," commands Omar, and Max obeys. With a swift movement, Omar secures the open handcuff to the steering wheel, and there he is – attached to the truck. "Until death do us part," he says. Omar stares at him for a moment, almost another recognition of humanity, like back in the chalet. But then he's gone, and the boy is climbing up into the passenger seat.

Max looks down at the aluminium box sitting to the right of the gear lever. It has four buttons, a gauge and a joystick, like some sort of homemade model aeroplane kit.

He can see Omar fiddling with the satnav. Seemingly satisfied, he now jumps up next to the boy and places the satnav on the dashboard, next to what looks like a small TV screen.

"Okay, let me tell you what's going to happen," says Omar, before pointing his pistol at Max. "You are going to drive into Rome following the instructions on the satnav. I will be right behind you, and any deviation will end in your deaths. Do you understand?"

Max says, "Yes." The boy seems transfixed by the aluminium box.

"When the satnav tells you that you have reached your destination, then the boy will set off the water cannon. The people it's aimed at won't be harmed – perhaps a few minor injuries if they slip over. This is simply an exercise in humiliation. No one will be killed. Understand?"

Max nods, but feels confused. Why would this man, who shows absolutely no hesitation in killing people, be wanting to hose them now with water? Is this his terrorist master plan, to soak a load of strangers? To force them to go home and take a change of clothing?

"Why?" he finds himself saying.

"The people you will firing the water cannon at are devout Catholics gathered in St Peter's Square to hear the Pope. This great act of sacrilege will be on global TV."

You're mad, he thinks. Why not shoot them dead, like in Paris? Or just drive into them, as in Nice?

"Okay, we're going to soak a load of old nuns and priests," he says.

"Yes," says Omar. "And tourists."

"And tourists…"

"But you mustn't start until the satnav tells you that you have arrived."

"Understood," says Max, who is wondering how any armed police stationed at the Vatican might react to a water cannon arriving in St Peter's Square and blowing people over with a jet stream, even if they managed to get that far. There's a steel mesh over the windscreen and he noticed earlier what looked like a sort of snowplough attached to the front. Some protection at least.

"What if the police try to stop us before we get to St Peter's?" he asks.

"Just smash on through, remembering your families back home. And then pray."

Oh, I'll be praying, thinks Max. But not to your God.

CHAPTER FIFTY-TWO

Nadia Pizzuto has hardly slept. By the time she did get to bed, just after two, restless dreams were interspaced with periods of anxious wakefulness, and by the time her alarm goes off at six o'clock, she isn't sure whether she has been lying there fretting or dreaming about lying there fretting.

Is there something more she can do? Of course a red alert, the highest level of warning of an imminent terrorist attack, has been issued to all the relevant agencies. The Vatican, which has its own army and police force, but which falls under the jurisdiction of the Italian state in matters such as this, has been informed.

Police checkpoints have been set up on all major routes into the city centre, with patrols at all city centre Metro stations and on trains. These patrols have been issued with gas masks, and with most of what little stocks of the sarin antidote that could be found at such short notice. The government has made a secret emergency application to Washington for further stocks, but Pizzuto doesn't know if and when these might arrive, and some wag in the office had suggested they approach the Mafia instead.

The investigation into the hotel has led to a 'Ndrangheta family in Reggio with a history of people-smuggling and sex trafficking, but already established wiretaps revealed nothing further. Forensics are still looking at the suicide vest found in the wardrobe.

Police all over Italy are on the lookout for a specific blue Audi A6, with number-plate recognition cameras primed to pick it up, while CCTV at the motorway toll booths tracked the car to eighty kilometres to the north of Rome yesterday afternoon, seemingly headed in their direction.

Swiss police finally stormed the chalet in Verbier to find two dead policemen and two dead British nationals – the chalet owner and an unidentified female. They have also picked up a small quantity of drugs, a load of spent ammunition but no guns, and a Mercedes people carrier that could be traced to Rome, to a luxury private rental company that deals mainly with super-rich Russians and Arabs. The owner has already been paid a visit, but refuses to divulge the names of any of his clients.

The two British fugitives are Maximilian Draycott and Harry Kimber, Kimber having already been detained on his arrival back in London on a flight from Geneva yesterday afternoon. Draycott's whereabouts are unknown, although he is thought to be a passenger in the Audi A6, along with a Saudi national, Aafia, who possesses a diplomatic passport.

Pizzuto has slept in the guest bedroom to allow her husband a decent night's sleep, and now slips into a dressing gown and pads downstairs. Her nine-year-old is already awake and she can hear him talking to himself in his bedroom, absorbed in some imaginary game. How much she'd like to join him and give him lots of cuddles, but she feels that there won't be much family time in the coming days and weeks.

Making a cup of coffee, she scrolls through the emails and phone message that have arrived while she's been sleeping, and two catch her immediate attention. The Saudi national, Aafia, caught a flight from Genoa to Frankfurt yesterday evening at eight o'clock. She was met at Frankfurt by a diplomatic mission that whisked her off into the night.

The second message again related to the Saudi national. Early yesterday afternoon she made a phone-call to a gymnasium in Civitavecchia, a gym belonging to a known member of the 'Ndrangheta.

"Strange," Pizzuto says to herself, taking a sip off coffee. "Very strange."

CHAPTER FIFTY-THREE

"Why were you carrying a gun?" asks the new man, who has identified himself as DS Philip Johns of the Metropolitan Police Anti-Terrorism Unit. He has joined the two detectives from yesterday, who both seem to defer to him.

The night in the police cell had been cold until he asked for an extra blanket and, to his surprise, was given one. The plastic mattress was hard, but he was tired, and he had slept surprisingly soundly until woken up for breakfast. Two slices of toast with margarine and a bowl of cornflakes.

"As I've already said," replies Harry. "The guy who claimed he was from the Saudi secret services handed me his gun after he untied me in that hell-hole in Rome."

"Saudi secret services... it's all a bit far-fetched don't you think?" asks DS Johns, a man of about Harry's age, trim-looking and with close-cropped hair disguising his premature balding. "Isn't the truth of the matter that, for perhaps good reason, you felt you'd been ripped off by the Saudi woman - Aafia, did you say her name was? – and simply went after her to kidnap her and get your diamond back?"

"What do the Italian police say?" answers Harry, eager to change the subject. "Do they say I'm imagining that place in Rome?"

DS Johns doesn't reply. Instead he tries a different tack.

"Why didn't you phone the police in Verbier until you were in Martigny, nearly half an hour away on the train? Why not simply find help as soon as possible once you'd escaped the immediate vicinity of the chalet?"

"I did phone the police from Verbier."

"Let me correct you... your call to the police was actually traced to Martigny, nearly thirty minutes away. You claimed to be in Verbier, but Harry, I'm afraid we've caught you out in a lie."

"Verbier... Martigny... it was all the same to me. I was in shock," says Harry. "Until the other day I'd never had anyone point a gun at me, but in the last two days it's happened twice, the second time I was actually shot at..."

"So you say..."

"Because that's what happened," says Harry. "When I got to the cable car in Verbier that takes you down to the train station I was in full flight mode. It was only when I got on the train to Martigny that I felt safe. And then I tried phoning the police, but couldn't get a signal. You can ask a Monsieur Remy if you can track him down, because he tried to help me. Also, when I was picked up by the VW camper van we passed a police car shooting past, and I assumed – or hoped – that they were headed to the chalet..."

"They were headed to their deaths," says Johns, reading through some notes. "Both men in their twenties, married with children."

Harry waits. Does this require an answer?

"I'm sorry about that," he says at length. "But what has that got to do with me?"

"But back to the VW camper van," says Johns. "The witnesses say that you were in good spirits. You don't sound like you were in shock at all."

"The witnesses were stoned," says Harry. "And drunk. But the point is that I was relieved to have escaped. If that's the same as being in good spirits, then I was in good spirits."

"I see," says Johns, and there's something about the way he makes that sound, as if Harry had incriminated himself, that bothers Harry.

"Have you heard of self-preservation?" he says against his better judgement that you shouldn't embark on a philosophical conversation with a policeman while under caution.

"I've heard of cowardice", says Johns, obviously glad of the opening.

"If cowardice is not wanting to die, then, yes, I was a coward."

"Cowardice is leaving your friend to die."

"Okay, I want a lawyer now," he says, then noticing the recording device, adds, "I've answered all your questions now, you're just asking the same ones all over again."

"What did you do with your gun?"

"I already told you," says Harry. "I left it on the table by the back door so that the others could use it."

"Did you tell the others that that's what you were doing?"

"No, because I hadn't decided to make a run for it at that stage," says Harry. "It was only when I saw Omar sitting in the car that I decided to leg it."

"Without warning the others," says Johns unpleasantly. "I think I'm beginning to build a picture now. But one question that I do keep coming back to is why you waited until you reached Martigny to phone the police?"

"I've already answered that. I want a lawyer."

"In shock, you say. Or just plain scared?"

"No comment," says Harry.

"And then to fly back to London when your best friend, as far as you know, is being held captive by a terrorist in Switzerland. Sounds a bit callous to me."

"No comment."

"Was Max your best friend?"

"No comment."

"You weren't sleeping with his wife then?"

"Who told you that?"

"His wife."

And there's an insinuating leer on Johns' lips as he stares back at Harry.

"Is that why you ran back to England, leaving... how shall we put this... your love rival in mortal danger from a murdering terrorist? Were you hoping that Max would in fact be killed, leaving the way clear for you and Rachel? Call me old-fashioned, but that doesn't sound like the actions of a best friend to me."

"That's not the way it is," says Harry, properly flustered for the first time in this interview. "It was over between me and Rachel."

"Really?" says Johns, leaning in towards Harry. "That's not the way she sees it. Have you told her it's over?"

*   *   *

Mary walks back from the newsagent with a bottle of skimmed milk and the morning newspaper. Every single paper is leading with the story, headlines ranging from *Britons slain in Alps massacre* and *Brits dead in Isis Swiss attack* to *Terror on the ski slopes* and *Murder in the chalet: Britons dead in Swiss terror attack.* All variations on the same theme.

Her own 'first-person' piece is on page three, following the news stories of the event. The headline reads: *My friend the British terror suspect. Are a stolen diamond and a mysterious Saudi beauty keys to the Swiss chalet massacre?'*

Mary stops walking to read the piece, half-cringing because she knows it was a rush job. Charlotte has tightened up the prose and punctuation, and added a couple of paragraphs to give some background information, while the picture desk have found a photograph of Harry looking very smart and rather smug, a publicity shot for Max and Harry's company. She had no idea that Harry's hedge fund was called Forward-Max Capital LLP. How vain of Max to name it after himself.

Next to her article is a short piece entitled *The Rise of the Concierges to the Super-rich,* a quick summary of the different ways in which enterprising Britons are making a good living from providing their services to the global nouveau-riche pouring into London.

She's just finishing folding the paper when her phone rings. It's BBC radio wondering whether she could come along to Broadcasting House to discuss her feature. She feels she ought to but instead tells a lie – a half-lie – that she's not in London. Actually she and Ben had set aside today to take a look around Sidcup and see if there was anywhere they could bear to buy a flat. God, how depressing.

CHAPTER FIFTY-FOUR

The first part of the journey is easy enough, round slip roads and on to dual carriageways, Omar in view from the rear-facing CCTV camera, following in his little Fiat Panda. The truck takes a long time to get up to speed, but, once it does, it trundles along quite nicely. Just about everybody in every car that passes stares out at the truck, and one driver even gives Max the thumbs-up signal. A fan of the riot police, presumably.

The boy keeps looking at the water-cannon controls, lightly touching the buttons and talking to himself. He seems to be taking his task extremely seriously.

The whole thing just seems increasingly bizarre to Max, and he can't help wondering if there is more to the exercise that merely giving the Catholic faithful a good dousing. But what else, unless it is something other than water that will be gushing out of the cannon on the truck roof?

As they approach the denser suburbs around Rome, Omar pulls out ahead of them and puts on his flashing emergency lights. Max eases up and pulls to a stop on the hard shoulder. Omar walks round to Max's door and pulls it open.

"I'm turning off at the next junction," he says, "but you carry on following the instructions on the satnav. Okay?"

"Okay," says Max.

"Don't forget. If you want to see your family again, do exactly as I have told you."

"Okay," says Max.

Omar slams the door closed and returns to his car. Off they go again, but at the next junction, Omar turns off. The satnav tells Max to continue for the next one-point-two kilometres and then to exit right on to the A90.

As he swings down on to a roundabout, Max notices two

motorcycle policemen standing next to their bikes surveying the traffic through sunglasses. The cops' gaze follows the truck as it approaches the junction to the roundabout and Max feels certain they are going to call him to a halt. Instead they turn their attention to a car that is following the truck, ordering it to stop. Max can see them on the CCTV, leaning in through the car's windows.

As they exit the roundabout Max finds that they are driving along proper city boulevards now, with cafes and shops and apartment blocks, and people on the pavement – all of them, more or less, stopping to stare as the truck rumbles past. The boy is still touching the water-cannon buttons like they were good luck charms, talking to himself.

Glancing at the CCTV, Max realises that he has been tailgated by the same black Range Rover for about a hundred metres now. Other cars are overtaking but this one – in fact two, there's another one directly behind it – are stubbornly sticking to the truck's slipstream. He'll soon have a better idea as to whether they're following or not, because in fifty metres he has to take a left down a more minor road.

The Range Rovers do indeed follow suit, down a one-way street lined with parked cars. Max pulls up behind a dustcart that doesn't seem to be going anywhere in a hurry. He honks his horn and then turns his attention to the two cars behind him. Several tough-looking men in jeans and bomber jackets, all of them wearing balaclavas, are emerging from the cars.

The truck doors swing open and masked faces appear, as do handguns. The boy starts shouting, but he's pulled out of the cab, a gloved hand clasped over his mouth. Max doesn't understand what's being shouted at him in Italian, but he can guess that he's been asked to get out of the lorry. A gloved hand reaches in and pulls the keys from the ignition.

As one of the men start pulling Max from the cab, he yells and shakes the hand that is handcuffed to the steering wheel. The man shouts something in Italian to his comrade, who shouts something back and heads off to the lead Range Rover. Swearing under his breath, the man puts the muzzle of the pistol right up against the handcuff.

"*Asptetta!*" shouts the comrade, passing up a large pair of bolt cutters.

"Thank God," says Max, as the cutters slice though the handcuff chain, leaving it dangling from the steering wheel.

Max now feels himself being lifted out of the cab. Two men half carry him to the rear Range Rover, as the man with the bolt cutters now jumps into the truck's driver's seat. The dustcart starts to move forward, followed by the water-cannon truck, as Max's head is pressed down, just like he's seen in the movies when a suspect is put into a police car, as he's manoeuvred onto the back seat of the Range Rover. The boy, he presumes, is in the lead car.

And now they are off, the whole operation having lasted less than a minute. As the dustcart and the truck take a left, the Range Rovers carry straight on, Max's minders obviously in no mood to make conversation.

"Police?" he asks, although something about the men suggests that they are nothing of the sort. The two men in the back with Max continue to look straight ahead through the eye-slits of their balaclavas, while the driver picks up speed, the front passenger on the lookout for other vehicles.

The two cars pull up near a large building that looks like a railway station, and the boy emerges from the last Range Rover. And then they are off again, the boy just standing on the pavement, a dazed look on his face. Max never did get to find out his name.

CHAPTER FIFTY-FIVE

In Fulham, Hugo Fairbrother has just had a rather vexing conversation with his sixteen-year-old son, Fergus. The morning had started out pleasantly enough, with the exchange of chocolate Easter eggs, and Radio Three in the background as Fairbrother sank his teeth into a slice of wholemeal bread, butter and marmalade made by his second wife, Lulu. And then the subject had turned to Fergus's choice of A-level subjects, which seemed unlikely to fit the boy for any worthwhile profession.

"English, psychology and art," he repeated. "Art?"

"Yes, art, Papa... you know, painting and drawing and things," drawled Fergus, slurping his tea. A shock of hair sat up vertically from his head. Had he forgotten to comb it, or was this the latest style? You really couldn't tell these days, like those youths he sometimes ended up representing who wander about with their jeans halfway down their legs.

"Painting and drawing? My word, that's very old school of you," said Fairbrother. "I thought they didn't teach those things any more. It's all video and conceptual and requiring absolutely zero amount of talent as far as I can see."

"Maybe I could try my hand at advertising..."

Saved by the bell, or rather his mobile phone, as Fairbrother takes a call from Stephen Cheswright, his fellow partner at Fairbrother, Cheswright and Burgess, criminal lawyers to the seriously rich. The Saudis had been in touch – there's a client that needs rescuing from the police down in Sussex.

"Crawley... do you know it?" asks Cheswright.

"Can't say I've had the pleasure," replies Fairbrother.

"Well, there's no pleasure to be had in Crawley as far as I know. When can you get down there?"

* * *

The custody sergeant has seen all sorts in his time, but this is a new one. For a start he is vast, by which he means fat or overfed, with a belly the size of a beached whale. The face is a ruddy ball, topped off by unruly ringlets of blond hair. He looks like Billy Bunter after the midnight feast to end all midnight feasts.

The man seems genial enough, but something about his manner tells the sergeant to beware.

"Can I help you, sir?"

"Oh hello," the man says. "I believe you are entertaining a client of mine."

"I see, sir, and what would be the name of your client that we are, er, entertaining."

"Ah, yes, thank you. The name is Harry Kimber and I believe that you are holding him under the misapprehension that he is some sort of terrorist. It must be bewildering for the poor fellow and I would so like to sit in and give him a helping hand."

The sergeant, who had rather been enjoying this show, reluctantly unpeels himself from the desk, "Hold on, sir, I will go and make further enquiries."

"If you would, that would be simply marvellous."

"Simply marvellous," the sergeant echoes with a chuckle as he goes to find the detective from the Met, Johns or whatever his name was, who had turned up this morning. "Simply marvellous."

* * *

Johns is less amused by the man's manner than the desk sergeant, but mainly because this enormous apparition knows full well how to make his life difficult. No grubby street brief this, or underachieving high-street solicitor, but a very dangerous, purring cat.

Here, in short, is the sort of brief who knows the ins and outs of every tiny clause of every bit of legislation and every minor piece

281

of case law – deep knowledge and experience, enough to scare off the CPS, but all wrapped up in a pretty ribbon – and the image he projects of a bluff fellow doesn't wash with the experienced detective.

Worse is that he reeks of what Johns called 'the establishment'. This Fairbrother had not only probably been to school with every other top judge in the land, he was probably godfather to their children as well.

"You may morally disapprove of my client's behaviour," the lawyer is saying now, jowls wobbling as he does so. "But that doesn't mean he has broken the law."

Harry is relieved to have this man on his side, because he was beginning to wilt this morning; he was beginning not so much to doubt himself than to dislike himself. That was very clever of Johns – even if he only sensed the half of it. Self-loathing – something that followed Harry like a shadow - might be dangerous in a situation like this. But what is making him feel uneasy now is the fact that the Saudi is paying for this eccentric but patently top-drawer solicitor. Why would that be?

Johns is digging in though. "Failure to report a crime is a crime in itself," he is saying.

"You know the ins and outs of Swiss law, do you?" Fairbrother hits back. "Goodness me, all those different cantons… all those different laws. Surprised they manage to make such elegant timepieces."

"I should think it's a pretty universal doctrine," says Johns.

"You should think? Or you do think? Or you know?"

"Yes, yes, yes," says Johns, determined not to be out-smarted. "Your client has been in possession of firearms."

"So has just about every Swiss citizen over the age of eighteen," says Fairbrother. "It's their patriotic duty. You're not an upright Swiss citizen if you don't own a gun and a nuclear bunker."

Johns decides to ignore the lawyer, addressing Harry instead on a point that he senses makes Harry evasive. "Why did you kidnap the Saudi girl?"

"I shouldn't humour the police by answering that question if I were you," says Fairbrother. "They're fishing. Goodness me, next they'll be claiming you're a member of Islamic State."

"Are you?" says Johns, instantly annoyed at himself for falling for this diversion.

"All right... enough," says Fairbrother, bringing his hands together like a particularly corpulent priest in prayer. "It seems quite plain to me that what you have here is a sensational story – one, by the way, that our friends in the media are all over so we had best write them all a stern letter of warning – but nothing else apart from that. My client has helped with all your enquiries, and now you must allow him to leave. Bail him if you must. He's plainly not a terrorist, but a victim of terrorism..."

"Sir?" The door has opened, and it's the badly dressed woman from yesterday.

"What is it?" asks Johns irritably.

"I think you should hear the latest."

Harry and Fairbrother look at each other as Johns leaves the room.

"Don't worry," the lawyer is saying. "We'll soon have you out of here."

"He says he can keep me here for twenty-eight days," says Harry.

"Well, that's a lie to start with – it's now a maximum of fourteen days, but only with the consent of a magistrate. There's not enough here to warrant that, I can assure you."

But when Johns returns he has a triumphant look on his face.

"Well, well, Mr Kimber," he says. "Your friend Max has just given himself in to the Italian police. He admits to have been executing an attack on St Peter's Square in Rome using sarin gas. Happy Easter."

CHAPTER FIFTY-SIX

Omar parks the Fiat on a side street near the Valle Aurelia Metro station – one of the reasons he chose such a small model being the potential need to squeeze into a small space on Rome's notoriously cluttered thoroughfares.

He feels like a man on a sunny Sunday stroll as he jogs up the steps of the graffiti-covered metro station. The infidels of the West are so careless of their public spaces. What does all this mess say about their state of their souls?

And then he spots the policemen – three of them, clearly scrutinising the passing public, more than likely on the look-out for a Middle Eastern-looking man with a prominent scar down his cheek. Omar also notices that two of the cops are carrying gas masks – he recognises the casing, a similar shape and styling to the masks he used in Libya while practising mixing the sarin.

Do they know about the chemical weapon? The Saudi whore will have told them, of course, and they're making an educated guess that the Metro system might be a target.

It was his fault for being greedy. He should have finished her off in Switzerland, along with the British spy, but she had promised him the diamond – the one worth £5 million. Stupid, stupid Omar. This is what you get for coveting riches down here on earth, when they are but dust. All the riches he could want await him in the next life.

He mustn't be too hard on himself, though. The money wasn't for its own sake but to finance the next stage in the jihad, whenever that was revealed to him. He had already seen how easy it is to buy anything you want if you have enough money and the right contacts.

And the diamond would have paid for the plastic surgery he now needs. And that isn't anything to with vanity. It's a necessity. If he is to continue with the Prophet's calling, he needs to get rid of that scar, or cover it up somehow.

He pulls out a street map from his jacket pocket and opens it out, head bent, scar away from the cops. He's already marked out the best route and now he looks round to get his bearings. The Via Anastasio II is over there, which loops down towards St Peter's Square. It's not very direct but he calculates that has about twenty minutes before the fun begins. Just time enough.

*   *   *

The water-cannon truck has been driven to a quarry on the north-eastern outskirts of Rome. High up and from a safe distance upwind, Gianni watches the flames lick the under-side of the vehicle – any moment now the fuel tank will ignite and there will be a loud bang, the sort of noise that comes ricocheting out of this quarry several times a day, although not usually on a Sunday.

When the explosion comes, it's far louder and more percussive than Gianni had expected. The shockwave hits him even up here, and bits of the truck are flying through the air, landing in a cascade of fireballs around what little remains of the vehicle.

"Mamma mia... it was booby-trapped!" he says to himself. "That was a bomb." He had better not tell the others, or they might be a bit upset with him.

A cloud of vapour sits above the smoking remains and gently disperses in the direction of the coast. In coming days, doctors will receive reports of villagers two kilometres downwind of the quarry having streaming eyes and noses – the first hay fever of the season it's widely suspected – and there was an outbreak of a sickness bug. Nothing too serious. No one required hospitalisation.

He taps a number on his phone, and receives the one-word reply: 'Pronto'. And in the far-off distance he can just make out the sound of a bulldozer engine being started up. The driver, wearing exactly the same make of biohazard suit that had been sold to Omar – after all, it was from the same stock – aims the bulldozer at the what remains of the truck, shepherding the bits of twisted, smoking debris towards a pit dug in the quarry floor. Having tidied up, the machine now drives rubble on top of this unmarked grave.

CHAPTER FIFTY-SEVEN

Nadia Pizzuto, Maurilio Marcone, a public prosecutor well known to them both by the name of Carlo Matteini, and a man from the Ministry of the Interior – name unknown – are looking at Max through a one-way window. He is side-on to them, unshaven, his left cheek badly bruised and a far-away look in his eyes. The handcuff is still attached to a wrist that droops down by his side. It's not that they don't believe his story, but they can't quite make sense of it.

He had walked up to a traffic policeman on the Piazza della Repubblica and tried to explain who he was, but the cop just thought he was a lost tourist and suggested he went to the tourist office. It was a civilian, a local florist, who had recognised Max from the television news and interceded in Italian. The traffic policeman suddenly became very interested and a little nervous, brandishing his gun around in a reckless manner. The florist, a sensible man, stepped in to say that Max wasn't armed and, as far as he could see, not dangerous.

So now they know how Omar intended to distribute his sarin – mixed with water and pumped out of a riot water cannon. Diabolical. But where is the water cannon now?

According to Signor Draycott, he had been handcuffed to the wheel of the truck, while an Arab boy of about twelve or thirteen – presumably the one that Omar had collected from the Mafia-owned hotel – had been trained to use the water cannon. It was all to have been a bit of fun, Omar had explained to the boy, while to Max he said that the humiliation of soaking and dispersing the Roman Catholic faithful on this, their most holy of days, would be a sufficient end in itself.

To Signor Draycott's credit, he hadn't quite believed Omar, but couldn't think what else he had in mind. What if he had known it was diluted sarin he was driving into St Peter's Square, with the potential to kill hundreds of pilgrims?

"That doesn't bear thinking about," Max had said.

"These men in the balaclavas and black Range Rovers," Pizzuto says now. "They were obviously tipped off in advance, but by whom? And who are they?"

"Well, leaving aside the police and the military," says Maurilio. "That just leaves the Mafia. They're the only other group with the organisational ability to pull this off."

"Agreed," says the man from the ministry, the first word he has contributed all afternoon.

Pizzuto and Maurilio look at each other, say simultaneously: "The 'Ndrangheta!"

"The Calabrians? But why?" asks the man from the ministry.

"We don't know," says Pizzuto. "But we do know that the Saudi national known as Aafia, before she fled to Germany, made a phone call to a gym in Civitavecchia owned by a 'Ndrangheta family boss."

"Any recent sightings of the water cannon?" asks the public prosecutor.

"Plenty – or rather too many," says Pizzuto. "We have witnesses that saw it leaving the centre of Rome in every direction except up into space. And I'm expecting an eye-witness account of that, complete with aliens, any moment now."

"What about verifiable CCTV?" asks the man from the ministry.

"We're working on it," says Pizzuto.

"Everything Signor Draycott has said tallies with Tariq's account," says Maurilio. "A part of my training in interview techniques was in spotting lies and evasions, and I am pretty certain everything he has told us is the truth. My instincts tell me this too. Without strapping him to a polygraph there's no way for certain of knowing, but I'd bet my apartment on his honesty."

"What now then?" asks the man from the ministry.

Pizzuto is staring intently at Max, who is now running his hand through his hair, and looking around the room, as if taking in his whereabouts for the first time.

Her phone rings. It's her deputy. They've heard from the English police and Signor Draycott's story pans out. His parents were indeed visited by gunmen.

"Let him speak to his parents," says Pizzuto. "Record the call, of course. Maurilio, you speak English – go down and listen."

The public prosecutor and the man from the ministry both nod their agreement.

*　*　*

"Maxi, darling, are you okay?" It's his mother's voice. He's glad she can't see him. He thinks of Nicky, and it gives him strength. There are worse things in the world than what he's been through.

"I'm fine, Mummy," he says; it seems funny to saying 'Mummy' in this police station after all that has happened. "The Italian police are holding me at the moment. But how are you? Your video message…"

"We're okay, darling. Obviously it was all a bit of a shock – they just barged in here with their guns. Two of them. Scary people… very rough and shouty, and incredibly young-looking. Like kids really."

"Did they hurt you?"

"No, they just scared us."

"I bet.

"How did you manage to get away? What happened?"

"Oh, it was quite funny really," his mother is saying, almost jauntily. She might be talking about something amusing that had happened at the local post office. "Well, did I mention that the Buxtons were coming over to play tennis?"

"Yes, you did," says Max, who finds his chin wobbling and his eyes welling up with tears at the mention of the Buxtons, this collision of his parents' friends, people he'd known all his life, with these extraordinary events. "Go on."

"Yes, well, they arrived and with Graham and Tony…"

Graham and Tony were the Buxtons' grown-up sons, Max's age or a bit younger, ex-Army.

"All of them in their tennis whites. It was so bizarre, Maxi…"

"I can imagine," says Max, tears rolling down his cheeks, his chin wobbling like crazy.

"So now there were seven of us to two of them. I have to say the Buxton boys took it very well. That's the army for you."

Max is laughing and crying at the same time. Usually his mother's stories bored him, but this one – told in the same tone of voice in which she relayed tales of village life – gripped him to the core.

"And then you'll never guess. Some friends of Tash showed up – four strapping lads, who'd been down the pub. Tash had forgotten she'd invited them over. So now we were eleven and to their two…

"Tash's friends took it pretty well too, I have to say. It was getting a bit like a drawing-room comedy at this stage, and it's really odd, despite these horrible men with their guns, I simply couldn't feel afraid. Perhaps I should have, because they could easily have killed all of us. You hear of these things going on in schools in America… everyone getting shot. And look at what happened in Paris…"

"Yes, quite, but then what happened to you?"

"Then – after all that – a police car rolled up the drive. They had come to question us because you were all over the news by this stage apparently, although we didn't know a thing about it. It's probably why the telephone also started ringing all of a sudden. It would ring for ages, stop, and then start again. Everyone's mobiles were also ringing like crazy. The gunmen were getting mighty agitated and told everyone to throw their phones into a pile on the carpet."

"Go on."

"Anyway I think these guys eventually got the funk – the situation just became too much for them, what with all these people turning up and now the police. They just did a run for it… out of the French windows, across the croquet lawn and over the hedge. I'm apologising like crazy to the Buxtons and Tash's friends for landing them in this situation, but they were all really nice about it. I think Tash's friends were drunk."

"Did they catch the gunmen?"

"No, that's the only downside. The two police officers who arrived by car called for backup because they weren't armed. That didn't arrive for ages, so they went round taking statements. They reckon they must have had a car hidden somewhere."

"Oh, God, Mummy – I'm so glad you're safe. And I'm so sorry for getting all of you into this mess. Say sorry to the Buxtons for me, won't you? I love you all."

"We love you too."

Maurilio took the phone from Max at this point, and nodded through the one-way mirror to Pizzuto.

"What now?" the man from the ministry asks Pizzuto. He hadn't understood as much of what the Englishman had said, except 'I love you all'.

"Now?" says Pizzuto. "Now we need to retrace the water-cannon truck's route back to wherever this warehouse is situated. Signor Draycott says it's not far from the airport. And we need to find the boy, who apparently got out of the Range Rover near the central station. Get some men down there now, and stop and question every Arab boy of around that age.

"And then I think Signor Dryacott deserves a shower and a hot meal."

CHAPTER FIFTY-EIGHT

The boy has decided to call himself Omar from now on, in honour of the man with the scar who had entrusted him with such important work.

'Omar', as he is now, asked to be let down at the central station. Or at least he kept repeating those two words until the men in the balaclavas seemed to understand. He had been angry with them at first for spoiling his mission, the work that he had been taught and that seemed like the most important thing in the world, but he now feels relieved.

If only there is some way in which he can contact his family back home in Syria. They would be proud of him, he is certain, but he wants to know that they are unharmed. Perhaps he should turn himself in to the police, but that might make big Omar angry, and little Omar respects big Omar. He's also scared of him, and what he might do to his family.

The boy goes to the wall where he used to sit with his friend, the other Syrian kid who sold himself to strange men. He's nowhere to be seen; perhaps he's with a man now, in one of the cheap hotel rooms round here.

The sun is hot and little Omar feels thirsty and hungry. His clothes, he notices now, are filthy and he imagines he must smell. He thinks he might go back home and join Isis; they're never hungry or thirsty, and they don't sell their bodies to strange men, which is a sin. He now knows that he won't be afraid to die – he has been through the whimpering and crying, and, as big Omar said, he passed the test.

If he were told to wear a suicide vest and walk up to a bunch of American soldiers, or, more like, some of Assad's militiamen, and blow them sky high, he won't mind. In fact he'll be happy. He will die and it will be for him like it is for the old men when they ejaculate over his body.

The sun is hot and he is hungry and thirsty, but he doesn't mind. He can sense rather than see that he is being watched. Omar turns and there he is – a well-dressed man, with a little dog on a lead. He smiles at Omar and Omar smiles back, and, emboldened, the man picks up his little dog and walks over.

"Do you like dogs?" the man asks, but Omar doesn't understand.

"One hundred euros. *Cento euros*," is all he says.

"Ooh, that's quite a lot for a little refugee boy, now let me see…" says the man, but Omar doesn't understand him, and doesn't care to either.

"One hundred euros," he says, before adding in Arabic, "and a hot bath."

*　　*　　*

"I don't know anything about sarin," says Harry, addressing his lawyer rather than the two detectives – Johns and the female cop from yesterday. "The last I saw of Max was yesterday morning in Verbier. He was alive and so was Kylie, Simon's girlfriend."

"But Simon was dead," says Johns. "You knew that."

"I knew that," agrees Harry.

"So what my client is saying," says Fairbrother, pressing the tips of his fingers together, "and, for the record, he has now repeated four times, is that he has no idea about the existence of any sarin, or a plot to use it in Rome.

"He has been to Rome… he is not denying that fact…where he and Mr Draycott managed to escape with their lives after the distinct possibility that they were going to be beheaded by a Arab gentleman who is possibly an Isis terrorist, and his associates. He was aided in his escape by an agent of the Saudi security services, now unfortunately deceased, and fled with Mr Draycott and the woman Aafia who had stolen his diamond and thus kick-started this whole escapade in the first place, and made their way to Switzerland, and the chalet belonging to Simon Fellowes. Most regrettably, Simon and his girlfriend of the moment, Kylie McDermott, decided it would be great fun to join them…"

"I think," interrupts Johns, "given the serious nature of the situation, that we will have no option but to detain Mr Kimber for a further period of time."

"And I will object most strongly to the unnecessary detention of my client, a man who is clearly traumatised by recent events, and a victim of terrorism, I repeat, and who is not himself involved in terrorism."

"As you keep saying. Shall we call it a day then?" asks Johns, his hand on the recording device.

Fairbrother nods, Harry shrugs and Johns turns off the tape recorder.

* * *

"Mary? It's Charlotte here, darling. Great work yesterday. Listen I've had a call from my counterpart on the daily. They'd like you to work with their team on this story, which, by the way, just gets bigger by the hour."

Mary has deliberately kept her phone off all day and avoided looking at the news websites. She and Ben had viewed five flats in their price range, and they were both now tired and dispirited. Two-bedroom, ex-local authority flats in need of modernisation, or next door to dogs they could hear barking through paper-thin walls, their owners telling them to "Shut the fuck up, you little fucker!"

"Let's go and live in Istanbul," she said as they left by the staircase because the lift was broken. Even the estate agent looked a bit nervous in this particular block.

They retire to a pub, where a football match is being shown on a big screen, and a lot of fat white men and their wives and girlfriends are getting smashed. Sunday afternoon in Sidcup.

"It's hardly cafe culture, is it?" says Ben, returning with a pint and a glass of white wine to the quietest table they could find. It is at this point that Mary turns her phone back on and notices six missed calls, all of them from Charlotte. She rings her at once.

"You'll get full whack for however long it takes," says Charlotte.

"I'm a bit out of the loop," says Mary. "Have there been any developments."

"Have there?" laughs Charlotte. "Just a bit, darling. Seems that Max has been arrested by the Italian police, preparing to gas St Peter's Square with sarin during the Pope's Easter address."

"No seriously," says Mary. "What's the latest?"

"I am being serious, darling! Max was driving a water cannon that was going to spray all those good Catholics with sarin. Crazy, I know. Except that the water cannon has gone missing, Max was abducted by men in masks, and, well, it's all a bit sketchy from there on in. We're getting all our information from an Italian stringer with connections in the Ministry of Interior, and I'm pretty certain he's working with just about every other news outlet in the entire world, so it's not terribly exclusive."

"Fucking hell," she says, looking at Ben. "I've got Ben here. Can I tell him?"

"Might as well, it's already been on Sky News, Al Jazeera and the BBC."

"What do they want me for?" asks Mary, sipping her wine, something cheap and nasty and not very cold.

"They want the personal angle, like the stuff you wrote for me. But go a bit deeper. What was Harry like? Did you ever meet Max? Lots of colour."

"I see... well..."

"Smash it, Mary. This could be the making of you."

CHAPTER FIFTY-NINE

By late afternoon Pizzuto's rapidly expanding band of detectives has been joined by two men from Europol and tactical assault teams from the Central Security Operations Service, and they are about to begin their search for Omar's warehouse when reports start coming in of a large fire at a disused trading estate about eight kilometres from Fiumicino airport.

"This looks interesting," Pizzuto tells the leader of the CSOS swat teams, a short wiry man with silver hair and skin like leather. "The blaze was reported two hours ago by a local farmer who went to investigate, but since the estate is in the process of being demolished, it had gone undetected and the flames had done their worst by then. There were also reports of a large explosion."

"Right. I'll send a team over there at once," says the CSOS leader.

"And I'll follow and bring the Englishman with me," says Pizzuto. "We also need to get forensics down there, if there is anything left to analyse."

"And I will go and have another chat with Tariq," says Maurilio, peeling himself from the wall against which he has been leaning. Having suddenly felt dog tired an hour or so ago, he is perking up again as the investigation resumes.

*   *   *

Having eaten a bowl of pasta with some sort of tomato sauce, followed by a yoghurt, Max curled up on the bed and drifted off into a doze. He has been asleep for what feels like about five minutes when he is woken by the cell door clanking open.

"Come," says a uniformed policeman, beckoning Max to walk past him through the open door. He is led down a corridor and into a room, where Pizzuto and four or five male detectives are standing in front of a window.

"Come here, Max, please," says Pizzuto, the first time she used his first name with him. Max takes this as a good sign.

The window looks into another room, brightly lit and where a line of boys of varying heights are standing. They are all Middle-Eastern-looking and all of them appear shifty and scared – all except a boy on the right end of the line, who is staring ahead, a hardness in his eyes that Max doesn't recognise from before. He does recognise the boy however.

"The 'ragazzo'… the boy in the truck… is he here?" asks Pizzuto.

"Yes," says Max at once. "The one on the right."

Pizzuto nods, leans forward and says something into a microphone, and the boys are led off – all except the one that Max has identified, who continues to stare straight ahead.

A uniformed policeman comes into the room and hands Pizzuto a slip of paper, a smile slowly spreading across her lips as she reads it.

"He was picked up near the central station, seemingly working as – how you say? – *prostituto*," she says in heavily accented English. "He had 100 euros in his pocket. If we can locate the truck, or anything is left of this warehouse, we'll check for fingerprints and DNA. It still is possible to extract fingerprints even after a fire. By the way, do you know what he's calling himself, the *regazzo*?"

Max shakes his head.

"He says his name is Omar."

*   *   *

Wearing rubber gardening gloves, Omar starts with the utensils – the knives, forks, spoons and plates, which he places in the bucket of bleach. He then pours on the food remains, and finally the dustbin bin liner they had been thrown into. He then drags the mattress and all the furniture and piles them into a great heap in the middle of the warehouse, and sets light to them.

The fire is slow to get going but that suits Omar, who picks up the various rags and ropes that he used to tie up and gag the Englishman and throws them into the gently licking flames. Finally he peels off his gloves and throws them on to the steadily strengthening blaze

He makes one last check for any odds and ends, before rolling the barrels of petrol so that they surround the bonfire at a distance of about two metres. Next to two of these barrels are IEDs of the type he used to use in Iraq, the ones the Americans called 'spiders'. Omar had felt almost nostalgic while building them last week.

He doesn't look back, but puts the Fiat into gear, lowers the handbrake and moves off. Only when he reaches the exit to this particular section of the trading estate does Omar slow down and lower his window. In his hand is a small black plastic fob, of the type used for opening garage doors.

A split second after pressing the device there is the muffled sound of an explosion, immediately followed by a flash and a louder bang, and a fireball rips into the air. He pulls away quickly and heads for the main road, only turning to look back briefly once. Black smoke is billowing into the cloudless sky.

There's a pair of leather gloves on the passenger seat, which Omar now slips on, and a packet of antiseptic wipes, which he uses to clean the steering wheel and gearstick as he drives. The shoes are deliberately two sizes too big.

About halfway to the airport he pulls in beside a wide drainage ditch that is full of weed and rubbish-choked water, and which he had scouted the previous week. Omar gets out and walks round to the boot, where the guns are stacked. He waits for a lorry and a car to pass before pulling them out carrying them to the ditch, dropping them one by one into the dark green ooze.

He drives to the car hire drop-off at Fuimicino, a young woman giving the Fiat's bodywork a quick inspection, before checking the fuel level and asking whether Omar had enjoyed his stay.

"Business, I'm afraid," says Omar, and the woman shrugs. He can see that she's not happy to be working on Easter Sunday.

"Thank you," says Omar. "Which way to departures please?"

CHAPTER SIXTY

Tariq is out of bed and resting in an armchair when Maurilio arrives at his hospital room. The window has even been opened slightly and the lightest of spring breezes is wafting into the room, along with the distant rumble and tooting of traffic.

"Glad to see you up," he says to the Libyan.

"You stopped him then?" Tariq asks as Maurilio perches on the end of the bed.

"Yes, we stopped him," says Maurilio. "Thank God."

"They had the television on in the nurses' room," says Tariq. "I see you're looking for the two Englishmen."

"Found them both," says Tariq. "What can you tell me about them?"

"Quite a lot actually," says Tariq, Maurilio trying hard not to betray his excitement. He waits, as the Libyan seems to collect his thoughts.

"They were sent by Aafia's father," he says at length. "They had been trying to get the diamond back that Aafia supposedly stole, and her father told them he'd pay them its value if they went to Rome and persuaded her to come back to the UK."

"I see," says Maurilio. "And was that likely?"

"No, not at all, and I don't know what his little game was," says Tariq. "He was sending the Englishmen to an almost certain death. Why would he do that?"

"I can't think," says Maurilio. "Have you given it any thought?"

"Maybe he wanted to create some sort of crisis," says Tariq. "He didn't approve of what Aafia was doing and he thought she was putting her life at risk. She's his favourite, you see. Perhaps he thought this would, as the British say, put the cat among the pigeons. Although in this case it was putting the pigeons among the cats. But, no, I don't know what he was thinking."

"What happened after they arrived?"

"Well, Aafia's father must have given them the details of the cafe where Aafia and I hung out, pretending to be thrusting young entrepreneurs. The owner loved us – we spent so much money there. We asked her to keep an eye out for any strange-looking foreigners who turned up, and she did. They turned up there last week – Max and Harry, and she tipped us the wink."

Maurilio isn't sure what 'tipped us the wink' means, but lets it pass.

"You must have known that you were leading them into an incredibly dangerous situation," he says. "Why didn't you just tell them to get lost and leave it like that?"

"Ah yes, and I regret that now," says Tariq, who lapses into silence. "You see..." he continues, before resuming his silence.

Maurilio waits, looking at the motes of dust that are dancing in the sunlight that is now glancing into the room, falling in a rectangle at his feet.

"There were two problems," Tariq resumes at length. "The first is that we were getting so close to finding out what the terrorists had planned. Or we knew in general terms what they had planned, we just didn't know exactly where and when. We were terrified of them getting cold feet, or changing their plans at this point, before we had more details.

"The other is that Omar was watching us. He didn't really trust Aafia and me from the start and had taken to following us and observing us covertly. We pretended we didn't notice him, but we got used to him shadowing us when we were out and about, and he was there that morning.

"We didn't give it too much thought, I'm afraid. We just acted instinctively. He would have seen us with the Englishmen and Aafia thought that if she took them back to the compound and told Omar that they had come to get their diamond back, then perhaps... I don't know."

"Did Omar know about the diamond?"

"Not at that stage, no."

"What happened next?"

Tariq sighs. What did happen before Omar caught him and nearly killed him with those hammer fist-blows to the temple? As if his body senses the approach of this event, he shivers and a feeling of nausea passes through him.

"We had a big argument about what to do with the Englishmen," says Tariq, after the feeling of sickness has subsided. "The Daesh wanted to kill them straight away, and we said that it would complicate matters to do that. We were just trying to buy time. There were plenty of places where we could hold them prisoner until after the event.

"Then Omar got really excited about not only killing them, but executing them on video – the video to be posted online immediately after the attack on Rome. He was the leader and so the others fell behind him and helped set it up. Actually, I think they rather enjoy this sort of thing.

"Anyway, it was then that Aafia went to talk to the guy from the Saudi secret services. They had to do something quickly. And I remember Aafia telling me to get out quickly, to involve the Italian authorities, and running down the staircase. But that, I'm afraid, is all that I remember."

CHAPTER SIXTY-ONE

"And now for the tricky bit," says Fairbrother. A CID officer had shown them round to a back door that opens on to the police car park. The lawyer has been allowed to leave his BMW here this morning.

"What is going to be tricky?" asks Harry, dressed in the clothes he had bought in that boutique in Martigny, and which he now feels look rather absurd. The weight of the Rolex rubs on wrists still sore from being bound in that place in Rome. Jesus, was that really only five days ago?

"Well you might like to know that you and your friend Max have been headline news since Easter Saturday," Fairbrother is saying. "The ladies and gentlemen of the fourth estate are currently congregated in an unseemly huddle in front of the police station."

Harry has got used to Fairbrother's florid way of speaking. In normal life he wouldn't have liked this morbidly obese solicitor – he was far too full of himself in more ways than one. But this wasn't normal life, and Harry is so thankful for his entitled manner and deep knowledge of the law, that his gratitude is almost akin to love.

Harry hasn't been charged with anything yet, although Johns kept citing 'reasonable grounds', Fairbrother shaking his head and later telling Harry to ignore him. 'Reasonable grounds' were just a form of words in this case, to make sure that they could keep tabs on Harry.

And so he has finally been granted police bail, although this proved slightly difficult because Harry didn't have what Johns kept calling 'a fixed abode'. Fairbrother had offered to put him up, but wasn't attracted to the idea of listening to the lawyer's flowery pomposity more than was strictly necessary in order to regain his freedom.

Harry himself had ideas of living it up on the company credit card, a nice little discreet hotel in Mayfair within walking distance of the office. Johns wasn't happy with that, of course, mainly because Harry had yet to book into one, but also on social grounds. He could see the old class resentment bristling in the detective.

In the end, since he was planning to visit her anyway, Harry gave his mother's address in Norfolk. He had to report anyway to Norwich police station, a week from today. And he must attend if Johns or any of the other investigating officers wished to question him further. Oh, and the safety-deposit key and associated documentation was still required as part of the ongoing investigation.

Harry now steps outside for the first time in over three days. It's sunny but with a cold wind whipping around the car park. Fairbrother indicates a blue BMW with tinted windows, against which is leaning a man in his mid-forties, fit-looking and built like a jockey. The man stubs out a cigarette as Harry and Fairbrother approach.

"Jim this is Harry... Harry, Jim," he says by way of introduction. The man nods, unsmiling, and pulls open a rear door for his two passengers.

"Jim's an ex-police driver," says Fairbrother. "The best in the business. How he keeps a clean licence I'll never know. Better put on your seat belt."

An unseen hand operates the gate to the car park, which slowly begins to slide open. Jim pulls the BMW around so that it's revving like it's on a racetrack starting grid. To the right, along the front of the police station, Harry can make out various vans with satellite dishes on their roofs, and a mass of people gathered around the front steps. As if in slow motion, the herd turns and starts rushing towards the BMW, but Jim accelerates off smoothly but speedily, taking the exit road in one.

Jim keeps a steady eye on the rear-view mirror as they become locked into the traffic moving through the clogged streets of Crawley, but once out of the thirty-mph zone he steadily starts to put a speed on. Very soon they are on the slip road to the M23 and speeding not northwards towards London, as Harry had expected, but south towards Brighton.

They move at a steady ninety-mph, Jim sticking to the slow lane where possible, overtaking if necessary and then cutting smartly back in. After maybe about fifteen or twenty minutes of this he indicates to come off at a service station called Pease Pottage.

"Righty-ho," says Fairbrother, who has been unusually quiet for the duration of the journey from Crawley, his plump hands gripping the seat edge. "We're going to pull up beside a car and you are going to jump out and into that car, and it will take you to London."

"I see..." says Harry.

"It's a very comfortable car," says Fairbrother as Jim navigates the service station car park. And there it is, the black on black Rolls Royce.

"I think I may have already had a lift in that one," says Harry.

Fairbrother smiles but doesn't say anything, as Jim pulls up beside the Rolls. He then jumps out smartly and opens the back door open for Harry.

"I'll see you in London later," says Fairbrother before the door closes on him. Jim has now opened the back of the Rolls, and Harry climbs in, his nostrils assailed once more by the smell of leather. The Saudi is seated at the far end of the rear seat, beaming moistly from his jaundiced-looking eyes. Some sort of bodyguard is up front, while the driver is an oldish bloke in full uniform.

"Harry... welcome," says the Saudi, indicating the seat beside him.

*   *   *

Rachel flicks through the copy of Italian *Vogue* that she bought at the airport. *Street style on the runways and fashion in the streets*, the headline informs her, but she's not really taking it in. In any case it's an article she has read a thousand times in different guises.

She likes Italian men: they're flirty and not too serious about anything. That is until they do become serious when they become very serious. There are some pretty poor specimens in this Rome police station, although there's one leaning over a desk, tidy bum sticking out, who keeps giving her the eye. So shameless. Quite cute.

She deliberately took a different flight to Tash and Max's dad, only meeting up with them in the offices of the lawyer recommended by the British consul. Massimo something or other. Massimo sounds like massive, she thinks, which is ironic because the lawyer turned out to be a tiny, birdlike man, bustling with nervous energy.

Rachel had picked up a smattering of Italian from her countless trips to Milan, and acted as unofficial interpreter any time that Massimo's English failed him, which was quite often. Basically, he said, the police and the public prosecutor believed Max's story, and that he was innocent of planning the terrorist attack, and had become a victim himself when coerced into driving the truck. And they believed he was ignorant of the fact that the truck contained diluted sarin. But still, this was a highly serious and very public case, so they must be extremely cautious.

Max was going in front of a judge later that afternoon, during which hearing the public prosecutor will recommend that the charges against him be dropped. If the judge agrees then Max will be freed.

"And if not?" Tash had asked. "Will he get bail?"

"There is no such thing as bail under Italian law," the lawyer replied. "If the prosecutor believes that the accused might flee then he can recommend what is called pre-trial detention. But since the prosecutor is of the opinion that Max is innocent then this won't be the case here.

"However the prosecutor is under an obligation to inform the victims of any crime if he is going to recommend that the case be dropped, and the victims can then file an objection. But since, in this case, it is unclear who the victims are, then I don't see this being a problem.

"Ideally the police would like to interview the Saudi woman, Aafia was her name, but she had disappeared – her diplomatic immunity making any likelihood of immediate detention highly unlikely at present. For you see there is one area where Max's involvement does not appear so straightforward and that is the initial journey from Italy to Switzerland. The evidence suggests the possibility that Aafia was taken against her will... under duress. Kidnap, in a word."

The policeman leaning on the desk straightens up and now gives Rachel the full stare. She sticks her tongue out and disappears smartly beneath the pages of her magazine. Tash and her father, who are sitting across from her like perfect strangers, are staring into space.

Rachel had never got on very well – or even a little bit well – with Tash. They were so different. Tash was one of those big-boned, home-counties boarding school girls that Rachel had met so many of, destined to turn into their mothers, keeping home at an old rectory along with a pair of large dogs and a quietly expanding white wine habit. She had Max's mouth and eyes and forehead, which was a bit weird for Rachel – her husband's female doppelganger.

Tash in turn thought that Rachel was a spoilt little daddy's girl. Only half right, thinks Rachel, because she was a spoilt little mummy and daddy's girl, an only child in a suffocating family triangle in which all attention, for good and bad, had been focused on her. The three of them in a huge house right by the park in Golders Green – so many rooms, so few of them lived in.

She had managed to get herself expelled from the Jewish Free School by the simple expedient of bunking off lessons, and sitting in cafes in Harrow smoking cigarettes and chatting up waiters. Then her parents tried boarding schools, places in Berkshire and Buckinghamshire full of girls just like Tash. She must have got through one of those a year, until, aged seventeen, her father had wisely given up. She had been given a small allowance – enough to rent a room in a house – and told to get on with her life. The best thing her parents ever did.

It had been the run-up to Christmas and Debenhams on Oxford Street were hiring extra sales staff. Shunted from department to department – handbags to kitchenware, electrical to toys – she soon found her spiritual home in ladies' fashion. Her enthusiasm and natural good taste were soon spotted and after Christmas she had been taken on full time.

By the time she was twenty-five and had met and married Max, she had been head-hunted twice by rival Oxford Street department stores, and by the age of thirty she was the chief buyer for a small chain of high-end women's fashion stores based in Bond Street. Amazingly, she managed all that while continuing with the delinquent lifestyle that had got her kicked out of three boarding schools. Max used to say that she had an iron constitution.

Tash looks over at her now, gives a wan little smile that doesn't make the journey from her lips to her eyes, and returns to staring into space. Max's father looks irritably at his watch.

At least Max's father isn't wearing that bloody old cricket jumper. In fact he looked quite dapper in a grey suit and club tie. Rachel had been down to the family home in Hampshire quite often in the first two years of their marriage, but she steadily came to loathe the place. All that forced surface jollity when she could tell they were all cracking up. Nicky's ghost was everywhere, and no matter how much they drank or how many tennis parties they threw, he just kept on haunting them.

They should have seen a therapist, Rachel always thought. She loves going to see therapists; it's great fun and well worth the money, just talking about yourself for fifty minutes. There was one therapist, though, who she had to stop seeing. It was too disturbing what he said about her sleeping around.

Rachel thought about what he had said about her promiscuity – except he didn't call it that – when she and Jess recently went shopping in Dubai. There she was, being pumped in bed by a French yacht skipper she'd met in the hotel bar, and all she could think of was her therapist.

She tried to get Max to see a therapist, but he did the typical public school male thing and claimed it was self-indulgent. Actually he became quite angry with her, which was unusual. God, he's going to need some serious therapy after this.

A door opens and their lawyer, Massimo, bustles over to them.

"We can see him now," he says. "Do you want to go in together?"

They look at each other, silently working out who has precedence – father, sister or wife.

"You two go first," says Rachel.

"Are you sure?" says Max's father.

Yes, she thinks. She hasn't worked out what she is going to say to him yet.

CHAPTER SIXTY-TWO

The Saudi raises his bejewelled hand and the engine purrs into life, the Rolls gliding past a gawping family, their arms piled with McDonalds drinks cartons and bags.

Harry is fighting with a mixture of emotions. There's an anger that has been steadily growing since his near execution in Rome and Verbier; fear of the Saudi's power, especially strong as he now found himself ensconced with him in his car, and there's hope – hope that he might be grateful for rescuing his daughter. Very grateful.

Harry's anger at least allows him to ditch the bowing-and-scraping etiquette. He won't be calling this podgy man 'your excellency', or whatever form of address Max had used all those weeks ago in Mayfair.

The Saudi is looking at him through his watery brown eyes, and Harry can't but notice again how yellow are the whites of his eyes. Is he ill?

"Are you angry with me?" he asks Harry.

"Well, yes," says Harry, taken off guard. "I… Max and I were nearly killed."

"Yes, and I am sorry. But I want to thank you for bringing my daughter back."

"Back where? Is Aafia in England?"

"Oh, no," says the Saudi, swatting the suggestion away with a wave of his hand, as if it was annoying insect. "She's safely back in the kingdom now, where she will remain."

"Saudi Arabia?"

"Saudi, yes… Saudi."

Harry thinks of what Aafia had said to him about life in Saudi Arabia, and how she hated its attitude towards women. "At least she's safe," he says.

"Yes, thank God. And so is Max," says the Saudi. "He's been released by the Italian police, you know?"

"No, I didn't know," says Harry.

"He will have to return to help with the investigation," "but these things take months and even years in Italy…"

"Like Amanda Knox," says Harry.

"I don't know," says the Saudi.

"Is Max back in England?"

"No, I don't think so," says the Saudi. "He's in Geneva, buying me a pretty diamond."

"A diamond?" blurts out Harry.

"Not that one… that one remains under lock and key for the moment, so I understand. But now, let's talk about you."

"Go on…"

But the Saudi pauses, seemingly absorbed in the motorway verge.

"You remember the Mayfair hotel where we first met?" he asks at length. "Well, there's a nice suite reserved in your name. It's booked for the next month, so use it as you please. There's also fifty thousand pounds in your personal bank account. We still have the details on file."

"O…kay," says Harry, wondering what file this is. Something to do with their former business transactions perhaps. The man continues looking out of his side window as he speaks.

"That is just a small retainer," he says. "There will be two-and-half million in your account as soon as you do what I'm about to ask, and we have a satisfactory outcome."

Harry feels suddenly light-headed and realises he hasn't eaten since the toast and cereal early this morning.

"Two and a half million pounds," he says. "Why that sum?"

"For your share in the diamond."

"But I've already brought your daughter back safely… that was what we agreed…"

"You kidnapped my daughter some might argue," says the Saudi, still looking at the countryside passing alongside the M23. A plane passes low overhead – an Easyjet plane in its orange and white livery, Harry notices. They pass a sign for Gatwick. How long ago since he'd made that landing in just such a plane?

"You're threatening me?" says Harry, after all we did for you?"

"Carrot and stick, Harry… carrot and stick. Wouldn't you like to hear some more about the carrot?" The Saudi is looking at him now. "Okay," he continues. "We're driving now to Claridge's hotel. Waiting in a room there is your friend Mary…"

"Mary?" Harry is beginning to feel seriously light-headed now.

"Mary, your friend the journalist, along with a photographer. You are about to give her the exclusive of a lifetime."

"How do you know about Mary?" asks Harry.

"Of course," smiles the Saudi, tapping on the glass partition. It slides open and a newspaper is handed back to him. "Mary Erskine has been making quite a name for herself in the past few days," he says, handing it to Harry.

The front-page story is marked as an exclusive, with Mary's picture byline attached. The story is about how both Max and Harry are to be released without charge. "We've been keeping her well informed," says the Saudi.

"The story you have to tell is quite simple and only omits two facts: The stolen diamond and the kidnapping. Let's call it mutually assured destruction – like in the good old Cold War. You mention a stolen diamond and Aafia starts claiming she was kidnapped at gunpoint. Oh, by the way, Max is fully onside with all this."

I bet he is, thinks Harry. It's the sort of deal Max understands. "What do you want me to tell Mary?" he says.

"It's simple really. You did some services for a rich Saudi– the press are all calling it 'concierge service' now, like you worked in a hotel or something – and this Saudi, a sick old man, asked for you to find his daughter. He wanted to reconcile himself with her before he died."

He is impassive as he says this, but Harry wonders whether he is trying to tell him something.

"It immediately makes me the good guy," says the Saudi with

a smile. "A terminally ill father wants to make up with his estranged daughter. Anyway, all the old man has is a photograph taken outside a cafe somewhere in Rome. A private detective he hired took it. Would Max and Harry do him this favour and try and persuade the daughter to come and see her dying papa?"

Harry still can't decide whether he is hinting at a truth, or being utterly cynical. He doesn't look well.

"Anyway, what you stumbled on in Rome was in fact a terrorist cell. My daughter, Aafia, who, by the way, has a proud record in campaigning for the rights of Muslim women…"

That's it, thinks Harry. The man is utterly cynical.

"She has infiltrated this cell with the aim of exposing it before it can do any damage. She has used her contacts in the secret service to get an undercover minder to join her – the man who was regrettably shot dead in Rome when you made your escape.

"And it was my Aafia who discovered the plot to spray sarin gas in St Peter's Square on Easter morning – a diabolical outrage that would have pitted Christian against Muslim for the next 300 years."

"I don't know what happened… what actually happened to stop the attack?" asks Harry.

"Saudi secret agents intercepted the truck and disposed of it. You don't know where."

"Is that what really happened?"

The man smiles. "You don't need to know that. Yes, that really happened, if you like. Anyway, can I tell you what headline I want to be reading tomorrow?"

"Go on," says Harry.

"*Saudis foil IS chemical attack on Vatican…* that sort of thing."

"I'll do my best," says Harry.

"You will," says the Saudi, a steeliness creeping into his sallow eyes.

"Can I just ask one thing, though?"

"By all means," says the man.

"Why?"

"PR," is all he says, returning to surveying the motorway verge. He doesn't say anything for the best part of a minute, and then he turns to Harry.

"How much do you know about Middle East politics?"

"Not a lot... I'll grant you that," says Harry.

"You're not alone in England with that," says the Saudi. "Well, there's a lot of nonsense spoken about the centuries old emnity between Sunnis and Shias, but that is all just camouflage for the real power-struggle, that between Saudi Arabia and Iran.

"Traditionally we, Saudi Arabia, had America on our side, while Iran had Russia, but things have been changing. America has lifted its sanctions on Tehran because they believe what those Iranians liars are saying about abandoning their nuclear ambitions, while we Saudis are getting a bad press for our supposed human rights violations. The West, for so long our allies in the region, is falling out of love with us.

"And there is IS. We started funding Islamic State in order to help get rid of Assad in Syria – a Shia by the way – but we have created a monster that now threatens us at home – it threatens the House of Saud, the bedrock of stability in the region."

"So you hope to discredit Islamic State and bolster Saudi Arabia's image in the West, all at the same time."

"There, you have it," says the man. "It's just one small piece in a complicated jigsaw."

"But I don't write the headlines," says Harry. "They're not stupid people. They'll write it as they see it."

"That is your job... to paint the picture that they see," says the Saudi. "Anyway, that is the desired outcome. Two and half million pounds or a charge of kidnapping depends on it."

CHAPTER SIXTY-THREE

Mary is staring into a huge spray of flowers that has just been deposited in a vase by a smartly dressed blonde housekeeper. She's not very good on her flowers, but she recognises roses, cream and pink roses, amongst the mix.

The weather in London has been bright and blue, but cold with it, for the past week or so, and a beam of sunlight is now illuminating the table with the flowers on it. On another table, against the wall, two silver platters have been placed, one piled high with sandwiches, the other covered in pastries. Next to the platters are bottles of water and Coca Cola and two thermoses, one marked coffee, the other marked tea.

Mary feels as nervous as a bride, good practice for when she and Ben attend the registry office in the summer. The photographer, Julian, is setting up next door; she can see him practising on his assistant, a young woman holding a collapsible reflector. Charlotte is talking on the phone outside in the corridor.

Mary turns once again to her list of questions, the result of a conference this morning in which the daily news team, joined by Charlotte from the Sunday and the daily editor, Miles Turner. Everyone is feeling both elated and suspicious about the approach from Harry's lawyer, Hugo Fairbrother.

What he had to say was quite simple. His client had received several high six-figure offers for an exclusive interview, but he wanted to go with his old friend Mary Erskine. He didn't want any money, but although he trusted Mary, whose recent reports he has been following, he does want copy approval.

"What do you think?" Miles had asked.

"Well, we never give copy approval… that's an article of faith on this paper."

"Mmm…" said Miles, clearly prepared to ditch this article of faith. "Is there some way around this?"

"Maybe I could talk to him," said Mary. "Journalist to ex-journalist."

"I don't want to lose this," said Miles.

The suite at Claridge's had been paid for by Harry's lawyer, which increased their suspicion even more, but sitting here now, Mary smiles at the irony. She and Harry had come to several movie junkets in this hotel, usually for visiting American actors. The journalists would sit in one room with the publicists, eating sandwiches and pastries just like these, waiting for their turn for fifteen minutes with some occasionally quite charming, but more often bored film star spouting generalised inanities.

And now it was Harry in the position of those movie stars. She just hoped that he isn't going to spout vacuous nonsense like them. Would the lawyer be present, acting like those film publicists and steering the questions away from anything too real or penetrating?

Mary gets her answer in less than a minute, as Charlotte strides in, followed by an enormous man, almost as wide as he is tall, with a belly like the prow of a ship. And there's Harry, a sheepish smile on his face, which broadens into a grin as he sees Mary.

"No personal questions please," he says, in memory of the PRs they both had to battle back in the day.

"I was just remembering all those film junkets here," says Mary standing to kiss him on the cheek and give his arm a squeeze. He is unshaven and wearing the oddest-looking clothes. "Did you remember doing John Travolta here?"

"Oh, yes," says Harry. "And Leonardo DiCaprio."

"Good day, Miss Erskine. My name is Hugo Fairbrother," interjects the mountain of flesh, proffering a warm, clammy hand. "My client will give you his account of what happened in Italy and Switzerland, and if you will just allow him to speak, without interrupting with questions."

"Is that the way you want to play it?" Mary asks Harry.

"Mary, I want you to know what's been happening, and it is extraordinary," says Harry. "But I am still the subject of a criminal investigation. Mr Fairbrother here will just make sure I don't give the police any cause to haul me back off to the cells."

"Fair enough," says Mary, switching her micro-cassette recorder to record.

"You still have one of those?" says Harry, laughing.

"And this," she says, sliding her iPhone across the table. "Belt and braces."

Charlotte too has the voice recorder app on her phone set to record.

CHAPTER SIXTY-FOUR

It's only a short walk from Claridge's to the hotel where the Saudi is paying to put up Harry, but instead he heads down on to Piccadilly and finds a cashpoint. He puts in his personal debit card and requests a balance. He does indeed appear to be £50,000 richer than he was last week.

A short walk takes him to Turnbull & Asser on Jermyn Street, where he uses the company credit card to buy two pairs of chinos, three shirts, a tweed jacket, three pairs of boxer shorts, eight pairs of socks, a pair of tan Derby shoes and a pair of suede loafers.

The assistant is very sorry but the credit card has been refused. Harry asks him to try again, and then hands over his personal debit card. No problem this time, thank you very much, sir, have a good day.

The cold wind is whipping down Jermyn Street as he trudges back carrying his shopping bags. He thinks he managed to convey to Mary the sort of story he wanted her to write. He stuck to the facts, her raised eyebrows registering her amazement as his story unfolded.

And then the questions. He knew a sticky one would involve the stolen diamond. No, he says, that had all turned out to be a huge misunderstanding.

"A misunderstanding?" said Mary, almost laughing with incredulity.

"A misunderstanding," deadpanned Harry. "You see, Aafia had actually given the diamond to her father, who presumed that the transaction had been completed and therefore took possession. He's paid up now, thankfully."

Mary just stared at him. She knew he was lying and she knew that he knew she knew. Luckily she didn't seem to know about the safety deposit box. The police haven't leaked that then.

And then there's the tricky question of his flight to England, leaving Max in the lurch. Fairbrother intervened at this point.

"Miss Erksine," he said, managing to sound like he's addressing an under-housemaid. "You can imagine my client's state of mind on being nearly killed not once, but twice. But that is not what is important here."

"What is important here?" That was Charlotte, standing in the corner of the room, staring hard at the lawyer. A bland smile spread across Fairbrother's face, and he bowed his head slightly.

"That is for you to decide… you're the journalists," he said. "You now have the facts laid out before you most generously, and now my client, as you can see, is in need of some rest and refreshment – or rest and recreation as they say in the military."

"I'm not really in the mood for the latter," said Harry.

"Well, time for your close up," said Mary, looking at his unshaven face, the eyes seemingly sunken and with dark rings beneath them. Harry appeared to have lost some weight as well. She had accompanied him next door, introduced him to Julian, and murmured: "What's this all about, Harry?"

"It's about survival, Mary. Survival and dealing with your past. You know?"

* * *

"I like the beard," says Rachel. "Not so sure about the clothes."

Max smiles. He is wearing a loose-fitting grey sweatshirt and a pair of jogging pants that the lawyer had brought him, and a pair of blue Crocs.

His wife is looking as immaculate as ever, and Max notices the uniformed guard giving her the eye.

"This room is probably bugged by the way," he says. "Just so you know."

"Yes, the lawyer warned me," says Rachel. "He also says he's confident that you'll be a free man by this evening."

"Yes," says Max, and they lapse into silence. It's Rachel who breaks it.

"Do you still want to carry on?" she asks.

"Christ… yes," says Max. "Now more than ever."

"Despite everything?" she asks, looking at him meaningfully. Max isn't sure he really wants to know what 'everything' entails.

"Yes," he says. "Despite anything."

She smiles, and he can see that her eyes are welling up. Their heads lean in together, their mouths meeting.

"No kissing!" shouts the guard, prising them apart. "Open your mouth please," he says to Max, who duly obliges. Rachel is laughing her head off.

CHAPTER SIXTY-FIVE

Harry takes a left on to Piccadilly, and walks down past Fortnum & Mason and towards the Ritz. Sitting against the wall, legs scrunched up, head wrapped in a scarf and buried beneath a hoodie, is the familiar figure of Nicola and her dog.

The dog looks up warily as Harry walks up and deposits his shopping bags on the pavement.

"You still here then?" he asks.

She looks up, bright blue eyes staring out from a raw, red face. Beneath her chapped lips there is a large cold sore, above them a moustache is sprouting.

"Where else am I going to go?" she asks in a northern accent. Harry realises that he's never really heard her speak before.

"I don't know," he says, and then he has a thought. He unclips the Rolex that has been hurting his wrist so much and drops it into Nicola's lap. The dog lifts its head defensively, as if about to leap to her mistress's defence.

"What's that?" asks Nicola, staring at the watch.

"It's a Rolex Submariner, worth at least £5,000," says Harry.

Nicola looks up at him suspiciously. "What am I going to do with that?" she says. "They'll think I've stolen it."

"You may have a point," he says. "There's a pawn shop up near New Bond Street… I'll take it up there. I'll see you later."

He scoops up the Rolex and slips it back on his wrist, which he notices still has the raw indent of whatever had been used to bind his hands in Rome.

Nicola watches him cross Piccadilly and disappear up Berkeley Street.

"What the fuck was that all about?" she says to Topaz, stroking her on the head. She looks back down towards the Ritz, hoping to see H, but he hasn't been around for days now. Anyway, he's always off his head on Spice these days. He's barely able to speak most of the time.

"It's a legal high," he had said, rolling it into a cigarette. But Nicola doesn't smoke – she never has. And she gave up drink to look after Topaz, so she doesn't want to get high.

She realises a woman – a well-dressed elderly woman – is looking down at her. "I hope you're feeding that dog properly," she says sternly, and turns on her heels.

"Fuck off!" Nicola shouts after her retreating back. "Just fuck off, you silly old bitch. What do you know? What do you know about anything?"

*   *   *

Harry checks into the hotel, where he's greeted with the sort of obsequiousness that the Saudi must experience everywhere he goes. It's a two-room suite and Harry is told to make himself at home with the bars and restaurants – it's all taken care of. Have a nice stay, sir.

While he's running a bath he rings the office, but oddly there's no reply – only the standard out-of-hours automatic message. He tries the office manager Fi's mobile, but goes straight through to her voicemail, the same with analysts Cyril and Tim's mobiles.

"While the cat's away…" he says to himself, adding some cold water to the bath, and then hitting the TV remote. BBC and Sky rolling news seem to have moved on to other stories – nothing yet about his release from police custody this morning. He checks his soon-to-be pawned Rolex. It's shortly after two. He tries the office again, and gets the same lack of response as before.

He rings Max.

"Dialled number not recognised," his service provider informs him.

He tries Rachel. What is he going to say? Christ, does she really have feelings for him?

"Dialled number not recognised."

"Perhaps I did die back there in Verbier," he says to himself, dipping a foot in the water. "Perhaps this is what death feels like – a free luxury hotel room where nobody answers your calls." And where you talk to yourself, he thinks.

At least room service seems to exist. He calls up for a medium rare steak, chips and salad and a half bottle of Côte du Rhône, and lays out the clothes he is going to wear. They don't match that well, he realises now, but at least they're smart. The shirt and trousers from the boutique in Martigny he consigns to the bin.

His phone rings.

"Hi, Harry… it's Fi here. Christ, are you all right?"

"I'm fine thanks, Fi. Where are you?"

"I'm at home."

"At home?" says Harry, desperately working out what day it is. It's not the weekend.

"Have you been to the office?" asks Fi. "The police took all the computers on Monday, and just about everything else that wasn't nailed down. It's a bit of a mess in there. Tim and Cyril buggered off – and I haven't heard from them since. Is everything going to be all right?"

"Have you heard from Max?"

"No, he's in prison in Italy, isn't he?"

"I heard he'd been released without charge."

"Oh, thank God for that," says Fi. "What happened?"

"It's a bit complicated to go into right now, Fi. But if Max makes contact, will you ring me straight away?"

CHAPTER SIXTY-SIX

"All's well that ends well," Aafia is saying to the moustachioed man behind the desk. They are in a fourth-floor office of the Ministry of the Interior in Riyadh, the inverted pyramid building that everyone seemed so proud of when it opened.

The colonel, as he styles himself, a career veteran of the Mukhabarat and Aafia's minder for the past two years, is actually a distant cousin of hers. Perhaps it was why he was chosen to look after her. She doesn't like him anyway. He is about forty, with sallow skin from sitting in this windowless, airless office for too long.

"Yes, but just think how badly it could have gone," he is saying now, twiddling his pen nervously. "Just imagine the implications if the Saudi secret service were found to have been actively involved in helping a terrorist cell carry out a sarin gas attack on the Vatican on the Christian church's most holy day. As a PR setback for the kingdom it would dwarf 9/11."

"Yes, but if we're going to supplant Iran in the affections of the West then we needed something big like this."

The colonel is smiling. "With you-know-who in the White House we don't need to worry about Iran just at the moment."

"We always need to worry about Iran", says Aafia, tugging at the headscarf that she had pulled down around her shoulders as soon as she entered the office. The colonel is her cousin after all. She didn't bother with an *abaya*, the long black dress worn by most Saudi women in public.

Aafia wasn't allowed to drive here so she had had to come by bus, which was annoying – or rather the men on the bus had been annoying because she was travelling without a chaperone. One old bloke, the same age as her father, kept on and on at her, threatening to call the religious police, until a glance at her identity card for the

General Intelligence Directorate shut him up.

"What's with stealing the diamond?" asks the colonel.

"Ah, yes, that was going to be my leaving present for Tariq," she replies.

"That useful idiot? Why – didn't you give him plenty of money for his schemes?"

"Yes," says Aafia, sensing an edge of jealousy in the colonel's voice. "But I felt guilty for using him." And I wasn't supposed to fall in love, or lust, she thinks to herself. She feels sad about Tariq, although she had gradually broken it off over the past year or so, made it feel like it was a mutual decision.

"You don't owe him a thing," says the colonel.

Just the last seven years of his life, thinks Aafia.

"Why did your father send those British men to Rome?" he asks.

"Oh, them. They just sort of fell into our hands. We needed independent witnesses and one of them had good journalistic contacts in London, so he seemed perfect."

"It's all so... so..." the colonel is waving his hand around as if the right word could be magicked from air around his head. "So Mossad."

We could do with a bit Mossad, thinks Aafia, who admires her counterparts in Israeli intelligence, and a lot less of these soft-skinned, well-connected pen-pushers sitting around in their air-conditioned offices. But this particular pen-pusher is still talking, and she doesn't like what she's hearing.

"I'm afraid we're going to have to withdraw your diplomatic passport... indeed any sort of passport. It is better that you remain in the kingdom for the time being..."

"But my father..." interjects Aafia.

"Yes, and how is your father?"

Bastard, thinks Aafia. You know very well how he is. Six months maximum, the Harley Street consultant had said.

"You must persuade him to come back," the colonel is saying. "And why not make him proud by marrying? Perhaps he can come back for the wedding."

"Did you have anyone in mind for my husband?" says Aafia, looking at the colonel full on. After all, Aafia would bring a significant dowry. He squirms in his seat, and shuffles with the papers on his ridiculously large desk.

"That Omar is very good at what he does", she says, turning the screw. "Quite good-looking if it wasn't for that scar. Any word on him?"

"Not yet," says the colonel.

"He's good... very good," says Aafia admiringly.

"You liked him?"

"Not my type." The colonel looks relieved.

"We need your passport... by sundown", he says. "Why you just couldn't stick at what you're good at – pretending to be a liberal, westernised Arab, attracting dissidents and then handing them over to us. Now that's a proper job for a woman."

CHAPTER SIXTY-SEVEN

Abdul is washing up his breakfast things in the cramped kitchen of his student house-share in the Portswood area of Southampton. He's being extra diligent because, although it's the Easter holidays, one of his housemates, Sam, a white hipster with a beard that makes him look like a Muslim brother, has come back early to start his revision, and Abdul has been putting up his friend Hassan since they got back from Stockbridge at the weekend.

Hassan has kept to Abdul's room, emerging only for meals and their five-times-a-day prayers, which they conduct in the main living room. Sam, who seems to revise in front of the television, on which he watches boxed sets of *The Walking Dead* while eating endless bowls of cereal, reluctantly shifts himself at the appointed times.

Hassan's real name, Abdul knows, is Jamal O'Rourke, and he's done time in prison, which is where he first received the Dawah. Jamal's father is Ghanain, long vanished, and his mother is English – more Irish really – from Willesden. Abdul met him at a mosque in Southampton, where Hassan had been sent to help see the light. They weren't interested, but Abdul and Hassan became friends of a sort, meeting afterwards in cafes in the city centre to discuss the war in Syria, their hatred of the West, their dreams of a true Islamic society and what could be done to help create the caliphate.

Abdul had managed to convert himself online without ever leaving his bedroom. He became more and more obsessed with jihadi websites, and what they had to say about the state of the world. His law degree studies started to seem ever more irrelevant, and he was even getting a name for himself for disrupting lectures with his arguments in favour of sharia. The girls on the course all hated him, except for one shy Muslim girl, who was always looking at him. "My life in the West is just study, eat, sleep, study, eat, sleep," he wrote on the blog he started. "It's so generic."

His one wish now was to travel to Syria and he's saving up for the price of a return ticket to Turkey. He knows there's a bride waiting for him – they been conversing on an encrypted messaging app. Her name was Julie, a blonde blue-eyed American who had become an IS fighter. Abdul could keep slaves for sex, if he wanted, Julie told him – because she's often away from home fighting and she doesn't want him to feel lonely.

It was Hassan who came up with the promise of money. They had a secret mission, he said, when he turned up at the house suddenly last week, and if they succeeded, then Islamic State would pay for their flights to Turkey and transport over the Syrian border. He then showed Abdul the guns, and how to use them, although he wouldn't say where he got them.

He had a car, an old red Ford Fiesta, and they were to travel to a place called Stockbridge, and to hold an English family hostage while they filmed them. The family's son was a British soldier who had been captured in Iraq, and IS wanted to extract information from him. By holding his parents at gunpoint they hoped to persuade him to talk. Hassan said he had a special number where to send the video.

Part of the reason Hassan won't come out of his room is that he's ashamed, thinks Abdul. They fucked it up by running away when they did. But it was becoming overwhelming – more and more people turning up – what were they supposed to do? Shoot all of them? He didn't think they even had enough bullets. The police turning up had been the last straw.

He stacks a plate on the drying rack and, lost in thought, nearly jumps out of his skin when the front doorbell rings. Hassan's face appears around the bedroom doorway. "Who's that, bruv?" he asks.

"Might be someone for Sam," says Abdul. "I'm not expecting anyone."

The doorbell rings again, and Hassan vanishes back into the bedroom.

Abdul opens the door on its latch and looks out. There's a tall, well-built Arab man standing there. His eyes are not unfriendly, but not anything else either. And he has a scar all the way down his face.

CHAPTER SIXTY-EIGHT

Harry walks into WH Smith at Liverpool Street Station and takes the newspaper from the revolving plastic cube. The banner headline is like something out of the glory days in Fleet Street, with its thick black font screaming: *How Saudis foiled Vatican sarin attack: exclusive interview with one of the two Britons held by ISIS in Rome.* Underneath is a picture of Harry, looking haggard, hollow-eyed and unshaven.

All the other serious newspapers had followed with the story, not that Harry needed to buy a paper to 'read all about it'. Mary's exclusive had broken on *Newsnight* the previous evening, with Mary in the studio, looking very new to television, but growing in authority during the course of her inquisition.

She revealed nothing about the circumstances behind the interview – 'protecting her sources' and all that – and was so obviously invested now in her exclusive that she didn't betray the scepticism she had shown in the hotel yesterday morning. An international affairs correspondent pontificated on the impact that this would have on the kingdom's hitherto deteriorating relationship with the West.

Harry had woken at six this morning and had immediately switched on the television in his hotel bedroom. Julian's photograph of Harry wearing those weird clothes from the Martigny boutique was all over the rolling news, until he was sick of the sight of himself.

There were also news teams outside the office, because there was the front door, with a female Sky News reporter saying something about Forward-Max Capital being a hedge fund and how owner Harry Kimber – the owner now was he? – acted as 'concierge' (that word again) for rich foreigners. Kimber's partner, Max Draycott, had been released without charge by Italian police and was expected back in Britain today.

Then Harry almost choked over his breakfast tray, laughing, as the bewildered-looking new owners of his house in Hammersmith met the world's press. Harry had been booked into the hotel under the name of 'Thomas Jones', he soon discovered, and grown used to being addressed as Mr Jones when he rang for room service. They shouldn't trace him here.

The lawyer, Fairbrother, had told Harry that there would be lots of big-money offers to talk to other media outlets, but that the sixteen-page document he had signed at the hotel was a non-disclosure agreement that restricted Harry from speaking to anybody about recent events, it seems. Not that Harry had any intention of speaking to anybody, since he was now two and a half million pounds to the good and he was only too glad to put the whole scary adventure behind him. As for Max, well, Max's manic deal making had got them into this situation in the first place, Harry reasoned to himself. And the Saudi had said that Max was 'on board', so he needn't worry about Max selling his side of the story to the media.

Only Fairbrother, the office manager Fi, and Harry's bank had the number of the brand new iPhone that the lawyer had given him – its caller ID blocked. Fi was to phone him at once as soon as Max got in touch, while Harry had updated his records with the bank.

With one glance at Harry's balance they had swiftly transferred him to someone introducing himself as Harry's personal wealth manager, who was keen to set up a meeting as soon as was convenient.

He steps out of the hotel foyer and on to the street. The pseudonym seems to have worked for there are no journalists waiting to greet him. His first destination is the pawnbrokers on New Bond Street, where he is loaned £3,000 for the watch, which he tells the man behind the counter that he will redeem the following week. He then goes down to Piccadilly in search of Nicola and her dog, who are duly slumped against the wall near Green Park underground station.

The dog sees him first, as Harry looms over them. He drops the £3,000, tied in a bundle with an elastic band, into Nicola's begging cap. The woman's fierce blue gaze meets Harry's.

"There's three grand there," he says. "Look after it. And yourself."

Nicola slips the wad inside her coat.

"What am I supposed to do with that?" she asks brusquely.

"I don't know," says Harry. "Where are you from originally?"

"Why?" she replies defensively. "Bolton. I'm from Bolton."

"Well, that would get you at least six months' rent up in Bolton," he says breezily. "Nice for you and the dog."

"Great," she says sarcastically. "And then what?"

"And then it's up to you, I guess," he replies.

She nods.

"Thanks, anyway, Gervaise."

"Gervaise?"

"It's what I call you."

CHAPTER SIXTY-NINE

Rachel is sitting by the open window of the six-star hotel on the island of Phang Nga Bay in Thailand. Freshly showered, and wrapped in a white towelling dressing gown, she is staring out across turquoise water at the limestone pinnacles that give the bay its picturesque quality – as the website put it.

They had spent the first night of Max's freedom in his apartment in Geneva, where they collected a suitcase of fresh clothes, after which they had paid a visit to Dieter. The gemologist had blanked Rachel as he provided Max with the certificates of ownership for the diamond – he so obviously fancies her husband, she thought.

The Italian police had provided Max with details of the Swiss safety deposit centre in whose vault the diamond was being held. The manager, having already received visits from the Swiss and British police, was waiting to greet Max and take him to the box in question. Max handed the gem to Dieter, who duly signed for it and took it back to his office.

Having paid sureties to return to Switzerland for further questioning in a week's time, Max and Rachel had then flown first class with Etihad to Bangkok by way of Abu Dhabi, arriving at this hotel yesterday afternoon, after an internal flight to Phuket and a rather tiresome ferry ride to Phang Nga. It would be a second honeymoon, said Max.

The seed investor had redeemed his money in Forward-Max Capital, citing the incapacitation of its partners, triggering its closure and forcing other investors to redeem their moneys. There was nothing to do now until the lawyers had sorted out the paperwork.

"What are we going to do about Harry?" asks Rachel, padding

back to the bed, where Max lies sprawled, one leg sticking out from under the duvet. "The bastard left you to die."

"Simon never believed that cock-and-bull about his dad dying in the Falklands," he says.

"But you did," says Rachel, sitting down on the side of the bed, and wrapping a towel around her freshly washed hair.

"I guess I wanted to. What about you?" asks Max.

"It didn't worry me one way or the other. Who cares if his father was some big hero or not? What else did Aafia say about him?"

"There wasn't much time to tell me anything," says Max. "Harry had just buggered off and we were waiting in Simon's kitchen for Omar to kill us all. She just said what I told you already, that he was the product of a one-night stand, that he never knew who his father was and didn't care, and that he had admitted to Aafia that he had been abused as a boy by his mother's boyfriend, a businessman, who then paid for him to go to our school."

"And do we believe that?" says Rachel.

"I don't know. Do you think he's a serial fantasist?"

"I know he's a liar... and a coward." Max ignores her pointed comment. It looks like it's going to be Nicky all over again, thinks Rachel. Something else not to be spoken about. Ever.

Max is thinking about what Dieter had told him many times, about the dangers of cutting diamonds. You never know what you might find inside – what tiny cracks, fissures and other weaknesses. They are hidden from the eye, and might shatter into tiny worthless pieces at any moment.

And then he surprises her.

"Actually I may need help", says Max. "I can't help thinking about her. Kylie I mean."

"The girl in the chalet... Max's girlfriend?"

"Girlfriend? Hardly", replies Max. Rachel doesn't think she's ever heard him speak so solemnly. "But, yes, her. I can't get her out of my mind. Omar shooting her... and Simon lying dead. But mainly Kylie."

"We ought to meet her parents", says Rachel. "There'll be an inquest, I suppose"

"I suppose", says Max absently.

Rachel joins Max on the bed, lies down beside him and snuggles into his chest. She closes her eyes and remembers last night – the intensity of their lovemaking. She knows. She knows. She knew as soon as he came inside her, Rachel straddling on top in order to get every single last millimetre of him deep inside of her. It was if she wanted to get him right up against the neck of her womb, deeper and deeper so that there should be no mistake. Don't ask her how she knows, but she knows.

*   *   *

His train leaves in twenty minutes, just in time for his last mission. He slips the cheque for £100,000 into an envelope, addresses it to Mary at the newspaper's office, which he has found printed on the letters page of that day's edition, and marks it 'strictly personal'. He then slips in a note:

Dear Mary, do with this what you will – but I hope that you and Ben will accept it as it is intended, as an early wedding present. Put it towards your new home. Best wishes, Harry.

He settles into the first class carriage, diagonally opposite from some sort of businessman in a suit, tapping away on a laptop. The man keeps sneaking glances at Harry, and Harry notices the newspaper with Mary's story by his side. Eventually the man plucks up courage, picks up the paper and asks in a pompous voice, "Is this you?"

"No, sorry, some mistake," says Harry, and turns to the BBC news website. He had read in the morning paper an item in home news about two young men being shot dead in Southampton, and hadn't thought anything about it. Now the 'breaking news' banner on the bottom of the BBC home page is saying: *Murdered Southampton men connected to Rome terror plot, say police.*

Two men who were shot dead yesterday morning in

Southampton have been identified as the same men who held a family hostage in Hampshire on Easter Saturday. Police say that the two men in their early twenties have both been positively identified by the family of Max Draycott, the British hedge-fund manager allegedly coerced into carrying out an attempted chemical attack on St Peter's Square in Rome on Easter morning.'

Fuck, thinks Harry. Omar.

He takes his wallet out of the inside pocket of his tweed jacket, and fingers his way through a selection of cards, finally finding the one he is looking for. Harry taps in the number.

"DC Andrews," a voice answers almost at once.

"Oh hello," says Harry. "My name's Harry Kimber. You visited my house in London a couple of weeks ago and left your card."

"Kimber… oh yes," says the voice, followed by a silence. "The same Harry Kimber that's been in the news recently, I believe."

"You believe correctly," says Harry.

"How can I help you then, Mr Kimber?"

"It's the case you came to visit me about. I'd like to be a witness for the prosecution."

AFTERWORD

My final draft of *The Concierge* was sent out to agents and publishers in March 2016, since when a number of horrifying events have occurred which echo those in this book. Most significantly in this context, the attack in Nice, France, in which eighty-six Bastille Day revellers on the Promenade des Anglais were murdered when a Tunisian man deliberately drove a truck into the crowd, along with similar atrocities using trucks and cars in Stockholm, a Berlin Christmas market, and on Westminster Bridge in London.

"Life imitates art," Oscar Wilde quipped, and while it didn't take great powers of prophecy to predict terrorist attacks on population centres in Europe – or indeed on the Catholic church – I was horrified to switch on my phone on the days in question and read, for example, of the killing of Father Jacques Hamel in his church in Normandy, or of President Assad's use of sarin against his own people in Syria. Sarin and a desire to confront Christianity are integral elements of the story in *The Concierge* – imagined beforehand and not simply ripped from the headlines to be exploited in a thriller.

What has become clear since writing this novel is that while some of the attacks, such as the ones on Brussels airport and metro in March 2017, have been the work of organised terror cells, most have been carried out by individuals inspired by, rather than connected to, so-called Islamic State. That's not to a say an Omar doesn't exist out there right now. In some form or other, he almost certainly does.

In the months between being accepted for publication and the final edit I have been able to include references to Nice and other atrocities, as well as other fast-moving world events that made 2016/17 such a difficult year in which to write a geopolitical thriller that referenced real-world events – Brexit, for example, or the unexpected election of Donald Trump. Many would have advised me not to, to keep such references vague, or to leave them out altogether. But if nothing else, they may provide a snapshot of these turbulent times.

I would like to thank here my friend Q, for his original idea, his sagacious editing, encouragement and constant badgering for more chapters; my wife Lizzie for her support and putting up with my absent presence as I dreamt up the latest twist in the plot; Ken Cowley and my sister Harriett Gilbert for reading the final manuscript and pointing out errors, omissions and inconsistencies before kindly saying that they enjoyed it. I hope you too.

Gerard Gilbert, 19 May 2017